Sign up for our newsletter to hear
about new and upcoming releases.

www.ylva-publishing.com

Books in The Teatime Chronicles

The Tea Machine
(Book one in The Teatime Chronicles)

Parabellum
(Book two in The Teatime Chronicles)
Coming 2017

The Tea Machine

THE FIRST OF THE TEATIME CHRONICLES

GILL McKNIGHT

non est ad astra mollis e terris via

"There is no easy way to the stars."

from *Hercules Furens* by Seneca the Younger

Acknowledgements

Many thanks to the team at Ylva. Especially to Astrid Ohletz and Sandra Gerth for having faith, and Jove Belle for being an excellent editor and friend.

This book had a long birthing, and a veritable who's who helped along the way. Joanie Bassler, Alena Becker, Jessie Chandler, Cate Culpepper, CK King and Victoria Villasenor—thank you for your advice and support.

Chapter 1

The battle for the Amoebas: hora IX:III

It was colder on the lower decks, and there was a cloying moistness that smelled of mould and corrosion. It clogged the lungs and made breathing an effort. Sangfroid's nose twitched as she sucked in the stale air. The quarterdeck had been breached. Her stomach knotted. That meant her mission was fried on its feet, and improvised escape plans were not her strong suit.

She moved forward signalling Gallo out to the left and Brassius straight ahead, while she remained on the right flank. In fan formation, they approached the Beta launch hangar. It had to be cleared and the escape pods activated to get the tech crew off.

"Gently people." Sangfroid breathed into her intercom. Vibration was dangerous. One thud from a military boot and it would be all over. "Little fairy steps."

"Twinkle, fucking twinkle." Gallo's grumble burped into her earpiece. They flowed forward silently. In the corridor behind her, the technical crew sat huddled on the floor afraid to so much as twitch. The doors to the launch deck slammed open and shut randomly, the wiring corrupted by the corrosive air.

Steel wall plates fizzled under layers of acidic ooze until angry red pockmarks glowed in the emergency lighting. It didn't take long for a ship to fall to pieces once one of these bastards got onboard.

"What do you see, Gallo?" she whispered.

"It's a big sucker, boss. Up on the ceiling. Most tentacular are on the other side; some poor bastard's keeping it busy over there." Gallo's voice crackled in her ear then cut out. Either Gallo's comm-piece was already disintegrating or her own earpiece was screwed. Their equipment was crumbling, making communication haphazard. She issued her commands quickly while she still could.

"Brassius, Gallo. Six inches above the eye. Give it all you've got. Travis, run those people to the pods once we open fire. Got it?" They were all that was left from her initial unit. Ten frontline troopers reduced to three in less than twenty minutes. Her rescue sortie had turned into a suicide mission. All she could hope for was to save the last of the techies and to get her people off Beta deck as fast as she could. Retreat was the only option now. The mission was a failure, and the Amoebas a goner. It was time to get the hell out.

Her crew responded with a faint chorus of "Aye, Decanus." She stepped out of her crouch and slid through the malfunctioning doors onto the launch deck. Above her a Colossal space squid quivered on the ceiling. Its moist oblong head was turned away, allowing her a few seconds to slip closer. Its mantle pulsated rapidly in the confined space. The fine textured skin fluctuated from the grey of the bulkheads to the olive green of the floor. It was trying to camouflage itself. A pointless exercise in a close combat situation. This was a young adult, inexperienced enough to leave its vulnerable mantle open to attack from behind. Sangfroid took full advantage.

Okay, Mithras, lets toast some slimy squid ass. She offered up a prayer to the soldier's god, stepped out of the shadows, and opened fire. Gallo and Brassius opened up with their laser rifles. Blue fire danced across the monster's body. It screamed; its liquid eye swivelled to find the source of pain. Tentacles whipped out towards them and globules of caustic slobber dropped from its panicked body.

In a synchronized move, Sangfroid and her unit divided their attack, drawing the creature's flailing limbs away from the entrance. Travis ushered the Beta lab technical staff through the doorway into the hangar. There were about twenty techies left in this sector working in the research labs, sequestered away from the main science deck. Once they were safely jettisoned into space, Sangfroid would throw her men into the remaining escape pods and make a run for it, too.

The squid's screams rang off the metal bulkheads. The walls roiled with the thrashing of its limbs. Brassius caught the wrong side of a tentacle and was crushed into a bloody blot against the far wall. Another huge tentacle found the fleeing tech crew and rolled them like skittles into an inky pool of squid blood. They floundered and wailed, trying to crawl from the choking mire, but the squid ink tarred them to the floor where they slowly asphyxiated.

Mithras, I'm losing them all! Sangfroid blazed her laser into the beast in desperation. Her mission was a big, fat, stinking failure. Travis flew past her impaled on a tentacle barb, shaken until every bone in his body hung loose and broken.

"Gallo. Get to the pods!" She bellowed into her comm-piece hoping it still worked. This mission was over as far as she was concerned. She'd take what she'd got and run. A half dozen tech crew were already floating away in their escape pods. The rest were either dead or dying. Her unit was decimated. "Retreat, Gallo. Run for it!"

She wheeled to the left, her finger glued to the trigger. Blue fire whipped crazily from her gun muzzle. Leaping over a severed tentacle tip and the sole of her boot came down on an inky bloodstain. The viscosity of it jarred her to a halt, almost dislocating her knee. She toppled forward. The weight of her fall broke the deadly adhesion. Gallo lay down covering fire as she scrambled to her feet and limped for the exit. Sangfroid could just about make Gallo out through the smoke. She was backing up slowly, drawing the beast down on herself. Behind her the last of the techies were running for the pods. Gallo was covering them, too.

Sangfroid lifted her laser and aimed for the eye. Well, the general area of the eye. Six inches above that sat the brain where the skin was toughest. She had to stop Gallo from getting cornered. Her shot hit its mark and sizzled across the liquid surface of the giant eye. The creature contracted in pain. Then it blinked away the discomfort and lunged in her direction. Space squid had notoriously bad eyesight. Blinding a squid slowed it down but didn't put it out of action. It sensed its prey in other ways.

She stumbled backwards, away from Gallo and the fleeing techies, drawing the squid's attention to the farthest reaches of the hangar. It would buy Gallo a few valuable seconds. She gritted her teeth. Her knee ached with every movement.

"Come on, you fuck faced son of shit—" A blur of celery coloured chiffon caught the corner of her eye. Sangfroid spun and took aim. Her trigger finger faltered. A young woman synthesized into solid form before her. The woman reached out and gently, but firmly, pointed the weapon away from her face.

"Now we'll do it my way," she said and grabbed Sangfroid's wrist. "Run!"

Despite her small size, she seized Sangfroid with a surprisingly steely grip and took off down the corridor, her long skirts swirling and heels clicking in a rapid staccato, clearly uncaring about the noise she created. She was drawing them away from the Beta sector hangar. Sangfroid stumbled along behind her, still stunned by the woman's sudden appearance but somehow compelled to run along with her. Instinct moved her feet. Her gut, with its uncanny predilection for survival, urged her onward.

Gallo's gunfire stopped. Sangfroid hoped that meant she'd managed to evacuate safely. The Colossal's screams echoed down the corridor after them. The walls reverberated with a deafening pounding. It was giving chase, pouring its limbs into the narrow corridor, following the vibrations of their running feet.

At the first junction, they skidded to a halt. The young woman looked left and then right, fussing and frowning. "Which way is it?" she demanded.

"To where?" Sangfroid asked. Who the hell was she? Where had she come from? Did Colossals have hallucinogenic weaponry?

"This way." The woman grabbed at her arm again and dragged her to the left towards the Beta research labs. "If we cut through here it should bring us out at Kappa sector," she said.

How did she know that? "Who are you?" Sangfroid asked.

"Oh, no." Her cry of dejection stopped them in their tracks. Up ahead two infantile squid sat glued to the walls on either side of the corridor. They blinked stupidly, quivering in alarm at the sight of humans. Sangfroid raised her laser, but too late. The smaller squid spat out ink. It caught her full in the face, and she immediately fell into respiratory arrest. She sank to her knees, aware the woman beside her had received a direct hit, too. She felt the woman's hand claw at her arm before it slipped away. Blindly, Sangfroid scrabbled about for her but couldn't find her. The woman was lying somewhere out of reach. She'd lost her.

"Oh bother, not again," came the soft sigh off to her left. Then the suffocating darkness squeezed the last ounce of life from her lungs.

THE BATTLE FOR THE AMOEBAS: HORA X:I

"Go, go, go!" Travis yelled at the techies as he threw them at the escape pods. Sangfroid moved off to the left and laid down a stream of continuous fire to draw the creature after her and away from Travis. The squid momentarily gave her all its attention.

"Gallo," she bellowed into her comm-piece, hoping it still worked. "Answer me, Gallo."

"Decanus?" Gallo's voice came through, thin and crackly. "All clear here."

"Grab Brassius and get out."

"Brassius is dead."

"Get out. I'm making for Kappa sector." She snapped out the order. "See you at the Parabellum." That was their good luck code.

"Damn better. After this shower of harpy piss, it's your round. Out."

Sangfroid grinned. She hoped Gallo was already running for a pod. Gallo was a seasoned soldier—hard headed, reliable, and best of all, she was lucky. Sangfroid had no doubt Gallo would be at the Parabellum tonight in time for half-price cocktail hour, but wasn't so certain about herself. A huge tentacle slammed onto the floor beside her. The reverberation shot up her legs making her shins ache. She sidled back, gun still blazing. The exit portal was somewhere behind her, crazily banging open and shut. She could hear it even if she couldn't see it in all the smoke.

A green blur caught the corner of her vision. The scent of light perfume momentarily overrode the stench of sizzling squid. She swung around, gun raised. A young woman in weird long skirts materialized before her. With a calmness and assurance that belied the bedlam around them, the woman reached over and delicately redirected the weapon away from her face. Confusion swamped Sangfroid. A cold fist of fear battered her belly, and the fear was for this woman, not for herself. Who in Hades was this, and why was she feeling so anxious for her?

"Let's try this again, shall we?" The woman grabbed her by the wrist and dragged her away. "Run!"

Sangfroid obeyed. There was no other option. A huge tentacle slammed into the ground where she'd been standing a split second ago. They ran through the exit portal and down the corridor. Sangfroid pushed through the pain in her knee, concentrating on the profile of the woman running with her. Who was she? Something about her was familiar in an excruciating, hopeless, gut-wrenching way. At the next junction they unerringly swerved right, heading for the Beta labs.

"Quickly. Pick up your feet," she scolded as she ran, her long dress a flurry around her ankles.

"Who are you?" Sangfroid easily kept abreast of her, curtailing her pace to match.

"This is neither the time nor place for introductions. Suffice to say, it's coming after us, and we must be brisk."

Behind them a dozen thickly muscled tentacles came crashing down the corridor. The reverberation of their running feet easily gave their location away, but it was too late for stealth. They could only hope to outrun it.

"Why are we heading this way? This deck's infested," Sangfroid said.

"Shortcut," the woman answered, out of breath.

Whoever she was, she certainly knew her way around a space corps research ship. With a tight turn they arrived at the Kappa sector launch hangar where row upon row of shiny egg-shaped escape pods sat in pristine lines. Sangfroid's heart sank. The pods were untouched. This part of the ship hadn't managed to evacuate at all. Gods only knew how many were dead.

"I don't know how this bit works." The woman turned to her, eyes wide with anxiety. Sangfroid didn't waste time.

Quickly she punched a key sequence into the control panel. The nearest pod slid open revealing a crisp white interior with a single seat.

"You get in this one," she said as she reached inside to switch the autopilot to standby. The woman came up behind her, and before Sangfroid realized her intention, she'd shoved her as hard as she could in the small of the back. Sangfroid's gammy knee unbalanced her enough to somehow be bundled into the pod.

"Hey!" The moment her backside hit the seat, the door mechanism began to close. The woman stepped back. "Sorry for the shove," she said. "But you're so stubborn sometimes."

Behind her Sangfroid could see a thick tentacle slide around the corner into the pod bay. It slowly groped towards the rustle of the woman's impossibly flounced skirts. She was totally unaware of the danger. Sangfroid lurched forward. Her rear lifted off the seat and the door mechanism reversed to swing back open.

"Oh, but, no—" The woman leaned forward to try and push her back inside. Sangfroid grabbed her roughly, pulling her onto her lap.

"No. No. You can't. You have to get away." The woman struggled fiercely, but fruitlessly, and soon gave up. She was small, and Sangfroid held her in place easily. She sank back into the seat, and the door slid closed with a satisfying swoosh as a blast of vile black ink slapped against the contoured window of the pod. Sangfroid thumped the eject button with her fist and the little egg shot out of its bay. A tentacle lashed out and slammed the pod sideways. It smacked into the ship's infrastructure and bounced twice before falling out the launch door into space in a weird corkscrew spin. There, it shuddered and stalled. Sangfroid and the woman held their breath. Above their heads the pod's console lights spluttered off and on again. They flashed and blinked and then flashed some more. Through the small window they could see the huge tentacle coiling back, ready for another punch at them. The pod spluttered, rebooted, and then, with a stupendous burst of speed, whisked them out from under the descending tentacle with only millimetres to spare. With a series of clicks and clunks, it whirled away from the Amoebas, and for a breathless second, the doomed research ship was framed in the escape pod's window. The Amoebas drifted drunkenly, listing to one side. Isolated fires and acidic scars marred the long, cylindrical hull. Debris littered her wake. Then the escape pod spun out into the huge void of space, calculated the nearest point of safety, and headed directly for it.

Sangfroid slumped back in the seat, her body slack with relief; unlike her captive who was scolding her again.

"You can't do this. This is terrible, terrible," she said, prizing Sangfroid's fingers off her waist.

Who the hell was she? The air around them cooled as the hiss of stasis gas filled the tiny cabin.

"This is not in the plan…" The woman yawned. "You're doing it all wrong," she grumbled, then curled up on Sangfroid's lap and fell into a deep and immediate stasis sleep. Her head was tucked under Sangfroid's chin, and her hair smelled of old fashioned flowers. It was a beautiful smell, and vaguely familiar, but she couldn't recall from where or when. For all she knew this woman might well be a mirage. An illusion made up of half-formed memories, or nothing more than an old centurion's fancies and fantasies. Sangfroid wondered if she was poisoned by squid ink or, more likely, having a nervous breakdown? Or maybe she was dead and this was some weird afterlife experience?

She encircled her arms around the woman's waist and allowed her eyes to drift shut. She was slipping away on a cloud of stasis gas and trying vainly to recall what the flowery scent meant. Dead or not, she had a suspicion that for once everything would be just fine.

Chapter 2

"He can't just lie there. He's making the room untidy. My paleobotany ladies are due any minute, and Hubert still has to set up the optical lantern."

"He's a she, Sophia."

"Nonsense."

Sangfroid slowly became aware of the world around her. Her head hurt. Coming out of stasis sleep was always rough, but this was very different. The temperature was all wrong, for a start. It smelled funny, too. Fresh cut flowers with an underlay of fire smoke. Where was she? And that noise. Mithras! A female was whining. Her reedy voice came from somewhere above her and cut through Sangfroid's brain like shrapnel. It didn't belong to the young woman she'd escaped with. Her voice was richer, more melodious. Sangfroid's military training kicked in, and she tried to make sense of her surroundings without betraying that she was awake. She lay flat on her back on something soft and overstuffed, and definitely not a pod seat.

"Please, Sophia, stop being so disagreeable." Now *that* was the voice of the woman from the pod. Sangfroid strained to listen while controlling her breathing to feign being out cold.

"I can hardly move her until she regains consciousness. I mean, she's enormous," the pod woman continued. There was a short silence, then, "Ah ha! How opportune." A finger poked

Sangfroid firmly in the ribs, and Sangfroid buckled with a grunt. So much for fooling them. Pod lady was a sly one.

"Up, you loiterer," pod lady said. "I can see you are finally among us."

The game was up. Sangfroid opened her eyes and swung into a sitting position. Much to her surprise she found herself in a stuffy, old-fashioned parlour furnished in a tumult of dark woods, heavy fabrics, and too much gilt. Practically every inch of floor space housed some elaborate and unnecessary piece of furniture. Side tables, footstools, and over-designed upright chairs gave the room a cluttered, claustrophobic feel. She felt trapped inside a museum exhibit like some wax dummy. All she needed was a cup and saucer in her hand.

A fire crackled in a large marble fireplace and threw out a pleasant heat. Sangfroid felt extraordinarily tired and depleted. The gloomy room with its cluttered warmth leeched the strength out of her, drawing every ache and pain to the surface. The battle for the Amoebas had lasted nearly thirty brutal hours. First, they had fought to take back the ship deck by deck. When that proved futile, the Imperial Fleet Senate ordered the total evacuation of all non-military staff. How many had made it? She looked around the strange room. And to where? What kind of rescue station was this?

She was sitting on an elaborate couch, all tapestry and tassels and about a million useless little cushions. Behind her stood two young women, both dressed in a flounced and fussy manner that mirrored the furnishings perfectly. The smaller of the two Sangfroid recognized at once from the Amoebas. She obviously had access to some sort of teleport technology, a dangerous weapon that was far beyond space corps capabilities. Sangfroid suspected she had mind-altering ability, too. Obviously, she was a very formidable character, but whether she was a friend or foe to the Empire was uncertain as yet. Sangfroid gave her a furtive, sideways glance. *She's very pretty.* Immediately, she snapped her thoughts back in order. There was business to perform here. Her life was in danger, and she was eyeing up the local talent? Her brains must be stewed by laser fire.

Beside the pretty pod lady stood another woman, the one that went by the name of Sophia. Sophia was taller, thinner, and glared at Sangfroid with bristling hostility. *Not a friend of the Empire, then.*

"Where am I?" Sangfroid asked, assuming she was most probably a prisoner of war. If so, there were rules and regulations to be followed.

"That's a rather ponderous question," pod lady answered. "In that it's weighty and requires much thought."

"Oh, for heaven's sake," Sophia muttered.

Pod lady gave Sophia a stern look, then turned her attention fully onto Sangfroid. "And by that I mean, are you referring to a point on a Euclidean plane, for instance?" she said, warming to her theme. She was incredibly earnest. In fact, she was wide-eyed with earnestness. Her irises were caramel coloured with little black flecks. This observation surprised Sangfroid. Usually, she didn't notice details beyond armed or unarmed, even in pretty women. If they had a gun in their hands she paid attention. That was as far as her interest in strangers went, but this woman kept dragging her attention away from the business in hand. That had never happened before. Again, Sangfroid wondered at the reality of her situation.

"...perhaps with a rotational angle around a pre-selected point..." Pod lady was still jabbering away. She did not adhere to any prisoner of war protocol Sangfroid was aware of. "...or as defined by a translational shift? What do you suppose?" The question was levelled at her.

Sangfroid blinked.

"Enough!" Sophia cried. Sangfroid wholeheartedly agreed.

"You, sir," Sophia turned her aquiline profile towards Sangfroid, "need to do a translational shift off this chaise before the ladies of my paleobotanical society arrive. They cannot find you lolling about looking so...so...unravelled. Besides, Hubert will be here any moment with the lantern, and he needs to move the couch."

"Sophia. How uncivil," pod woman said. "My guests are more than welcome in my parlour and on *my* chaise longue."

Sangfroid struggled to her feet from the low chaise. Her thigh and lower back went into spasm. She gritted her teeth and pushed through the cramp. The Sophia lady was right; she was unravelling faster than a wonky warp drive. She tugged her uniform jacket into some semblance of order and stood as straight as possible given she felt dislocated in several places. The ladies ignored her efforts and continued to squabble.

"This is Hubert's house," Sophia said.

"And *my* chaise longue."

Sangfroid cleared her throat. "Sangfroid, R.J." She officially introduced herself to pod lady. She was the only one she wanted to talk to. The Sophia creature did not interest her in the slightest. "Decanus, first class, of the IX Imperial Space Corps Marines, ma'am." Her memory was cloudy, but she knew they'd definitely left the ship together, crammed in a single escape pod. The scent of her hair was still on Sangfroid's shoulder. "How exactly did we get here?"

"Good. He's upright." Sophia gave her a dissatisfied glare. "Please, Millicent, take Mr. Declan away and have him cleaned up. We can't present him to decent company looking like that."

"It's decanus, not declan," Sangfroid corrected. "It's a military rank." So pod lady's name was Millicent? She liked that; it had a nice ring to it. Mill-*ee*-cent. Millicent. Nice. Then she pulled herself together. She could be in danger here and, instead of doing something sensible about it, she was mewling over nice names?

"Looking like what, exactly?" Millicent rose to her defence, and she liked her a little bit more. "And he is a *she*, as you have been previously informed."

"He's got blood all over his uniform." Sophia carried on regardless, her whisper almost as loud as her speaking voice. Sangfroid squinted at her. Was she gender blind?

"Of course, *she's* got blood all over her uniform. She's a soldier. She's been in battle. Why, she's practically a hero."

Practically? She damned well was a hero! She'd more decorations hanging off her than the cushions on this ridiculous settee. Her esteem for the Millicent woman dropped like a dog down a well.

"Is that ink?" Sophia rudely pointed out black splotches of squid ink on Sangfroid's uniform sleeve and across her chest.

"Yes, it is," Millicent said. "What of it."

"Perhaps he's been heroic in a post office?" Sophia snorted.

"There is real blood, too. Look here and here." Millicent pointed out several other colourful stains.

"Then it is most rude to make a house call directly after battle. One should change one's uniform first, or at least scrub up." Sophia was not going to back down.

"Excuse me, ladies," Sangfroid interrupted with her most authoritative voice. It was time to take control. "I have some questions—"

"Pardon me, Mr. Declan," Sophia spoke over the top of her. "I did not mean to be rude about the blood on your uniform. I am sure you attained it under the most valorous of circumstances, and I sincerely hope it is not your own. But I really do need to rearrange the furniture for my meeting. All these chairs have to be in rows, you see, and Hubert has to place the optical lantern right there." Sophia pointed to the spot where Sangfroid stood with a disapproving finger.

"It's decanus, not declan. It's a military rank," Sangfroid repeated firmly. "And I'll be happy to remove myself once I have some answers." The thought occurred to her that maybe she really was dead, and this was some sort of entry exam for the Elysian Fields. There was usually some tricky test for newly deceased warriors to pass before they were allowed access. Then again, her leg hurt abominably, and it would hardly be fair to be dead and still ache all over. Maybe she wasn't dead. Maybe she was hallucinating? She wondered again about the possibility of squid developing hallucinatory weapons.

"Exactly where am I, and who are you?" Her words were curt and crisply delivered.

"Oh, please forgive me." Millicent touched her sleeve, despite the encrusted blood. "Decanus Sangfroid, may I introduce Miss Sophia Trenchant-Myre."

Sophia gave a light, disinterested curtsey. "Sangfroid? Sounds French." She sniffed. Sangfroid bowed stiffly in response. The hand on her arm became insistent, and she was aware Millicent wanted to draw her aside. If it provided her with more information, then so be it.

"Better French than Declan and Irish," Millicent said and, with that final snub, led Sangfroid to the door. "I am Miss Millicent Aberly," she said once they were in the hallway. "If you would care to come with me, I shall attend to your wounds." She blushed beautifully and seemed annoyed at doing so.

Yep, Sangfroid decided. She was definitely dead. Women did not blush beautifully at her in real life. This had to be some glorious Hesperidian maiden come to carry her off to the Isles of the Blessed. Or more likely trick her into the lower bowel of Tartarus. Hesperidian maidens were sneaky like that.

"Is this some sort of test?" she asked outright, mystified that she was once again following this woman around like an unweaned runt. Millicent gave a delightful, tinkling laugh as she ushered her down a wood-panelled hallway. Her laugh was magical and turned Sangfroid's synapses to goo. So much for her stern self-control, iron-clad will, and twenty-three years of the toughest military training in the cosmos; it all amounted to nothing when Miss Millicent Aberly laughed.

"Sophia can be a trifle trying," Millicent said. "But she's hardly a test. Lord only knows how a pass mark might be determined. In here, if you please."

"What's the paly…pala…?"

"Paleobotanical?"

"Yes. The paleobotanical thing she was going on about?"

"Oh, her latest amusement. Her lady friends gather the first Friday of every month to see glass slides of plant fossils and suchlike. It lasts for about fifteen minutes before they get bored, stop for tea, and gossip away the rest of the evening. Broadens the mind." She grinned impishly. "It's very important they sit in rows, you know. Makes them feel intellectual."

They entered a darkened room towards the end of the hall and Millicent lit a porcelain gas lamp. The light flared and revealed a room much smaller than the one they had left. This room was sparsely furnished but somehow more intimate and comfortable because of it. Even in the soft glow of the lamp, Sangfroid could see the colour scheme was light and mellow. This room had an airier, more feminine feel after the oppressive formality of the room they'd just left.

"This is my day room," Millicent said and fussed about drawing the drapes against the dusk. A few coals smouldered in the fireplace. She rammed them about with a poker until they looked livelier and added a few more with the coal tongs hanging by the hearth. There was a ruthless efficiency in her movements, and though Sangfroid couldn't take her gaze off Millicent, she managed to take in the rudiments of the room with a military thoroughness. A small bureau was squeezed into the far corner, positioned to take in the view from the window, had the drapes had been open. On either side of the chimney breast, shelves were piled with books and magazines. Before the fireplace sat a small couch and close by a comfortable looking high-backed armchair. Needlepoint rested on its padded arm. From the chair's position, turned towards the fire, yet close to the table with the gas lamp, Sangfroid guessed this was Millicent's favoured chair.

She glanced at the needlepoint. She had darned her own pants often enough to view a threaded needle as a loathsome chore, rather than a pastime. But then she had fought her way through enough solar systems to expect the strange and unnatural wherever she landed. The Empire had conquered worlds much more archaic than this one. Here, it was the constant call back to her own heritage that threw her. This world looked like it had popped up from the pages of a history book, and that made Sangfroid extra suspicious. It had to be a trap. The Colossals had somehow wormed into her mind and pulled out this version of home; except it was so woefully wrong it was laughable.

"Hubert and I have an arrangement of rooms. I use this one for my reading and relaxation, and he keeps his laboratory in the larger room to the front of the house that used to be Papa's library. Now, about that leg." Millicent opened a small cabinet and examined a collection of apothecary bottles.

While she fussed over her bottles, Sangfroid flicked the drapes and peeked outside. She tried to look casual, but the room and its furnishings were so bizarre she had to see what lay beyond. The view offered little interest. There was a small garden with orderly flowerbeds and high hedges. Beyond these, the yellow glow of gas street lamps shone weakly against an evening sky. She'd have to get out there at some point and explore. It was all so intriguing, like the living history museums back home.

"Let me see. Pyretic saline. Laudanum, no, that's no use." Millicent clinked her way through the medicine cabinet.

"Where is this place?" Sangfroid asked. "And where's the pod?"

"Ah, here it is. Carbolic infusion." Millicent ignored the question, which didn't surprise Sangfroid. She recognized this mulish mindset. In fact, a lot of Millicent's mannerisms seemed familiar. Sangfroid turned away from the window to watch her uncork a bottle and splash the contents on a pad of lint.

"The pod?" she asked again, ignoring the swab held out to her. She wanted answers, not liniment. Millicent waved the wad at her, and still she refused to take it. "Answer the question," she said.

"Will you please apply this?" Millicent sounded stubborn, but Sangfroid refused to give an inch.

"No. You'll find I can be just a mulish as you." She placed her hands behind her back and stood up straighter.

"There's a difference between being mulish and being an ass. Will you take the swab if I promise to tell you all I know to the best of my ability?"

"Deal." Sangfroid took the swab from her and brusquely rubbed her knee through the tear in her pant leg. "So? Where's the pod?"

"I've no idea," she answered. Sangfroid glared at her. She'd cheated. She was supposed to have the answers! But, in all fairness, she continued her explanation with genuine frustration on her face. "We materialized in the parlour, sans pod. I didn't mean for you to come all the way home with me. If you hadn't interfered everything would have gone to order. It's all your fault."

"My fault? Lady, I think you'll find I was minding my own business, blasting squid, when you popped up and started bossing me about."

She sighed as if Sangfroid were the problem and set the carbolic bottle back into its slot in the cabinet. "Hubert will explain everything just as soon as he's freed from Sophia's requirements."

"Who's Hubert?" This Hubert was obviously important. Both women had mentioned the name with something akin to reverence. Maybe this was as good a place as any to start. She had to unpick this mystery somehow. "You mentioned a Hubert before. So did Sophia."

Millicent blinked at her in surprise. "Oh, I am sorry. Of course, you haven't met him yet…this time around, I mean. Hubert is my brother. He'll be along shortly, except that he has to set up the accoutrements for Sophia's little gathering. Sophia and Hubert are betrothed, you see."

Sangfroid nodded, as if this was a pertinent fact, which it wasn't, but any little piece of this crazy puzzle was welcome.

"What do you mean by this time around—" A loud crash interrupted her next question.

"That will be Hubert now." Millicent hurried into the hall, and Sangfroid immediately followed. Millicent Aberly was the key to this mystery, and Sangfroid wasn't going to let her out of sight for one second.

Chapter 3

"Hubert! You've broken my eggs." Sophia's scolding voice floated down the hallway.

"Only the shells, dearest," came Hubert's cheerful answer.

An egg rolled along the Persian runner and came to rest against the toe of Sangfroid's boot. She picked it up and examined it. It was dyed cerise and had a lurid face painted on it. Cerise hardboiled eggs lay all over the floor. A man of a similar age to Sangfroid was scooping them up into a beribboned wicker basket.

"Sorry, dearest. The leg of the lantern caught on the handle." He scrabbled around the floor collecting pieces of shell.

"They were for the orphanage." Sophia wailed, clearly distressed.

"What is this?" Sangfroid asked quietly, showing the egg to Millicent.

"An Easter egg," she said. "Sophia had arranged a basket for the orphanage."

"What's an easter?" Sangfroid guessed it was probably a festival for chickens, much like the bull festivals back home. Millicent tutted distractedly at the question and turned her attention back to her brother. Hubert had finished rescuing the eggs and re-shouldered his optical lantern. It was a beautiful affair of polished brass lens and mahogany casing with collapsible tripod legs, and it was almost as tall as Hubert. Sangfroid had seen similar items in science museums. It was interesting that this man owned a working example.

"The hall carpet is a mess. My ladies can't see it this way. Where's Edna?" Sophia wasn't about to be placated. "Millicent, for goodness sake, call for the maid."

"Edna's busy preparing the refreshments for your ladies. I'll clean it up. It won't take a moment." Millicent stepped forward, a hint of exasperation in her movements. "Hubert, let me introduce Decanus Sangfroid, *first class*," she gave a gracious nod with the slightest hint of condescension towards Sangfroid, "of the IX Imperial Space Corps Marines. Decanus, this is my brother, Professor Hubert Aberly of Her Majesty's College of Engineering and Physics."

Sangfroid stepped forward and gave a curt, military bow.

"Splendid." Hubert shook her hand warmly. "Imagine meeting you here, Sangfroid," he said as he gave Millicent a sly sideways look. She blushed, and Sangfroid felt she was the object of a joke between them. It immediately put her back on the defensive, and she was annoyed to find all this charming distraction had lulled her off guard. She couldn't afford to relax. Not even for a nanosecond. These peculiar little people may be strange and engaging, but she had to be careful; they could very well be extremely dangerous.

"Sir. That's a fine machine you have there." She indicated the lantern, determined to keep up a friendly facade.

Hubert smiled. "Oh, yes. A beauty," he said and patted his lantern lovingly. He was a short man, only an inch or two taller than Millicent. His sandy hair was beginning to recede from his forehead and temples, and he carried too much girth around the middle to be a sportsman. Aside from that, he seemed inordinately jovial, and his eyes, the same caramel colour as Millicent's, twinkled intelligently from behind tiny wire-rimmed spectacles. His clothing was as strangely quaint as the ladies'. He wore plaid trousers and a worsted wool jacket with handkerchiefs, pencils, and protractors poking out of every pocket. "Just look at the workmanship. It's a Newton, you know," Hubert said.

Sangfroid nodded as if that meant something to her.

"Let's set her up, shall we?" Hubert indicated that Sangfroid should accompany him to the front parlour. "Leave the ladies to sort things out here, 'eh?"

Sangfroid got the impression Hubert couldn't get away fast enough.

"But what about this mess?" Sophia said.

"I told you, I'll get the brush and clean it up," Millicent replied curtly.

"And where exactly is the brush, Millicent?" Sophia's high whine followed them into the front parlour.

"Oh please, you don't even know where we keep the maid." The door closed on their conversation with a well-oiled click.

"Good to see you, old chap." Hubert winked at his little gender joke. "How's the leg, by the way?" He immediately threw himself into assembling the lantern without waiting for an answer.

"The leg?" Sangfroid was a little taken aback by the warm familiarity of Hubert's words. She didn't know what to make of the wink. Her hand dropped towards her tricky knee. "It's fine."

"Good. While I do this, move those chairs into rows, will you?"

It took Sangfroid mere minutes to swing the heavy dining chairs into order. "How many ladies are you expecting?" She set out three rows of five chairs apiece.

"Oh, a veritable flock. We're expecting a muster of ladies this evening. I'm afraid word of your visit has circulated, Sangfroid. My intended is neither discreet nor discerning in matters of this nature. Sophia needs the limelight. And whether it's by hosting evenings of pretentious twaddle like this one or indulging in inane tittle-tattle, she will have it." He fussed about, fixing a white cloth screen in front of the chairs. "That is why Millicent is fuming. She hates the attention. Millicent can't bear to have her actions audited."

"I don't understand any of this." Sangfroid frowned. Actions audited? What did that mean? Though her soldier's gut told her these people were essentially harmless, she was far from happy with the situation. There was too much subtext she couldn't decipher. Too many currents wriggling away beneath the surface. She had no idea where she was, who they were, or whom they represented. It was time for answers.

She opened the door to the hallway. Millicent was sweeping the last of the eggshells into a dustpan. She looked heated and dishevelled and muttered angrily to herself. Sophia was nowhere to be seen, which was probably for the best, Sangfroid decided.

"Millicent, would you come in here, please?" Sangfroid liked the sound of Millicent's name on her tongue; it sounded exotic and intriguing. Millicent looked surprised but complied, shaking the dust from her skirt before joining them.

"I need answers. And now, please," Sangfroid said, solemnly turning to face them. Standing side by side, the family resemblance was unmistakable, except Millicent had darker hair. Their mannerisms were similar, too. Both seemed anxious, earnest, and unnervingly intelligent.

"Well, yes," Millicent answered, carefully. "I suppose it's only fair."

"Yes, I suppose it is." Hubert sighed, then stepped up to the mark with a direct question. "Tell me, Sangfroid. What year is it?"

Sangfroid's frown deepened. She wanted to ask the questions, and what was worse, this particular one reverberated somewhere at the back of her mind. *What year is it?* It had weight and purpose. This question was somehow no stranger to her, and how she answered was important for all of them. Then the crazy notion slipped away as quickly as it had come, leaving her feeling foolish and unfocused. She caught Millicent's calm but concerned gaze and knew she had witnessed that flashing moment of unease and understood it better than Sangfroid did.

"It's anno VI in the reign of Hadrian X," Sangfroid said.

"She can't go around saying that," Millicent murmured to Hubert.

"Let me see." Hubert went slightly walleyed and stared at the ceiling. His lips moved silently.

This went on for several seconds until Sangfroid felt obliged to ask, "Is he praying?"

Millicent laughed. "He's calculating. He's absolutely brilliant at mathematics. The best in England. In all of Europe, I'd venture."

"1957," Hubert announced. "That's what it would be in our calendar." He looked directly at Millicent.

She stared back, alarmed. "1957! That can't possibly be correct, it's less than a hundred years away. They can't have advanced that much in such a short time."

"I agree. It's as if there is a rogue branch somewhere in our timeline where something has gotten rather out of place."

"What has gotten out of place?" Sangfroid asked. She was becoming frustrated with these two and wished she disliked them enough to apply torture or at least a good garrotte. "And what is 1957?" She put an edge to her voice to warn them her patience was wearing thin and that she was a dangerous adversary.

Sombre chimes rang out from the hall. The parlour door flung open, and a harassed Sophia bustled in to join them. She had changed into an aubergine velvet gown with cream lace, and pearl studded cuffs. A monocle hung on a black ribbon pinned to her breast. Her hair was set in a severe fashion and bedecked with black feathers and black velvet bows. Huge ones.

The ensemble was intended to give her a sophisticated and scholarly air, but with her gaunt height and aristocratic nose she favoured a plush crow.

"The first of my ladies are arriving." She waved her hands about. "Where is Edna? We can't keep them waiting on the doorstep." The whine was back in her voice. "And they're early. Everyone is usually terribly late; it's the fashion." Sophia sounded vexed at the faux pas. "How maladroit."

"Maybe it's a vanguard action," Hubert said, merrily. "Prepare yourself to be breached." He gave Sangfroid another conspiratorial wink.

"I hope everything is ready, Hubert?" Sophia asked, though it came out more like a demand.

"Yes, my dear. All is ready." Hubert's smile dropped, and he stood at attention by the lantern, a tray of glass slides on the table next to him.

"Best we retire," Millicent whispered and indicated for Sangfroid to follow her.

"You can't go now." Sophia was shrill with anxiety. "People will expect to be introduced to our guest. The ladies know you've a visitor, Millicent. It's all very exciting," she said in a voice that suggested the opposite. Then taking a good, long, horrified look at Sangfroid, said, "Oh, look at the state of him! I thought you were cleaning him up! Has he no other uniforms? Something less gory, perhaps with epaulets?" She glared at Sangfroid with supreme dissatisfaction.

Sangfroid gawped at her. Did Sophia really think she was a houseguest? And a *man*? Sophia wasn't as bright as the Aberlys, that much was certain. Not that Sangfroid blamed her; there couldn't be many people as bright as the Aberlys. It occurred to Sangfroid that the true nature of her arrival was being kept secret from Sophia. But why?

Millicent kept a firm hold of her arm. Sangfroid could feel the anxiety pulsing off her and decided to let her take the lead.

"Introductions will have to wait until later, Sophia," Millicent said. "Decanus Sangfroid would hate to divert attention from the latest riveting news from the paleobotanical world. Meanwhile, I shall search father's wardrobe for anything with frogs or tassels that may pander to the vacuous foppery you favour so well. Rest assured, we shall return ready and prepared to share tea and proper introductions with your ladies of science."

Sangfroid spared a glance towards Hubert and, on seeing the suffering in his eyes, edged a little closer to Millicent, determined to retreat with her. Their escape, however, was foiled by Edna's alacrity. She had already opened the front door to a throng of Sophia's scientific sorority. Their excited trills and warbles echoed down the hallway.

"At least cover the bloodstains on your chest!" Sophia exclaimed. "Here, carry Millicent's shawl." She grabbed a shawl off the piano stool and pressed onto Sangfroid's chest. Sangfroid grabbed it and held it over the worst stains.

"I have never needed for my shawl to be carried in all my life!" Millicent was outraged. "It's *most* presumptive and gives out quite the wrong message." Her protestations were drowned as a gaggle of ladies massed in the doorway. They stood judiciously halfway in and halfway out, waiting for the flustered Edna to officially announce their arrival. Unfortunately, their excited whispers were clearly audible to those present.

"Is that him?"

"Goodness me, he's a giant!"

Sangfroid was mortified at being the object of speculation for a half dozen owlish spinsters.

"Hush, Velma; he'll hear you."

"Foreign, I should imagine. I understand foreign gentlemen can be very tall."

"I hear that the men of the Urals are the tallest of all."

There was excited tittering at this.

"Isn't he handsome? Just look at those regimentals."

Sangfroid clutched the shawl tighter to her chest. Why were they calling her he?

"My dearest friends, please do enter." Sophia boomed out a welcome to her guests, and the awkward moment passed. The ladies bustled into the room as if a singular entity. Salutations were dutifully exchanged with both Miss Millicent and Professor Aberly, before the ladies' unified attention was once more riveted upon Sangfroid.

"Major Sangfroid," Hubert began the introductions as man of the house. Sangfroid frowned at the deliberate change in her name. What the Hades was a major? "May I introduce Miss Bench, Miss Hove, Miss Surplus, the Misses Thrace-Bartley Holmes, Miss Ogilvy, Miss Fitzpatrick, and Mademoiselle Beaulac," Hubert announced in a breathless rush then ducked behind his lantern and tried to look preoccupied. "The vanguard," he muttered for Sangfroid's ears only. "You're on your own, now."

Vanguard my arse; this is an entire heavy armour division. "Good evening, ladies." Sangfroid swooped into a low ceremonial bow. She wasn't sure of the exact status of these ladies, but decided to be ultra polite in case they were priestesses of the local cult.

Millicent thankfully inserted herself into the introductions. "Major Sangfroid serves with the First Prussian Dragoons and has kindly come to call on us whilst in London. He is a close friend of Hubert, as you know. It is wonderful to see him again and so unexpectedly."

Sangfroid was dumbfounded at the blatant lies tripping off Millicent's tongue. She had even more gall than her brother. Her identity must be a serious issue for the Aberlys to hide it at every turn. And her gender, too? But why?

Excited tittering followed Millicent's words, and Sangfroid felt the ladies scrutiny increase tenfold. She bowed again and politely smiled. She had no idea what was going on, but her instinct told her to play along. On some intrinsic level, she found herself trusting Millicent and Hubert. The ladies chattered freely now that the courtesy of introduction was over.

"Prussian! I told you he was foreign. Tall. See. It's all in the colouring."

"He is very blond."

"And tall."

"Yes. Ever so tall."

"Is Prussia near the Urals?"

"What brings you to London, Major?"

"Is the rest of your battalion here, Major?"

Sangfroid had no idea. An unexpected ache rattled in her chest. She had no battalion. She was a decanus not a major, whatever that was. She'd led a unit of ten centurions. Her soldiers, her friends, had died on the Amoebas. If this place was some strange, lunatic, afterlife, then where were her comrades? Why was she here alone? Her gaze strayed to Millicent certain she held the answers. If only she'd share.

The ladies continued their onslaught.

"You must sit and tell us all about the Urals, Major," one requested.

"Perhaps we could combine with the ladies of the Geographical society for a specialist talk?" another said.

"Oh, do say yes to a specialist talk, Major Sangfroid."

Followed by yet another. "You really, really must, Major. The Urals sound fascinating."

They pressed her to agree. She looked over at Millicent beseechingly, but she looked pale and stiff and equally adrift.

"Ladies, ladies." Sophia clapped her hands and began to corral her guests. "We need to begin. Hubert has an appointment on the hour and must leave. Millicent and the major will rejoin us for light refreshment later."

"Millicent and the major. How adorable." There were spinsterish giggles, and Millicent turned scarlet.

"See how he carries her shawl? He's so gallant, so romantic," said another, *sotto voce,* and Millicent looked as if she might explode.

Sophia ushered the ladies to their seats. The lights were lowered, and Millicent whisked Sangfroid out of the room at lightning speed, still blushing furiously.

"Millicent and the major? The prussian dragoons? And what are urals?" Sangfroid demanded as soon as they reached Millicent's little study. "What the hell was all that about?"

"Language, please. I will not have the H word used in this house."

Sangfroid assimilated this and decided to ignore it and carry on, without the H word. "What was all that about?"

Millicent bristled. "What else could I say? You can't be a decanus here; no one knows the term. There is no military equivalent. I made an informed guess, a presumption, on your rank and came up with major. And the Prussian Dragoons were the closest I could get to Imperial Space Corps Marines in that they both sound exotic and have over-elaborate uniforms."

"And why does everyone think I'm a man?"

"Well, you're very tall." Millicent looked flustered. "And board shouldered. And your short hair doesn't help."

"So? You and Hubert get it?"

"Hubert and I already know you. Sophia does not. To her, with your size and bearing, and…and attitude, you are masculine, and she simply can't perceive you any other way. Neither can the ladies."

That didn't make things any clearer to Sangfroid. So what about her hair? Long hair got matted with blood and guts and stuck to your face. She wasn't particularly tall either; everyone and everything in this world was tiny! Millicent was being ludicrous.

"How do you and Hubert already know me?" That was the issue she should be concentrating on. The answer would be interesting. She accepted there was a strange reverberation when she was around them. There was a link between them she had yet to understand.

"It's a long story, and I do intend to tell you." Millicent held her hand up to stave off any interruption. "It's just that we have bigger problems at the moment. You most definitely should not be here."

"For the last time, where is here!" Her patience evaporated. The tension of the past hour combined with the growing pain in her leg brought her to a standstill. Hesperidean maidens, space squid, drugs, and whatever damnation lay behind this mad house...she was going to find out what it was, once and for all.

Millicent sat upright in the chair nearest the fireplace. "You are in London, England," she said.

"Londinium?" That did surprise her.

Millicent's fingers plucked at a loose thread on her needlepoint. "Yes, I suppose it is your Londinium, except that it is also my London." She wouldn't look at Sangfroid, instead giving all her attention to the stitches. "And the year is 1862," she added.

"1862," Sangfroid repeated slowly. Examining the words for clues. They held none. This was stupid. The woman talked in riddles. Except Sangfroid's gut roiled in that way it did when something was terribly, terribly wrong. Old soldiers listened to their guts, and hers was currently singing opera. In warfare, the gut tended to assimilate information much quicker than the brain. Especially bad information. "What exactly is 1862?"

"It's the year in accordance with the Gregorian calendar that we use in this timeline. And that means there is almost one hundred years between the timeline where we are now and the timeline where you come from."

"One hundred years?" Sangfroid was incredulous. She looked around the room, at the gaslight, the ticking timepiece on the mantel, the open fire. There was no technology here worth spit. "There's more than a hundred years difference. More like a thousand. This place is primeval." It was worse than Sparta. "Are you saying I've travelled backwards in time?"

"Yes and no. And don't be so judgmental. I'll have you know you are in the heart of the British Empire, an advanced industrial society acclaimed worldwide for its engineering and entrepreneurial ingenuity. Why Hubert has—"

"Excuse me, but yes and no? I asked if I'd travelled backwards in time, and you said, yes and no?"

"*We* have. Remember I was with you. I went back to rescue…well, forward to rescue you. But somehow it went wrong, and you ended up here in my timeline. The proper one." She watched Sangfroid carefully as she delivered this latest bit of nonsense. "I knew you shouldn't have dragged me into that pod thingy, but you never listen." And as usual, no matter how nonsensical her speech, there was a reprimand in it somewhere.

Sangfroid looked around the room again. "I think you'll find my…timeline…is the proper one." She had problems with the word *timeline*. It was alien, farcical. "I was born on moon base Alpha Zeta IV. This place…this…" She waved a hand at their surroundings. "I don't understand any of this. Time travel is purely theoretical. It cannot be practiced, ergo it doesn't exist. Yet you're telling me that *you*, someone who burns fossil fuels, can do it? That *you* can do what the entire Imperial Science Consortium can't? I don't think so, lady."

"What do you think, then? How do you explain away your current surroundings?" Her colour was rising, and her eyes flashed. "Theory is the hypothesis of general principles backed by hard evidence that eventually leads to practice. Hubert has successfully exhibited this through the fact that *you* are *here*. Perhaps the Imperial Science Consortium needs to talk to Hubert if it wishes to catch up?"

Sangfroid snorted and flung herself onto the couch. It creaked alarmingly.

"And show some care for my Chesterfield! It was Mother's and not designed for brutish behaviour," Millicent scolded.

Sangfroid glowered at her, then squirmed uncomfortably on the stupid couch. She really was a giant here; everything was so…so… She looked over to where Millicent sat prim and proper on her own little wingback chair. Everything here was so bleeding delicate.

"Look, either I'm dead and in Hel—the place beginning with H, or you're a hallucination, and I've been captured by the enemy. Which is the same as being in the H place."

"Well, those things did happen, so I suppose you are right. But I'm right, too. We are a hundred years apart but in two different timelines. And yours is terribly out of step, even for an alternative one."

"I was captured?" She sat bolt upright. The Chesterfield gave another loud crack.

"Mostly…you were killed more than captured. But both things happened." Millicent frowned at the noises emanating from her settee.

"Millicent. You'd better explain what's going on. This isn't a game. I can't afford to play along with something I don't understand."

"That's true." She sighed. "And I always intended to tell you. But it's a long, complex story, and you can't interrupt."

"I won't interrupt." Sangfroid eagerly grabbed at this breakthrough. She thought she'd never get any sensible information from the Aberlys. This was her big chance.

"You will interrupt. You always do. You're most annoying," Millicent said. "I'll tell you everything. Well, almost everything. As much as I know. And then you will see how you ended up here. But you have to be patient and let me tell it in my own way." The more she spoke, the more her distress showed. "Or else none of it will make any sense."

Sangfroid nodded in agreement and sat back and waited, watching as Millicent took a calming breath and began. The fire glow caught the chestnut hues of her hair and threw her rounded cheeks into soft shadow. Her caramel eyes blazed, and her lips were full and pink. Sangfroid fixated on them as she spoke, following every curve, pout, and twitch, for Millicent was an animated talker. Her hands were never still; they fluttered here and there, cutting the air as she described this and explained that. And as she spoke, something Sangfroid had secretly suspected all evening came to full awareness. She loved her.

It was not a breathtaking revelation; it was more a factual, deep-seated knowledge. She was certain Millicent wasn't aware of the feelings she had for her, and Sangfroid was at peace with that. It was her secret. It belonged to her alone, and she softly wrapped her secret around her like a warm old cloak. And once she realized she loved her, she realized she had for some time. Yet, they had only just met? How had that happened?

"It all began last Wednesday. Hubert's birthday was several weeks away, you see." Millicent's hand drifted towards her needlepoint. "So I decided to embroider him an Ogopogo cushion cover for his present—"

"What's an Ogopogo?" Sangfroid interrupted.

"You promised!"

"Sorry. Carry on."

Chapter 4

LAST WEDNESDAY, LONDON 1862

MILLICENT SET ASIDE *THE ILLUSTRATED Cryptozoologist* and lifted her needlepoint. She held the sewing hoop inches from her nose and squinted at the fine stitching on her Ogopogo. There was no doubt about it. According to the periodical, she had placed the dorsal fin too far forward. With a sigh, she began to unpick the stitches. It was most disheartening. She'd spent the better part of the morning adding the fin, and now it seemed to be in the wrong place! The Ogopogo may be a supposedly extinct sea serpent, but that was no excuse for sloppy workmanship. If she kept losing concentration, she'd never have the cushion cover finished in time for Hubert's birthday, which would be a great pity as he loved cryptids.

"Millicent? Millicent. Don't be so tiresome. Come here at once."

The cry came from the hallway. Even if she hadn't recognized the strident voice, it could only be Sophia. Only she would call to the mistress of the house as if she were a servant girl.

Though I suppose I'm only the mistress until Sophia marries Hubert. Lord knows how I'll be called then. Millicent was not as enthusiastic about her brother's forthcoming nuptials to Miss

Sophia Trenchant-Myre as she ought to be. For someone who had little to add to any intelligent conversation, Sophia could be incredibly vociferous.

Millicent set aside her needlepoint and rose to answer the summons, knowing from past experience Sophia was disinclined to go away once her mind was set. She would bellow like a bull all morning until someone saw to her requirements. She was a tiresome visitor at the best of times, but when she had a thought in her head, she could be utterly atrocious.

"You called, Sophia?" she said calmly on entering the hallway. Sophia stood at the bottom step staring anxiously up the curved stairwell. She seemed bewildered to see Millicent emerge from farther down the hall.

"Oh? I thought I saw you on the staircase. You ran away from me," she said.

"How ridiculous. I did not run away from you. I was in my study as I always am at this hour." Millicent was mildly disapproving. Sophia should know the workings of the house by now. She had been affianced to Hubert for over four years, yet paid very little attention to anything to do with his household that was not immediate to her own needs. The hands of the Baroque grandfather clock inched closer to the eleventh hour, indicating a particularly important household ritual was almost upon them, and yet Sophia stood on, totally heedless of the time. It was as if the Aberly morning schedule was beyond her comprehension or interest.

Every morning, without fail, Millicent and Hubert breakfasted from exactly six thirty to seven o'clock. They then went their separate ways. Hubert to his laboratory, which was actually two rooms made one by the removal of the doors dividing the library from their father's old smoking room. Millicent retired to a much smaller room at the rear of the house with a pleasing view of the gardens. This had previously been the morning room because of the light it received early in the day. On Papa's passing, Millicent took this room for her own use. She was an intelligent woman who enjoyed her own company. Her only requirement was to have a defined space for private reflection and personal study. This room was her haven.

Every morning, excepting Sundays, Millicent took along a tray of tea and scones to Hubert at eleven o'clock on the dot. The servants were not allowed to enter his laboratory under any circumstances, so it befell Millicent to deliver the tea tray. She would serve morning tea, and they would relax for a short time to discuss their current projects or any items of interest in the newspapers and circulars delivered earlier that morning. It was a pleasant break; one they both looked forward to.

Behind Sophia's shoulder, the grandfather clock showed eight minutes to eleven. From the direction of the kitchen Millicent could hear the rattle of china as Cook assembled the morning tray. She wished Sophia would hurry up and explain her unexpected visit and be on her way before elevenses began proper.

"Whatever is it, Sophia?" she asked. She smoothed her skirts to hide her agitation. There was no point in being short tempered with one's soon-to-be sister-in-law. There would be plenty of time for that later when they had to share the same roof.

"I have organized for two dozen eggs to be delivered. Can you have Cook boil the lot, and perhaps Edna can dye them some pretty colours. Pinks and blues, though I'd prefer a primrose yellow."

"Excuse me. Coloured eggs? But why?"

"It's for Easter. I want to send a basket of boiled eggs to the orphanage."

"To constipate the orphans?"

"Really, Millicent. You're such a curmudgeon. It's called charity, and it's all the rage. All the most modish ladies are doing it." Sophia tut-tutted as if Millicent were being deliberately dense. "Why, the Partridge sisters are sending Easter posies to the lepers."

"We have lepers? In London?"

"Well, somewhere out in Hampshire." Sophia waved a hand vaguely in the direction she assumed Hampshire to be. "Or maybe its amputees? Yes, amputees. Anyway, they're getting flowers, and the orphans are getting coloured eggs. It will all be so merry."

"Hardly. Those children live in the poorhouse, Sophia. It is only called an orphanage because they have been forcibly removed from their parents. They troop down to the workhouse each morning to begin a fourteen-hour shift at the looms. It would be more charitable to challenge what is really no more than child slavery than to send them coloured eggs." Millicent warmed to her subject, hoping Sophia's new charitable interests might be channelled towards a greater purpose. "I am attending a meeting at the Creswell reading rooms this evening. The primary agenda is child exploitation and strategizing social action to protest against it. Why not come with me?" Millicent was most eager now. Finally, here was an interest she and Sophia could bond over. At last they had something in common.

Sophia snapped closed the pearl buttons on her gloves and wriggled her fingers to settle the calfskin comfortably around them. The rattle of china came closer from along the hallway. Edna was approaching with the eleven o'clock tea tray. Millicent wondered if she should invite Sophia join her and Hubert for tea so they could talk more about possible social action, but decided not to. Hubert would have a spasm if Sophia appeared in his laboratory.

"Remember, pink, yellow, and blue," Sophia said. "I'm attending church with the Partridge sisters this Sunday, so I'll need them by then." She hefted her parasol onto her shoulder and left in a flurry of philanthropy. Millicent bristled. Her offer of a social conscience had been brushed aside. She should have known better.

"Two dozen eggs for 140 children. How will they decide who gets the protein?" Millicent called after her, but the door closed sharply on her question.

"I have the master's tea tray, Miss Millicent." Edna appeared before her and wobbled into an unnecessary and ungainly curtsey. The tray tipped precariously, and the china rattled alarmingly. Millicent grabbed the tray from Edna's panicked grasp.

"Thank you, Edna. Remember our rule? No curtsies while you are holding things. Now, Miss Sophia has organized a delivery of eggs. Ask Cook to boil them, please."

"Yes, Miss. I'll tell her."

"And could you dye the shells, Edna."

"Dye the shells, Miss?" Edna looked as agitated as she was mystified. "How? I mean what colour, Miss?" She sounded very unhappy with the task.

"Drop them in a bucket of beetroot water. Red will do splendidly."

Edna wandered back to the kitchen looking as perplexed as ever. With a sigh, Millicent headed for Hubert's laboratory, tea tray in hand. She tapped at his door with the toe of her shoe on the last chime of eleven o'clock. All was well. The morning ritual, with all its continuity, had been rescued.

"Come," Hubert called cheerfully. Millicent used her elbow to tip the handle and pushed the door open with her hip. It swung wide to reveal Hubert's sanctuary, a sober, high-ceilinged room. Under Hubert's tenancy, the bookshelves burgeoned with scientific apparatus, intricate engineering models, and all sorts of wonderful gewgaws. These shared the mahogany shelving alongside large leather tomes and bound periodicals. The floor, and nearly every other available flat surface, was haphazard with piles of books and academic papers, and strewn around the lot, lay a variety of mechanical curiosities Hubert was either building or pulling apart. While it was a large and extremely interesting room, Millicent much preferred the snug simplicity of her own little hideaway.

In the winter months, her study was warm and welcoming with its flickering fire and cosy proportions. The huge windows in Hubert's laboratory let in a dreadful draft in the wintertime, and in direct contrast, the same large windows allowed the sun's full glare during the summer months. On some summer days, it was so blindingly hot that Hubert had to close the drapes to stop from being cooked. Outside the birds sang, roses bloomed, and throngs of cheerful Londoners jostled along the sunny streets of their capital, while poor Hubert sat perspiring in the gloom.

Not that anything as distasteful as jostling occurred on the sun-filled pavements of Christie Mews. The mews was one of the more desirable addresses near Green Park, Westminster, and the nearest that any cheerful Londoner got to jostling along it was to deliver goods to a trade entrance. Truth be told, this exclusivity affected Millicent and her brother very little. As long as they were left in peace to follow their intellectual pursuits, neither felt compelled, nor inclined, to bow to the social dictates of their class. They were known to be rich, which was a good thing, but also eccentric, which was not. Their behaviour and interests were too irregular to be of good taste, so therefore they were often socially shunned by their peers and mostly left alone, which suited them very well indeed.

Papa had made his fortune importing diamonds. Number five Christie Mews bore testament to his business acumen. Arthur John Aberly's investment portfolio had left a sizable trust fund for his children. He had left his son and daughter well provided for, and this enabled each to live their lives unencumbered by such trivialities as earning a living or marrying for advancement. And that also suited Millicent and Hubert very well indeed.

Millicent set the tray on a small side table and frowned disapprovingly at her brother's rear end. Hubert was enveloped waist deep in his latest passion. His legs dangled out of a huge, blocky machine built from brass and wood. His torso was buried in what Millicent could only imagine to be the engine compartment, though it had little resemblance to any that she had seen before. There was no funnel or furnace, and if it had any cogs and pistons, they were well hidden. Rather, it looked like an enormous snow sleigh with multiple heavy-duty levers and a curious vertical disc, almost a tall as she was, balanced at the rear. It was a ridiculous ensemble and looked suspiciously like a pile of badly abused furniture. Millicent had noticed the disappearance of several household items recently, and her suspicions were now confirmed. Hubert and his new contrivance were behind it.

With dismay, she noticed Papa's smoking chair positioned in the centre of the ugly contraption, its ornate mahogany legs sawed off to make it fit. Millicent was most vexed. The chair had been a genuine Georgian piece, and their father had been very fond of the red velvet cushioning.

"Hubert, kindly re-surface and join me for tea," she called. With a grunt and the clunk of a carelessly dropped spanner, Hubert extracted himself.

"By Jove, I could do with a scone right now," he said and wiped his hands on an oil-stained handkerchief. "Engineering sharpens the appetite. Any cherry?"

"Hubert, I strongly object to you mutilating the furniture. Is that the occasional table from the drawing room?" She nodded towards the wooden disc propped on the rear of his machine. "I've noticed it's gone missing." She glared in steady accusation all while pouring tea without spilling a drop. Hubert had the grace to look guilty. He hid his sheepish grin behind the rim of his teacup.

"I promise to put it back once I get the replacement copper disc made. This is just a prototype." He nodded at his machine and bit into his cherry scone with relish. "It's all about precision. I need to calibrate the measurements before I send the templates off to the engineers."

"A prototype what?" Millicent asked. She had watched the apparatus being slowly assembled over the last few weeks and had asked this question frequently, never once receiving a satisfactory answer. She didn't expect one now.

"I told you before. It's an automated heuristic simulator," Hubert mumbled with a full mouth, his greedy gaze already fixed on a second scone.

"I am certain that you didn't tell me any such thing." Millicent sipped her Lapsang Souchong thoughtfully, then said, "You mean it's a sort of timepiece, like a clock." She cast a dubious glance at the machine crowding the centre of the room. She'd thought the Baroque grandfather clock in the hall, over-sized and showy. It looked positively demure compared to this…this conversation piece. Its brassy curlicues gleamed in the light streaming through the windows. The sun was beginning its midday arc across the rooftops to the front of the house, and already the room was becoming uncomfortably hot. "If it is a clock, it is uglier than the Baroque. And I'll tell you here and now, there is no room for it in the vestibule," she said.

"No. It is not a clock, though perhaps it could be called a *time* piece of sorts." Hubert looked pleased. He loved to make riddles, but Millicent wasn't in the mood.

"Forgive my ignorance. At the moment it looks like a sleigh with half our furniture piled upon it, as if we were refugees in a snowstorm. How is it a timepiece of any description?"

"Because it can take you to any *piece* of time."

"Pardon?" His riddling was growing tiresome. She moved the plate of scones out of reach and fixed him with a steely glance. Hubert stopped his games at once.

"It's a time machine, Millicent. Imagine it! A machine capable of transporting a man to any pre-selected moment in history." His voice rang with enthusiasm. "Well, almost. I still need to work out how to power it. If my algorithms are correct there's no reason why it shouldn't work." He settled in his seat, brows furrowed, considering his problem.

"What powers the engine?" Millicent asked. She was curious, now she understood what he was working on. Hubert always had some interesting invention at some stage of development sitting around his laboratory. This one was more thought provoking than usual.

"That's the problem; what fuel type to use. Gas delivers such an unstable current. I've tried pressurizing it to a higher ratio but it doesn't work very well, and it smells dreadful."

"I know. Cook was complaining. What are your alternatives?"

"Coal?"

"No, Hubert. I will not have it. Last time you experimented with combustion, we had coal coming out of our ears and the heat was unbearable."

Hubert strolled over to the windows overlooking the Mews. "I do have another idea," he said. "But it is very radical." He paced back and forth before the window until Millicent found she was squinting at the sunlight that haloed him.

"Do come away from the window, Hubert, the light is too bright." She shielded her eyes with her hand. "Whatever do you mean by radical?"

"I mean radical as in harnessing the power of the cosmos!" He turned and tugged on the cord to close the window drapes. The heavy velvet swung shut like the curtains in a theatre production. The room was plunged into cool shade. "Solar power will fuel my machine, Millicent. Even as it powers the earth on which we stand," he said.

"Solar power? How ingenious. And how will you manage that?"

"Copper. Huge copper plates." He indicated the wooden disc already mounted on his time machine. "And a water tank." He showed her a cistern hidden behind the driving seat. It had multiple funnels with copper piping running to the cylindrical pistons at the front of the machine in what Millicent had imagined as the engine bay. "The water is heated by the condensed rays of the sun on the copper disc, and steam is carried thus to the pistons." Millicent could see how the piping fitted in with his scheme.

"The water would eventually evaporate and the tank run dry." She pointed out. "And whereas I can understand how the pistons could derive motion, however short lived, I cannot see how this will propel a machine of this size through time?"

"In answer to your first question, the disc will spin and, in doing so, will circulate the water as it enters the pipes and pistons. Only a fractional amount of water will be lost as the circulatory system harvests any run off." Hubert was rocking on his heels, enjoying the conversation. "And secondly, I cannot prove—"

"Okay, okay." Sangfroid broke her promise and interrupted the story. "So the guy's a genius. Do we really need all this scientific boo-yah?"

"I knew you would interrupt. You are very inconsiderate." Millicent puffed in frustration. "You need to know some of the *boo-yah* in order to understand what I'm telling you."

Millicent's annoyance curiously didn't feel unusual. Whatever their connection, on some level Sangfroid was clearly used to being the object of her exasperation.

"May I continue?" Millicent asked, waspishly.

"Please do," Sangfroid conceded with an overly charming smile. Millicent gave her a sharp look, cleared her throat, and resumed her story.

"I shall leave you with your conundrum, Hubert." Millicent gathered the cups and saucers onto the tray.

"What are you doing today?" he asked. Millicent heard the real request in his voice.

"What do you need me to do?" she sighed.

He produced a thick binder and waved it vaguely in her direction. "It's just that I could do with your opinion on my latest thesis. It may shed some light on this." He nodded towards his machine. "It deals with curved time waves."

"So, you are really considering travelling through time as opposed to space?"

"Let's call it space-time, shall we, and consider it an abstract? And then, let's assume our destination, as well as our current locale, is both a temporal and a spatial point. Now, what would happen if we applied velocity? That is all I am asking you to consider." He tapped the binder. "My outline is in here."

Millicent took it from him. "I will look at it, but only after I finish my needlepoint." She warned and tucked it under her arm. "I look forward to seeing how you deal with gravitational fields. That should dampen any supposed velocity."

"Ah ha. Already I can see you are smitten." He gallantly opened the door for her to exit.

"I am *not* smitten. I am curious, Hubert, merely curious. However, any hypothesis that prevents you from buying coal by the tonnage will always deserve my inquiry." Then she—

Sangfroid lunged to her feet. The Chesterfield creaked like an old whaling ship but she didn't care. She was tired of resting. Tired of listening. Tired of nothing making *any* sense. "You can't expect me to believe you and your brother have built a time machi—"

"That does it. I refuse to tell you anymore." Millicent slapped her hands on her lap. "And it is obvious you will not be satisfied until you've broken my mother's furniture to matchsticks."

"I am not sitting here and listening to this…this babble. It's nonsense. A time machine built out of a table. And what's all this temporal velocity thingy? What's that about?"

Millicent sighed and raised a hand to her temple. "I knew I should have bypassed the theory. You never were very good at it. And now I've got a headache."

"Stop talking as if you know me. This is some sort of trick. You're working for the enemy."

"Sit down, Sangfroid. You asked for the story, now please bear me the courtesy of listening to it."

Sangfroid glared at her resentfully. Millicent looked very pale, and she did believe she had a headache. Perhaps she was pushing her too hard? She shouldn't do that. After all, she was coming from a position of zero intelligence. She winced, the phrase was a little too close to the mark, especially in this house. She was coming from a position of zero *information*, she amended, and if this was an enemy trick, she'd only find out by keeping calm and letting this bizarre game play out.

She went to the small sideboard and poured a glass of red wine from a cut-glass decanter that felt satisfyingly heavy in her hand.

"Here. See if this helps." It was a peace offering, and Millicent accepted the glass with a polite thank you. Sangfroid poured a second, larger dose for herself. Ye gods, she needed it. Carefully, she sat back down and tried to look composed though she seethed with a hundred questions she could barely formulate because they ran so quickly through her mind.

"Are you ready?" Millicent asked. "I need to tell you about last Friday."

"What about last Friday?"

"You are becoming anxious, so I will move on to last Friday; that is the crux of my story."

"There's a crux?"

Millicent looked offended. "Of course there's a crux. There's always a crux. Now sit still and listen and maybe you can identify it."

Chapter 5

LAST FRIDAY, LONDON 1862.

THE LABORATORY WAS EMPTY WHEN Millicent arrived, tea tray in hand. There was no answer to her polite toe tap. It was then she realized Hubert had to give a lecture that day, and she'd forgotten all about it. Frustrated by her own oversight, she entered the laboratory and settled into her favourite chair. The tea was made and the scones warmed, so she may as well enjoy them, though she would have preferred Hubert's company. She had listed several questions on gravitational fields for discussion and was crestfallen he was not present to hear them. Disappointed, she poured a cup of Earl Grey. The curtains were open and dust motes danced in the bright light. Although it was still not midday, the heat was building up to intolerable levels for the afternoon. Poor Hubert, he'd be sitting in the dark again.

Idly, she rose and wandered around the room. She sipped her tea and perused her brother's bookshelves to see if he had any new acquisitions but found nothing of interest. She drifted over to his time machine. It was hard to ignore, so huge and unwieldy in the middle of the floor. Thoughtfully, she examined it from all angles. A copper disc now replaced the tabletop.

Copper piping fed from the disc to the cistern and from there to several gleaming brass pistons. Papa's chair did look elegant nestled in the centre of it all; its red velvet offset the burnished instrumentation beautifully, though she still resented its dwarvened state. Something twinkled at her from the heart of the machine. She moved closer and gasped. The handle of her best Sunday parasol protruded from the instrument panel! Sunlight gleamed off its golden bevel. Her cup clattered against its saucer. Hubert, the magpie, had adapted it into some sort of lever and embedded it in the brass control panel. Oh, how he would rue the day!

What else of hers had he purloined for his Frankensteinian creation? Millicent was outraged. She reached across and yanked on the handle to try and free it from the instrument panel. It slid down a level until it notched into a new position with a satisfying clunk. The copper disc slowly began to rotate. Sunlight glanced off the whirring face and bounced back through the window, throwing rainbow prisms around the room.

Oh dear. Millicent pulled the lever back up to what she thought was its original position. The handle rose easily and clunked into a slot higher than she intended it to go. The copper piping began to hum as hot water flushed into the pistons, and with a sharp hiss, they began to rise and fall, slowly at first, but with gathering momentum. *Oh dear me.* She forced the handle back down a notch. Everything sped up. Millicent let go of the lever. *What a pickle.* Hubert would scold her terribly if he knew she had meddled with his machinery; but really, it was her *best* parasol. Whatever was he thinking?

The disc spun faster, and the pistons fell into a galloping rhythm. She had to admit she was impressed. It all looked so precise and purposeful. Hubert must feel very proud of his invention—

The machine lurched. Or was it the room?

Millicent suddenly felt quite queasy. She tightened her grip on her cup and saucer. The room was spinning, and the copper disc shot out shards of strong light that blazed into every corner of the room, then swirled away to another area as if she were sitting inside a lighthouse. She closed her eyes against the glare and dizziness. The pistons hissed, and the pipes hummed. Her head throbbed in time with it all. She was overheated, nauseated, and distressed. She took a step back on weak, shaking legs, and felt a hand on her lower back. With a distinct push, she was propelled forward into the machine with great force. Her head hit the plush seat of the chair, her thigh scraped against a brass curlicue. The air was forced out of her lungs then whooshed back in with a violent, sickening surge. Only this was a clingy, sour, malodorous air not the dusty warmth of Hubert's laboratory.

"Aim for the head." Someone roared in her ear. Thunderous noise overwhelmed her. The wails and screams of human voices. The banging of a hundred drums. Her head rang with it. Her body shook with the force of it. Millicent opened her eyes and—

"I think I know what happens next." Sangfroid leaned forward, her eyes gleaming. "This is when we make a run for the pods."

"No, that was later. Much, much later. We've been through this many times. You only ever remember the last attempt. Now, please hush and let me continue."

Chapter 6

MILLICENT OPENED HER EYES IN time to see a huge blue-grey tentacle flash past, inches from her face. She ducked, partly out of instinct and partly because her knees gave way under her, and landed heavily on her bottom behind a metal bulwark. Beside her— looking on with a mixture of horror and dismay—crouched a soldier. His face was ashen. He had lost his helmet and his filthy blond hair stuck to a bloody gash across his forehead. He had that wild-eyed look Millicent had often seen in the men returned from the Crimea. His uniform hung tattered and bloodied from his broad shoulders. A tiny curl of blue vapour rose between their startled faces from the odd looking handgun he pointed at her.

Millicent recoiled and dropped her cup and saucer. The crash of breaking porcelain shook him out of his stupor.

"Where the bloody hell did you come from?" He barked at her.

"The laboratory," she answered, flustered at his rudeness. There was no need for the H word. Or the B one, come to that.

"But you..." He seemed confused and very unfocused. He stared at her dress and then at the broken crockery. He looked deranged and incapable of stringing more than two thoughts together. "Why aren't you at the pods?" he finally demanded in a very accusatory manner.

"To what pods you are referring?" she said. "I was in the laboratory when—"

"Decanus. We're getting decimated over here." A voice crackled from somewhere near his ear. He shouted to no one in particular that she could see, "Get the hell out, Gallo. Kappa sector, now!"

Yet again he proved incapable of polite conversation or volume control, even when talking to himself. He yelled all the time and grossly overused the H word. He was, all in all, very unsavoury.

A tentacle thundered to the floor beside them, making the whole room shudder and creak. The noise was deafening. The metal floor under them vibrated violently long after the tentacle had reared up and away. That caught her attention completely.

"Goodness. That is an extremely large mollusc." Her blood raced in a healthy mixture of fear and excitement. *How often did one witness such a creature up close! Well, maybe too close.* "Can I assume it's a member of the genus Architeuthis?"

The soldier glared at her and, in answer, let off another loud volley of gunfire towards the tentacle which only seemed to infuriate it further.

"You can assume it wants to kill you." The retort was brusque to the point of rudeness. It was then that Millicent noticed something else. With a blink of surprise, she realized this big, burly bear of a soldier was a woman! A cussing, fighting, very angry woman! There was no time for conjecture as a vast shadow reared over them and more clubbed arms thundered to the floor drumming out an unholy tattoo. Every fibre of Millicent's body protested at the vibration pouring through it. She felt shaken to bits. It was obvious she had materialized into a brouhaha involving a sea monster of some sort. She was flabbergasted. Hubert's devilish machine had landed her in the middle of a battlefield! All around her, weaponry fired and men screamed. It was brutality of the greatest order.

"How the hell did we miss you in the first sweep." It was not a question. The soldier seemed quite upset. "You're not exactly missable." This statement was accompanied by a disapproving glance at her dress.

Millicent self-consciously smoothed the fabric; it was already grimy from the torrid battle conditions. The soldier's uniform wasn't much better. It was a bizarre costume, with trousers of all things! Navy trousers—with a rather nice maroon strip down the outside of the leg that matched her tunic top—which covered her very long legs and disappeared into boots; boots that were slick and shiny with all sorts of glutinous muck. Millicent appreciated the fashionable co-ordination of the uniform, if not the over-all bloodiness of it. Maroon was a good, sensible colour, given the amount of gore splattered across the woman's chest. The epaulets, however, were a catastrophe; one was missing and the other partially torn away.

She was about to counter with a scathing comment on this when she was grabbed by her upper arm and dragged away. This manhandling was just too much! She tried to shrug the soldier off, but she tightened her grip. She clearly had no intention of letting Millicent go.

"Will you stop dragging me about," she snapped. "I am capable of animating my own limbs."

The soldier glared at her. "When I give the word, you *animate* for the exit. Got it?" She waved vaguely to the left. Millicent could see nothing but a wall of thick smoke.

"Okay. Go." The soldier lurched upright and blood seeped from her leg wound as she limped heavily forward, pulling Millicent along with her. Millicent froze. She was in a huge metal hanger. No wonder the banging was deafening as drums; she was as good as inside one. The floor was littered with the bodies of soldiers. Men and women. They lay before her, banked up three or four deep, broken, dismembered, and lifeless, in pools of a thick, viscous liquid that stank with a sulphuric sourness. It stung her eyes and caught at the back of her throat. The bodies lying directly in the liquid were dissolving into one big, misshapen lump of bone and tissue. Knots of massive serpentine tentacles coiled across the walls and ceiling, groping blindly for the living.

A soldier sprinted past them. He was bolting for a distant doorway when a barbed tentacle snared the back of his uniform and flung him in the air. He landed in the seething nest of tentacles and was instantly torn limb from limb. Millicent gagged. Her legs refused to work, and she slumped back onto the floor, pulling the unbalanced soldier down with her.

"Hallowed Hades, woman." She threw her useless pistol to the ground in disgust and clutched at her knee. Fresh blood welled from her wound. "Look. I've no idea who you are or where you came from, but you look human and you speak scientific, so I'm taking you to Kappa sector whether you like it or not. I've got my orders, and it's to get the tech crews out. We're done here. This deck's a goner. Your laboratory's a goner. You have to go and now!"

"I'm not resisting you. I wish to vacate the immediate vicinity as eagerly as you do, but you have a leg wound, your weapon looks the worse for wear, and to be frank, I am so terrified I can barely stand, nevermind run." She pushed a strand of hair from her face. Her neat chignon was unravelling almost as quickly as her mind. She fumbled for the lace handkerchief tucked up her sleeve and dabbed at her stinging eyes. It allowed her a moment to think.

"Lady, we gotta run. That thing is coming for us. It knows we're here, and it will never give up until this ship and every living thing on it is mush."

They were on a ship? Of course they were. Why had it not occurred to her they might be at sea? How else could a monstrous Kracken-like cephalopod attack?

"If I may say," she sniffed away the last of her anguish and settled her mind on the business of escaping, "that poor soldier we just saw killed by that…that thing." It was really far too large to be a cephalopod. Unless it was a sort of prehistoric, cryptid cousin, and wouldn't that be exciting! If only it weren't killing everything before it. "That soldier was running in precisely the direction you want us to go. It's obvious the creature is guarding that exit."

"Of course it's guarding the bloody exit! That's why we're trapped! We have to make a run for it." She gathered into an awkward crouch and looked ready to dash off at any moment. Millicent placed a hand on her arm to stall her.

"No," she said, in a calm, level voice. This warrior woman's logic was as stunted as her vocabulary. "We have to go in the opposite direction. If it's of the cephalopod species, and I have every reason the presume so, then it will have a lens eye similar to vertebrates. And judging from the size of the beast, I'm hoping it's a Colossal squid and not the Giant type." This was the exciting bit, and Millicent became duly animated. "The Colossal has stereoscopic vision whereas the Giant is capable of seeing a full 360 degrees."

"Look, lady." The soldier was unimpressed with the importance of this information, which disappointed Millicent greatly. She was obviously not very well-informed regarding molluscan physiology, despite being in mortal peril from them. Before the soldier could pooh-pooh her plan, she changed tack to a more straightforward explanation.

"These walls are riveted in horizontal panels about six feet apart. See?" She pointed to the scorched, blood splattered walls that soared to almost fifty feet above them. "The riveted edges provide small ledges we could move along. That would keep us off the floor and away from that…that inky stuff that seems to…melt people. And also we will be creeping along on its *blindside*, so to speak."

"Blindside?" The soldier squinted at the wall, a deep frown darkening her smoke-smudged features. Millicent hoped she was seriously considering her proposal.

"As I said, if it's a Colossal squid, it will only have forward-looking vision which is currently focused on the left hand exit, yes?"

The soldier shrugged. "You're the one studying them."

Millicent frowned at this. It was true she was a cryptologist and was particularly fascinated with the Ogopogo, but that was hardly a mollusc, most probably some sort of Basilosaurus anomaly—and anyway, how could this grubby soldier possibly know what it was she studied?

The soldier shrugged again. This seemed to pass for conversation. When Millicent didn't respond she said, "So, you tell me what its eyes do."

"But I have told you," Millicent answered, losing patience. "We should climb the wall ledges to a safe height and make our way along the ridges behind the creature's back. I assume there is an exit to the rear of this room? We can escape that way."

"There is, but it leads back to the labs and we need to get to the escape pods in Kappa. We're taking the long way round if we go that way."

"Does that matter?"

"Yes, because the ship is rigged to self-detonate at meridies."

"Oh, I see. Meridies as in noon." This was unwelcome news. "How soon is that?"

"Too soon."

"Well, we better get on with it." Millicent began to crawl out from their shelter towards the nearest wall. The soldier clumsily caught up and shouldered her to the side.

"I'm guarding you. It's my job to get you techies off this stinking rat hole. You keep behind me unless I say different. If that thing grabs me; promise me you'll run like hell."

Millicent sighed. The H word again. Between Hs and Bs, she really was foul mouthed. It must be a military thing. "If that thing grabs you, I promise I'll run, but like a lady."

Chapter 7

"This wall is sticky." Millicent squinted at the ooze squeezing through her fingers.

"The metal is corroding. Squid stink rots everything. A perfectly good ship starts to mold like an old sock once one of these buggers gets on it."

Oh dear, another B word. How many are there? "I'm not sure squid stink is the correct terminology. But it is less corrosive than the gore those poor people are lying in." She nodded at the human waste of war almost twenty feet below, though her vertigo did not allow her to look. The soldier glanced back at the dissolving cadavers.

"That's squid blood. It's like acid. You better be dead when you hit it. This stuff," she flicked the tackiness from her fingers, "it corrodes the fabric of the ship, metals, alloys, and all sorts of wiring. Weapons, too," she said. "The squid somehow adapt the atmosphere to suit them and wreck anything manmade. But the stink alone doesn't melt flesh, just metal. Keep moving." She gave a sharp cough. Millicent could feel the corrosive air tickling at her own lungs. There was a sour, metallic taste in her mouth. She felt contaminated. This enemy invaded on every level.

Her plan was working. They were edging along the wall high enough up to keep out of the line of squid vision and any haphazard weapon fire from the deck below.

"It *is* a Mesonychoteuthis, and so it has binocular vision!" She was pleased to discover her guess had been correct. This greatly increased their chances, especially as the creature was currently focused on a series of loud explosions on the other side of the hangar.

"Thought you were the expert." The soldier was setting up a brisk pace, forcing her to hurry when she really wanted to pause and observe. The beast was fascinating this close up.

"Hardly an expert." She watched the drift of colour fusing across its bulbous mantle. The subtle texture of the skin, with its map work of dark, pulsating blood vessels crisscrossing under the epidermis, mesmerized her. "It's so beautiful."

The soldier snorted. "Only a scientist would find these buggers beautiful. What do you do with them in the lab? Are you working on that infant we caught off Scorpius Major?"

"When you say laboratory, do you—Oomph." Her foot slipped, and she nearly toppled. The soldier grabbed for her, pushing her back up onto the bulkhead.

"Thank you," Millicent muttered into the metal. She was flustered; the soldier's hand rested on her waist in a most inappropriate manner. The heat from her palm seeped through Millicent's clothing, and her face flushed in what she knew was a most unbecoming manner. She quickly regained her grip and waited for the soldier to relinquish her hold, but she was slow to do so.

"Careful. Can't go losing the brains of the outfit. I'm here to round you up and herd you home. The senate hates losing its clever clogs," she said. They were coming up to a badly corroded section. She kicked at the crumbling metal edge and frowned.

"This stretch is bad." Her grip on Millicent's waist tightened. She seemed totally unaware of any discomfort. Millicent wiggled a little to try and dislodge her hand when, much to her mortification, the soldier swung behind her, cupping her entire body with her larger one. The woman was exceptionally tall, and her long limbs easily encased Millicent on either side. Heat flew to her face, and she could feel the tips of her ears scorch. No one had ever pressed against her that way. The soldier smelled strongly of sweat and a sharp nitrous odour she put down to some sort of gunfire residue. Her uniform with its elaborate straps and buckles was torn and scorched and smelled coppery with blood. She'd noted the limp earlier, and now Millicent wondered how many other wounds the soldier had.

"We'll go slow, okay." Her voice rumbled just above Millicent's head. "I don't want you to fall." Then she felt the press of the soldier's chest against her back. Millicent gripped the vibrating metal with white-knuckled fingers. Her toes curled in her light house shoes for extra purchase. Falling was not the immediate problem. She could feel the stir of the soldier's breath against her scalp, and heat radiated off her into Millicent's spine and hips. She puffed a strand of loose hair out of her eyes, hoping to cool her burning cheeks. What on earth was this soldier thinking, squashing a lady like this? It was very improper, even if she was trying to save her from the morass below.

"This is a complete overreaction," she said. "I can manage perfectly well."

"No, you can't. Not over this next bit. Let's go." There was no more discussion, the soldier began an awkward crablike shuffle, edging them slowly past the Colossal's mantle. A tentacle flailed by, too close for comfort. The soldier flattened her body against Millicent, knocking her against the bulwark so hard it took her breath away. The air around them roiled, then whooshed. Millicent closed her eyes, certain they'd be swept to their doom but the huge barbed club sailed on leaving them to exhale softly with relief.

"Hold still," the soldier whispered directly into her ear.

"Of course I'll hold still. I can barely move. You're squashing me." She was indignant. It was the only way to cope with her fear and the annoying fluster the woman soldier threw her into.

"Sorry." She eased back a bit, but not much. "Nearly there."

"We're at the exit?" Millicent peeped out from under her arm. Up ahead she could see what she hoped was the exit. A green glow flashed erratically over huge metal doors that shuddered open and slammed shut in manic malfunction. The wall they clung to vibrated with each slam of the doors and made her fingers ache. She desperately hoped they'd soon be free of the hangar. Her body was weakening, and the enforced proximity to this strange woman wasn't helping her concentration any. With a grunt, the soldier started up their crablike creep again.

It was a relief when they finally reached the exit light. The descent to the floor was tricky, though. The climb up had been easy compared to this. For one thing, they were closer to the creature, and she was very aware of a stagnant dampness that oozed from its moist, semi-translucent skin. It lost some of its beauty now she was alongside it. The chill stink of death and decay saturated her throat and sinuses, and she could almost taste its vile ink. The air was so cold and clammy it clung to her skin and made her shiver with discomfort. She was afraid. It was the old, primordial fight-or-flight fear, and she was glad the woman beside her was making the decisions for her.

The soldier went first and guided her down the bulwark step by step. She was grateful for it, as the fullness of her skirts did not permit her to see where she was putting her feet. The noise was incredible; with each step she was descending into a nightmare. The floor trembled violently under her when she finally reached it. It was like stepping onto an earthquake. Her vision blurred, and her head ached with the endless cacophony of screams and weapon fire. The ceaseless hammer of squid arms breaking the hangar to bits was driving her close to madness. Millicent felt nauseous and disorientated and was nearing the point of exhaustion, both mentally and physically.

The soldier grabbed her hand and hauled her unceremoniously through the slamming exit doors and into a murky, ill-lit corridor. The air here was a little more breathable, and she sucked it in with great gulps.

"I...I didn't realize how dizzy I was getting back there."

"Squid stink rots your head. If you're in it too long you get confused and make mistakes. We have face masks for it, but they fall apart in no time."

"Do you mean a sort of gaseous hallucinogenic? Or maybe a phosphorus based poisoning of the nervous system?" *How interesting.* These squid had a gruesome arsenal.

"I mean it makes you stupid. Now come on," she said. Millicent remembered the soldier's wild-eyed stare when she'd materialized beside her, and now doubted that she was the primary reason for it. The soldier could easily have been in the thrall of "squid stink," as she so succinctly put it. Her gaze was much more focused now that they were in cleaner air. Her eyes were gunmetal grey, hard and flinty, and for the moment, squinting cautiously into the gloom ahead. Once again she grabbed Millicent by the hand and drew her along behind, keeping to the shadows.

Despite her earlier misgivings, Millicent clung to her hand. The corridor was wide with a low ceiling and sweeping bends, and the slam and slide of broken doors clanged along the length of it. Smoke hung in lazy pockets, pierced by tiny red and green lights blinking randomly from melted electrical panels. Overhead, the lighting strips flickered weakly, distressing the walls with long, eerie shadows. It became clearer to her by the second that Hubert's machine had deposited her not only in the middle of a weird, interspecies war, but also considerably into the future. If she ever got home again, he was so going to hear about this.

She watched how carefully the soldier moved, her body tense and on full alert.

"Are there more?" she whispered nervously.

"Yup, there's always more. We beat them off, but they always sneak back in."

"Oh dear." She glanced about anxiously.

"We should be okay here for a while. We cleared the Beta deck when we got your lot out."

"My lot?" She frowned and took a deep breath. This was going to be a difficult question. "Why do you think I belong to this ship?"

But the soldier wasn't listening. Instead she raised a finger to her lips for silence. Millicent strained to hear what had caught her attention. From around a corner came a sharp click, then another, and another, and then someone said in disgusted exasperation, "Ah, fuckamo, fuckamas, fuckamant."

The soldier let go of her hand and stepped forward around the corner. "Gallo?" she said. "That you?"

"Well, blow my war horn, Sangfroid, is that you?" came the answer.

Intrigued, Millicent followed. She saw another soldier crouched over an abandoned pile of weaponry.

"Sangfroid! Hey, you made it!" This was followed by a happy guffaw. The soldiers collided in a rough, shoulder-slapping embrace.

Sangfroid? So that was the name of her rescuer. Millicent watched the comradery from a polite distance, all the time glancing over her shoulder for sneaking squid.

"Well, I managed to make it back to where we started," Sangfroid said ruefully, and stepped back. "Maybe not the smartest move. What about you? Why are you grubbing around out here?"

It was only when the soldiers separated that Millicent realized Gallo was a woman, too. Another giantess! Wherever this place was, her gender had come a long way.

Gallo held up two handguns from the pile of discards at her feet. At least Millicent assumed they were handguns. They were very complex weaponry but similar to the one she had seen Sangfroid throw away in disgust.

"These fuckers are still juiced." Gallo grinned.

Millicent pinched the bridge of her nose. *Oh, dear. I think I may have an F word to add to the list. Perhaps I should start a lexicon?*

"Excellent." Sangfroid grabbed one from her.

"Hey. Where'd ya get the frock?" Gallo nodded at Millicent, who bristled at the impolite tone. She had similarly noted Gallo's strange attire but had thought it not polite to pass comment. Gallo was almost as tall as Sangfroid. She had mannish short, dark hair and a swarthy Mediterranean type complexion. She was dressed in a similar, equally grubby uniform. It underscored her leanness of hip and rather unfeminine shape. Millicent recoiled from her catty thoughts with a stab of shame. She should be above such demeaning judgment of another woman's figure. Even if the woman was rude.

"She's a scientist." Sangfroid jerked a thumb at Millicent. "We need to get her to the Kappa pods." Her casualness annoyed Millicent immensely, almost as much as Gallo's rudeness. She felt like a parcel that had to be delivered rather than another human trying to survive the same living nightmare.

"She looks weird, even for a scientist." Gallo frowned at Millicent's dress. "Teeny wee thing, too."

"Excuse me." Millicent straightened her back. "I happen to be the average height for an English woman, and furthermore I—"

"Don't get her talking." Sangfroid turned her back on them both and looked along the darkened corridor. "Any idea what's up there, Gallo?"

"Well, really." Millicent had never seen such ill-mannered behaviour.

"Bastards are creeping back," Gallo said. They both ignored her.

That did it! Millicent reached for her reticule and drew out a small notebook with attached pencil. She was going to keep a record of this insolence and report it to their commanding officer—if she ever had a chance to meet him! She jotted down Gallo's latest obscenity. Between them they had the manners of the gutter, and it would be addressed later.

"They're really determined to crack this deck. Rest of the ship is still intact last I heard." Gallo said.

"Your comm-piece still up?" Sangfroid asked, surprised. "Why do you think it's only this deck?"

Gallo shook her head. "Lost it ages ago. Melted like butter. And I don't know why they're concentrating on this deck, but they want it." She turned to face the hanger Sangfroid and Millicent had come from and readied her gun. "Okay, I'm up for it."

Sangfroid shook her head. "No go. It's a big bastard and it's bedded in for the foreseeable." She nodded in the opposite direction. "We're heading for Kappa," her voice brooked no opposition, "via the labs."

"The labs." Gallo looked uncomfortable with this idea. "Aw, man."

Sangfroid nodded at Millicent. "It's okay. We got a brainiac to lead us through."

Gallo still didn't look happy. "I hate the labs," she said glumly.

Sangfroid nodded at the hangar doors. "We're mincemeat if we go back there."

Gallo's frown turned to a mutinous scowl.

"Plus, it's an order," Sangroid added, her voice taking on an edge that reminded them all who was in command.

"Aye, Decanus." Gallo turned towards the labs in a huff.

Decanus? Millicent struggled with the word. It was Sangfroid's military rank, she supposed. She had heard her called that earlier, through what she now realized were their communication objects. Her fingers itched to draw the small wired box away from Sangfroid's ear and examine it. How fascinating. Hubert would love it here if it were not so deadly.

"If the Beta launching deck is jammed with friggin' Colossal, I suppose we've no other choice." Gallo was still grumbling about the shortcut through the lab. "But anything so much as twitches, lady," she turned and glared at Millicent. "I'm fucking popping it."

Good Lord, Millicent thought. *Why on earth do they insist I'm one of their scientists? Surely they can see I'm not of the current timeline. And whatever is in the laboratories to make them all so jittery?*

Chapter 8

THE LABORATORY WAS SEALED TIGHT. At first Millicent didn't consider this strange, despite all the other doors on the deck crazily slamming open and shut. She assumed they had corroded wiring.

"Stand back," Sangfroid ordered her. Brash blue light flamed from the pistols she and Gallo pointed at the command panel.

"What kind of weapon is that?" she asked when they stopped firing to examine the damage.

"Hand laser."

"Fascinating," she said. Then after a moment, she asked, "What is a laser?" But her question was drowned out by a second onslaught on the panel.

"Wish they put this much security into all the door locks," Gallo bellowed over the sizzle of fried wires. "Might be nice to keep a squid out for once."

The wiring popped and then surrendered, and the doors slid quietly open. Sangfroid and Gallo stopped firing, and in the silence that followed, Millicent mulled over Gallo's words. *"Nice to keep a squid out for once."* Did that mean... "Are you intimating there are squid locked *in* here?" she asked.

Gallo and Sangfroid looked at her with growing incredulity. "It's the lab," Sangfroid said, unhelpfully.

"Well, you're the scientist," Gallo muttered gloomily. "What else do you keep in a lab, 'cept squid?" She stared warily through the open doorway. "Don't tell me there're worse things than squid in there."

A thunderous bang echoed down the corridor behind them. Something ominous was occurring farther on up.

"We need to get going." Sangfroid stepped inside, laser raised. She signalled for Millicent to stay close to her. Gallo automatically took up the rear.

"So. Where do we go?" Sangfroid asked Millicent.

The room was a brightly lit wonderland. A perfect oasis of calm, unperturbed by the brutal battle going on outside its sterile walls. Sterile walls that were covered with hundreds of wiring panels and glowing lights. Millicent stared, awed by the glory of it all. Long, wide benches, in a shiny translucent material Millicent didn't recognize, stretched the length of it, and complex machinery sat on the bench tops or was suspended from overhead racks. Everything looked sharp and bright and gloriously intriguing. Millicent's fingers itched to touch.

"Where do we go?" Sangfroid repeated in a tight voice.

"Oh. Let's go here." Millicent headed directly to the first bench to examine a magnificent example of a gyroscope. "Goodness me, I've never seen such a small one, or so precise. Hubert was considering the possibility of a gyrocompass, you know. He hoped the new electric motors could help him create an indefinite spin. He has a rudimentary prototype assembled at the moment, but if he could only see—"

"How the hell do we get out of here!" Sangfroid yelled. Millicent jumped back from the gyroscope as if it had burned her.

"I have no idea," she answered curtly.

"But this is the lab," Sangfroid said.

"It's not my lab."

"Not—" She looked like she might explode, and Millicent was glad there was a workbench between them.

"Well, fuck that." Gallo was equally aghast.

"I have not, at any point, stated that I worked in *this* laboratory." Millicent felt compelled to redefine what was quickly becoming a dictate from these two. "That was an assumption on your part entirely."

"What! But!" Sangfroid spluttered and then sighed heavily. "Okay. Let's just find an exit and get out of here." She turned away and led them deeper into the lab.

"Good gracious, look at that." Millicent gasped.

"What? What is it?" Gallo raised her weapon. Millicent gently pushed Gallo's firearm away.

"It's already dead," she said. She walked over to a huge glass tank covering the far wall from floor to ceiling. It was filled with a thick viscose liquid, and multiple wires emerged from the tank to disappear into various electrical wall panels. The other ends of the wires were attached to a severed, heavily muscled, squid tentacle. It was at least fifty feet long, and at its thickest point was about five feet deep, which meant it was nearly as tall as Millicent herself. This close, Millicent found the physiology fascinating.

"That's unusual. The squid you're fighting have more tentacles than arms," she mused. "This tentacle, for instance, has multiple hooks and serrated suction rings. An uncommon amount, despite the size."

"That's 'cos it's a soldier squid." Gallo came to stand beside her.

"A soldier? So you're saying these squid have a social structure, or a caste system, like an ant colony? What an intriguing concept."

Gallo shrugged, looking far from intrigued. She was less tense now that there was no immediate danger. Her hand strayed to her neckline, and she plucked absently at a gold medallion and muttered what Millicent took to be a short prayer. Or maybe it was an oath; it was hard to tell with Gallo. The medallion glinted in the overhead lighting.

"Is that an amulet?" Millicent asked, noting her companion's fidgeting.

"It's the goddess Looselea." Gallo shoved the medallion towards Millicent so she could take a better look at the golden cameo. "She's the goddess of engineers, not soldiers, but the medallion belonged to my mother so..." She shrugged self-consciously and tucked it back into her tunic. "Brings me luck," she said as she snapped her top button.

"You mother was an engineer?" Millicent was fascinated.

"Yeah. Damned good 'un, too. See them hooks?" She awkwardly changed the subject and pointed at the rows of vicious tentacle barbs with her handgun. "They can rotate. Rip you in half in a second."

"In less than a second." Sangfroid joined them.

Millicent shuddered. She had seen them in action. It still felt like a dream, but her hand against the cold glass of the tank and the warm, sweaty smell of Sangfroid and Gallo standing beside her reminded her it was not. It was a nightmare. She was in a place where she should never have existed, experiencing things she fervently believed belonged far into the future. And what an Armageddon of a future it was. What had mankind become? Why, these people standing beside her could even be her own progeny!

Gallo burped and tapped the glass with her toe. "Smelly fucker," she said.

"Hell, yeah," Sangfroid agreed.

Millicent sighed. Perhaps she would remain childless.

Gallo wandered off to examine other tanks nearby, and Sangfroid moved closer to Millicent. She regarded the severed tentacle with interest.

"I've never seen one of these things up close. Well, this still and up close. Why is it in there?" Sangfroid asked.

Millicent's gaze followed the trunk wiring. It wound from the tank to the panels in the wall above. The wires were thick and of various colours, all twisted and flexed, making the cord appear almost umbilical. "I think it's a type of electrical animation," she said. "I'm unsure how the circuitry works, but I'd guess the electrical impulses trigger muscle responses in the limb. Interestingly, this was first proven by Galvani in the late eighteenth cen—"

"Okey-dokey." Sangfroid sounded distracted. She turned away and shouted at Gallo. "What's up ahead?"

"—tury," Millicent concluded. If she couldn't be bothered to wait for the answer then why ask the question? She glared after Sangfroid, but then her thoughts returned to the tank and its lurid contents, and she bit her lip. She considered experimentation on living specimens cruel, but this looked like an attempt to reanimate dead tissue. The question was how did the specimen reach the tank? She hoped the tentacle had not been dismembered from a living organism.

"Do all the laboratories do this type of experimentation?" she asked.

Sangfroid grimaced. "You're the brains. I'm just the shooter who keeps you alive and thinking."

"There's babies," Gallo called from another tank. Millicent's heart sank as she went to look.

"Larvae," she said with some relief. Hundreds of the translucent little molluscs floated in a deep vat. They tumbled and fell in a myriad of pearlescent blues and whites, swirling like liquid jewels in a kaleidoscope.

"Squirmy little buggers," Gallo said.

"They're dead." Millicent's voice was flat. "They're only moving because the liquid's vibrating." She moved away, disappointed and distressed. This part of the lab was almost entirely stocked with tanks filled with various parts of squid anatomy. There was an awful gruesomeness to it, an urgency to try and understand these creatures, though most probably only to research their weaknesses rather than wonder at their magnificence. Hubert had often bewailed that the greatest scientific advances were so closely associated with, and financed by, warfare and cruelty, rather than a sincere and altruistic thirst for knowledge. If this was the future, then he would be disappointed that so little had changed. The work in this laboratory was not so much *know thine enemy* as, quite literally, *divide and conquer*.

"Let's get out of here." Sangfroid was back to guide her away from the tanks. "Kappa sector's this way." Her grip on Millicent's elbow was curiously gentle as if she sensed her distress. A quick glance at her fixed profile told Millicent that Sangfroid was also affected by the laboratory's research.

They moved on, weaving through the wide benches with their array of fantastical instruments and machinery. Millicent would often stop and dither by a particularly marvellous contraption, but could do little more than ogle before Sangfroid pulled her away and kept them moving.

"I think we can exit through there." Gallo pointed off to the left. "It leads to Kappa through the aft decks."

Sangfroid hesitated a moment then redirected them to the door Gallo had identified. They approached a separate wing of the laboratory guarded by even more locked doors which were covered with vivid iconography that Millicent took to be warning sigils. Gallo muttered an oath, and her hand strayed to her medallion. Both she and Sangfroid raised their handguns and blazed away at a nearby door panel.

"Get ready to run when I tell you," Sangfroid roared over the din of her weapon. The panel was on fire, and the doors were slamming open and shut like a sideways guillotine. Would the danger ever cease? Millicent had not appreciated how tiresome adventuring could be.

"Gallo, you go first. When she says it's clear, you're next. Okay?" Sangfroid shouted at her. Millicent snapped out of her reverie and watched in alarm as Gallo timed her leap and passed through the slicing doors unscathed. Weapon at the ready, Gallo scoured the room beyond before giving Sangfroid an affirmative that all was safe.

"On three," Sangfroid told Millicent. "One, two…three." She counted down, then pushed Millicent so roughly she sailed through the gap with her feet barely touching the floor. Sangfroid followed hard on her heels, slammed her flat onto the floor with her huge body sprawled flat over her. They lay nose to nose, and Millicent found she was momentarily transfixed by the grey of Sangfroid's eyes; they had little green flecks, and the irises were expanding at a rate of knots until her eye was almost black.

"Kindly remove yourself at once, Miss Sangfroid," she blurted, embarrassed by her flushed face and light, shallow breathing that she was certain were only too apparent. The woman's clumsiness around her was absurd. She always seemed to be slamming into or falling over her. Sangfroid scrambled awkwardly to her feet and dragged Millicent up with her. Gallo guffawed. Millicent glowered and dusted herself down with sharp agitated movements. Though Lord knew why she bothered; her lovely eau de nil day dress was destroyed.

"It's not miss; it's decanus, my rank." Sangfroid's rough cheeks flushed. "Call me Sangfroid," she said, her gaze darting away. Millicent rubbed her bruised shoulder, and her jaw clenched in censure. Awkwardly, Sangfroid reached out and tucked an errant strand of hair behind Millicent's ear. "I guess you've earned it, I've done nothing but beat up on you all day." Sangfroid's fingertips were hard and calloused as they scraped against her cheek. She moved her face into the touch, but only for a pulse beat. Sangfroid felt so safe, so solid and reassuring, and after all, any fleeting solace in this mad world could only be welcome.

"I'm just going over here to throw up a little." Gallo stomped off while making yakking sounds. Then she called,

"Hey. There's another tank in here." She peered into a darkened annex. "It looks different from the—" She pulled back startled.

"Different?" Millicent was by her side in an instant, curiosity outweighing concern. Gallo's arm barred her from moving any farther forward.

"Careful, I thought I saw something move." She squinted into the darkness. Their movements or perhaps even the sound of their voices seemed to automatically bring the annex to life. Overhead lighting flickered on, but it was soft and low-level compared to the brash lights in the outer laboratory. The walls began to glow pink, a reflection of the colour pulsing out from a shallow tank that sat on a central bench. The wires leading to and from it hummed. This tank was active, in contrast to the others that had been switched off. Perhaps this room ran from a separate power supply.

"I think the room reacts to us," Millicent said, amazed at such a marvel. "That's the movement you saw. It was the room responding to you," she told Gallo, who still looked leery.

"Live specimen." Sangfroid read a sign on the annex door. "That's what you saw." Her voice was grim. "There's something in there, all right."

"Security status triple Alpha." Gallo read another sign.

"Detour time," Sangfroid snapped, and she and Gallo turned back the way they'd come. Millicent watched their retreating backs for a split second, then kept her course straight into the triple Alpha lab. She was drawn as if magnetized. If there was a live specimen here, she wanted to see it. Her skin tingled, and she imagined her hair crackled with the frenetic energies that ricocheted around the room.

"Wait!" Sangfroid came running back, but it was too late. Millicent stood in the middle of the annex by a small tank, wracked with horror. This tank was shallow and circular, not unlike a huge lab dish, and filled with a clear gelatinous liquid. Inside, a small squid lay staked out with its arms and tentacles all stretched to their utmost and clipped to electrical grip devices that hummed menacingly. The squid's mantle was coral, and the colour filtered along the tentacles to a pearly pink that finally paled to white at the tentacle tips. The gentle undulation of colour reminded Millicent of rose petals fading as summer passed. Its suction rings were a deeper pink, and there were no barbs on the fragile arms. Its single squid eye, a glassy pale blue with a huge black pupil, watched her cautiously. It blinked, and Millicent blinked back in surprise.

"Be careful." Sangfroid was at her side, ready for the unexpected. Behind her, Gallo hovered by the door, weapon raised.

"I think I will be perfectly fine." Millicent watched a translucent ripple spread across the vulnerable pink flesh. The large eye blinked at her again, and she believed it was filled with fright. The creature was scared of her? Her gaze locked with the wide-eyed stare, and she felt herself tumbling towards that fear. It mirrored her experiences of the last few hours, the terror and brutality, the disorientation. Empathy filled the space between herself and the little pink squid.

"I think it's communicating with me," she murmured.

"What? Get it out of your head," Sangfroid snapped. "I told you they mess with your mind."

"It's not dangerous. It's…hurting," she said.

Gallo flicked a glance at the dish. "Of course it's hurting," she said. "Look at the state of the poor little bugger." There was a grain of compassion and disapproval in her voice, but only a grain; suspicion smothered everything else.

"Why is it here? Why is this one alive when all the others have been dismembered?" Millicent asked.

Sangfroid shrugged. "I don't know. The senate ploughs zillions into bio-weapons research and uses grubs like us to keep the research ships safe." She indicated that she and Gallo were the grubs. "I've no idea why they didn't kill it. Maybe they ran out of time?" She looked at the quivering specimen before them. "Pretty, isn't it? In a gross sort of way."

Gallo snorted. "Ain't you the lover-gal today? Why don't you fall on top of it?"

"It's a she, Sangfroid, not an 'it,'" Millicent said. "And this is deliberate." She waved a hand at the apparatus. "They intended to keep her alive, and for a long time, from the looks of it."

"It's a she? How can you tell?" Sangfroid regarded the squid with even greater interest. "I know, I know," she suddenly crowed with satisfaction. "Because it's pink!"

Millicent gave a slow, sad sigh. "It's communicating with me, and I sense this is a female. A young one, too," she said. "However, should we find a baby blue one, I'll concede to your theory."

The far off rumble of explosives shook the floor under their feet. The lights temporarily blinked off and on, and all the glass and steel around them rattled ominously.

"Hull breach! Can we please just go?" Gallo demanded.

Sangfroid grabbed Millicent by the arm. "Come on."

She struggled free. "We can't just leave her here. It's inhumane."

"We can't take her with us," Sangfroid snapped. Gallo waited for them at the exit, rocking impatiently from foot to foot.

"But we could free her and maybe the other squid will find her and save her?"

"Ah, I see. You've missed the bit about the whole ship self-detonating anytime now. We need to get to the Kappa escape pods, or we'll go up with it." She began dragging Millicent away.

"No." She shook herself free and ran back to the bench. "Please. It won't take a moment, and I have to do something. I can't walk away from this. No one with a speck of decency could. This is torture, plain and simple." She began to unclip the grips holding small tentacles in place.

After a slight hesitation, Sangfroid pushed her aside and grappled for the clips.

"Okay, but only because it's a tiddler, otherwise I'd leave it to fry. Go cut the power." The small squid rippled, and warm colours swam across her mantle illuminating Sangfroid's face with a healthy rose flush. "Sorry."

Millicent heard the muttered apology as one particularly awkward clip cut at the tentacle tip and a spot of inky blood smudged the gel in the lab dish. It was as if Sangfroid, too, was in communication with the creature, though in her haste, she did not realize it. Millicent did notice and stored it away for future reference.

While Sangfroid took care of the clips, she went to sever the electrical current to the tank. The cover came away in her hands, and the mass of circuitry inside nested around one large blinking, red switch. Millicent pulled it, since it seemed the most obvious thing to do. Immediately the main laboratory hummed and every light lit up in a blinding blaze.

Gallo shielded her eyes. "You hit the friggin' main."

Machinery whirled and blipped into action. Vats began to bubble, and everywhere banks of red and green electrical lights stopped blinking and shone out steadily. The entire lab reanimated as if driven by an invisible workforce. In a tank beside Gallo, a disembodied squid's heart shuddered then thumped once, twice, and then beat as steadily as it would inside a living creature. "Fuckamo!" Gallo leaped away from it.

In other tanks organs began to twitch. Huge floating squid eyes began to ricochet off the glass walls of their prison. A liver wriggled and frothed to the surface like bloated flotsam. Other organs blew inky bubbles up through the liquids in their containment tanks. It was as if a gruesome carnival had sprung to life, and it chilled Millicent to the bone. Gallo went pale, her weapon ready, and her body tense.

"You've activated the whole damned lab." Sangfroid appeared beside her. "Out! Now!" She grabbed Millicent again with a hold that said she was not letting go.

"Sangfroid!" Gallo called in warning.

There was a thunderous crash behind them and a wall of liquid and shattered glass exploded into the room. The little pink squid curled into a tight ball, distress radiating off her. Millicent and Sangfroid turned towards the destruction. The huge severed tentacle had broken through the walls of its tank and flailed crazily around the laboratory, smashing benches, machinery, and experiments to matchsticks. Its serrated suckers snapped open and shut as if tasting the air, and its vicious barbs quivered and flexed along the muscular arm. With alarming speed, it lurched its way across the lab towards the annex. Sangfroid pushed Millicent behind her and raised her gun to join Gallo in a volley of fire. Together, they fell back farther into the annex; there was nowhere else to go. The lasers tore into the tentacle, gouging out lumps of necrotic flesh, but the thing was blind and mindless. There was no stopping it. It jerked and spasmed under the gun fire, but kept on coming.

The annex doors disintegrated under the weight as it struggled to spill through into the small room. With one almighty shove, Sangfroid sent Millicent sprawling towards the other exit, the one that led out to the corridor.

"Go!" she yelled. "Get out."

Gallo stepped forward to shield her as she scrabbled on the floor. "When you hit the corridor keep left all the way to Kappa," she shouted over her gunfire. And then the tentacle was in the annex with them. Sangfroid fired non-stop, moving backwards, drawing the tentacle away from Gallo and Millicent and towards her.

"No," Millicent screamed when she realized what Sangfroid was doing. Sangfroid was on the wrong side of the annex. She was cornered. The tentacle reared once, higher than before, and crashed towards her. She had nowhere to retreat. It coiled around her in thick, lumpish contractions as she roared out in anger and pain and, before Millicent's horrified gaze, tightened its hold so its barbs sank deep into Sangfroid's flesh. Then in one huge, rippling spasm, it tore her into a hundred pieces.

Chapter 9

"What!" Sangfroid sat bolt upright. The Chesterfield went into spasm. She ignored the groans and glared at Millicent instead. "I was killed?" She took a large swig from her wine glass. Then another.

"I know." Millicent gave a look of deepest sympathy. "It was horrid."

"I've just been ripped apart by a severed squid arm. I'm sorry it was so horrid."

"Now you're being facetious, which, by the way, is neither charming nor witty," she said. "Do you want me to continue or would you rather sulk?"

"There's more? Don't tell me it ate me."

Millicent tutted disapprovingly and sank back into the story. "As you can imagine, there were bits and pieces of you all over the annex—

Gallo let off a hail of gunfire, all the time pushing Millicent towards the exit. The tentacle turned its attention towards her.

"Hit the green button. This is the emergency exit; pray to Looselea it still works," she yelled at Millicent.

Millicent found the button and hit it with numb fingers. Sangfroid's image filled her mind with horror. She couldn't speak, couldn't think. The door slid open soundlessly. She and

Gallo fell into the corridor and Gallo slammed the door closed to gain them temporary respite from the monster on the other side.

"Now run. We've got to reach Kappa before the Amoebas self-destructs," Gallo ordered and took off down the corridor. Millicent tried to run with her, but her skirts caught at her heels and her legs were uncoordinated. She felt dizzy, as if her head was bloodless with shock. Sangfroid was dead. She was gone. Forever. And Millicent had orchestrated her death. She had refused to obey orders and had delayed their escape. She had done this! *She*, who shouldn't even have been there in the first place!

"Hurry up, woman!" Gallo was waiting impatiently a little way ahead. Millicent staggered onwards and Gallo turned once more to lead the way. The cold metal walls around Millicent began to melt and the floor lurched up to meet her. The stale odour of the corridor faded, as did the distant booming warfare. For a moment she thought she was swooning, her knees buckled, and then she wondered if the ship had exploded, making it too late for Kappa.

"I got you." Gallo's hand gripped hers "Come on, stay with me." Millicent sank farther. Her legs refused to move. The inky, bloody stains on Gallo's uniform became a blur, and the corridor spiralled away from her. Her world was spinning wildly, and then she smelled the warm tweed of her brother's jacket, and Hubert was calling her…and Hubert was calling her…and—"Hubert!" she screamed and clung to his arms.

"Oh Millicent, Millicent." He cradled her, tears coursing down his puffy cheeks. "In God's name, what happened to you? I thought I'd lost you for good." He was babbling in his distress.

He led her to a settee, though she still needed his support to sit upright. She gazed around her incredulously. She was back in Hubert's laboratory with its smell of leather, pipe tobacco, and chemicals. Familiar books lined the walls, and Hubert's no-nonsense desk sat squat and solid by the draped windows. A lamp had been lit and cast a welcoming glow. In the hearth a fire crackled happily. She was home at number five, Christie Mews.

"Get rid of that thing!" She pointed an accusing finger at his time machine.

"Yes. Yes. Anything you say," he agreed at once. "Oh, Millicent. Here, sit up, dear. Let me get you tea. Or perhaps a sherry?"

"Brandy," she ordered. "A large one." She sniffled into the back of her hand. Tears coursed down her cheeks unchecked. Her hair hung around her in tatty wisps, and her dress was torn and covered in oil and dirt…and blood. Sangfroid's blood! Sobs wracked her. She covered her face with shaking hands and still the tears fell through her fingers. Hubert raced to her side and flung himself down on his knees beside her.

"Oh, my dearest sister. Tell me what has happened. When I came home to find no sign of you, the tea tray abandoned, and the machine running wildly with the gears locked… Why, I nearly went mad! It was only by the gravest good fortune I remembered the original gear setting and was able to re-engage the lever. You came into focus soon after. You were only an outline, like a photographic print taking form, then suddenly you were here, solid and in the physical." He was wringing his hands, distraught by her appearance and tears. "It was extraordinary. You sort of…oozed back into this world, finally solidifying, but looking like this." He waved a hand at her dishabille. "Are you well? What on earth happened to you?"

She sniffled and took small sips of her brandy as he festooned her with large cotton handkerchiefs he managed to disgorge from every possible pocket.

"Thank you," she said, dabbing at her eyes. "Hubert, take a seat please and let me tell you a most fantastical and harrowing tale of a discordant and brutal future, and a very, very…" Here she broke down into tears again. Her brother sank into the settee beside her and waited for her to compose herself. "A very wonderful, brave hero," she sobbed.

"You were crying for me, right?" Sangfroid asked, as if she needed to be sure. "Not Gallo?"

"*Of course* I was crying for you. You'd just died horribly or had you missed that bit?" she snapped. "It's the crux you are supposed to be looking out for. You're the one who demanded to hear the story."

"Just asking." She seemed a little abashed. "There's a lot of heroes out there." Though that came out as false modesty to Millicent's shrewd ear.

Millicent sighed. "I apologize for being snappish," she said. "But you must understand, I felt *terrible*. I knew I was responsible, you see. But for Hubert's infernal machine, I should never have been there, and you would not have died trying to rescue me. I do hope Gallo got away."

"She was fine the last I saw her. Depending on what timeline it was, I suppose."

"And where exactly was that?" Millicent asked.

"In my version of events, I last saw Gallo in the hangar. We were joking about meeting up at the bar later. It's our go to place." Sangfroid said. "The night before the battle, we were hanging at the Parabellum. It was helluva night, actually. We got totally smashed with some legionnaires Gallo knew from Cygni Gamma, and then we hit the casinos and bordellos." She stopped when she noticed Millicent's arctic stare.

"I knew it!" Sangfroid was on her feet again. "This is an Elysian test, and you *are* a Hesperidean maiden come to test my worthiness."

"I am no such thing. I am not even sure what a Hesperidean maiden is, and I have no wish to know." She held up a hand to stop any further explanations. "And rest assured your worthiness in neither here nor there to me, Decanus Sangfroid."

"So…" Sangfroid sat back down. "If I'm dead, how come I'm sitting here talking to you in this timeline?"

"Because I interfered," she said. "Somewhere out there is a timeline where you hopefully survived the battle on the Amoebas and went on to meet Gallo at the Parabellum club."

"Bar. The Parabellum is a bar, not a club." Sangfroid snorted in derision at the idea. "You should see it; it's the biggest booze hole for every reprobate species in the galaxy. All the troopers from around—"

"Bar, club, they're all places where nothing of any good ever happens," Millicent declared. "So, we have two timelines. This one, which is mine. And then there is the timeline where I arrived on the Amoebas and you were violently torn asunder."

"Are you sure about that? I don't feel dead. Maybe I can stay here in one piece until you figure out how to get me back to the Parabellum?"

"No, you cannot stay here. It can't be like that. Hubert is working on getting you back to your proper timeline. Preferably in one piece and staying that way," she said. "You don't belong here, and I can't go around inventing military ranks and imaginary platoons for you; someone is bound to notice you don't fit."

"Those ladies didn't notice."

"Those ladies wouldn't notice if the house was on fire as long as there's a servant to put it out."

Sangfroid took a chance. "They seemed to think Millicent and the major fit well enough. If I recall correctly." It was a clumsy attempt to flirt, and Millicent blushed violently, as Sangfroid sort of hoped she would. Maybe Millicent liked her back? A smart rat-a-tat on the door ended their conversation before she could explore further. Hubert entered, his faced wreathed in a relieved smile.

"Just popping in to let you know I've managed to escape the paleobotanists, but it won't be long before tea is served, and they'll be baying for Sangfroid, heart, mind, and soul," he said and shot Sangfroid a mischievous glance.

"I haven't managed to clean her up yet." Millicent gave Sangfroid's filthy uniform a disappointed look. "We've been too busy talking."

"And how is that going?" Hubert asked.

"Unsurprisingly difficult," Millicent said. "And we've only just started."

"There's more?" Sangfroid was disconcerted.

Hubert held out a black drape coat and a rather natty top hat. "These were my father's. He was a large man, and some of his stuff might very well fit. Well, almost fit." He ran a calculating eye over Sangfroid's frame. "Let's go to upstairs and see what we can find." He looked to Millicent for approval, and she nodded in agreement.

"She can't go about dressed as she is. She'll get arrested. I'll have her uniform sent out and laundered for the morning," she said.

"I don't need laundering." Sangfroid suspiciously studied the coat Hubert held out. "This stuff just sponges off. See." She scratched a fingernail over a particularly crusty patch to prove her point.

Hubert paled as a nodule of human skin pinged off. "It will take more than a sponge and scratch to get past the doorman at the Prometheus club."

"We're going to a club?" Sangfroid perked up. "Is that like a bar?"

"No, the Prometheus club is for gentlemen of a scientific persuasion." Hubert led her to the door. "What say you try on a clean pair of trousers and maybe a shirt, then we'll head for my club, and I'll explain more over a brandy, 'eh?"

Sangfroid hesitated and plucked her uniform, obviously loath lose it.

"The ladies will be disappointed to have missed you," Hubert said, noting the lack of enthusiasm. "Of course, if you'd rather stay here and have tea with them instead?" he added. Sangfroid shrugged out off her uniform jacket in double quick time and dragged on the proffered coat.

"This fits fine." She tugged hard at the short sleeves. "Let's go."

Hubert and Millicent's father may have been a big man, but he was no match for Sangfroid's dimensions.

"Good man," Hubert approved.

"But I'm not a man." Sangfroid lips twisted in disapproval. "Why does everybody get that wrong?"

"Because, for this age, you are so far removed from the feminine norm, I suppose," Hubert said. "And it's best to keep it like that for as long as you're visiting. 'Eh, Major, old boy?" He winked. "Now, what say we find you some clean trousers and a shirt, and then we'll be on our way."

"So, we're going to a club?" Sangfroid refocused on the interesting part, giving up the battle over civilian clothes. "And that's not the same as a bar?"

"It has brandy." Hubert patted her on the shoulder. "And I'll wager you need some."

"Please be careful," Millicent called after them.

"Oh, we will," Hubert reassured her.

"Hey, I'm dead. What else can go wrong?" Sangfroid looked over her shoulder and gave Millicent her most inappropriate grin.

Chapter 10

Sangfroid checked out the Prometheus's reading room from over the rim of her snifter with a certain amount of satisfaction. This was definitely a bar. Okay, so there weren't any bar girls or even a dice table, but not all bars promoted prostitution, and they had passed a huge billiard room on the way in, so some gaming was allowed.

The journey over had been fascinating. Hubert had hailed a transport vehicle pulled by horses! A hansom cab, he'd called it. Sangfroid hadn't seen horses since a childhood visit to a zoological garden. Though a few of the very privileged patricians kept them as pets.

She'd stuck her head out the window for the entire ride. Hubert had complained about the chill, but she'd loved sucking in the damp night air with its smoky smells and the sharp sourness that came after a rainfall in the city. Hubert told her there was a river nearby, the Thames, and she thought she could detect the oily stench of it. Gas lights gave the streets a sickly glow. The houses were tall and cramped together, and the thoroughfares were cobbled and narrow as if they had run out of room to build. The city shadows were long, and anyone who emerged from them walked quickly, bundled up in warm clothing with their heads covered against the cold. They seemed anxious to reach their destinations. Everything was exciting and intriguing, and for once, Sangfroid felt part of the foreign cityscape. Usually, she was stomping all over it as part of a war machine. This time she was like a tourist, a kinder version of invader.

They alighted at the Prometheus club. A low, unadorned building as square and solid as the men who frequented it. It smelled of leather and tobacco and the mustiness of too much thought and too little action. Sangfroid approved. A centurion could truly relax here, and a recuperating one could rally her energies before the next campaign. Just like at the Parabellum. The thought brought her full circle to her current problem. Millicent's story had confounded her and she needed to consider the implications. The choice being she was either mad, dead, or had indeed time travelled. And each possibility needed a stiff drink to accompany any in-depth contemplation. Sangfroid found a certain relief in the austere furnishings of the Prometheus club after the feminine clutter of the house. There was something refreshingly solid and right about the wingback chairs Hubert had claimed for them.

The room was eerily quiet with only the occasional cough and the rustle of newspapers. Sangfroid found it quaint that the news of the day was circulated on sheets of printed paper, and that there were places like this to just sit and read them. It was a nicer way to assimilate information than the constant stream of senate propaganda that poured through her comm-piece night and day. She took an appreciative sip from her glass. The brandy was exceptional. She'd noticed that the wine she had served Millicent earlier was also excellent. Hubert's timeline obviously didn't stoop to the bland but potent synthetic alcohols that hers did.

"What are your intentions regarding my sister?"

Sangfroid's brandy shot down her nose. "What?" she asked, pinching her stinging nostrils as she regarded Hubert through watery eyes.

"After all, Millicent has died for you on countless occasions. That says something about a gal, you know." Hubert's cheeks were bright pink, and his nose glowed rosily. Sangfroid doubted the man's capacity for drink and wondered why he was forcing this bonhomie over a brandy.

"You mean Millicent's dead, too?" She didn't like that idea. Not at all. It was okay for her to be dead. After all, she was a soldier. It was in the small print. But she didn't want anything or anybody to hurt Millicent. Millicent was her secret love, and she'd be damned if she was harmed in anyway.

"Not at the moment. But she has passed away on several occasions trying to rescue you on the Amoebas." Hubert stretched out his short legs in front of the fireplace. Sangfroid wished she could do the same, but her borrowed pant legs only came halfway up her shins and had to be tucked into her boot tops. She felt pinched in by the scratchy, irritating fabrics of this world. One miscalculated stretch, scratch, or yawn, and they'd burst apart.

"What do you mean she's passed away on several occasions? Hey, you know about the Amoebas?" she asked, then realized what a stupid question it was. Of course Hubert would know. Millicent would have told him everything.

"I have *been on* the Amoebas," Hubert informed her. He looked excited as if he was itching to talk about it. "Wonderful vessel. I'd loved to have seen her in her hay day, and not when she was being torn apart."

"What the hell? When were you on the Amoebas?"

"You don't really believe Millicent would have settled back into her own timeline knowing she had contributed to your death? Helped you get torn apart? She could never have left a thing like that alone. Oh no. She went back to save you." Hubert took another sip of brandy. It was loosening his tongue nicely. All this time butting heads with the sister when all she had to do was pour a drink down the brother's throat.

"She did that for me?" Sangfroid was touched and immediately felt stupid for being so sappy.

"Often. She had trouble saving you from the squid, you see, so insisted on going back time and again until it worked. Though strangely enough, it was your own interference that made it finally turn out well, in that you didn't die, you merely turned up here." Hubert ordered a refill of their glasses from a passing waiter then continued, "But no. Millicent would not be swayed by any argument to the contrary. She had to go back, over and over again, to try and save you. And so, you see, I had to go back with her."

Sangfroid sank back in her chair and closed her eyes. Oh, no, not another Aberly wandering through her timeline. It was a mockery of every scientific principle she was barely able to grasp.

"Tell me everything," she said grimly, bracing herself for the worse.

"I was just about to, old boy," Hubert said, cheerily. He took a healthy swig of brandy and cleared his throat. "Now, where shall I begin? Ah, I know exactly the place!" And then Hubert took up his story again—

"You can't possibly destroy it!" Millicent howled at him.

"But…but you distinctly told me to." Hubert was confused. They had just spent a harrowing hour as Millicent recounted the events of her time travel adventure. His initial self-congratulations at the success of his invention soon dissipated at his sister's desolation. After she had finished, he sent her away to see to her toilette and immediately began to disassemble his evil creation. She had returned with a fresh gown, redressed hair, and like any woman, a complete change of mind.

"You said to get rid of it," he said.

Millicent removed the spanner from his hand and caressed his cheek. Her eyes still overly bright from her earlier tears.

"You truly are the most wonderful of brothers," she said. "And I can see clearly why you flounder as lesser colleagues surge to prominence as so-called men of science. They carry not a whit of your intelligence, while you carry the morality for a thousand of them."

"I will not wantonly hurt another creature, Millicent." Hubert's heart beat fast and shallow inside his chest. "And no part of this invention is to remain in this house if it has endangered or frightened you in any way." He felt wretched for what had happened to her. "I have been selfish and blinded by stupidity. I did not foresee that we could meet with such awful monstrosity and nihilism. If any of it should return here…why, I dare not even think of the consequences! It could mean the end of civilization, Millicent."

"In that other world, it seemed as if our civilization had not begun. Or else been totally passed over. I saw no trace of it," Millicent said. "There were undertones of the Roman Empire everywhere. I mean their uniforms were dripping with aquiline regalia. And they're all polytheists!" She frowned and bit her lower lip. "Perhaps there are parallel timelines. And each history wends its own course like a stream, subject wholly to the landscape, or obstacles, of the world surrounding it. Does that sound plausible?"

"Don't tantalize me with your provocative presuppositions, Millicent. I built this devil apparatus stimulated by nothing but the abstractions of my own mind, of parallels and paradoxes, of the limitless potential of a space-time continuum. I thought I had a vision, but now I see it for a folly."

"Really, Hubert, stop being so poetic," Millicent said with stern disapproval. "You had a good idea, and it worked."

"You will not sway me. I should have seen the man in the machine. I should have realized where this would lead. Wherever mankind goes, the Four Horsemen follow." He lifted the spanner and turned to his machine, shoulders slumped. "It has to go."

"No." Millicent pulled at his arm. "We cannot dismantle this machine, at least not yet. I have been the *force-majeure* in the untimely death of a brave soldier. We have go back and undo what I have done. She died horribly because I was meddling with her timeline like some freak of nature. I may have done irreparable damage, Hubert. Damage that may ripple on forever through time."

"Impossible."

"I remember the lever sequence I used to begin my journey. We need to return at a time that overlaps with my primary visit."

"Buy why? That will mean two of you running around. Won't that be a little grotesque, not to mention overcrowded?"

"I need to be there to make sure Sangfroid leaves the hangar by climbing along the wall, otherwise she will try and make a run for the door and die."

"If that is to be her fate, does it really matter whether you go back or not?"

"Do you want to see this ship's laboratory, Hubert?"

"Yes," he admitted somewhat shamefaced.

Millicent nodded. "If you promise you can bring us back, then I am determined we go to that exact point in time and make good. I swear that Decanus Sangfroid will not go into the annex with me, we will divert her somehow—"

"And you just couldn't say no?" Sangfroid interrupted Hubert's story. "You couldn't just pull the damned thing to bits right there and then? Let me tell you something, I was going to die anyway. Millicent stopped me from making a death run across the hangar. That's when I would have died if my number was up. It makes no difference that it happened later in the lab. She had nothing to do with it. I was doomed from the moment I pulled on my boots that morning."

"So, you're saying Millicent is no more than a bit player in your theatre piece of doom?" Hubert asked.

"Gods, you are poetic. I dunno. Maybe." Sangfroid was uncertain. She felt a greater pull to Millicent than she was prepared to admit to her brother.

"Good luck with that," Hubert said. "I think you'll find she's given herself top billing."

"And you let her go back?" She was still astounded. Hubert seemed like such a sensible man. "Because she told you to."

"What could I do?" Hubert argued. "You know Millicent. She can be very stubborn. Best of all, I knew I could preset the machine to return its occupants automatically. You see, I decided it was best that I went along with her. And needless to say, I was agog to see the laboratory as she described it. I had to go." He signalled the waiter for more brandy. "Look, let me cut to the quick of it. I persuaded Millicent to let me tweak the navigation slightly, she…we…did not need to go through the hell in the hangar; we only had to arrive at the laboratory ahead of you. It went like this—"

Hubert hung on to Millicent's arm, still giddy from the slide of his own world distorting into this one. And what a desolate place it was. They were in a long bleak corridor built from an unidentifiable metal plate. The walls were an ugly nondescript grey colour, and the floor a very unbecoming olive green, neither colour added to his stomach's sense of well-being.

"Are you all right, Hubert?" Millicent asked, anxiously checking out the corridor fore and aft. "We must be quick."

"Where are we?" Hubert asked, becoming aware of a tremendous hammering and screaming from farther along. At first he thought the frightening noise was part of the travelling process, a phantasmal outpouring of his mind's distress. Now he realized it was entirely local.

"I'm sure this is the corridor I was running along when you transported me back to my own time." Millicent glanced around. "Yes. The exit from the annex is this way."

"Are you sure? We seem to be moving directly towards that awful noise?"

"That's the hangar battle. Sangfroid and the other me will be beating a retreat to the laboratory soon. We have to hurry."

"But towards it?"

"Come along, Hubert." Millicent tugged him by the sleeve. "Here it is." She stopped before a huge, recessed metal door. "Something is troubling me."

"Just something?" Hubert squeaked, and sweat coursed down his brow. He mopped at it with a large handkerchief.

"What happens if one of us dies and we return to our own time as a corpse?"

"I have no idea," Hubert looked at her blankly. "And I hope to never find out."

Millicent took a deep breath and slapped a green button by the door. It began to slide open, and she stepped back, tense.

"Beware," she said. "If we've timed this wrong a huge severed tentacle will emerge at any moment."

"What do we do if it does?" Hubert whispered.

"We answer the corpse question."

The door opened fully, and nothing terrible emerged. They tentatively entered the dimly lit room.

"We're not here yet," Millicent whispered with relief. "The main laboratory is empty." No sooner had she spoken that a soft pink glow began to suffuse the room. "Oh, Hubert." She moved quickly to the central workbench. "The little squid is still here."

Hubert could barely move. His greedy gaze devoured the wonders around him. The benches, the shelves, and even the floor were awash with the most beautiful instrumentation he had ever seen or dared to imagine. This was paradise, nirvana, and fairyland all rolled into one. To his left, his right, above, and below…everywhere he looked he saw the most magnificent scientific paraphernalia that far outstripped the meagre gruel served at his own table of knowledge.

"Hubert. Will you please wake up and come over here." Even Millicent's sharp call could not snap him out of his delirium. He went to her in a haze of transcendent bliss. He could not stop his gaze from roving now that the annex glowed brighter. The walls shone with a celestial pearly pink that reminded him of a glorious new dawn, and then he saw what Millicent was calling him towards. His joyful heart faltered, and he was cast from Eden into the cold world of scientific endeavour and all its demons.

A pink blob was stretched out heinously tight in a shallow tank filled with some sort of sterile electrolyte. He recognized it as a vivisection station, and his blood pressure plummeted. The inhumanity of the situation physically pained him even though the specimen pegged out before him was alien and looked nothing like any mollusc he had ever seen before.

"It's big," he murmured.

"Pah!" Millicent spat out, startling him. "Come closer. Tell me what you see."

"Well. It's obviously a member of the cephalopod family." He began his prognosis then declared in astonishment, "It's sentient!"

New thoughts, both radical and instinctual, exploded in his brain. If he closed his eyes and stoppered his ears, he was sure there would still be fireworks sizzling his synapses. His mind popped and fizzed as illumination flooded its darkest, dullest corners with enlightenment. "And I do believe it's a female, though for the life of me I can't say why? I don't understand how I should know?"

"I think she has a sort of psychological communication ability." Millicent was pleased with his perception.

"You mean she is communicating with us."

"I suspect this whole room illuminated when we entered and alerted her thought processes. It happened before when I went to turn off the current running through her tank. The front of the wiring panel fell away at my touch whereas all the others had to be shot off with laser pistols." She was very excited about this.

"You're right," Hubert exclaimed with increasing awareness. His head felt as if a dozen closed doors had suddenly slammed open, and the rush of fresh air through his brain nearly blew him off his feet. "And she was waiting for us."

"She's communicating with you directly?"

"Yes. And her name is Weena." Hubert was beside himself.

"Weena? How delightful. She communicates with you much better than with me." Millicent's eyes were alive with wonder. "Do you think she needs us to have a certain level of intelligence for satisfying discourse? She spoke to Sangfroid, and she didn't even notice."

"All these thoughts are flooding my head. If I look at something," Hubert went over to an instrument on a nearby shelf and picked it up, "I can understand what it is and how it works. Not necessarily how to use it, but the basic premise behind it is in my mind." He was awestruck. "And Weena is telling me all this." He held up the apparatus in his hand to demonstrate. "A multimeter for measuring electrical impulses!" he announced delightedly—

"Like the one in your pocket?" Sangfroid tapped Hubert's coat pocket. "Don't tell me you've been pilfering from my timeline. How's that going to work out?"

Hubert looked shamefaced. "Please don't tell Millicent," he said. "I confess I have been back many more times without her knowledge."

"Oh, boy."

"You see, the laboratory became like a drug to me, I had to go back and explore thoroughly. I found I could manipulate the time machine so that I had more and more freedom to browse before you entered the laboratory. And there was another reason." He could not meet Sangfroid's eyes. "And I am a terrible man for it. Please understand I love Sophia, but in a different way now from when I first proposed. At that time Papa was dying, and he dearly wanted to see his children settled. Millicent point-blank refused to wed. She wouldn't even entertain the thought. Can't say I blame her. It's different for a woman surrendering her wealth and independence to a future husband. And with her bluestocking tendencies and Chartist politics, I can't see that Millicent would ever have found a mate to compliment her interests." He gave Sangfroid a beady look that made her prickle.

"So?" Sangfroid did not like discussing Millicent's marriage prospects, slim as they were. She wondered at her escaping marriage so easily though. Where Sangfroid came from marriage was a social necessity for the upwardly mobile and always advantageously arranged. Matchmaking was a very lucrative industry.

"Because Millicent wouldn't entertain the thought, I stepped up to the mark," Hubert said morosely. "Godfrey Trenchant-Myre was a business acquaintance of my father's. The Trenchant-Myres were a well-respected family, and it seemed the simplest thing to pledge my troth to Sophia. Of course, our families were delighted. It made the last few weeks of Papa's illness happier." He stared moodily into his glass; always a bad sign in those who couldn't handle their drink. Sangfroid decided to push it a little more before setting Hubert on a homeward path.

"I'm not sure I understand what you feel so bad about?" It was a lie. If she'd have been betrothed to Sophia, she'd have volunteered for a suicide squad at once.

"Because I love Weena."

Sangfroid stared at her companion, unsure what to say. This little man dressed in blobs of brown tweed had just told her he was in love with a squid? A dirty, big, evil, melt-your-face squid. His round, flushed face with his high, cerebral brow that curved back into his receding hairline shone in the firelight. He looked like he might cry. Clearly she was not going to get any sense out of him in this state. The conversation had swerved into an area Sangfroid had no idea how to deal with, and she bet Hubert would forget his confession by tomorrow morning. She dearly hoped he would. Any more talk would only be embarrassing; best to duck this and move on.

"Come on, sport. Home with you." Sangfroid hauled her companion to his unsteady feet. "Where do we pay?"

"I've a tab." Hubert led the way out. His head was bowed, and he wobbled and wove a little, but she kept a firm hand on the small of his back and guided him towards the door. "I say, it's not really that far, do you mind if we walk home?" He sounded despondent.

"Sure." A walk in the night air was just what her cramped legs needed. It would be nice to experience this weird little city first hand. She was drunk, too. And she didn't care if it all was a hypno-therapeutic-thingy the squid were playing on her mind. Whatever it was, and wherever she was, it was damn fine.

They stepped from the Prometheus onto slick, wet pavements, the heels of their boots slapping out loud in the night air. The streets shone waxy under the yellow lamplight that cut crazy patterns across the puddled cobblestones.

"You see," Hubert spoke up as they strolled along. "Every time I went back, I spent more and more time conversing with Weena." He was determined to complete his confession. Somehow, now they were free from the smoky confines of the club, Sangfroid didn't mind. The fresh air made her head lighter and clearer, and everything looked and smelled exciting and different. "She's so smart, Sangfroid. So intelligent and sweet, and those blighters were hurting her. She always knew when I was coming, and she'd help me understand things. Not just in the lab, but about her world and the way it worked."

"Wonderful." Sangfroid was more interested in her surroundings than in squid talk. She already knew how smart the squishy buggers were. Hadn't they decimated her entire unit and then turned the Amoebas into a barbecue? She stopped to pull at a privet hedge and sniff the wet foliage. "Can you eat these?" Her tongue gently tapped the dark green leaves.

"I've never tried. Anyway, Weena and I…slowly we became friends, and then, somewhere along the way, I fell in love." Hubert cried and flung out his arms to embrace the night sky. This was different. Hubert had been almost apologetic up until now. Sangfroid smiled. The fresh air was having its effect on Hubert, too. She perfectly understood. This was a *wonderful* night. The brandy had been superb and plentiful, and now it charged through her blood like a thousand chariots. Hubert was drunk and happy, and Sangfroid had the feeling this did not occur often enough for this compact little man.

"Love is a mighty good thing, Hubert," she said, noting the slight slur in her voice. A *happy* slur. "Never be ashamed to love. Even if it is inter-species. And a deadly species at that."

"The female of the species is always deadlier, Sangfroid. Everyone knows that. I used to be terrified of women. In fact, I still get a little nervous, especially on Sophia's paleobotanical nights." His face darkened.

"Tell me about it. So what's with all those ladies?" she asked. "They were so damned nosy."

"Millicent was badly caught out. She had no idea Sophia had informed half of London's polite society that she had a "gentleman" caller. As you probably know, Sophia has a deep set neurological condition with seeing you as female. Her nerves just can't take it, so she redefines you as male. The little ladies of her inner circle will, I'm afraid, share a similar disposition. They simply cannot cope with a true life archetypal fierce woman warrior such as yourself. You will always be a handsome, debonair major in the Prussian Dragoons because that's what they want to see."

"And on some level, that's what they want for Millicent." Sangfroid felt a little more sober. "A gentleman admirer, maybe an engagement, and a suitable marriage."

"Well, yes. They are all despairing spinsters with barely a farthing or good feature between them. I'm sure they only attend Sophia's ludicrous evenings for the decent supper Millicent lays on for them. She is the blue-eyed baby to them, a sort of favoured niece, if you like. She is wealthy and wise, and all she needs is a good husband to be truly complete, and that's what the little ladies want to see."

"Sophia's hardly a little lady." This was cruel, but Sangfroid held her fully responsible for this evening's fracas. To have arrived in the Aberly house with only Millicent and Hubert present would have been a totally different and much more pleasant experience.

Hubert sighed. "Sophia has her own cross to bear. Don't be too harsh on her. Over the years since our betrothal, she has taken up a role in our little family circle. She is the speck of sand in our well-oiled cogs, and sometimes it is good to feel a mild hesitancy in the streamlined running of things. It makes one appreciate the machinery better when it does run right."

Sangfroid had never heard such a "well-oiled" criticism, but stayed silent. Sophia was Hubert's intended, even if he was having an extra-curricular romance with a Colossal space squid. Who was Sangfroid to pee on the pompa? Hubert and Millicent had so far offered her nothing but friendship and security in this weird world. She would let it ride for a while and see what developed. After all, there could be worse things than playing a dragoon major from the Prussias or the Urals or wherever, for Millicent's lady friends. They had been a little swoony around her. Sangfroid liked that.

Hubert stopped dead in the street, so that Sangfroid bumped into him almost bowling him over. He recovered himself and looked up to the stars pushing through the overcast sky above. They were small tinny specks. "How disappointing they look from here once you have travelled among them. You are so lucky Sangfroid, to be born when and where you were, in whatever timeline that was."

"The stars may be mysterious to you, but your world is just as strange to me. I mean, these Urals where I'm supposed to come from. What are they?"

"Oh, just a wild, expansive place where nothing ever happens. But it sounds exotic enough to explain you away. I do think Millicent was quite clever there. And that brings me to my original question. I haven't forgotten, you know. Mind like a steel trap." Hubert went to tap his temple with a forefinger but poked himself in the eye instead. "What are your intentions towards my sister?" He drew up to his fullest, slightly lopsided, height.

"Is this your street?" Sangfroid easily steered the conversation to safer waters. She didn't want to talk about her "intentions." As far as she was concerned, she had none. She barely knew the woman who had landed her in this insane situation, even if her brother spoke with assurance of a possible connection. The idea of a future with Millicent left an unexpected bubble of warmth in the pit of her stomach, however. A bubble that expanded every time she saw Millicent or spoke to her or thought about her. It made her blood heat and her step lighter, but then again, that could just as easily be the brandy. Either way, she wasn't prepared to think about it anymore than that. She loved Millicent, but it was her business. A business that scared her blind.

"So it is! This is my street!" Hubert said in wonder and wobbled around a corner, and Sangfroid followed. "Number five, I think."

A row of hansom cabs lined up outside number five. The horses stirred impatiently in their traces, and the drivers huddled on the pavement smoking and talking with each other.

Bemused by the gathering, Sangfroid and Hubert mounted the steps to number five Christie Mews. Before they reached the top step, the door was flung open and a fretful Edna greeted them. "Oh sir, am I glad to see you."

"Why, whatever's wrong, Edna?" Hubert dumped his overcoat into her waiting arms and weaved across the hall towards his laboratory. Sangfroid set her top hat on Edna's head and gave her a wink that made her jump.

"It's the ladies, sir. They won't go home until they meet Miss Millicent's gentleman again. All their carriages are waiting for them, but no one will be the first to leave. And Cook is fed up making tea and cake and has gone to bed." She was close to tears.

"But the ladies have already met Major Sangfroid," Hubert said, turning a little too sharply towards the parlour and almost unbalancing. The tintinnabulation of ladies voices could be heard from behind the great mahogany doors.

"More of 'em came afterwards, sir. Many more. They won't go because the others have already met the major, and now the rest want to meet 'im, too." Edna was wringing her hands.

"Don't worry, Edna. We'll sort it out." Sangfroid felt sympathy for the girl though she couldn't understand why she was in such a fret. It was only ladies after all. Nosy, little, spinstery ladies. She'd give them something to talk about!

"We'll see to it. You go on to bed, Edna," Hubert instructed her kindly.

"Oh, thank you, sir." She bobbed a clumsy curtsey and disappeared as quickly as she could.

"Come on." Hubert's face had lost its melancholy sheen and taken on the look of a reckless man. Sangfroid had seen that look many times in the Parabellum the night before a battle. It was a thing of beauty, that ephemeral moment when the rationale flees, but despair has yet to arrive and take up residence. It was the void of chance where *anything* could happen if a centurion was brave enough to act and not think. A place where life and death were played out on the dice and, in the morning, on the face of the enemy.

"I've got your back, matey." She gave Hubert an imperial salute. "Mithras, give strength to our right arms!"

"Right arms!" Hubert shouted and gave a sloppy salute back.

Sangfroid braced herself, then swung both parlour doors open with great aplomb and a mighty crash. In a happy daze, she took in the whole room in an instant and saw Millicent sitting bolt upright with eyes hollowed out by tiredness and ennui. Beside her, Sophia was tight-lipped and seething. And around them perched a black-frocked murmuration of paleobotanists, twittering gossip and tidbits over their china cups. The room fell silent as she and Hubert entered.

"Ladies!" Sangfroid sailed into the parlour, her arms spread wider than an ascending eagle. This set off a whirl of excited trills. She puffed up her chest under their adoring gaze. She'd spin them a yarn they'd never forget. "Let me tell you *all about* the Urals, with its vast and wild expanses," she declared loudly, "and amphitheatres full of mighty lions!"

Chapter II

"Amphitheatres full of mighty lions! Mighty lions?" Why were women's voices so much shriller in the morning? The thought rumbled through Sangfroid's mind as the window drapes were torn open with such rattling bad humour as to split Cerberus's heads apart. It felt as if all the hammers of Vulcan were pounding in her skull. Her eyelids flickered against the cushions where she lay face down. She carefully inched her head upwards. Then the full splendour of morning fell through the window and cut into her squinted eyes like shards of glass, and she prayed Vulcan would deliver the killer blow right there and then.

"Mighty lions!" Millicent shrilled again for added measure. Her decibel output had to be equal to the biggest, meanest, most bastard commanders Sangfroid had ever served under. How did she do it? She was tiny. A wee, wee, tiny thing. Where was all this noise coming from?

"You preformed the *dance* of the Urals." She continued to screech like all the Harpies of Thrake. "Do you even know where the Urals are?"

"Augh. Ack." Were the only sounds her acrid throat could utter.

"What on earth got into you last night, apart from too much brandy?" Millicent ground out the words, cold and hard. "It was *shameful*. No, shameless." She must have thought about this, as there was a moment of blessed silence before she cried, "Shaming! In fact, it was all three." She was not to be appeased. Millicent sailed over to her hearth and began to savagely shake coal on the embers, creating a new avalanche of hell in Sangfroid's head.

"Ack."

"Up, you ne'er do well. Up." Millicent's full attention turned to Sangfroid, now that the drapes had been ripped apart and the fire battered to buggery. "How dare you defile my mother's Chesterfield with your drunken prostrations! Arise, you vulgarian and drag your sorry carcass to the dog's bed, it will suit you well."

Sangfroid creaked to a sitting position and found she had indeed defiled Millicent's mother's Chesterfield by passing out on it face first. There were drool marks on the vermilion silk cushions. She vaguely remembered Millicent stomping off to bed not long after Sangfroid began regaling the ladies with phantom stories of her service in the Prussian Dragoons and Ural life in general. They'd loved it! And yes, there had been a dance. A little bip-boppy thing she had picked up during some downtime on a starship circling the Wolf-Rayet nebula. The ladies had clapped along in time. It had been a wonderful evening. Wonderful. But now her face itched, her eyes burned, and her head felt like it had been kicked around a bear pit for bait.

She tried to apologize. It was usually the quickest way to make a woman happy and, hopefully, quieter.

"Ack," she said, then coughed and tried again. "Sorry." She needed water. Just enough to drown in.

"Sorry? Sorry?" And Millicent was off again. "You sat there and *lied* to those ladies. Blatantly *lied*."

"No." Her voice might be croaky, but it was warming up nicely with her growing irritation. "I sat there and *embellished* to those ladies. Embellished on *your* lies." And she was on her feet stumbling for the door. She could not bear an argument this early in the morning, and Millicent knew that. Except... except, she hesitated, how could she know that? But her head was too fuzzy to think it through. She had a weird synergy with Millicent; she could acknowledge that much. Millicent was spooky for Sangfroid to be around. It felt as if she lived inside Sangfroid's head half the time. She generated feelings that pushed and pulled Sangfroid in all directions at once, and that did not mix well with a hangover. She drew herself up to her full, impressive height. "Excuse me," she said as formally as possible, "while I go and drown myself."

"There's a wishing well in the garden."

Sangfroid would have loved to slam the door on the way out, but she was an old pro at hangovers and knew not to make that rookie mistake. The hallway smelled of cooked bacon, and it made her stomach protest, which seemed to be the morning's theme. She met Hubert coming carefully down the stairs. He looked a lot sprucer than Sangfroid felt in that he'd had a shave and managed to wet down his hair, but he had the eyes of a suffering man.

"Mornin'," Sangfroid rasped.

"Ack," Hubert rasped back, then cleared his throat and pointed to the stairs. "Toilette, wash, stuff. Left, end of corridor. Your clean uniform is set out." With that he limped off towards the breakfast room.

Hubert had directed Sangfroid to his father's suite of rooms. The washstand was neatly laid out with the late Mr. Aberly's personal grooming tools. It was an astonishingly kind gesture on Hubert's behalf. The water was tepid but Sangfroid stripped and washed thoroughly, then turned her attention to the curious array of implements set out on the dresser before her. Quaintly antiquated as it was, Sangfroid soon found her way around the manicure set. Frontline troops were resourceful, and she had a thousand uses for anything pointy. She liked the cologne. The sharp cedar tang did a lot to refresh her pallid sinuses and sting some colour back in her flesh. She pulled on her freshly laundered and thoughtfully mended uniform, satisfied to be back in her own skin.

When Sangfroid stepped out onto the landing, she felt revitalized and ready to face breakfast. The door to Hubert's bedchamber lay ajar. Sangfroid hesitated. The multimetre Hubert had removed from the Amoebas sat in full view on a bedside table. What else had he purloined? And how might this kleptomania affect both their timelines?

Sangfroid nudged the door open a little farther with the toe of her boot. She hesitated at the threshold and gave the room a cursory glance. She felt guilty for snooping, though it turned out she was right to do so. She noted at least two more objects that she would hazard weren't from this world. One she knew to be a bio-thermometer—she'd seen enough of them in the medical wards—and the other was the small gyroscope that had so entranced Millicent on her first visit.

"Hubert, you naughty boy," she murmured and entered the room feeling fully justified in doing so given Hubert's indiscretions. "What else have you got squirreled away here, 'eh?"

It was a large room, bigger than Sangfroid's entire living quarters on the Quintus Prime. She wondered momentarily if she was now classified MIA and if her quarters had already been re-allocated to the next boob to fill her Decanus boots. She hoped Gallo was still around to collect her things. She'd get some good gear, and Gallo would no doubt sell or gamble away the rest of her crap. Gallo was practical like that. She'd raise a beer to Sangfroid's memory, then sell her spare pants.

She gave Hubert's room a 360-degree examination and approved. Good solid, no-nonsense furniture. The bed was old and mahogany and nearly six foot wide. If it were hers, she'd fill it with all the floozies she could buy. She'd be hard put to break a fine bed like that with a tumble or two, but she'd love to try. Beside the bed stood a dresser, its top littered with coins, fossils, lumps of curious rock, and all sorts of other boyish things. Hubert had never outgrown collecting what Sangfroid classified as junk.

There was a huge armoire stuffed with tweed suits in an exciting palette of brown. Next to the tweeds hung rows of white cotton shirts, and to the left of those, trays of starched collars, bow ties, and cuff and collar studs. She was amazed that all this gear was Hubert's alone. All Sangfroid had to her name was two uniforms and a ceremonial toga for feast days.

Life onboard the Quintus Prime was frugal. It was a dilapidated old turd tub of a ship. A small city rattling around in space with all the beauty and grace of an iron lung. It wheezed along, dragging over one million troops and support staff to wherever they had to go in order to kill things. It had shops, bars, casinos, and brothels. It had sports arenas and circuses. It also had hospitals and crematoriums, as well as a vast fleet of assault craft to help fill both up as fast as possible. But it was home, *her* home, and had been since she was a child soldier.

Am I really dead?

She remembered that last night at the casino tables. Gallo had been on a mean streak with the dice and treated them all to gallons of plasma ale with her winnings. According to Sangfroid's fading memories, they'd been drinking when the mayday from the Amoebas had come through. Suddenly they were sober, grabbing their gear, and running for the assault ships that would carry them into battle.

She perched on the edge of Hubert's bed. Sangfroid didn't understand these timeline thingies. How could a person be in one place at one time and die only to pop up in another place and time hale and hearty? If it were truly possible why did anybody have to die? *We could all live forever, right? Maybe that's why the gods keep these timelines apart?* This time travel science had the stench of disaster all over it. She hoped Millicent and Hubert knew what they were doing. It took a big pair of centaur balls to mess with the gods.

The soft splash of water drew her attention to a separate door leading from Hubert's bedroom. She guessed a bathroom lay beyond, and Hubert had left the water running. Sangfroid gave the door handle a rattle. It was locked. The splashing on the other side ceased. Sangfroid frowned. Water taps did not turn themselves off.

Now, where would a brainiac like Hubert leave the key? A nearby chair had the impression of two shoe soles on the cushioned seat cover. Sangfroid smiled and reached for the top of the doorframe and found Hubert's hiding place. She slotted the key into the lock and carefully opened the door. All was silent, no more watery splashes, not even a drip. Sangfroid stood blinking at a single blue eye that blinked back at her.

A pink squid sat in a copper bathtub surrounded by various apparatus from the Amoebas lab. The sunlight shone through the open window, and a light breeze danced along the healthily glowing pink flesh. The squid was content and happy, though Sangfroid had no idea why she should think that? And she was *huge*!

Sangfroid thundered downstairs taking three steps at a time, flew past Edna and startled her into dropping a duster, and burst into the breakfast room where Millicent and Hubert were eating in silence. The atmosphere was frigid. Millicent looked murderous, and Hubert woebegone. Sangfroid had no time for the Aberly's domestic drama. She needed answers. She needed information. She needed the Fates to weave her a new life, one where she'd never met these two.

"Right, you," she shouted, pointing at Hubert. "What in Hades do you think you're doing?"

Millicent's fork clattered to her plate, while Hubert's sat suspended with a piece of sausage on it, inches from his open mouth. Millicent recovered first.

"Has something interesting happened in the Urals, Decanus Sangfroid?" she said frostily. "Perhaps they've invented a new dance?"

"Something interesting is happening in Hubert's dressing room," she returned just as coldly.

Hubert went white.

"Did you really think you could hide her? This is insanity. Don't you understand what she could do to your planet?" she bellowed.

"What on earth are you talking about?" Millicent looked alarmed. "Who is in Hubert's dressing room?" Her confusion told Sangfroid that she had no part in this…this squid abduction, and that gave her some relief. At least one of them was possibly sane. She turned her withering gaze upon the sole culprit. Hubert stared back, wide-eyed and ashen.

"Weena is upstairs," Sangfroid said.

"Who on earth is—Weena!" Millicent was on her feet immediately. "Weena? The little pink squid." She looked at her brother in horror as he wilted in his seat.

"Little pink squid my a—" Sangfroid caught her angry glare and changed tack mid sentence, "atoms! She nearly fills the room. She's a Colossal, for Jupiter's sake. A *Colossal*, not a miniature squid. They don't come in miniature. A Colossal! She'll soon be as big as this house. *Colossal!*" She knew her voice was borderline hysterical, but she had to get it through to them. "Big-As-A-House!" And she widened her arm span as far as she could stretch to underscore her point.

"Hubert." Millicent turned to her brother. "Is this true? Is there a Colossal space squid in this house?"

Hubert hung his head. "I couldn't leave her there. They were hurting her."

"How could this have happened? I was there with you, and you most certainly did not have Weena with you when we returned."

Hubert did not reply.

"Hubert, I demand an answer," Millicent said sternly. "Were you secreting space squid?"

Sangfroid knew the answer but waited for Hubert to confess; better it came from him.

"I went back and got her later," Hubert admitted wearily.

"You what?" Millicent was flabbergasted and sank into her chair. "You went back without me?" Her eyes held so much hurt Sangfroid actually flinched. She did not like to see her upset. Deflated after her initial announcement, Sangfroid sat down at the table and listened to Hubert's leaden-voiced confession.

"I went back many times, Millicent. At first I wanted to explore the laboratory and to do that I needed to converse with Weena. She helped me understand things. Over time I became more aware of her plight; those experiments were pitiless, and…and I began to worry and care for her." Hubert looked wretched. Millicent reached for his hand. It was obvious she understood what he was really saying. "I couldn't leave her there," he said softly. "She asked me to bring her here, to this timeline. So I did."

"They're planning an invasion." Sangfroid dropped her head onto the table. The crisp linen tablecloth was clean and cool against her overheated brow.

"Why do you think that?" Hubert asked. "Squid are peaceful creatures. Your Roman Empire attacked them first." His voice gained an edge Sangfroid didn't appreciate.

She looked up. "We did not. They came after our ships." She straightened in her seat. Truth was she had no idea of the political reasoning behind the wars Rome waged. Insight wasn't something the common soldier was entrusted with.

"And where were your ships?" Hubert asked.

"In Scorpius Major."

"That is the squid's home galaxy. It's a huge gas system. The Empire just came forging through without so much as a by your leave." Hubert was beginning to sound indignant. Millicent stepped in.

"Why were you in Scorpius Major, Sangfroid?" she asked. "Usually one warring faction invades the other to acquire resources of some sort or to advance its civilization in some way. What exactly did Rome require from a gaseous galaxy?" She was genuinely interested, and Sangfroid genuinely had no answers.

"To get to the other side," she said with a shrug. "If we see it, we take it, and move on to the next offensive. It's Rome's way. Veni, vidi, vicious."

Millicent looked aghast while Hubert nodded knowingly. "Tell me, Sangfroid, given that you are possibly a trillion light years from Earth, have you even seen the eternal city you fight for so valiantly?" he asked.

Sangfroid knew she had a blank look on her face. A few hours hanging out with the Aberly's, and she was beginning to recognize the facial muscle set, but this time the question was really hard.

"What's an earth?" she asked, determined not to feel stupid. Now it was Hubert's turn to look blank. Sangfroid would have felt smug if she'd understood how exactly her question had confounded him.

"You don't come from Earth?" Millicent asked, obviously confused.

"I was born on moon base Alpha Zeta IV."

"Yes, you told me that before." Millicent was impatient now. "But what planet does that moon orbit? I had assumed it was our own."

"It's Rome's moon," she said.

"You mean Rome is actually a planet?" Hubert looked confounded.

"Yes. Of course it is." These two never failed to surprise her. "Rome is the home planet. Every citizen is allowed to see

Rome once before they die, if at all possible. We do tend to die young. But no matter where you were born in the Empire, you're expected to get to Rome at least once before you pay the ferryman," she said proudly. "Rome conquers all and is all," she quoted the mission statement.

"You mean to tell me there is no planet Earth, only a planet called Rome?" Millicent looked to her brother. "Of all the puffed up, arrogant… Words fail me."

Sangfroid squinted at her suspiciously. Words failing Millicent was probably a bad thing.

"I have no idea what has happened to your timeline," Hubert shook his head in wonder. "I only know the squid will stop Rome. You will throw all your resources into this war and lose, and then you will fall into decline. It will take centuries but it will happen."

"It will not."

"It will so."

"It will not."

"It will so."

"It w—"

"Gentlemen, please," Millicent interrupted. "We have a Colossal squid upstairs, perhaps we need to address that first and then you can continue your playground squabble?"

Hubert removed his napkin from his collar and rose wearily to his feet. "I'll take her back."

"And I'm going with you in case something else adheres to your jacket, like a lab bench or a refrigeration unit." Sangfroid huffed. Hubert was not her friend anymore. He had decried the Roman Empire, so now Sangfroid didn't give a monkey's anal gland about dropping him in it with his sister.

"What does she mean, Hubert?" Millicent, as usual, missed nothing.

"She's alluding to the fact I had to bring some equipment back with me for Weena's welfare." Hubert shot Sangfroid a hard look that made her momentarily reconsider the wisdom of upsetting her host, a man a million times smarter than herself. Then she reverted to not giving a monkey's anal gland and sat back smugly. Hubert would get his good and proper, his harpy-tongued sister would see to that.

"Hubert." Millicent stood on cue.

Here it comes. Sangfroid readied herself. Glad someone else was in Millicent's bad books. Hopefully her turn was over and Hubert's about to begin. *This isn't going to be pretty.*

"I want a word with you in my study. In private." Millicent turned on her heel and marched out of the breakfast room leaving Sangfroid feeling a little cheated. Why was the flamethrower tongue for her only?

"When you come begging me for my sister's hand in marriage, and believe me you will, I shall laugh in your face," Hubert hissed as he passed Sangfroid's seat. "And I shall say 'No.'" He bent close to Sangfroid's ear and whispered, "Nooooooo."

Sangfroid sat bolt upright. "Wait!" she said. "Why would I ask you?" Not that she was ever going to ask for Millicent Aberly's hand. Sangfroid was a frontline soldier, and frontliners never married. She was too hard-nosed to settle down in a nice little villa with a vineyard by the sea as her parents had dreamed of on their moon-dirt farm.

"Ask?" Hubert was bitter. "Ask? You will have to *beg* me and hope that I am kinder than you. And you had better believe I shall not be!" And with that Hubert slammed out of the room.

Chapter 12

Millicent awaited Hubert in her study. It was unusual for him to visit her here, but there had been those rare occasions when he had outstripped the mark with some experiment or other. Then she would haul him in to stand fidgeting on her Persian rug before a blazing fire and an equally blazing sister. This was one such occasion, and she could hear his footsteps dragging along the hall to her study door. She sat on the edge of her chair as he entered. He looked miserable and defeated, and she was annoyed that Sangfroid had not been more circumspect with her disclosures.

"Hubert," she said when he at last stood before her. "I do not think it is proper for you to love a squid."

He started, his eyes alight with defiance and a little shame.

Millicent immediately softened her tone as his pain was all too apparent. "It is obvious you care very deeply for Weena," she said.

As expected, he came back with the only argument open to him—the one that wounded her the most, though she refused to show it.

"And is it proper for you to love a soldier from the future? And furthermore, one who soldiers for a tyrannical war machine," he cried. "And has died at least a dozen times? Why, the woman is as good a ghost."

He was justifiably angry at what he reasoned to be Sangfroid's betrayal, but Millicent knew this was more than a simple fall out of friends over inter-species galactic warfare. This argument was really about the heart and how Hubert had to abandon Weena to a cruel fate in dangerous and uncertain circumstances.

"No, it is not proper for me either," she agreed. "I am a pacifist, and you had only to rest at the word *soldier* for it to be improper. The word *woman* is also quite conflagratory, but the less said about the Sapphic elephant in the room, the better." Her answer directed him to the core of his upset—the impropriety of the human heart. He sank onto the Chesterfield with his head in his hands.

"Forgive me, Millicent," he said. "That was cruel. I do like the big gal tremendously, you know. She sort of grows on you."

"And I like and respect what little I know of Weena. But our hearts are silly creatures," she continued, kindly. "They see things simplistically, always looking into the mire of everyday life and trying to magnify any small thing that will make us happy, and in doing so, our logic becomes distorted."

"I'm sorry," he said. "Not because I brought Weena here; I've always known she'd have to go back. But not to that laboratory," he added quickly. "I've been trying to surmise the best location to return her to, where she would be safest. Rather…" and here his shame clearly showed on his face. "Rather, I'm sorry that this whole damned time travel adventure has turned our lives upside down and set both of us adrift on emotional seas we are barely able to navigate." He looked at her with anguish in his eyes. "You and I are intelligent, rational creatures, Millicent. And now our safe, little, orderly life here at Christie Mews will never be the same again. We have crossed our Rubicon."

She took his hands in hers. "And we crossed it shoulder to shoulder as we always do and always will. Now, take me to see Weena. As lady of the house, I should like to welcome her to our home," she said. "Has she really grown that much?" They linked arms and moved together into the hallway.

"Don't believe Sangfroid. She is nowhere near as big as a house. She fills Papa's old bathtub; that is all." He smiled at her in weary relief, and she was glad they had not fought.

"Sangfroid is an idiot," she reassured him. "Squid terrify her."

"Hey, I heard that." Sangfroid joined them as they passed by the breakfast room.

"Is it not true?" Millicent teased her in an effort to dispel any residual awkwardness between her and Hubert.

"It is true." She conceded with good nature. "But I didn't survive in the frontline as long as I have by not having a healthy terror for them." She caught Hubert's eye, and the look they swapped convinced Millicent all would be well. Soldier and scholar, each stood by their own experience and formed as honest an opinion of their separate worlds as possible. And that was that. They were far too good of friends to fall out for long.

"We are going upstairs to see Weena," Hubert said. "And discuss with her what is to be done next." He hesitated a moment, then said, "Would you care to join us?"

Millicent was proud of his quick forgiveness. Hubert arose from his earlier shame on wings of white—a man of vigour, prepared to grasp the stinging nettle and set things right. Sangfroid was just as quick to let bygones be bygones and slapped Hubert on the shoulder in a stout, friendly fashion.

"Sure, I'll join you," she said happily.

Millicent's smile remained as she led the way upstairs. She was happy for the robustness of their growing friendship and how quickly they had resolved their differences. They gathered together in Hubert's dressing room—three humans and a young Colossal squid. Weena was probably adolescent in size, Millicent surmised, if her previous state were to be classified as juvenile. Also her pinkness had faded. There was a greyish hue underneath her iridescent sheen that reminded Millicent of the patina of the adult squid. It was interesting to witness these initial stages of development. She could understand Hubert's fascination.

Communication with Weena had improved and was a much more fluid affair. Now it was clear to Millicent when Weena was conjoined with her mind and when she was having an independent thought of her own. It was a sophisticated process, and Millicent felt she had attained the level where Hubert had been on his first meeting with the little squid. His greater intellect had allowed an intimacy of understanding from the very start, whereas Millicent was still adapting to it. Though she suspected this was not due to any advance in her own skills but rather the maturing of Weena's. There were no changes in Sangfroid's ability to communicate that she could see. She stood on the threshold looking ill at ease, completely unaware of the thaumaturgic interaction Millicent, Hubert, and Weena were engaged in.

"So," Sangfroid asked, "what's the plan? Are we just going stand around looking at each other intently?"

"Weena is reminding me of the time I went back and almost got caught by one of your techie chappies in the lab," Hubert said, his face wreathed in smiles. He and Weena were inordinately fond of touching one and other, Millicent noted. They exchanged little pats and taps of fingertips and tentacle, and once he even gently touched her mantle. He was much more demonstrative with her than he had ever been with Sophia. *And that's the difference between a squid and a cold fish.* She immediately chastened herself for being mean minded and focused on what Hubert was saying.

"You mean you calibrated your arrival to a time before the ship was attacked?" Millicent suddenly realized the significance. "Before Sangfroid and the space corps centurions arrived?" She turned to Sangfroid. "Can you remember where you were before the attack?" If it were somewhere safe, maybe she could go there and somehow prevent Sangfroid even beginning her fateful journey to the doomed ship? How simple. Why hadn't she thought of it before? All those attempts to save Sangfroid in the heat of battle when all she had to do was stop her getting anywhere near the fray.

Sangfroid shrugged. "Funnily enough, my last true memory is of being in the casino with Gallo before we were deployed. Then we go to the Amoebas to shoot up squid and poof, you're there and my memory gets wiped." She tapped her temple. "It goes all hazy for me the minute you turn up. Like uncorking the tequila."

"So we can move to either side of Sangfroid's arrival on the ship." Hubert and Millicent both spoke at the same time.

"That was spooky." Sangfroid looked at them warily. "I was thinking the same thing."

"That is because it was really Weena's thought transmitted to all of us," Millicent told her. "I think she's finally found your wavelength. You must have a very low frequency."

Sangfroid stared uneasily at Weena. "I'm not sure I want a squid inside my head," she said, then turned to Hubert. "Okay, so you can arrive on the Amoebas anytime you want, so what? All you do is steal stuff."

"More importantly, we can arrive before the squid attack," Hubert said, ignoring the jibe.

"I still don't get it. Why does that matter?"

"The squid attacked for a reason," Millicent told her.

"Yeah. The Amoebas was a Roman ship and the squid are our enemy." Sangfroid was impatient. "They attacked a peaceful scientific research ship."

"You can hardly call the work carried out in those laboratories peaceful," Hubert said. "They're more like floating torture chambers. Also, the Amoebas had a special cargo onboard." He reached out and stroked Weena's coral arm. "Your scientists had stolen a juvenile queen from the squid spawn. Weena is royalty," he said proudly.

"She's what?" Sangfroid blinked in confusion. A large, singular, blue eye blinked back at her.

Somewhere in the house, a clock chimed out eleven, and the rattle of china on a tea tray could be heard downstairs. Growing squid apparently needed a lot of rest, so Hubert shooed them out of his dressing room and down to his laboratory for elevenses. Millicent poured tea while Sangfroid gave the time machine a lingering examination with Hubert as her guide.

"So how did Weena get here?" she asked, eyeing the dimensions of the machine sceptically.

Millicent handed her a delicate china cup and saucer and winced as she clumsily handled the wafer-thin material. "We think it's by being in close proximity to the traveller. By touching, in fact."

"But that machine could barely hold me, never mind Weena. She's gotten big." She juggled the cup before she gave up on the teeny little handle. Ignoring Millicent's consternation, she wrapped her hand completely around the porcelain cup.

"Don't worry," she told Millicent. "I'll be careful. I remember how upset you got when you broke the other one in the hangar."

"Yes," Millicent said, drily. "A pinnacle moment. All else pales."

"It doesn't matter what size you were." Hubert got them back on track. "You didn't materialize in the machine with Millicent. You popped up on the settee in the evening parlour, remember?"

"Rather inconveniently, too," Millicent murmured.

"But it gave me the idea that maybe I could transport Weena the same way." Hubert sipped his tea. "All I had to do was assure she materialized when the house was quiet. I chose an evening when Millicent was at her Chartist meeting and that Edna had off. Cook always goes to bed early."

"You brought Weena here the day before yesterday?" Millicent was surprised.

"But she was on the ship yesterday when we were fighting in the lab?" Sangfroid said.

"No, I brought her here last week. It's time travel. Remember? Different rules."

"I can't keep track of all this." Sangfroid stared moodily into her cup. She hadn't met Hubert before yesterday, yet he felt like a good, long-standing friend. Her feelings for Millicent were more complicated. They went deeper, to places she had never known existed inside of her, constricting her with panicked palpitations until her breathing grew shallow and her skin slick with sweat.

"It's harder for you," Hubert said. "Millicent and I are firmly rooted in this timeline along with the time machine. Try and see this room as a sort of terminus. We can get on and off the time machine as we would an omnibus, but we're always circling our home route and ending up back here."

"Whereas you have hopped on the wrong bus entirely," Millicent added. "And Hubert and I have to deduce where you got on and how to make sure you get off again at exactly the same stop. Understand?"

Sangfroid thought about this for a moment and said, "No." She bit into her third scone and wiped her sticky fingers on her pant leg, ignoring the disapproving look Millicent gave. "So, can we send Weena back on the bus the way she came, especially now she's bigger? She'll break the lab bench if we don't do it soon."

"I don't really want to send her back to the lab as—" Hubert said.

"Hey," Sangfroid interrupted. "Maybe I can go back with her?"

Hubert and Millicent exchanged glances.

"What?" Sangfroid demanded. "You said we could go back at any time which means we can go back to before I died."

"Sangfroid, I have often gone back, and believe me," Millicent said. "It just doesn't work. In fact, the only reason you are here now is because you pulled me into the escape pod with you. Despite my best efforts, I sincerely doubt you would have been saved at all." She sighed. "I have become quite despondent at your lack of longevity."

"You mean…" As usual Sangfroid grappled with a bottleneck of ideas until Millicent gently uncorked her.

"I mean I have never once managed to save you," she said. "I thought you were going to explain all this at the club?" She accused her brother.

He went red. "I tried," he said. "But events took over."

"You mean you got drunk," Millicent gave them both a hard look. "And imbecility took over. I shall never forgive you for that dance."

"I thought it looked very virile and Cossack like," Hubert defended Sangfroid, though rather lamely.

"It's all in the thighs." Sangfroid slapped her own. "You should see how high I can bounce when my knee's not ban-jaxed."

"Can we please get back to the subject in hand," Millicent said sternly.

"But you saved me; that's why I'm here," Sangfroid said. This was met with silence. "Well, isn't it?"

"When Millicent and I went back, that initial time, it didn't exactly go as expected," said Hubert.

"Not that we had any defined expectations," Millicent added. "We didn't know what would happen."

"We hadn't much of a plan at all," Hubert agreed.

"In fact, it was all very *laissez faire*," Millicent said.

"What happened?" Sangfroid sighed and settled back in her chair with a defeatist slump.

"Well," Hubert began, "as I told you last night, we arrived on the Amoebas and went straight to the laboratory where I met Weena for the first time. Then suddenly, the doors of the main laboratory burst open with lots of smoke and noise and the like."

"That was us coming in, right?" Sangfroid looked to Millicent for confirmation.

"Yes. I warned Hubert that we had to detour you away from Weena's annex. You couldn't find us there. And then I had a wonderful idea—"

Weena managed to sit still while Hubert awkwardly detached the clips from the ends of her tentacles to free her from the oppressive machinery surrounding her.

"Quickly, Hubert." Millicent waited by the wiring panel, her hand poised on the red switch. "Once I pull this, the lab outside becomes a death trap, and we have to leave immediately. Do you understand me?" she hissed.

"Yes. Death trap, I think I can remember that," he hissed back and unclipped the last of the tentacle attachments. "What about Weena? Will she be safe?"

"I assume so, seeing as the harbinger of death and destruction is most probably a piece of her big brother." From the corner of her eye she watched as Sangfroid, and her other self, entered the lab. The other Millicent began to linger over the apparatus on the benches while Sangfroid grew more and more abrupt. She hadn't realized before how nervous Sangfroid had been, hovering over her anxiously while bossing her about. It saddened her to see how exhausted and beaten down they already were, for she knew there was much worse to come. It also disturbed her that her chignon was in a terrible mess, and as for the state of her day dress!

"All done. Pull the switch," Hubert said. She did so, and as before, the main lab lighting and all its machinery came to demonic life.

"Good Lord!" Hubert exclaimed, agog at the transformation going on before him. The huge tentacle twitched as electrical current began to run through it. Millicent grabbed his sleeve and pulled him under the nearest bench as they watched Sangfroid bundle the other Millicent towards an exit on the other side of the lab and away from the annex. She breathed a sigh of relief. It had worked; Sangfroid was out of danger and moving away from the dismembered tentacle. She had saved her!

"Quickly, we must leave before the tentacle comes after us." She pushed Hubert towards the annex door.

"What tentacle?" The glass tank exploded, and the severed appendage began its rampage across the lab, jerking, twitching, and destroying everything in its path. Hubert went sheet white. "Look at the size of that thing," he squeaked.

"Yes. And though it is severed from the brain it still has some sort of faculty. Soon it will sense we are here and come after us."

"How fascinating," Hubert said. "Do you suppose it's a sort of reverse innervate syndrome?"

"Out. Now." Even as she shoved him towards the door, she sensed his reluctance to leave Weena despite the avenging severed tentacle destroying all before it.

"She'll be all right," she assured him. "They are of a kind. I truly believe that in some way it is trying to protect her." *Much as you wish to.* The thought surprised her, but she knew it to be true. Hubert was inordinately attached to the little creature, but there was no time to dwell on the thought. She dragged him out into the corridor where they had originally materialized.

"Surely it must be time for the machine to bring us back?" she said. She was anxious about this part of the proceedings, much more so than Hubert who apparently had every faith in his calculations. For the first time, he looked calm and in control. He fished his pocket watch from his waistcoat and announced, "We have seven minutes. Plenty of time. It's a straight run from here."

"Seven minutes could be a tad too generous." She was anxious. They could hardly run around the ship for the next several minutes and remain safe. She looked around for a place to wait it out, except the corridor had changed in their absence. It was no longer empty and abandoned; now it was filled with smoke and the noise of the battle echoed louder as if it was no longer contained by the walls of the hangar. The thud of booted feet came thundering towards them.

"In here." She pushed Hubert into a shallow recess and squeezed into the space beside him. Several men and women in white overalls ran past escorted by a lone soldier.

"Come on you lot. Run. The escape pods are straight ahead." The soldier bellowed at his charges. Acrid smoke shrouded the corridor farther on up. They ran on into it, and no sooner had they disappeared into the gloom, than horrible screaming began. There came an ugly shuddering, and the metal walls shrieked in protest as the whole ship lurched.

"I don't think we should go that way. Do you know another route?" Hubert asked, looking anxiously after the soldier and his doomed charges. He mopped his brow with his handkerchief. Millicent dithered, thinking hard, before taking off again with Hubert at her heels. "I suspect the corridors are built to a grid system," she said. "If we go down here and keep taking the right hand side we should re-emerge at—Oh." She broke off. On the floor at their feet lay a pile of abandoned weaponry. "Gallo was checking through these when I first arrived." She stooped and picked up a hand weapon.

"Who's Gallo?" Hubert asked.

"Oh, look. A laser pistol! I've always wanted to see one up close." Millicent picked up the weapon and hefted it in her hand. "It's lighter than I expected. Look, Hubert, isn't it fascinating that—"

Sangfroid barrelled around the corner, heading straight for her with her own pistol raised and at the ready. She staggered to a standstill, pop-eyed with shock at seeing Millicent standing before her playing with pistols and not tucked away safely behind her where she ought to be. Millicent also gave a start, equally as shocked at Sangfroid's sudden appearance—and the gun in her hand went off. A blaze of burning blue hit Sangfroid square in the chest at point blank range—

The silence hung heavy. Millicent and Hubert watched Sangfroid in anticipation, their expressions guarded.

"You shot me?" she said, then stood and began pacing. "You shot me. I can't believe you shot me." She paused and glared at the time machine and then at Millicent. "Actually, I can."

"I am truly sorry. It was an accident." Millicent felt terrible. "You startled me, barging about like that."

"Yes. I can see how barging about in a war zone would be inconsiderate."

"Now you're being silly," she said. "I thought Gallo had taken all the working guns with her. I had no intention of shooting you."

"Who is Gallo?" Hubert asked but was ignored.

"I'm beginning to see a pattern here," Sangfroid said. "Whenever you're around, I die. It's as simple as that. How do I know it won't happen here, 'eh? How do I know you won't massacre me in this timeline, and then I'll be dead everywhere! In fact, why don't I just go outside and hurl myself under a hansom cab and save you the bother."

"Who is Gallo?"

"Really, you are such a theatre piece. Listening to you is like a bad night at the opera. I have apologized for shooting you; what more can I do?" Millicent said.

"Who is Gallo?" Hubert shouted. They both turned to look at him.

"My best buddy," Sangfroid said. "And a damn fine soldier."

"You saw her in the lab, Hubert," Millicent said. "She came in with myself and Sangfroid."

"No I didn't."

Millicent frowned. "Actually, now I think of it…" She turned to Sangfroid. "On that second occasion, I don't think Gallo came into the laboratory with us. At first I assumed she was off to the side looking at something or other. But I can't recall seeing her even once. Was she with us?"

Sangfroid shrugged. "Haven't a clue. You've messed with my timeline so often my memories are about as concrete as baby food. In this version, the weapon you so carelessly aimed at me was working, as if Gallo never picked through them?"

"As if Gallo was never there." Millicent was worried. A principle player had just walked off stage. Could that happen?

Chapter 13

"Millicent," Sophia said later that afternoon. "I am feeling frightfully left out. I called this morning with more eggs for Cook only to find all three of you ensconced in Hubert's laboratory, and that silly creature Edna simply refused to disturb you. She turned into a quivering wreck when I mentioned rousing you. What can you all possibly have to talk about that I can't contribute to?" She glared at the assembled company until both Millicent and Sangfroid shifted uncomfortably in their seats. Hubert had so far managed to avoid this visit by loitering all afternoon at the university. Millicent seethed at his deliberate absence; she was always being tricked into entertaining Sophia.

"Oh." She wracked her mind for a topic that would bore Sophia rigid so she would go away. "We were talking about suffrage for women. It's a movement that is gaining momentum on the Chartism manifesto."

"Really? I can't see Declan caring in the least for that." Sophia sniffed.

"Decanus," Sangfroid corrected and slurped her afternoon tea. She looked irritated and distracted. Boredom oozed out of her every pore, and Millicent itched to kick her ankles to make her at least sit up straight, instead of listing in her seat like Pisan architecture.

"Major Sangfroid has the greatest interest in women's suffrage," Millicent said, bristling at Sophia's impropriety.

It was only last night she had been introduced to Sangfroid properly. Far too soon to assume first name terms, even if it was the wrong first name.

"Decanus," Sangfroid corrected her, too.

"We agreed you were a major," she whispered. "You cannot be a decanus here. It means nothing."

"Maybe it's an old family name from the Urals—ouch!" She broke off with a yelp. "You pinched me." She examined a small red mark forming on the side of her wrist.

"You deserved it. We've had enough of your Urals," Millicent said.

"What you bet this goes septic." She rubbed her wrist. "And I die."

"You really should be in an operetta," Millicent said.

"You really should be on a death squad."

"Enough of this ineffectual flirting," Sophia said. "It should be curtailed to the front parlour chaise, where it belongs."

Millicent's face flamed.

Sophia sailed on heedless of her insensitivity. "I have been inadvertently eavesdropping at Hubert's laboratory door for some time now," she said. "And I think it reprehensible of you to not include me in your scientific discussions. I am a highly educated lady, easily a contemporary of Millicent, and yet I'm always left out."

"How can one inadvertently eavesdrop?" Millicent was so astounded by this admission she let the fantastical nonsense about their intellectual parity pass.

"By arriving at a door, hearing voices, and not going away," Sophia said. "You see I come from a large family, Mr. Decanus." She turned to Sangfroid. "For all its size, it is impossible to acquire any information worth having unless one uses one's ingenuity. Why, I was unaware of my eldest sister's wedding until the week before. Factual advisement is in short supply, and the rest is all assumption. It's so easy to be disabused in the Trenchant-Myre idyll."

"I can't imagine you being disabused at all," Sangfroid said. "And it's decanus, no need for the mister."

"Oh, in my family, I am quite the scholarly wallflower." She fluttered back and Millicent bristled. Sophia was being almost coquettish, and it jarred horribly with her usual brusque, blunt, and essentially humourless nature.

"Sophia, what exactly did you overhear at the door?" Millicent asked and leaned over to pour more tea, but with very stiff shoulders to convey her disapproval.

"That you are planning to travel. And very soon." Sophia added two lumps of sugar with the silver tongs and stirred delicately. Sangfroid offered her cup for a refill. Millicent shuddered at the sight of her mother's chinaware in the Neanderthal grasp.

"Something about Paradoxees and Quantumphysex." Sophia took a sip of tea. "Which I am sure are in Africa. And I will not allow it."

Millicent stilled and cast a look towards Sangfroid who looked back blandly. "I'm sure you misheard." Millicent tried for a light laugh. Sangfroid did not join in, preferring to sulk.

"No, I did not." Sophia brushed imaginary crumbs from her lap. "You are planning a journey with Hubert. And it is unfair not to tell me. I should know when the house is to be empty so I can keep an eye on the staff and ensure there is no scally-wagging or loitering. Staff always loll about when the master is away."

Millicent frowned; it was a relief Sophia had no clue as to the true nature of their travels, but still worrisome she knew of it at all. The drawing room door opened, and Hubert finally joined them.

"How was the university, dearest?" Sophia asked with little interest.

"Busy, as usual. Ah ha, I thought I heard the tinkle of china," Hubert said merrily looking the tea set. "Any scones?"

"Sophia is aware of your travel plans, Hubert." Millicent sweetly laid the problem at his newly arrived feet. He paled a little but managed to accept a cup of tea and a buttered scone.

"Oh?" he said and then began to eat robustly as if chewing heartily would save him from adding further to the conversation.

"I should have no wish to travel abroad." Sophia primly began her lecture. "I see no advantage in such an enterprise." She regarded Millicent's plaid fan-front day dress with a sly eye. It was much less stylish than Sophia's three-piece, peacock blue silk, and both ladies were acutely aware of that fact. Millicent hated her frumpy old dress. Her frequent exploits to Sangfroid's timeline had denuded her wardrobe of her more fashionable garments. She was now reduced to reaching into the nether regions of the armoire to find anything at all respectable to wear. A shopping expedition was looming, and that disheartened her greatly. Dress shopping was not her forte. Had Sophia proven a more agreeable companion, Millicent would have asked her to come with her and give advice. Sophia knew quality, had taste, and was well up on the latest fashions. But her overbearing nature was too much for Millicent and so she depended on the recommendations of shop girls and her own rather narrow palette of favoured colours.

"I mean, it's not as if one brings back anything worthwhile, like news of the latest fashions," Sophia continued. Her barely concealed barb at Millicent's day dress hit its mark.

"Indeed." Millicent simpered, trying to control her temper. "I declare you would not like it abroad, Sophia. Their language is atrocious. There were H words, and Fs, and on at least one occasion a B." Her fingers tightened around her reticule where she had composed a list of all Sangfroid's unsuitable language so it could be addressed later, if there ever was a later.

"A bee?" Sophia was curious.

"Yes, a B."

"I do not like bees. I do not like any creatures. Not even cats and dogs." Sophia was very firm on this. "Nor do I have time for horses."

The Tea Machine

"Then I am certain you would not like abroad at all," Millicent said, thinking of the giant squid upstairs.

"Rather," Sophia continued as if no one had spoken, "it is more probable that you shall all return with some dreadful disease and die. It is very foolhardy of you, Hubert, to die before we are wed and you can make me a widow."

Hubert choked on his scone.

"I so admire your thinking, Sophia," Sangfroid told her. "I mean, who knows what strange souvenirs a man might return with?" She glared at Hubert and let her gaze drift down to his pockets.

"Yes," Millicent agreed, seething at Sangfroid for siding with Sophia, so she, in turn, sided with Hubert. "There is always the worry of some *organism* following one home," she said and glared blatantly at Sangfroid so there was no doubt as to which organism she referred to.

Hubert finished his scone, apparently unconcerned by all the glaring going on. "A very valid argument, my dear." He smiled at Sophia who smiled demurely back.

"So we are in agreement, Hubert," she said. "No more travel. I can't have you haring off whenever I need you here to help with my societies. If you were to go away, I would be sure to need you, and you would have to return at once, which begs the question why go in the first place? It is all so fucking awkward."

"Pardon?" Hubert started in his seat.

Millicent sat bolt upright. "Pardon?" she echoed. They all regarded Sophia in stunned silence. "Sophia," she said, "I want you to think carefully about this. Have you been travelling yourself, recently?"

"Of course not. How ridiculous. I think I should buggering well know if I had done such a silly thing," she answered. She gathered her gloves and stood. "Now, I must bid you all farewell. I have to call on the Misses Partridge and help them choose hymns for the church flower festival. It should be frigging fantastic this year."

Millicent led Sophia out to the hall. "Sophia," she said, taking her arm in hers. "It's been wonderful to see you. I've been meaning for us to have tea and tell each other our news."

Sophia regarded her with suspicion. They never swapped news.

"Perhaps you could advise me on purchasing a new dress?" Millicent continued to lay bait. "I do so admire this three-piece you are wearing. Is it a Charles Worth?" She squirmed under Sophia's narrowed gaze. She hated deceitfulness, but this was for a necessary cause.

"It is a Worth," Sophia replied slowly. "My sisters and I—"

"What fun," Millicent interrupted. "You do have such an exciting life." Sophia tensed and Millicent sensed she may have gone too far. She knew Sophia was sensitive to being the youngest, plainest, and probably the most boring female in her large family. Millicent tried to remedy the situation. "I mean has anything…new…happened recently?" She began to reel Sophia in.

"Well," Sophia said. "I did have a purpose for my visit this afternoon, but I found it inappropriate to speak of it in front of the gentlemen."

"Oh, and why would that be, dear?"

"It's about your coal hole," Sophia said in a conspiratorial voice.

"My coal hole?" Millicent repeated.

"Yes, I've been investigating your domestic arrangements regarding the delivery of coal, and I recommend you get the hatch from the street fixed. You can't have people falling down there," Sophia said. "And I may have found you a new footman, too." She seemed very pleased with this.

"A new footman?" Millicent was lost. Did they even need a footman?

"Except he speaks Latin, not English. But he learns very quickly." Sophia elaborated. Her colour heightened, putting an unnatural rosy glow onto her sallow cheeks.

Latin? Millicent tightened her hold on Sophia's arm and eased her into the brocade settle in the hallway.

"You must tell all," she said, trying to sound delightfully intrigued rather than heinously alarmed.

"Remember, I called earlier this morning, and as I said, Edna greeted me," Sophia began, leaping at the chance to have Millicent's ear. "I found her in a terrible state, yet far too fretful to disturb your elevenses, as I have also stated." Her disapproval surfaced, but she soldiered on. "She was so relieved to see me, bless her. She needed guidance and advice, and really who better to turn to than her soon-to-be-mistress. Who else was there to take the helm while you were all ensconced in the laboratory?"

"What did she want?" Millicent tried to keep Sophia focused on the facts.

"It was most intriguing," Sophia continued. "She said to me—"

"Oh, Miss." Edna, clearly distressed, met Sophia at the door. "There's something awful in the coal hole, and Cook is too busy straining soft fruits and says it's none of her business what goes on in the coal hole and if Master Hubert hadn't sacked the footman for diddling the port, then there'd be a man about the house to go down into coal holes and the like and see what's what." Then she sniffled tearfully into her apron and blinked moistly at Sophia.

"And until a new footman is employed, I assume it's your chore to see 'what's what'?" Sophia asked as regally as she could muster, making a mental note to remind Hubert to hire a man as quickly as possible. Lord only knew how many 'what's what' had been left to Edna's slippery attention span.

Sophia sighed heavily. She had been hoping to forgo these sort of domestic situations until long after she was married. She was the fifth and last daughter out of nine children, and very far down the chain of command in the Trenchant-Myre household. From an early age, Sophia had to struggle for every soupçon of attention she could garner. Nor did it overly concern her parents that their youngest daughter's education was cobbled together from her siblings' scholastic leftovers. Tutors had been set up for the boys until they came of an age they could be jettisoned off to boarding school, only to return for weddings, funerals, and an occasional Christmas. The young Sophia relied on her brother's cast-off books and purloined volumes from her father's library in order to learn anything at all.

Her older sisters had been taught the rudiments of household management from their mother, including the literacy levels needed to keep the books and make sure one's servants weren't bleeding one dry. But in Sophia's case, her blessed Mama delivered these lessons less frequently. With nine children behind her, and an age gap of ten years between her other daughters and Sophia, Mama was quite worn out by the time it was Sophia's turn to learn womanly wiles. The result was Sophia had little knowledge of domestic economy. Her greatest shame, one of many, was that she came to Hubert totally unprepared to run his house and was secretly hoping Millicent would continue on in that capacity. Though she'd rather choke on her own tongue than ask.

"Where is Miss Millicent? Surely she should be taking an interest in the coal hole?" Sophia asked Edna.

"Miss Millicent and Master Hubert are currently indisposed," Edna answered unhelpfully. "I went for Miss Millicent first, but she was not to be found. I think they are in the master's laboratory taking tea and I am not allowed to 'so much as knock on the door,'" she rhymed off by rote.

As much as she wanted Millicent to run the house, it still irked Sophia that she should take centre stage, especially when it came to Hubert. Sophia had never once set foot in the laboratory, yet Millicent swanned in and out as if it were Claridge's. She filled the most important roles, leaving Sophia in the shadows. Sophia already had a multitude of siblings doing just that, and it was tiresome that the pattern continued into her new life. Why did everyone refer to Millicent in a crisis? Sophia decided that on this occasion she would take command. After all, in the absence of Millicent and Hubert, it was up to her to keep the house flag aloft. She may have little to give in the way of domestic advice, but that didn't mean she couldn't offer it anyway, if only for effect. She cleared her throat and launched into action. "What exactly *is* a coal hole, Edna?"

"It's the cellar where we keep the coal, Miss."

"And what is amiss with this cellar?" Sophia was losing interest already. Coal cellars sounded like disgusting places.

"I think someone's in it, Miss." Edna was wide eyed, and her hands trembled.

"Well, it's obvious that they should not be. Have you asked them to remove themselves from the coal hole?"

"No, Miss. I ran away when I heard the moaning."

"Moaning? Dear Lord, woman, they're probably hurt. Maybe they fell in or something." Sophia was unsure how people presented themselves to a coal hole, but if there was moaning then something was awry.

Edna turned chalk white, and it dawned on Sophia that she would have to go and call into this cellar herself to ensure this moaning ne'er do well got on his way. He had better not be a drunk. She had no sympathy for intoxication or merriment of any kind.

"Take me to the coal hole this instant." Sophia warmed to the idea of solving a domestic dilemma and giving a scoundrel a good telling off at the same time. It would please her to inform everyone how she had taken charge while Millicent malingered over tea in the sacrosanct laboratory.

Pleased with her contribution to the crisis, she followed Edna to a small door adjacent to the steps that led to the kitchens. It was on the same level as the boot room, and the whole area had a strange, unfamiliar odour that Sophia could only put down to human industry. She pushed open the cellar door to reveal a flight of narrow steps that descended into darkness as black as pitch. She was definitely not going down there. It was filthy!

"How on earth do you get the coal into such a place?" she asked.

"The coal man delivers into the hatch in the street, Miss. This is where I fill the buckets in the morning to set the fires." Edna fidgeted with her apron, staring down the stairwell.

"How abhorrent. I can only assume someone has trespassed by falling in from the street. I hope the coal has not been damaged."

"Cook says it's haunted."

"Nonsense. You are not allowed to believe in ghosts. Do you understand me, Edna?"

"Yes, Miss."

From the bowels of the basement, a guttural moan swirled up at them. It was low and forlorn and as desolate as the wind in a winter graveyard. Edna squeaked and took flight, leaving Sophia rooted to the spot in blind panic.

The slither of avalanching coal told her something was moving down there. Then came the drag of footsteps; first one, then another, and another. Slowly they moved from the bottom of the stairs towards where she stood. She felt faint. The steps drew nearer, scraping on the stone stairway. Her knees weakened, horror clawed at her heart, and yet she couldn't move. Below her a young man's face surfaced from out of the gloom. He was dark haired and sooty skinned, and his eyes were a fierce angelic blue that pinned her in place in a spasm of Gloriana, rather than fright. He was beautiful. Absolutely beautiful. His hair was blacker than the coal-strewn hell from which he ascended. He was tall, and noble, and gorgeous, and

The Tea Machine

Sophia's heart joined her sagging knees in a betrayal of all that was upright and moral. *Lord Byron is in my coal hole!*

And then he spoke in a marvellous, foreign tongue. He spoke as they did in Babel, with words strange and uplifting, and Sophia found that if she concentrated hard, really, really hard on the movement of his wondrous sculpted lips...it made no difference at all. She understood not one word but was happy to stand transfixed in ignorance. In fact, the movement of his lips weakened her knees further.

He mounted the stairs gazing at her with equally rapt attention, bordering on disbelief. His long, silky eyelashes blinked in the bright daylight, and she wanted to count each and every lash that surrounded his cerulean irises. How long had he been down there? The poor, poor, beautiful man. Oh, Edna would pay for this!

Sophia was thrilled that he was her discovery and hers alone. It could so easily have been Millicent who found him. Millicent already had a handsome, mysterious gentleman admirer from the Urals. It was only fair that Sophia advocate for this one. Especially as he was much more handsome and definitely more interesting than Mr. Decanus. Sophia was elated with her find.

Then it dawned on her that the language he was speaking was Latin, and her heart sank. Millicent had been taught Latin, but Sophia hadn't. Oh, she pretended to have some knowledge of it, but in reality it was gleaned from her father's gardening journals and not from proper language lessons. She could not bear for Hubert, and especially Millicent, to know how undereducated she was. Still, she so wished to communicate with her beautiful stranger, she just had to try out what little she knew. It would not be long before her precious discovery would be ripped from her grasp by the Aberlys.

"Lonicera alpigena," she said, using her meagre Latin.

"Alpine honeysuckle?" he repeated, admittedly confused. He reached the top stair and towered over her, a primitive, powerful beast forged in the lusty fires of Lucifer. His eyes held the blazing blue of foreign skies, his hair the inky gloss of a raven's wing. She looked up at him until her head swam.

"Galanthus nivalis," she said, breathlessly.

"Common snowdrop?" He was frowning now, and she was running out of Latin plant names. She'd have to resort to her brother's old school motto, if only she could remember it. Fidelity and…books, under…what, a unicorn? Oh, dear. Then she realized he was answering her, or rather repeating her words, but in English. He was translating her Latin into her own tongue. How clever!

"Do you understand me?" she asked. In answer he dropped to one knee and lifted the hem of her dress and kissed it. Now it wouldn't matter if he spoke double Dutch with an Irish accent and a kilt. He was wonderful.

"Vaccinium oxycoccus." She sighed, dreamily.

"Cranberry." He smiled back at her.

Chapter 14

"Cranberry?" Millicent was appalled. Who was this strange man? What had Sophia been thinking not to report this intrusion to her sooner?

"Yes, we share a mutual love of gardening." Sophia smiled and sighed.

"You wouldn't know a flower bed from a paddy field," Millicent snapped.

"You are too cruel," Sophia objected. "I may well know the difference—if I were to see them side by side. Besides, I have taught him English, after a fashion. The study of linguistics also binds us."

"It is not English; it is some horticultural gobbledygook that may well have you both arrested if you step foot outside of this house," Millicent said, and added as an afterthought, "or into any convenient florist. Where is he now? Please don't tell me he is still in the cellar."

"No, he is not." Sophia sniffed haughtily. "He is in the kitchen with Cook. She says he has cleaned up well, is industrious, and would make an excellent replacement footman."

"And this new…effervescence in your language? Is this the result of your cross-cultural linguistic studies?" Millicent asked, wondering at the ease they all had in understanding each others native tongue. She would have to ask Hubert for this thoughts on the matter.

"Whatever do you mean?"

"The Fs and Bs you are using so freely and frequently, my dear." Millicent dipped into her reticule to retrieve her pocketbook of curse words. She tapped it with an indignant finger. "I, too, have a study underway."

"The Fs and Bs?" Sophia looked genuinely puzzled. Then her expression brightened. "Oh, that is Latin, silly Millicent. I teach him English and am learning Latin from him in turn."

"Then desist from learning more. I fear your Latin is more Anglo-Saxon than you realize."

"Can he be your new footman?" Sophia blushed. "Please say yes."

Millicent suspected Sophia had developed an inappropriate fascination with this stranger. "I will pass on Cook's recommendations to Hubert, and he will decide if the young man is suitable," she said, manoeuvring Sophia towards the front door.

"Please convey my best wishes to the Misses Partridge," she said and ushered Sophia onto the doorstep. She was about to close the door when a thought occurred. "Sophia," she called. "Please, no Latin with the ladies; they are elderly, and it would only," she grappled for a suitable word, "confuse."

Sophia gave her a bright smile and went on her way.

"Do we know anything about the coal hole?" Millicent dashed back to the drawing room in a flurry of skirts and high colour. Sangfroid and Hubert looked at her blankly, so she explained further. "Sophia has just this minute told me she found a strange man in our coal cellar." She threw Sangfroid a look. "Could another organism really have followed us back?"

"I did *not* follow you here. I was minding my own business killing squid and getting killed in return, when the next thing I know, I woke up on your bloody-damned-ugly couch."

"Hyphenated swear words now," Millicent scolded and scribbled in her notebook. "I see your vulgarity is evolving semantically. Just what we need. I am keeping a list so we can work on your diction."

"Who is in the cellar?" Hubert asked.

"My diction works just fine for my timeline, lady, which is where I wish I was right now. You think I followed you?" Sangfroid said. "If anything, I was kidnapped."

"Who is in the cellar?" Hubert asked, again.

"Kidnapped! Oh, for Goodness sake!" Millicent snorted. "Who would pay a ransom for you?"

"Who is in the cellar?" Hubert shouted. They stopped arguing and looked at him. He took advantage to elaborate on his question. "Who has Sophia unearthed in the coal cellar? Did she say?"

"She gave no name. Apparently he speaks Latin and likes gardening. Oh, and she highly recommends him as a replacement footman."

"What do you mean, he speaks latin? What's latin?" Sangfroid asked.

"Latin was the ancient tongue of your culture. Rome was the chief city of the Latium region, so its language is Latin," Hubert explained. "The Roman Empire has come and gone in this timeline. It was once mighty, but now it is obsolete. All great empires come and go throughout history, and in this age the force to be reckoned with is ours. Rule Britannia, and all that."

"Britannia? An empire?" Sangfroid broke into loud guffaws. "Britannia. That dump? It's a prefecture of Gaul."

"Oh dear," Hubert said. "Please don't say that to anyone outside of this room. Relations with France have always been fraught."

"And I don't speak Latin. I speak Roman," Sangfroid said proudly.

"How is it we understand each other?" Millicent asked Hubert. "It's alarming how easily we seem to fall into a mutual understanding. As if our minds are being somehow manipulated from afar?"

"I honestly don't know, but I suspect it's something to do with proximity to the Colossals. The Amoebas was full of them. If they have some sort of organic ability to speak mind to mind, maybe they can act as universal translators? Or perhaps pass the skill on to us?"

"But Sophia and her society ladies can understand Sangfroid, and they haven't been near a squid." Millicent pointed out.

"I think we would have heard about it if they had," Sangfroid said.

Hubert shrugged. "Again, I'm not sure. Perhaps it's because Weena is in the house? Perhaps it's a contagion between us? I wish I knew, but really there is so much to understand. I have barely scratched at the surface, nevermind plumbed the depths," he said. "Where is this man? I don't like the idea of him in the house. We need to talk to him. He could be dangerous. Should we be armed?" he asked Sangfroid.

Sangfroid pulled a nasty looking dagger from her bootleg.

"I say." Hubert looked both unnerved and impressed at the same time. "Has that been down there all along?"

Millicent looked alarmed. "What on earth are you going to do with that?" she asked.

"Hubert will summon the man, and I'll wait behind the door. If he steps out of line, I'll gut him."

"There will be no blood spilling on my Seljuk carpet." Millicent was adamant.

"Perhaps there's another room you prefer to gut strangers in?" Sangfroid said.

"There is. Follow me." Millicent led them into Hubert's laboratory and proceeded to roll up the Persian silks. "Will this suit?"

Ignoring her sarcasm, Sangfroid took up position behind the door. "I want you out of here for safety's sake," she said, "but there's no hope of you going, is there?"

"No." Millicent yanked on the bell pull by the mantelpiece. Edna appeared at the threshold of the doorway a few minutes later and lurched into her awkward curtsey, careful that not one toe should cross into the forbidden territory of the laboratory.

"Yes, sir?"

"This man Miss Sophia found in the coal cellar, Edna," Hubert asked, "is he still in the house?"

Edna went beet red, and Millicent suspected this so called footman had woven his seducer's spell around Edna, too.

"Why, yes he is, sir," Edna said. "He's downstairs with Cook polishing the silver."

Millicent was surprised. Cook guarded the silverware like a dragon its eggs. Had she been enthralled by this cad as well?

"Send him along will you," Hubert said, and Edna left, her feet skittering along the hall tiles.

He's a bounder, thought Millicent. She could see it now. He had to be some sort of devious charmer to inveigle his way so cleverly with the women of her household. Heavy, measured footsteps echoed along the hall. She braced herself for an onslaught of artful charm and seductively honeyed words.

The man entered the room and immediately saw Sangfroid. "Fuckamo, if it isn't our Froidy!"

Gallo? Millicent was aghast.

"Gallo, hah!" Sangfroid threw herself at her comrade, and they crashed together in a hug that would put battling grizzly bears to shame. "I was wondering if you made it."

"I didn't," Gallo said happily. "I'm dead. And let me tell you, the afterlife is nothing like they said it would be." She stood back, all seriousness. "I was in the deepest pit of Tartarus, Sangfroid, but the goddess came and cast her light down on me and set me free. Now I'm tasked with shining up her treasure. And not in the usual way." She winked and slapped Sangfroid on the shoulder. "But hey, you died too. Bloody squid, 'eh?" Then she saw Millicent. "Hey, the frock didn't make it either! It's like a friggin' reunion."

Millicent glowered.

"The froc—Millicent is not dead, and neither are you and I," Sangfroid told her.

"Good Lord, another one, and she's enormous." Hubert sidled up to Millicent to whisper in awe. "What is it with these women from the future, are they Amazons?"

"No, the Amazon's are even taller," Millicent answered, rather peevishly.

"How do you know that?" Hubert asked.

"I'm not sure. I just do." Millicent turned her attention to the reunion before her.

"Are you sure we're not dead?" Gallo squinted suspiciously at Sangfroid. "I feel dead. I'm working my butt off downstairs for some Hesperidean maidens, and the big fat one is mean." Then she grinned. "But she likes me."

"They all like you. Nothing changes." Sangfroid laughed. "How the hell did you get here?"

"Dunno." Gallo shrugged. "Last I remember, I was running down the corridor with the froc—Millicent, and then I woke up in Tartarus."

"That was our coal ho—cellar," Millicent said coldly. "I'll leave Sangfroid to explain how you got here and where you are. The woman who found you was—"

"A Goddess!" Gallo's eyes shone. "Sangfroid, I was lying in this black pit of despair when suddenly there was a shaft of light, and I followed it and ascended to meet Looselea."

"Looselea?" Sangfroid looked surprised.

"Looselea?" Millicent tried to keep the mockery from her voice but was too scorched from the frock remarks to have much sympathy for Gallo and her naive beliefs.

"Who's Looselea?" Hubert asked.

"You mean the goddess on your mother's medallion?" Millicent said, gesturing at the fine chain glinting from beneath Gallo's collar. "The Goddess of Engineers?"

Gallo's fingers strayed to her medallion. She pulled it from her shirt and kissed it. "Yes," she said. "I have seen the goddess, and she is as beautiful as she is wise."

"Don't tell me we've imported a goddess as well," Millicent said. "Just how many stowaways were there?"

"Do you mean the woman who found you in your pit?" Sangfroid asked. "That woman? Skinny and kinda weird, with a big nose?"

"Hey. I don't poo-poo your Mithras. Leave my Looselea alone." Gallo scowled.

"Good Lord, you think Sophia is Looselea?" Millicent said.

"Who is Looselea?" Hubert asked. "And tell me now before I have to shout. Why does…Gallo…" He said the name carefully, still intimidated by the size and musculature of the woman soldier. "Why does Gallo seem to think Sophia is a goddess? I mean, it's the last thing she needs to hear." His brow was glistening, and he mopped it with a large handkerchief.

Sangfroid peered at the medallion in Gallo's hand. "It sort of looks like her, except the hair's all piled up suggestively," she mused. "And that toga is a little risqué. Nice décolletage, though."

"Let me see." Millicent elbowed her out of the way. On closer inspection, this deity looked far too carefree and undone for Millicent's liking. "I can see similarities in the profile. Sophia does have a distinctive nose." She was reluctant to admit.

Hubert crowded in to examine the medallion. "The nose fits, but little else matches. So who is this Looselea?" he asked. "You said she was the Goddess of Engineering?"

"Looselea is the patron Goddess of Engineers. In the pantheon, she's the Goddess of Steam Power," Sangfroid said. "She's one of the older gods, been around forever."

"Steam power? In ancient Rome? Rome, BC? You're saying that in ancient Rome you had steam power?" Hubert looked incredulous.

"What's a BC?" Sangfroid asked. "Is that in your book?" she asked Millicent.

"How perfectly awful," Millicent said, ignoring her and turning to Hubert in dismay. "How on earth did the early Romans discover steam power? Aside, of course, for bathing."

"This explains the wild trajectory the Roman Empire takes in Sangfroid's timeline." Hubert had an excited look. "By discovering steam power out of context with normal industrial and cultural evolution, they were able to make a massive technological leap forward and skewer world history as we know it!" He was obviously having an epiphany, but it was a solitary one. The others merely stared.

"Hey. We did everything right," Sangfroid said. "It's *your* culture that's the museum piece. You're the primitives."

"We are not," Millicent said. "You cheated. You had to have some goddess show you a shortcut; we did our empire building all by ourselves."

"Weena has already stated that you are out of context as a species," Hubert told Sangfroid. "You are an anathema to the universal continuum."

"Universal what?" Gallo looked questioningly at Sangfroid. "What's he on about? And why's he dressed funny? Update, please."

"He's a professor, the boss of the brainiacs," Sangfroid told her. "He invented this machine." She pointed at the contraption in the middle of the laboratory. "It lets you travel through time, so they decided to come visit us and screw us over." Next she pointed at Millicent. "She's managed to kill me at least 300 times, and I bet she's done you in, too." She concluded with, "And he dresses like that because he likes brown."

"That's a hell of a list," Gallo said. "What did we ever do to them?"

"Oh, you gave us straight roads," Millicent snapped back, "and space squid from another dimension." She turned to her brother. "They all have to go back where they came from, Hubert. It's as if we've opened a portal, and now anyone or anything can just wander in. It has to stop."

Hubert looked bewildered. "I've no idea how to stop it. As far as I'm aware, Gallo was running down a corridor with you, and when I brought you back, she must have been caught up in the time flux. Much like Sangfroid was when you were in the escape pod together. But I have no idea why Sophia, or a likeness of her, should be a deity in another timeline."

"Then she must have travelled into the past, though why she hasn't mentioned it is beyond me. Usually I hear the inane minutiae of her every living minute," Millicent said. "I'll send an invitation for dinner this evening, and we'll see if she can enlighten us under direct, yet discreet, questioning."

Chapter 15

"The Misses Partridge were very resistant to Latinization," Sophia said and watched warily, napkin at the ready, as Edna poured wine into her glass with a tremulous hand. "But we did settle on "All Things Bright and Beautiful" and "Ride on, Ride on in Majesty" for the flower service. We use the *High Anglican Hymnal*, you know," she informed Gallo with a dewy-eyed look.

Across the table, Gallo smiled in approval. This seemed to be Gallo's entire repertoire for the evening since she'd discovered the wine. Millicent was not amused.

Hubert paid no attention to anything, content to furtively scribble in a small notebook by his elbow. Millicent recognized this behaviour as a sign he was on the verge of some breakthrough or other, and this meant he was beyond any conversational capability save the odd grunt. Therefore the brunt of the evening's entertainment fell squarely on her unhappy shoulders. She glanced around the table. Gallo and Sangfroid were rapidly becoming red-nosed. After deliberating on the quality of the wine for several moments, they proceeded to drink a bottle each in no time at all and were well into the third. It seemed all beverages were substandard in their world, except for tea, which was highly lauded and apparently more expensive than gold, crassium-magnate, or the Tyrian dyes the

Emperors used. Millicent kept only the best Ceylon tea in her house and was amazed that they were unimpressed with it. Timeline tea was obviously something to behold.

"Sophia, dear. It was most fortunate that you retrieved, Gallo, our houseguest, from the coal cellar. She was really quite lost," Millicent said. "It is a rather roomy house after all." She had to start her inquiry somewhere, and it was best to explain Gallo's presence at the table before pressing Sophia on possible forays to Mount Olympus and inadvertent deification.

"Mr. Gallo is more than welcome." Sophia simpered. Millicent frowned. Along with all the other women in the house, Sophia seemed to blank out Gallo's gender. She had seen a similar response towards Sangfroid. Gallo was nearly as tall as Sangfroid, though leaner and just as well muscled. She wore her dark hair mannishly and was certainly very handsome, but there was no doubt in Millicent's mind that she was a woman. So why were Sophia, Edna, and Cook so blind to it? Was it a sort of social conditioning? Perhaps social conventions eroded common sense, ergo if it didn't wear a bustle, it must be male? What a delicious experiment. If only she had the time to explore it farther. This put her into a deeper grump. There had been no time to pursue any of her own interests since becoming a full-time assistant to Hubert's time travel debacle.

She kicked his shin under the table, and he lurched into some semblance of awareness. He looked up, blinking like a night owl, noting with confusion he was sitting at his own dining table and hosting a dinner party. She glared at him.

"Ah, Gallo. Yes. Gallo..." Hubert spluttered into action and then ran out of ideas. Millicent delivered a second, more brutal kick. He yelped and finally focused.

"So, Gallo. You served with Sangfroid in the Prussian Dragoons, 'eh?" he said, sticking to the tall story they had agreed upon.

Gallo sat up straighter and cleared her throat. She was a terrible actor. "I certainly do, Professor Aberly," she said. "And

I am enjoying my visit to Londiniu—I mean, London, very much," she said. Sangfroid grinned in red-nosed approval.

"Call me Hubert, please. We're all friends here."

"Thank you, Hubert. My name is Captain Gallo of the First Prussian Dragoons, and I was born in the U...Urals?" She checked this detail with a furtive look at Sangfroid.

"I thought we'd agreed you were a 2nd Lieutenant?" Sangfroid murmured, though not quietly enough.

"If a nob like you can be a major, then I can damn well be a captain," she hissed back, also not quietly enough.

Millicent narrowed her eyes at this new N word. She was uncertain of its provenance, but suspected it was one for her list. She glanced across at Sophia to see how she had received this version of Gallo's appearance. The way their house was filling up with Prussian Dragoons, they'd soon be a military outpost.

She need not have worried. Sophia was looking considerably flushed. Millicent realized Gallo had been refilling her glass with alarming frequency, and they had only just started on the soup course.

"Captain Gallo. How thrilling." Sophia sipped her wine. This worried Millicent as Sophia rarely drank. It would not do for her to return to the Trenchant-Myre household merrier than she had left it. One did not reside at the Trenchant-Myre household in a state of merriment. It was forbidden. All merriment, along with tradesmen and wet umbrellas, had to be left at the door.

"I suspected you of great things the moment I set eyes on you." Sophia stared at Gallo over the rim of her glass.

Like being the new footman? Millicent suspected her pet budgerigar had more wit than her future sister-in-law.

Edna arrived with a fish course of brown trout in a caper and chervil sauce. Millicent had been pleased when the fishmonger filled her last minute order, though now the pleasure was beyond her. The dinner party was doomed. Hubert was again lost in his notes, and his food sat untouched. Sangfroid scraped the sauce off her fillet and poked at the fish underneath suspiciously. Millicent glared at her and got a cheerful grin in reply.

"Are you a religious man, Captain Gallo?" Sophia asked. It seemed her party prattle was going to be the only conversation this evening. So much for finding out why Gallo had mistaken Sophia for a goddess, Millicent thought mournfully. No one seemed to care a fig about that once the wine was decanted.

"Yes. Mars, Bacchus, and, of course, the divine Looselea are my private pantheon." Gallo answered with a dazzler of a smile, the full force of which obviously caused Sophia's ears to seize as she seemed not to hear not a word of the bizarre answer.

"You must join us for the flower service this Sunday." Sophia cooed like the dove she would be consuming in the next course. "I think I may even have some spare hymnals in the hallstand. I keep several there for Hubert as he is always losing his."

Millicent was fuming. Everyone was inebriated, bar herself and Hubert, who might as well be, as he was lost to reality anyway. And he did *not* lose his hymnbooks. Rather he scribbled formulas in them all through the church service, and they inevitably ended up in his lab desk doing anything but uplifting the soul with song.

A thump from upstairs caused the chandelier to rattle. The crystal on the table vibrated into a pleasing tinkle. Millicent blinked in surprise. Then another more ominous thump followed the first. Fine particles of plaster floated from the ceiling and dusted the table like an April snowfall. There came a distant rumbling, and then silence. Gallo blew plaster off the fish on her fork and took a healthy bite. "What was that?" she asked with a full mouth.

"Dunno." Sangfroid looked uncomfortable. She glanced across at Hubert who had barely registered the disturbance. "Should I go check?"

"Hubert, your rooms are directly above the dining room," Millicent said, nudging his elbow. "Perhaps you should ensure that everything is as it should be?" Her gaze caught Sangfroid's in shared concern.

"Yes. Of course." Hubert got to his feet and hurried away, a look of distraction etched on his face. He was clearly on to something, and Millicent ached for the times when their evenings consisted of a simple meal and a discussion of their latest hypothesis. She turned her attention to the reason for this miserable social occasion.

"Sophia," she said. "As you know, we have been talking recently about travel. I find the whole idea captivating. Captain Gallo has come a long way to join us in Londini—London, and so has Major Sangfroid, who kindly shared stories of the Urals with the ladies of the paleobotany society." She gave Sangfroid a smile of sugared cyanide.

"I am considering a new society, Millicent." Sophia tore her gaze away from Gallo for a second. "A Latin society," she announced proudly, "for ladies who wish to learn this wonderful tongue."

Millicent coughed into her napkin and tried to gather her rapidly fraying thoughts. She decided she could only deal with one crisis at a time. "What an engaging idea, and I'm sure we will discuss it later. In greatest detail," she said. "To refer to my earlier question, have you re-considered travel now that we have such good friends in the Urals? Perhaps we should consider a journey to Italy? It is, after all, the home of the Latin language."

"I do not like travel. I do not like Italy," Sophia said firmly. "Although I am warming to the Urals."

Millicent sighed. The Looselea conundrum would never be solved in this way. Sophia was most probably not the timeline deity. She bore a slight resemblance to a crude rendering of some slattern dressed goddess, and that was all. This evening was a waste of time.

"I want to get a hymnbook from the hallstand for Captain Gallo. So he can accompany me to church on the morrow," Sophia said.

Millicent held back a snort of derision. She looked at Gallo's drunken, happy-go-lucky face. "What a wonderful idea. I'm sure the captain will adore the flower festival."

Sophia rose to her feet slowly and took small but deliberate steps out of the room. Millicent noted how she trailed her fingertips along the dining room dado rail to help her negotiate her way to the door. Sophia couldn't have taken more than two steps into the hall when her scream brought them all to their feet.

Sangfroid and Gallo made it into the hall in seconds, with Millicent hard on their heels. They were brought up short by the spectacle before them. A large tentacle was draped over the stairwell. It stretched down to the last stair and spilled out onto the tiled hall floor. If its source was Hubert's dressing room—and Millicent suspected it was—it had to be at least thirty feet long. It was heavy and well-muscled, a pearly grey with pink undertones and thankfully without barbs.

"Jupiter's dick! Squid!" Gallo yelled.

"I told you." Sangfroid turned to Millicent raising her arms into the bragging fisherman pose. "Big as a house, I said, and did you listen? Centaur balls, you listened."

"What is it?" Sophia backed up to the hallstand in terror.

"Um. Hubert has been experimenting with molluscs," Millicent said, though knew she could never explain this away. She was in shock herself. Could this really be Weena? How much did a Colossal squid grow in a day? As she spoke, a second smaller tentacle looped over the upstairs gallery. The last several feet of the tip coiled into a perfect spiral on the floor just outside the breakfast room.

"It's a monster, not a mollusc." Sophia wailed. "Where is Hubert?"

Where was Hubert? Sangfroid and Gallo whipped long daggers from their boot tops and ran at the stairs, pushing past the pearly flesh and its clammy suckers. The tentacle lay inert; unconcerned with the commotion it had caused, though the suckers flexed open and closed as if examining the environment. Millicent could only wonder at what Weena had become. This humongous squid limb seemed so removed from the tiny pink shrimp-like creature she had first encountered. And Hubert was in the lair of this gigantic beast! She grabbed the nearest weapon to hand—a parasol of the finest Battenberg lace—and followed Sangfroid and Gallo into the fray.

"I'm going with you," she called.

"Stay there. That's an order." Sangfroid pointed her back down the stairs.

"Now you're being silly." She elbowed past her and proceeded after Gallo. "Hubert's up there; I must go."

With a hiss of frustration, Sangfroid grabbed her by the waist and bodily deposited her firmly on the stair tread beneath her.

"I said stay there." She shook her gently. "If you were serving under me, I'd have you flogged and flung into the nearest lake to cool down," she said, her voice thick.

"You must be lovely to work for," Millicent muttered. Sangfroid's gaze was fierce, and Millicent tried to hold it, only to feel her face flood with colour. She was too aware of the smell of soap and wine mixing with Sangfroid's natural smell. Of the smoky heat in her eyes. The span of her hands around Millicent's waist was steely. There was no doubt she had the strength to toss Millicent out in the street if she wished. Millicent desperately wanted to find Hubert, so she held her tongue and slipped from Sangfroid's grasp to take up her place a pace behind.

"Don't leave me," Sophia cried from the hallway.

Millicent was unable to comfort Sophia, distracted as she was by the enormous tentacle crushing her staircase. She and Sophia would have to address some serious issues later. It was time Sophia was told the truth about their recent travels, and that Quantumphysex was not an African destination, but a complex, and ultimately dangerous, scientific principle. Resolute, Millicent pressed forward and ignored Sophia's cries, content that at least she was out of harm's way in the vestibule.

"You can't leave me." Sophia wailed again, and then her lamentation was interrupted by the arrival of Edna with the bird course. The maid concentrated fully on her salver of dove and quail. She walked the entire length of the hall, swerving around a quivering tentacle tip and sailing unperturbed under the arm draping from the gallery railings. She observed nothing, wholly intent on her tray. Triumphantly, she entered the empty dining room un-phased by the calamity in the hallway behind her.

Millicent regarded Edna's stoic rejection of reality with jealousy, while Sophia took advantage of her distraction to slip gingerly around a flaccid tentacle and attach herself to Millicent's back. Her hymnal readied to slap the word of the Lord onto anything that so much as twitched in her direction.

"I do not like it, Millicent, but neither will I be abandoned," she said, her voice full of quivering resolve. "If you are determined to press forward, then I shall go with you."

"I don't like it either, Sophia. I am worried for Hubert."

"And the Axminster is ruined." Sophia eyed the stair carpet with a malevolent eye.

All four moved slowly past the languid, serpentine limbs to find they did indeed originate from Hubert's bedroom door. Or rather, where the door had once been before monstrous tentacles had burst through the wall sheering the door and its framework away. Outside the gaping hole, Hubert's shoes sat neatly side by side, as if awaiting a boot boy to remove them for cleaning.

"What does that mean?" asked Gallo, her suspicious pagan mind making her spook at anything odd or new. "Dead man's shoes?" she suggested.

"It doesn't mean any such thing." Millicent objected to any reference of her brother's demise. "He's just tidy."

They clambered over splintered wood and plaster into Hubert's bedchamber. Here the writhing limbs were much more animated. They bunched and seethed across the floor. The solid bedroom furniture was smashed to pieces under the heaving weight. The source of the outlaying appendages was the dressing room. There, the entire wall had disintegrated against the sheer size of Weena. The knotted contortion of her limbs was even greater near her bulbous, frantically pulsating mantle. Occasionally, her eye, now dimmed from its baby blue to a dull slate colour, appeared through the gyrations to blink at them. Her rippling convulsions shook the remaining walls and under their feet the floorboards thrummed with her agitation.

"It's a big bugger." Gallo crouched, knife at the ready. The weapon seemed too puny to be in any way effective.

"What are you going to do when her tentacles hit the street, huh?" Sangfroid asked Millicent. "Tell the neighbours it's a mollusc experiment?"

"Don't hurt her," Millicent said to them. "We need to find Hubert. Until then we have no idea if Weena is friend or foe."

"I thought you could talk to her," Sangfroid said.

"At the moment my brain is all confusion. I'm seeing flashes of places I know I have never been. I'm not sure if she's conversing with me or if I am eavesdropping on her and Hubert. Oh, where is he. He'll get hurt in all this crush." She scanned the coiled mass for any sign Hubert might be among the melee.

"Hubert!" Sophia screeched, and for a moment, he crested from the seething swell as if thrown up by sea surf. He raised his arm and waved, rising and falling on the curl of a grey tentacle. Once, twice, three times he waved. Until finally, with a quick smile, he disappeared under as if pulled down by an unseen current. He arose again, in one final majestic surge, and was rolled slowly, gently, but determinedly towards the moist, black maw of Weena's beak and was swallowed whole.

There was a stunned silence until Sophia's scream started them from their horrified immobility. Gallo leaped on the nearest tentacle, while Sophia swatted the grey limb with her hymnal. Sangfroid barked out an order to retreat. Gallo followed his command immediately, grabbing Sophia as they backed off. With swift, compact movements Sangfroid removed them from the room and redeployed them to the top of the stairs.

"Get her out of here," she ordered Gallo, pointing at Sophia who was already sinking to her knees in a faint. Gallo lifted Sophia in her arms as if she weighed nothing at all and carried her down to the drawing room. Millicent followed, her hands numb, her mind stalled with shock. She trailed behind Gallo to the drawing room. Sangfroid came after her and slammed the doors shut.

"Hubert's gone." She could barely utter the words. They came out in a hoarse, breathless whisper. Then Sangfroid's arms were around her, and she leaned into her and wept.

"Millicent," she whispered into her hair. "My Millicent. I am so, so sorry." Sangfroid's cool fingers found the nape of Millicent's neck and caressed her gently.

Gallo laid the unconscious Sophia on the couch and then knelt beside her. She looked over to Millicent with battle-hardened eyes that had seen many cruel things. "I hardly knew him," she said, "but I could see the prof was a good man. I'm sorry, Millicent."

Millicent pulled away from the comfort of Sangfroid's arms. She took out her handkerchief and wiped at her tears, trying to recover her composure. Holding onto Sangfroid was not helping her think. And she had to think.

"Thank you." She acknowledged Gallo's kindness. "He was a great man, so gifted and clever. He was taken from us too soon. He had so many wonderful ideas and theories. So much to give to the world. It's so unfair he's not here anymore to… to…" Her tears flowed freely. "And he was always so happy."

She sniffed into her lace handkerchief. "Up until the last he was waving and smiling." A vague hope glimmered in the back of her mind. *He was smiling?* And hard on hope's glimmering heels, came understanding.

"He was smiling," she said, brightening.

"I thought it was more of a grimace," Sangfroid said.

"No, it was most definitely a smile." Millicent moved towards the door. "And he carefully placed his shoes on the landing by his bedroom. It was as if he knew what was about to happen. As if it was part of a plan, and he'd no time to warn us. But he knew what was about to occur, and he was waving and smiling so as not to alarm us."

"Well, it didn't work," Gallo said. "I was very alarmed."

"Where are you going?" Sangfroid followed Millicent to the door.

"I'm going to the dining room," she said. "Hubert was preoccupied all evening with his notes. I have to see what he has written down. Hubert would never allow himself to be ingested by a space squid without a good reason. And especially not without his shoes."

"Whereas countless others were rude and kept theirs on." Sangfroid snorted. "Hey," she said when Millicent opened the door a crack to peep out. "Wait up. What do you think you're doing? We're in lockdown."

"I told you. I'm going to the dining room."

"Oh no, you don't. That's clear across the hall, and the hall is enemy territory. You're staying here. Understood."

Millicent peeped out. "The coast is clear," she said, gathering up her taffeta evening dress. "Run!" And with a swirl of petticoats, she left Sangfroid standing.

Chapter 16

THERE WAS NO REAL NEED to run. Weena had gone. The stairway was clear of alien tentacles, though the path of destruction was clear to see. Sagging stair treads, snapped banisters, and the newel posts pushed outward at awkward angles. Nevertheless, Millicent lifted her skirts and sprinted for the dining room as fast as she could. Sangfroid easily kept pace beside her.

The dining table heaved under the weight of the food piled upon it. Edna had duly delivered each and every course at the required time and, finding no guests present and the previous course uneaten, had simply deposited her new platter on the table top. Neither had she cleared away the previous untouched courses. The resulting food mountain was an insult to both eye and stomach. *What on earth was the girl thinking?* Millicent had no time to ponder the befuddled workings of Edna's mind. She snatched up Hubert's notebook and began to pour over its contents.

"How can you read that? It's nothing but hen scratches." Sangfroid loomed over her shoulder. "Hey, look, is that two monkeys fighting over a pineapple?"

"When we were children, Hubert and I developed a hieroglyphic shorthand based on pictorial representations of mathematical values. It comes in very handy," she answered curtly and moved the book away from Sangfroid's ignorant gaze.

"I just bet it does." Sangfroid absentmindedly grabbed a breaded quail breast and began munching on it. "So, what does he say?" she asked with her mouth full.

Millicent squeezed her *vert de terre* taffeta into Hubert's carver seat and began to pour over his notes. Sangfroid chewed noisily and poured herself another glass of wine.

"It will take time to decipher this," she said. Sangfroid's presence annoyed her. She always seemed to be hovering around her, taking up too much space.

"It'll take centuries. You could read cave daubs easier."

"I understand most of what it says, but I'll have to look up some of the more obtuse scientific references," she said, defensively. "Now either eat quietly or go away. You're distracting me."

"I'm going back upstairs to see what Weena's up to," Sangfroid said and dumped the half-eaten bird on the table. A certain stubbornness had entered her voice that Millicent knew best to ignore. In this type of mood, Sangfroid was resolved to get her own way, so she let her have it. Millicent did, however, give a disapproving sniff and kept her nose buried in her book.

"Her tentacles are still retracted." Sangfroid checked the hallway before going out. "It makes me wonder if this whole visit was all about her becoming big enough to eat Hubert."

"Why on earth would she do that?" Millicent stared at her. "Why wait at all? Why not arrive when she was big enough to eat the lot of us? Eat all of London, for that matter?"

"Maybe she will. I've a feeling we've not seen the half of it," Sangfroid said. "I mean, no offence, but it's hard to believe this pokey little era is where time travel technology popped up. I think you and Hubert are being manipulated from afar."

"Pokey little era." Millicent bristled. "I'll have you know that you are at the very heart of the British Empire. We are the world leader in science, engineering, and industry, with my brother being at the foremost in *all* those disciplines. It is totally conceivable for time travel to be his invention. He's a genius. And what do you mean, *manipulated from afar*. Whom do you suspect? The space squid? Your war mongering senate? Or perhaps another of your ludicrous gods?" She returned to her notebook, dismissing Sangfroid entirely. "Please inform Cook should we need a sacrificial lamb."

"Virgins work better," she said. "More meat on them."

Millicent blushed violently at the impertinence and concentrated harder on the pages before her, not letting Sangfroid see how unsettled the remark made her.

"There's something going on here," Sangfroid said. "Something spooky. And I think Hubert knew about it. Try and make some sense of those scribbles. I'll be back in a moment." And she turned heel and left.

Across the hallway, Sophia was beginning to come around.

"Drink this." Gallo eased her upright and lifted a glass to her lips.

"I had the most ghastly dream that I lost my betrothed to a huge squid." Sophia moaned and held a hand to her temple. She became aware of their proximity and tried to move away. The pain in her head was too much, and she felt incredibly nauseous. She sagged back against Gallo's shoulder and sipped from the offered glass.

"Yeah. It ate him, all right," Gallo said, easily managing the extra weight. "The buggers do that."

"Good Lord. Is it true?" She coughed into the glass. "And is this hard liquor?" She was horrified on both counts.

"It's Scotch. I reckoned you'd need it for the shock, cos it's true enough, the prof was eaten by a Colossal squid. Sucked him straight down like spaghetti."

"The house is infested with giant squid, and my fiancé has been consumed. Of course I'm in shock." Sophia struggled on to her feet. Her face was hot, and her legs felt woozy and weak. "I'm shocked that number five Christie Mews has gone to such wrack and ruin and taken my Hubert along with it. And I know exactly who to blame! Where is Millicent?" she demanded. "And Mr. Sangfroid? He's responsible for this. There were never any squid in this house before he arrived. I'm certain he brought them with him from the Urals." She was close to tears and fought to hold them back. Hubert would have liked those grieving for him to keep a stiff upper lip.

"They went that way." Gallo pointed to the hall.

"I am going to tell him I am very unhappy and hold him entirely responsible for this mollusc infestation. He has to remove them at once." Sophia tried to sound resolute, though her stiff lip kept trembling. "I do not like it at all."

Without further ado, she strode into the hall and made her way to Hubert's laboratory. It was high time she spoke up. She had been the quiet, timorous one for far too long, while Millicent and her beau, Major Sangfroid, ran riot. Christie Mews, Westminster was not the place for giant molluscs.

"I do not like it." She cried bursting into the laboratory, only to find she was alone. Millicent and Sangfroid weren't there, and it was boring to make a scene with no one to witness it. Sophia contented herself with a quick inspection. She'd never been in Hubert's laboratory, despite her greatest insistence. It had always irked her that Millicent could so casually access this room while she, Hubert's betrothed and now as good as his widow, had to remain outside.

Immediately her senses flooded with the vacuum left by his sudden demise. The laboratory carried the queer scent of chemicals and compounds, and the sandalwood soap that impregnated his tweeds. His pocket watch lay on his desk bedside the onyx inkwell she had given him for Christmas. She remembered his ink-stained fingers as he scribbled his lecture notes. Oh, how Her Majesty's London College of Engineering and Physics would miss him. Oh, how *she* would miss him. He had not been a very passionate man, but he was clever and kind, and he would have made her a good husband. Her tears flowed freely.

"I do not like it." She sniffled into her lace handkerchief. It was unbearable to lose a fiancé in such a cruel and unusual way. Lord only knew how it would be reported in the obituaries.

In the middle of the floor sat an ugly contraption. His newest experiment, no doubt. A sleigh made from a muddle of copper and bronze. It was coated in sinuous tubing and shone in the lamplight like the sousaphone of Beelzebub himself. It was an unholy, accursed thing, and she was sure all the talk of travel had to do with this and not Italy at all. Everyone had been deceitful towards her, and now Hubert was devoured. That's what happened when people told fibs.

Sophia lifted the fire poker from the hearth and ran to the machine, walloping it several times across the plump, velvet seat.

"I-do-not-like-it!" she cried, her face awash with tears. The machine responded with an errant puff of steam from the water cylinder at the rear. Sophia took this for mechanical back-chat and walloped the contraption further.

"Hey. Careful." Gallo prised the poker from her fingers. "I'm not exactly sure how it works, but I'm sure you're not supposed to hit it like that," she said gently and lowered Sophia onto the red velvet seat. "Rest here, and I'll call for tea, okay? Do I tug on this thingy here?" She moved to the bell cord by the mantelpiece.

Sophia slumped in the machine's driving seat, totally defeated. Her life had turned a corner, and the corner led back to the Trenchant-Myre front door. Behind that door lay everlasting spinsterhood. She had been inordinately fortunate that Hubert had proposed. Sophia was under no illusions as to the quality of her face and figure. Millicent was by far the better beauty, and yet, up until Major Sangfroid appeared, she'd had the audacity to display no interest in marriage whatsoever. Meanwhile Sophia, like any younger daughter of a large, well-to-do family, hung on grimly in hope of a marriage proposal and a home of her own. It was the only escape. Plain, unwed daughters had no other purpose than to look after their aging parents and the reams of nephews and nieces their more successful siblings dumped on them. She could see her future stretching ahead of her. She'd be the frumpy spinster sister who became the unpaid nurse and governess to the whole family, until she grew so old and worn, she'd finally be useless and left to crumble away in an attic all alone. *Like a dried up old fruitcake.*

Even without a husband, Millicent still had it all—independent wealth, fine looks, a home at a genteel address. She had dresses and jewellery galore, even if her taste was too conservative to be fashionable.

As she wallowed in self-pity, Sophia's attention was caught by a sparkle in the centre of the machine control panel. A kaleidoscope of light blurred before her teary eyes. She recognized the hilt of Millicent's good Sunday parasol with its wonderful inlay of gemstones and mother of pearl. *Even her parasol is beautiful, and yet she allows it to be debased by this crude, steam-puffing machine.*

It was unbearable. Millicent with her intelligence, her wealth, her handsome beau from the Urals, and no one to look after, save her pretty self. Especially now that poor Hubert had…had…gone. With a sob of despair, Sophia threw herself forward. The parasol handle dislodged with a clunk, and the huge disc whooshed into a slow rotation. The water cylinders bubbled, then boiled. Steam began to belch at the ceiling, gathering in volume and vigour until a huge, wet cloud hung around the chandelier. Gallo edged to the door, not taking her attention off the spectacle.

"Hey?" she called into the hallway. "Sangfroid? I think you should come see this."

Footsteps thundered down the stairs. "Weena's gone. Not a sign of her," Sangfroid shouted back. "It's as if she just went poof."

"I think Sophia is about to go poof if you don't get in here and do something," Gallo yelled back. "The furniture's gone weird. Does it do that here?"

Alarmed by the strangeness going on around her, Sophia twisted around to stare in disbelief at the spinning disc. What on earth was happening? Her fearful gaze locked with Gallo's.

"Make it stop," she called. Even as she spoke, the room faded in and out of focus, and she feared another swoon was upon her. Darkness framed the edge of her vision, and she saw Gallo dive towards her, but slowly as though in a dream. At the same time, Millicent and Sangfroid burst through the doorway, their faces masked in horror. They too flew towards her. She felt Gallo's hands on her shoulders trying to lift her up, though she couldn't actually see Gallo anymore. Then Millicent's cool touch was on her wrist, dragging at her, trying to move her out of the seat. Millicent also faded from view, though Sophia could hear her calling, her words disparate and shrill. She could also hear the sea, birdsong, and the drone of old men's voices. Heat and dust assaulted her senses. Her sinuses flooded with the itchy scent of cedar and wood smoke. Her skin prickled, and her heart jumped with fear.

She did not like this.

She did not like this at all.

Chapter 17

THE SMELL ASSAULTED HER FIRST, followed closely by noise and heat. Millicent was in a market place, and it was chaos. Donkeys brayed. Dogs barked. Children cried, and men and women roared out their wares. Which was fish, of every size and variety.

Fish stalls surrounded her on all sides. And flies of every size and variety filled the air. They crawled over everything, living or dead. Opened-mouthed tuna and limp-limbed calamari lay atop avalanches of whitebait and mackerel. Huge barrels of salted sardines sat row upon row. Hundreds of milky eyed fish stared blankly up at her, while behind them the stallholders glared at her with slit-eyed suspicion. Their stares were surly rather than questioning, so she assumed her impromptu arrival had gone unnoticed in the bustle of the busy market. She noted the simple clothing and blunt, guarded faces of the people surrounding her. Where on earth was she? And why was there a tangible feeling of ill will pulsing towards her? A quick look told her she was alone. Neither Sangfroid, Sophia, nor Gallo were in sight, which was very worrying. Was this the sort of place a lady should be unchaperoned? Sangfroid should be here. For all her annoying habits, she would never leave Millicent alone in an untested environment.

Unsure where to go or what to do, but inclined to move away from the hard looks, Millicent took a step forward. Her heel skidded on the glutinous miasma coating the cobblestones. A filth of fish guts, swill water, and Lord only knew what oozed around her feet, and her heart went out for her kidskin slippers, now ruined beyond redemption.

"Careful, my little urn." A hand caught her elbow and steadied her. He spoke in Latin, and she was momentarily amazed that she understood him as easily as she could Sangfroid or Gallo. Was she in Rome? It was not that hard to imagine. This was the civilization where their two timelines seemed to separate. Her startled gaze met with the curious but kindly one of her benefactor, and she was grateful for it after the hard-eyed looks surrounding her. *A little urn?* Had she heard him right? She detached from his grip and steadied herself.

"Thank you," she said politely with what she hoped was the right amount of respectability.

"Please, let me escort you to the temple," he said. "Perhaps it is best to move away from the populous. They are not in a very forgiving mood towards the tea. After all, it is taxes time." He was perhaps in his late fifties, bedecked in a crisp white tunic that shone like a beacon amid the filthiness of the marketplace. The sun glinted off his carefully coiffed, silver hair, or rather the resinous substance that held it in place. He was scented with cypress oil, which, though sharp on her nostrils, was a balm against the smell of fish. She almost moved closer for that reason alone. He exuded a mannerly and courteous concern, which was reassuring.

Millicent dithered. Tea and temples? She was certain the Romans did not drink tea. It grew far to the east, well beyond the borders of their Empire. Did they trade for it? Maybe this wasn't Rome after all but some other ancient city? How intriguing. More to the point, should she trust this strange man? What were her options? She was not in the most salubrious of places and not very welcome at that.

"Please oblige me." The man held out his arm to lead her away, and Millicent felt compelled to oblige. She draped her hand through the crook of his elbow, and he led her towards the edge of the square where gullies washed away the worst of the muck around their feet.

"Thank you for your help. I am Miss Millicent Aberly." She may as well begin her investigations while she had his attention. "And you are?"

"Cassian Titus Atticus, at your service." He grabbed at her fingers, trapping them under his arm.

She tried not to pull her hand away and look rude. Instead she continued with her questioning. "You mentioned a temple?"

He laughed. "The High Tea Temple of Rome is just around the corner. I assume you are lost? You have that lost look about you."

"I am a little disorientated." So she was in Rome after all. A Rome with a high tea temple? That sounded as promising a place to start as any, especially if it removed her from this smelly marketplace with its disagreeable vendors.

They walked along the edge of the square, tiptoeing around the messier gullies and several glutinous puddles. The din from the fish market was slowly drowned out by a loud clanking noise. Millicent noticed smoke hanging low over this corner of the market. As they approached the source, the clanking became more mechanical to her ear, and when Cassian delicately led her around a large stack of unused barrels, she found a noisy but glorious steam powered machine. It was made of bronze; a squat box-like structure resting on four large cartwheels. The fluted funnel chugged out plumes of steam, not smoke as she'd at first supposed. Steam clouds hung hot and greasy above them until the breeze shredded them to pieces.

"What on earth?" Millicent breathed. This was not what she had expected to see in ancient Rome. Her companion seemed very at ease with the machinery. Her question was answered.

She had materialized in the version of ancient Rome that was at the root of Sangfroid's civilization. She was torn between delight at the discovery and trepidation at her vulnerability.

This was time travel in its truest form. She had no knowledge of this place or what would be expected of her. It was totally different from projecting into the future to arrive by Sangfroid's side where she felt safe and protected despite the dangers of that age. Sangfroid always made her feel secure. Here she was alone, adrift on dangerous waters. Wouldn't it be wonderful if Sangfroid were to appear now? Simply walk around a corner and find her and make everything immediately better. And Hubert walking along with her! How wonderful if he were to come back. Her brother would explain everything to her. He would have loved this machine, and it would be Sangfroid who escorted her to safety instead of this clammy-handed stranger.

She imagined the elation of the moment, but it didn't last, and desperation draped over her like a sodden blanket. Hubert was dead. She was lost in an alien world, and Sangfroid and the others were probably as lost as she was.

A naked urchin ran past her to the machine and opened a heavy, ornate door. Clouds billowed out, only these were frigid with cold, not hot and steamy. The child's flesh mottled under its bite. To her astonishment, he began to dig out ice with his bare hands and throw it into a huge pail almost as tall as he was.

"An ice maker?" she said in awe. "It actually makes ice." Her awe soon changed to agitation when she noticed the child's fingers were black and disfigured with frostbite, and still he clawed at the impacted ice until the pail was full.

"Of course it's an ice maker." Cassian laughed. "You can't have a fish market without ice. Well, maybe in the provinces, but not in Rome." They watched as the child staggered off under his load.

"That poor boy," Millicent said. "Did you see his hands? Why not give him a small shovel, or at least some sacking to protect his skin?" Her voice was tight with her upset.

"I see you are new to Rome," Cassian said. "The child is a slave. He costs less than a shovel. In Rome there is an abundance of labourers. There are more people than actual work. It's not like the provinces. Where are you from, by the way?"

Millicent's skin prickled. There was something about her companion that set her on edge. He was canny enough to sense her discomfort and glide her away from the ice machine. She disengaged her hand from the crook of his arm, sliding her fingers out from his acquisitive grasp.

"It's just that your dress is so…unusual, even for a tea maid. Is it ceremonial?" Cassian chatted lightly, as if nothing unpleasant had occurred. "Perhaps there's a festivity at the temple that I am unaware of?"

Tea maids and temples again. Ought she inquire further, or was this something she was expected to know?

"I am rather new to the city," she explained cautiously. "In that I cannot seem to locate the temple. Perhaps…" As she had hoped, he jumped at the chance to escort her, and she found her arm once again seized in a most inappropriate way.

He led her away from the market through a side portico and out into a broad and sunny colonnade lined with spice stalls. The odour of fish was immediately masked with huge swathes of competing incense.

"It's best to exit from the east side of the market square. The scents are enchanting, and they clear the sinuses." Cassian smiled at her, wafting the fug towards his nose with flapping hands. Millicent relaxed enough to take interest in these new surroundings.

"This colonnade leads to the Trajan baths, and as the spice masks the smell of the fish market so well, the spice merchants are allowed to trade along the entire walkway," Cassian told her.

Millicent was fascinated. The stalls were adorned with colourful flags. Bright red, orange, and vivid green silk banners snapped and danced, advertising their seller's wares on the wind. Spices spilled from out of copper bowls onto worn tabletops. The vibrant colours competed with the swirls of silk above. Platters were piled high with the yellow hues of ochre, umber, and cadmium as pure as the sun's rays. They bloomed next to other platters of earthy reds that held the blunt heat of their homelands. Nutmeg, pepper, turmeric, ginger, clove, and cardamom, exploded upon her sense of smell like fireworks. Colour splattered the stone cobbles where passing feet trod the spices into the dirt and threw up a whirl of fragrance.

A multitude of exotic languages assaulted her ears. The deep-set smiles of the Indian and Asian spice vendors were wonderfully cheering after the glowering locals in the fish market. The cultural fusion confounded Millicent. This version of Rome had trade routes as far flung as her British Empire. She began to take mental note of the anomalies. Sangfroid's ancient capital was much more advanced than its counterpart from her own timeline. Oh, how she wished she had someone to share it with.

Her thoughts immediately turned to Hubert, and she shut them down sharply. She was too emotionally raw to dwell on his death, especially in such a dangerous place. There was a mystery to Hubert's demise she had as yet to unravel, and until she had, she would be careful with his memory and the disillusion his loss brought to her. She must focus on the task at hand in a progressive and robust research manner that would make her brother proud. Determined of her goals, she focused on the sights before her and collected her evidence.

Contrasting with the happy faces of the spice vendors were those of Rome's citizens. Wealthy women shopped along the colonnade. Their children, all healthy and clean clothed, gathered around a small steam powered theatre shrieking with laughter at the antics of a clockwork monkey as it danced to a reedy tune piped by its master. For a moment, Millicent paused to enjoy the show until the monkey screeched and flung itself up a pole to escape from its audience. It was tugged back by the chain around its neck, and she saw it was not a clockwork toy at all. It was a real animal with mechanical parts interwoven with its physiology. A leg had been removed and replaced with a tiny bronze limb, the little knee pistoned up and down manically in time with the music. She could see the metal ball of a hip joint rotate in the bony cusp of the monkey's pelvic socket. The skin on its belly and chest was pared back to show the biological workings inside the torso. The gullet, stomach, and bowels were all real enough, but its heart organ was no more than a metal and leather box that bellowed in and out belligerently. The owner gave the animal copious cups of hot water that somehow fuelled the beating heart-box.

Millicent was equally repelled and fascinated; she itched to hold the creature and examine it further. And then she looked into the crazed eyes of the little monkey and saw his torture for what it was. He glared back, and she knew he didn't see her or the children or the gay banners blowing in the wind. He was beyond the visions of this world, and his insanity had locked his mind into a safer place. He opened his mouth and screeched and the rows of blunt copper pegs that replaced his teeth gleamed in the sun. It was a terrible, agonized leer. The children yelled with laughter. Millicent recoiled, bumping into Cassian who giggled along with the children.

"I love the dancing monkeys," he said and kept on watching the show while Millicent stepped away to compose herself.

The children's mothers stood nearby, gossiping with each other or haggling with the spice sellers. Millicent could feel their sharp, disapproving looks that always slid away as soon as she turned to face them. Whatever she represented in this city, she was as welcome on the streets as she had been in the fish market. She refused to be flustered and concentrated hard on the magnificence of her surroundings. She raised her eyes to the soaring architecture and let it momentarily lift her spirits up from the cold, hard people of Rome and yowling children with their deformed monkey. From under the covered walkway, the towering arches of a vast aqueduct cut across the blue skyline. Elegant with its sheer stone-clad lines, it cradled the cityscape, dominating the buildings and streets and trailing through the city like a bold, white ribbon.

Millicent wished with all her heart that Hubert were here to accompany her exploration. He would have been fascinated and appalled, and he would probably still fall in love with this macabre city. It took the bloom from every new discovery that he was absent from her life. She blinked back sudden tears.

"The Aqua Claudia." Cassian was back at her side, following her upward gaze. "Splendid, isn't it? I envy those new to Rome; the city is a cornucopia of wonders, each waiting to be discovered like the sweetest morsel. It's not called the glory of the civilized world for nothing."

"It's beautiful." Millicent shifted under his gaze, uncomfortable with the way Cassian glanced sideways at her when he said sweetest morsel. He made her skin prickle. She had to concentrate on finding the others and then devise a way to get back home. Her sense of unease was growing.

On the horizon, she made out the curved white dome of another majestic building. It reared over the terracotta roofs, dwarfing even the highest tenement buildings. The sun gleamed off its gilded crests, making it beautiful against the cerulean sky. She was in Rome. And Rome, in any era, was magnificent.

"That's the Basilica Valeria." Cassian pointed to the dome. "Come, you can see it better from the south side," he said, and together they wove through the spice stalls and out from under the colonnade and into the full heat of the day.

Millicent regretted they had not come across a parasol stall, she knew they were definitely a Roman commodity. Every lady in any era had fought the same battle with the sun, and she would have loved the relief of shade right now.

"We are now on the via Phocas." Cassian continued his tour. "To the left, a few streets down, flows the Tiber, and beyond that, you can see the Quirinal Hill and the top few tiers of the Belly."

The Belly? What a curious name. She had not heard of that particular piece of ancient architecture, perhaps it belonged to this world only? There must be many such buildings. He led her into a narrow street, hemmed in on all sides by tall tenements so that the strong afternoon sun thankfully became no more than an oblong on the cobblestones. She was fascinated with the architecture and the atmosphere of the city. The street names sounded so exotic, and she was overawed to see famous buildings in all their finery that in her time were nothing but ruins. The Coliseum! The Trajan baths! She was swept along at his side mesmerized.

"If you look to the right, you can just about make out the highest part of the temple Castores," Cassian said. The Temple of Castor and Pollox? Oh, she could barely believe it.

"And if we go down here," he pointed towards a wide street, "we will see the High Tea Temple of Rome across from Fruit Scone Square." He finished his tour with a flourish.

Millicent stumbled.

"Excuse me? Did you say fruit scone?" she asked.

"Yes. I—Careful." He pulled her to the side as a small steam powered engine chugged past them. Its rattling wooden wheels dipped and swayed over the cobbles. It was a squat, square machine in dull bronze with a plank bench seat. Several men in shining breastplates and crested helmets sat perched on top. Behind them, tethered to the rear of the machine, came a string of wretched men and women blinking teary-eyed in the smoke belching directly into their faces. There was no breeze in this narrow street to blow the fug away; it hung directly over them as they wheezed and gagged for fresh air.

"Those are soldiers?" she asked about the men in armour sitting on the machine.

"Arena guards. That's why they're so shiny. It's not as if they fight." There was derision in his voice. "They're talking prisoners to the circus for the games." He brightened up at that.

"Oh." Millicent had a good idea what that meant. These poor people were to be fodder for the bloodthirsty gladiator games. She looked away. She had neither the heart nor stomach to witness the sad and scraggly procession. Rome was rapidly losing its fascination. In this timeline, and with this rate of industrial expansion, it was easy to see how Sangfroid and Gallo came to be in the outreaches of space a few thousand years later. And with the vicious things she'd seen—the slave child's twisted hands, the monster monkey, and now these felons led away to be massacred for sport—she understood how thin the veneer of technical sophistication actually was. The smallest scratch, and the brutality of a callous, ravenous, war machine oozed out. This was what Weena had meant when she warned Hubert about planet Rome's skewed evolution. This Rome carried its immorality and monstrosity before it like an Aquila. It had advanced all right, but out of balance and harmony with true time. The pugnacious, brutal mindset of one nation, combined with unprecedented industrial advancement, had empowered an entire world towards universal dominance. And it had managed it all through timeline chicanery, making huge technological leaps while the morals and social conscience of the Roman race had failed to develop in tandem.

"Come away." Cassian guided her around a corner. "Prisoners are diseased. It's best not to breathe the same air," he said. "Ah. Here we are."

They stood in a small square. Sunlight washed over the warm sandstone brick of a trim and tidy building. It was one storey high but looked taller due to its elevation. Several granite steps lead up to a marble portico, and on each step sat large urns filled with brightly flowering plants. It was a soft, feminine building. Beguiling in its simplicity and artful decoration. The square before it was clean, sun-filled, and airy. Curiously, a few goats with tinkling bells wandered wherever they liked. Millicent wondered if they were destined for some sort of pagan ritual or other, but didn't want to dwell on it. Braziers filled the air with apple-wood smoke. There were a few stalls selling baked goods. Hence the name, Millicent thought, spying scones and breads of all shapes and flavours.

The square was far from crowded. An old woman, bent double with age, idly swept at the cobbles with a large, twig broom. The stall holders here differed from those Millicent had seen previously, in that they were all young, pretty women. They wore long white tunics that flowed down to delicate sandals decorated with seed pearls and brightly coloured gemstones. As she approached, she was astonished to see that, under their outer dress, the young women wore what looked to be an attempt at a bustle and petticoats. Surely that was not correct for the period? This anomaly satisfied her that there was a connection to her timeline and this version of Rome. There was now no doubt. There had been tampering!

"Would you like a fruit scone as an offering?" Cassian, as ever, crowded in at her elbow. "Or maybe a sponge finger?"

"No, thank you." The cakes did not look particularly appealing up close.

"Of course not, silly me." He rushed to apologize. "You are an urn, after all. You should offer up tea leaves, not baked products."

Millicent would have loved to question Cassian on this urn business, but her unease around him caused her to hold her tongue. They were mounting the steps to the temple, and she decided to wait and hope things would become clearer to her once she was actually in the building. Part of her also hoped, on a vague, illogical level, that she would find Sophia safely ensconced within and most probably responsible for all this nonsense. There were too many coincidences with home. The signs were everywhere—tea, baked goods, and petticoats. Three things Sophia adored.

Millicent had reached for Sophia and grabbed her even as her body dematerialized in the time machine and had been pulled into the vortex after her. If they had travelled to the same place, it made sense that Sophia had arrived slightly ahead of her. But surely only by days, or weeks. How had she had the time to set up a lunatic religion? It didn't help that Millicent had no notion of how they were to return to their own time. Hubert had always organized their return trips. If she dwelt on it too long, she became almost incapacitated with worry.

She was relieved to step out of the blazing sun and into the shade of the temple doorway. The atrium was a cool airy room, heavily marbled, and contrasted beautifully with the hot, dusty sandstone of the exterior. A large domed ceiling helped circulate the cooler air. It was so high that doves flew in and around the blue-eyed oculus that opened up to the heavens beyond. The clear blue of the Roman sky contrasted beautifully with the delicate ceilings, painted to resemble the inside of shimmering seashells. It was a gorgeous effect that took her breath away.

"Cassian Atticus." A voice rang out, none too welcoming. He stooped into a low bow before the woman rapidly approaching. She was a wide lady in a long and voluminous toga, complete with a bustle that only exaggerated her size. However, she moved lightly enough on her feet to appear before them almost immediately. "I am surprised to see you here so soon after your last visit." She spoke to reprimand, and Cassian squirmed like a guilty schoolboy.

"Best wishes, my lady. I found this young devotee lost on the streets and thought it best to return her," he said. The matron turned her attention to Millicent. She had a broad, flat face, all dull edges and blunt features. Her hair, dyed a harsh and unnatural red, was piled into ludicrous twists and rolls that did not compliment her in any way. For all the dullness of her features, the lady's eyes were as sharp as knives and just as steely.

"I don't recognize her," she said, looking Millicent up and down. "But we have new girls arriving from the provinces all the time." She seemed unimpressed with the provincial specimen she was looking at.

Millicent did not trust the obsequious change in Cassian's manner. Nor did she like the way she was being discussed, as if she were a bartered object. She levelled her gaze with the matron.

"Excuse me," she said in her most frosty, formal voice, "but I don't believe we have been introduced. I am Miss Millicent Aberly."

The matron gawped at her with an expression of shock that very quickly turned to red faced anger. Without warning she slapped Millicent across the face. The crack of her hand against pliant flesh startled a dozen doves into flight. Cassian twitched involuntarily, and Millicent was vaguely aware of his struggle to keep composed as she collapsed on the beautiful marbled floor.

Chapter 18

"Not another friggin' coal hole." Gallo swore into the gloom. She lay curled in a corner as if tossed there by some great force. Slowly, she unfurled her long limbs and sat up. Nothing was broken, but everything felt bruised and aching, and her head banged like a war drum. She groaned in protest. This was exactly how she'd felt the last time she'd been sucked from reality and dumped in a black pit. She wondered if she really had died this time and made it to Tartarus.

It was so damned hard to tell these days.

Somewhere to her right, she could make out the faint glow of smouldering embers. It was a small, inconsequential light but enough to throw elongated shadows; much to Gallo's dismay, the shadows began to seethe and crawl. They flickered across the walls and ceiling, creeping slowly towards her, stick-like and eerie, hemming her into the corner. She slithered back until the rough stone bit into her shoulders. Her knife was not in her boot, and she vaguely remembered leaving it by the couch when Sophia fainted. Now she cursed her carelessness. *Okay, bare knuckles it is.* She lurched to her feet, hunched in a boxer's stance. It was a crazy way to face demons, but Gallo was out of options. All she knew was she was a legionnaire, and she had promised her dear old mother she would die on her feet.

The glow in the far corner flared, then blazed up into a good sized fire. It threw out heat and enough light to see clearly. Gallo found she was surrounded and, to her consternation, dwarfed by several warriors of the Amazon nation. Her shoulders relaxed. *I must be dead and on the Elysian fields. Score me!* She was on the field of warriors with the Amazons. She had finally arrived at her happy-ever-after, eternal resting place.

Oof! A punch to the stomach doubled her over.

"Spying scum! How long have you been hiding here?" The nearest Amazon kicked at the hamstrings of her left leg. Gallo fell to the ground, and a foot pressed down on her windpipe.

"Speak, or I'll crack your neck like a dung beetle." Extra pressure was applied, and Gallo's eyes bulged. She spluttered weakly, and the pressure eased enough to allow her to swallow.

"I just got here." She gasped. The pressure was mercilessly reapplied to her throat, then eased off. "I'm not spying," Gallo said, before she was silenced again. One of the warrior women leaned over and glared directly into her face.

"Explain," she said. She was the boss. A quick nod from her and the boot was withdrawn.

"The goddess Looselea brought me here." Gallo coughed. It wasn't *that* much of a lie. There was certainly some correlation between Sophia and the goddess, and touching Sophia in that infernal machine had somehow catapulted her into this mess. Ergo, she was on a godly mission. She'd love to know exactly where she was. She worried that Sophia might be in similar trouble. After all, the Amazons were vicious, tree hugging bastards.

"Looselea?" At least the lead warrior recognized the name. "She's not one of our goddesses," she said dismissively.

"Well, she's one of mine. And she sent me here." This was another half truth and was received with a frown.

"She definitely wasn't in here before." An Amazon warrior spoke up. "We checked out the cell when we arrived, and she wasn't here. And there's nowhere she could hide, tiny as she is."

Gallo bristled, but she could feel a general assent among the group. She had not been here before. Ergo, she had just arrived. Ergo, she was not a spy. And ergo, she was a bleedin' divine messenger.

Get with the cosmic order, sisters. My gods are better than your squirrely, tree hopping ones.

Relief ran through her. She might get away with this. An act of divinity was a hard sell, especially to hard-nosed heathens such as these. At least she had them thinking about it. It was bad mojo to kill a god's minion; any god, even one that wasn't your own.

Cell? The word pricked into her consciousness. "Did you say we're in a cell?" she asked. It made sense. There was a rough floor under her back, and what she could make out through the barrier of Amazon legs was enough to tell her this wasn't another coal hole. Her heart sank. The bellow of an angry bull echoed from some place not too far away. At least that was different. "A cell where?"

"A cell in the Belly." The lead warrior stepped back and allowed Gallo get to her feet. "So, messenger of a goddess we don't believe in, why are you here? What brings you to the Belly of the Beast? Come to save us?" There was a sneer on her lips.

"Who is the Beast?" Gallo asked, though the churning in her stomach already told her. The Belly of the Beast was the nickname for the most bloodthirsty gladiatorial arena in all of Rome's long history. The Beast was always the current Emperor in his sporting guise. It was his prerogative to wear the golden lion's mask at the celebratory games. But the one, true, most monstrous Beast, was the man who had built the Belly arena in the first place; the Emperor who had created the bloodthirsty games for his own glory. He'd been the most callous and vicious of all Rome's early Emperors. In Gallo's own timeline, his name acted as a curse for the clean living and an oath for the debased. He was worshiped by secret cults who gathered in dark temples on stark, lonely hillsides, or in the heart of deep, damp forests.

"What rock do you live under not to know that Severus ex Machina is the Beast of Rome," the Amazon said, amused at Gallo's question.

Gee, of course it is. She had guessed right. She had landed in the depravity of Rome's darkest age, governed by its cruellest ruler. She was indeed in the coal hole of Hell. "Oh, shit," she said.

"Easy to smell when you're neck deep in it."

"Why are we in the cells?" Gallo asked.

"A messenger of the gods who doesn't know where she is or why she has been sent? We are lucky, indeed," the Amazon leader said. Behind her, the warriors laughed. She stepped back and gave Gallo a rude, once-over glance, before saying, "I am Alkaia of Thermodon." She drew herself up, dark and proud, to her full, impressive height, and glared at Gallo with shrewd, narrowed eyes.

"Gallo of…of the Prussian Dragoons." Gallo played it canny. Common sense said it would not be wise to be an Imperial soldier in a cell full of the Empire's prisoners. If she'd had to use a fake identity for Londinium, then maybe it would be smart to use it here, too. Until she was back in her own time, she would follow Sangfroid's advice. And if she ever caught up with her again, she would break both her legs and wrap them around her neck like a snood. Decanus or no, she was one pig-swilling turd of Circe. Gallo was not sure how or why any this had happened, but she knew it was somehow Sangfroid's fault.

"I haven't heard of Prussian Dragoons. But you are a warrior? You have the bearing of a warrior," Alkaia said. Gallo took it as a peace offering.

"Yes. And you are Amazons." Gallo tried to dampen the natural awe she held for them, but the wry smile she received showed she was unsuccessful. A shift ran through the throng surrounding her; the body language relaxed, and she realized they had accepted her quietly spoken respect and were pleased. Initial antagonisms had been dispelled with a few careful words.

"Eat with us," Alkaia said. "Hipp is a good cook, even with the meagre provisions we've been given."

The Tea Machine

A younger woman tended a pot hung over the fire pit. She smiled at Gallo and nodded for her to sit. Gallo counted six Amazons in all, crowded cross-legged around the cook pot, passing around an apple-wood pipe filled with a crude dung tobacco.

"So why you are in a cell in the Belly? Are you prisoners?" Gallo asked Alkaia. She took a lung-churning toke from the pipe. It hurt her throat more than the boot stomping had. She choked down a cough and tried to look composed.

"We're here for Severus's annual games to the glory of his own sweet ass. Every nation has to send gladiators as an act of allegiance," Alkaia said.

Outside their cell, the corridor shook with the howl and snap of the pit animals and yells of their keepers. Gallo tried to ignore it just as her companions did. They calmly puffed on the pipe and stared at the flames, talking softly as the stew bubbled. Someone handed her a cup of ale. It eased the ache in her throat, and finally she let herself relax, confident that she may not be among new friends, but at least they weren't going to gut her anytime soon.

"But the Amazon nation was not part of Severus's Empire? I mean *is* not part of his Empire," Gallo said.

"All nations send warriors to the games, unless you want Severus and his army knocking on your door." Hipp snorted and threw more herbs into the pot.

"It's a token," Alkaia explained. "It keeps the peace with a man who does not like peace. And manages to push an Empire spinning out of control away from our borders."

Hipp splashed stew into coarse wooden bowls and handed the first one to her leader, and the second to their guest. Gallo accepted it, grateful for the gesture. These women had little enough to share.

"Eat and be eaten." Hipp laughed as she served them all.

"To a death well met," the others chorused back and slapped cups of weak ale together in a joking toast.

"You fight tomorrow?" Gallo asked and supped from her stew bowl. The first mouthful was rich and strong and she could feel it doing her bones good.

"We fight tomorrow, messenger. I believe you are a sign after all," Alkaia said, watching Gallo carefully over the rim of her bowl. "I think tomorrow you will work the magic you were sent to do, and make sure we die honourably."

"It is Severus's way to try and shame our nation," another warrior called Toxis explained. "Every year he orders bigger and better games, and the games master devises more macabre ways for us to fight, but we are never cowed. We fight hard and die bravely. The Amazons will never die easy."

"They treat the tribute fighters like toys. They delight in destroying us," Alkaia said. "And as we are a strong, masterful nation of women, they are especially vindictive towards us. We fight hard to uphold the honour of our nation. The longer we can survive in the arena, the better for Thermodon."

"If the contestants die too quickly or fight poorly, then Severus takes it as an insult and annihilates their homeland. Genocide is nothing to him. He boasts of it as a cleansing. To prove worthy of existence each nation must send the best warriors it can," Toxis said.

Gallo's appetite was lessening. She had no magic to combat this. Looselea was no longer a talisman on a cord around her neck. She had become Sophia, a silly, sweet woman, and Gallo worried for her. What part of this ancient world was she in? She could be in the next cell for all Gallo knew, or a thousand miles away. What if she had landed in the sea, or a volcano? It was funny how, in the middle of this madness, her first priority was Sophia. The only option was to get out of this cell, search for Sophia and the others, and hope that somewhere out there they were looking for her, too.

"Where are your weapons?" She could see none in the cell.

"They were confiscated. We get them back before we go into the arena. Until then, we are treated like this. All the tribute fighters are herded down here with the animals. It's a psychological test, but we are strong up here, too." Alkaia tapped her temple with a forefinger and winked. Considering they faced a death match in the morning, Gallo found her companions very upbeat.

"Has anyone ever won and walked away?" Gallo asked out of interest.

"It's a rare as a red moon. The odds are stacked against you."

"But it *is* possible to fight and go on to live a long and happy life?" she persisted.

Alkaia shrugged, and the other Amazons looked at each other. "That's a bit of a radical theory," Toxis finally said. "Is that your divine plan?"

"I don't have a plan. I'll fight and see what happens." Gallo raised her bowl to salute to her new comrades. She was here, and she was required to fight, and that was all she had ever done. If she won, she would go free, and if she died honourably, then that would be good, too. Gallo had always expected to have a shorter life than normal. All legionnaires did. She had lived well and had no regrets except one, and it shadowed her heart. For one magical moment, she had met a woman who transcended all others and then lost her almost immediately to another, darker magic. She would get Sophia back. She would save her. She had no idea how, but she vowed it to herself.

"Tomorrow we die." Alkaia cracked her bowl against Gallo's. And for Gallo that was a right and natural salute. She would die. But only if she had to.

"With honour!" The Amazons roared, and Gallo's voice roared with them. And along the corridor, strange and dangerous creatures roared back.

Chapter 19

THE MARBLE FLOOR WAS COLD and hard. And not as pretty when her nose was pressed up against it. Millicent lay clutching her stinging face. The patter of bare feet rushed towards her, and she was hauled up by hands more concerned with haste than care or courtesy. From the corner of her eye, Millicent could see that the matron and Cassian had moved aside and were in deep discussion, ignoring her prone position.

"I know I still owe you from the last time, but I would really like this one for myself," Cassian spoke in a pleading, urgent voice. "Couldn't you keep her aside, just for me? I'm bringing a few friends back after the games." He pressed a small bag of coins into the matron's hand. "I'll bring the rest with me this evening," he added, rather desperately, as she weighed the bag thoughtfully. "And we'll have a pound of your finest Oolong in honour of the goddess."

"Come this way. Quickly." A voice whispered in her ear. Millicent was manhandled away by a young woman dressed in a short tunic. "If she notices you're still about, she'll hit you again harder," the girl said.

"If she so much as touches me, I'll…I'll…" Millicent didn't have words for what she would do; she had never been physically assaulted before and felt a little in shock.

"Come." The girl led her through a doorway and down a chilly corridor. Sunlight did not penetrate this part of the building, and the shadows loomed long and gloomy from the flickering tallow candles. From far off, she heard the splash of water, and the farther they progressed down the corridor, the noticeably warmer it became.

"Where are we going?" Her heart was still thumping, and her face felt hot and bruised. She was thoroughly agitated by the assault and unsure how much danger she was in. Why should she trust this girl? "Where are we going?" she repeated, trying to squelch the panic in her voice.

"The bathing rooms." Her guide relented.

The answer was not what she had expected. It did not reassure her either. They could be about to drown her for all she knew. Her travels into Sangfroid's time had been dangerous, but she had always been more or less in command of her own destiny, if only because Hubert was in the background engineering her exit. Here it was different. Here she was trapped and vulnerable. She had felt it in the streets, and now she had been attacked by that fat slattern! Lord only knew what else awaited her. The muted whispering between Cassian and the broodmare, who seemed to own the place, was another worry. What she had overheard was calculated and menacing, and she knew it concerned her.

The girl pulled her into a side room. Fragrant heat bloomed around them.

"We're in the caldarium. Leave your clothes there." The girl pointed to a stone bench on the far wall. Millicent looked around her. The room consisted of a small pool wreathed in delicious clouds of scented steam and surrounded by stone benches. The walls were garishly painted with forest scenes filled with romping nymphs and hoary centaurs.

"Oh, you are slow." The girl began hauling at Millicent's clothes. "Where are you from? Your colouring is unusual; are you Gallic?"

"I can manage myself." Millicent slapped away the groping hands.

"Well you better get on with it then. Matron will be here in a minute to see how you clean up." The young girl was equally irritated. "I'm Jana, by the way. What do they call you?"

"Millicent," she muttered and tried to decide what to do. She was overheated. Her undergarments stuck to her body, and her hair had escaped from its pins and now fell around her shoulders. She was certain her cheek was black and blue, but she absolutely refused to cry. The scented water called to her. Flower petals floated on it, for heaven's sake. It was irresistible. Surely a quick wash could only help her refresh and re-focus? Not that she would let Jana assist with her toilette. She was no more to be trusted than any of her Roman counterparts.

Millicent fretted for her friends. Were they going through equally bizarre experiences? She particularly worried about Sophia. She was least equipped to cope with the vagaries of time travel and could be in mortal peril. She hoped either Gallo or Sangfroid were with her, looking after her.

"Come on." Jana's hands were pecking at her again, twisting and tugging her clothes loose. "I'll get in trouble because of you."

"Who is that…that woman? The matron?" Millicent could think of a better name for the hard faced harridan, but desisted. She began to reluctantly undress.

"Cybele is the tea matron. She manages the temple and the tea maids, and she's a bitch. Don't be getting on the wrong side of her or you'll suffer and then some." She sighed. "Gods, but you wear a lot of clothes. Is it cold where you're from? Where was that; did you say?"

"Britannia." Millicent took a chance on mentioning her homeland as the last of her clothes fell in an ungainly heap at her feet.

"Britannia!" Jana exclaimed in horror. "No wonder you're bundled up. I hear it would freeze the teats off a pig up there."

Millicent had no answer for that.

"Get into the water, and I'll send these off to the laundry," Jana instructed. She was a bossy little thing, but Millicent complied.

"When will I get them back?" she asked, wondering if the steam mechanization she saw everywhere allowed for extra quick laundering.

"You'll wear a tunic like mine during the day, and then there'll be a toga for the evening when the worshipers arrive." Jana indicated her simple mustard coloured tunic with its plaited belt of stringed leather. Millicent was aghast, she didn't want to wear that…that horse blanket, not even for one second. Nor did she like the way Jana said *worshipers*, as if it left a bad taste in her mouth.

"I prefer to wear my own clothes," she said, reaching for them.

Jana whipped them out of reach. "No way; they stink of fish. Did you come here in a trawler?"

"You don't like these worshipers, do you? Who are they?" Millicent asked to distract her while she attempted to snag back a garment. It was turning into a game where she was outsmarted by Jana's sneaky twists and turns every time she made a lunge for her clothes.

"They're the creeps that come here for evening worship and buy tea so they can fill up the urns." The derision was clear in her voice.

Cassian had called her an urn. "What exactly do you mean by urns?" She suspected it would be something distasteful.

Jana spluttered with bitter mirth before realizing Millicent wasn't joking. Her face fell serious. "You, and young women like you, are brought here to be urns. You entertain the worshipers with your bodies," she said plainly. Millicent recoiled in horror, and Jana took the opportunity to deftly whisk the clothes out of her reach once and for all.

"That's why the matron bought you. Some girls are selected to be urns, and others, like me, see to the domestic chores. Let me tell you, if I had your looks, I'd be tempted. Some urns end up marrying well. Granted the old coots are knocking on Hades door, but even so—"

"I have absolutely no intention of being an urn!" Millicent made a doomed grab for her clothes. She had to get out of this heinous house of iniquity. How on earth had Sophia managed to build a cult around tea and debauchery? They hardly went hand in hand.

"Oh no, you don't," Jana said. "I've had enough of this nonsense. I've got work to do. In you go, little urn." And she pushed Millicent into the pool.

Millicent surfaced spluttering angrily. The water came up to her chest. Above her Jana slipped out of her own tunic, collected a dish, and joined her in the water.

"I made this fresh this morning," Jana said and began to rub an exfoliate over Millicent's back and shoulders and then her upper arms. It was lovely. Millicent stopped surging about to appreciate the luxuriant massage. The oil smelled beautiful.

"What is that?" she found herself asking. It felt wonderful to have the sweat and grime scrubbed off so deliciously.

"Olive oil and sea salt. And I added some neroli." Jana began to sluice Millicent's back and arms. "Fresh is best. If it's left too long the olive smell is overpowering." She handed Millicent the bowl. "You can do your face. Mind your eyes though, the salt stings." She began to lather Millicent's hair with an equally divine smelling product. "This is my own recipe," she said. "The stuff they use here is shocking. Lye soap, I ask you? No wonder their hair looks like rats nests." She massaged up a surplus of lather, and Millicent moaned at the luxury of it all.

"This is why Matron keeps me on," Jana continued. She was obviously in a chatty mood for her hands became less brisk and she took her time. "I mayn't be a beauty, but I'm indispensable to her. I manufacture all the soaps for the urns." She began to rinse. "Keeps me on her sweet side, otherwise I'd be down the market quicker than a whiplash."

Having seen the matron's unsweet side, Millicent could only agree with Jana's philosophy.

"Don't annoy her. She's dangerous," Jana warned. Then said, "Now hold your nose." She forcefully ducked Millicent under the water. When she spluttered back to the surface, Jana was still yammering on about the abuses young women underwent to partake of the tea. "We sign our lives away to come here."

"Like a nun." Millicent wiped the water out of her eyes. The correlation popped into her head and out of her mouth at the same time.

"An *urn*." Jana looked at her as if she were stupid. "Young women come here from all over the Empire hoping to either make a fortune, or marry one. Even the temple slaves can make enough to buy their own freedom, if Matron approves, that is." She seemed cheered by the thought of wealth for all.

"I thought the temples belonged to the state?" Millicent recalled her school lessons from long time past.

Jana shrugged. "The tea temple is different. It's a franchise and Matron owns this one." A sliver of pride crept into her voice. "And I make it smell good. Now, out." She was all business again. "We need to get you dry as toast."

This time Millicent did as she was told. Jana clambered out, and Millicent followed her to an adjacent chamber. There was no pool and the room was heated to a high temperature. Millicent assumed she was to stand here until her body dried. Instead she was given a cup of water and ordered to sit down.

"It's best to keep drinking in the heat. Now sit quietly while I get my oils and give you a nice rub down." Then Jana was gone.

Millicent considered sneaking away, but she was naked and lost and the lethargic heat was sucking the last ounce of resistance from her weak limbs. The stone seat was warm under her bottom, and she leaned back against the painted wall. This time, the murals were an elaborate seascape of shells, waves, and fantastical fish. Instead of drying off, she found she was perspiring, and her bones were melting with the delicious, relaxing heat. Tension oozed out of her. She sat and sipped her water in an exhausted stupor. Her resolve was at an all-time low, completely outflanked by circumstance and the dull, perpetual nag of not knowing what to do. She needed to find the others and somehow organize an escape, yet the task felt gargantuan, and she felt so small.

"No snoozing." Jana appeared beside her. "Let's get you to the unctorium before you nod off. I've got the oil warmed and ready. Then you can have a bite to eat and afterwards take a nice nap."

The unctorium was next door. Millicent sprawled face down on the stone slab as Jana liberally covered her from head to toe in sweet smelling almond oil, and then massaged it deep into her muscles.

Millicent moaned. She had never felt anything so luxurious, or so decadent, in her entire life. This had to be the work of the devil, but she was beyond caring. She would happily burn in hell for such a wonderful, relaxing experience. A cold knife blade touched her skin and made her jolt. Fear coursed through her. She had let her guard down and was about to be stabbed to death.

"What's wrong?" Jana asked. "This is the best bit."

Millicent turned over to find the girl standing beside her with a strigil in her hand waiting to scrape the excess oil off her body. She felt silly. She knew how Roman baths worked.

"Are they all as jumpy as you in Britannia?" Jana grumped and went to work with the curved blade. "Now, roll over so I can do the back of your legs."

It was another seductive temptation, and Millicent fell into it with shivering bliss. *I am a weak, ineffectual woman,* she scolded herself, but gently.

"That's you all done. Shiny as a new kettle, you are," Jana said eventually. She helped pull a simple linen tunic over

Millicent's head. It was pure white and practically glowed beside the drab yellow one Jana wore.

"Use this to gather it in." Jana handed over a thin plait of leather that knotted at the waist.

"Follow me," she ordered and took off down another long corridor. They were moving into the bowels of the temple, and the air grew cooler and quieter.

"This is a huge building," Millicent said. "It didn't look half as big from the outside." As Jana was a friendly, talkative type, Millicent began to question her, hoping not to reveal the true complexity of her alien status.

"It's Rome. Everything has to be the biggest and the best, or Severus will tear it down. This is the High Tea Temple of Rome. There are thousands of them all over the Empire. Sure, weren't you were recruited from one in Britannia?" She cast Millicent a curious sideways look.

Millicent didn't answer. She was too busy trying to orientate herself. It was becoming clear to her the temple had a web-like layout, with a central hub she had yet to see.

"Or were you bought at the market?" Jana asked, slyly. "You were, weren't you?" Surprise showed in her eyes before turning to sympathy. "Nevermind. I was, too," she added, taking any sting out of her words.

Millicent hesitated. She was more aghast than stung. Bought? *Oh, good Lord, Jana's a slave, and she thinks I'm one, too.* It never occurred to her that this might be the case. This was not good; if she was supposed to be a slave, then it could seriously limit her mobility in this world.

"Was that why the people at the fish market were giving me harsh looks?" she asked. Perhaps a female slave should not be out and about without a chaperon?

Jana snorted. "Most of the vendors are freedmen; who are they to give harsh looks?" She glanced over playfully. "You talk quaint. Is that the way they speak in Britannia?"

"Then why were they so upset with me? They looked nasty. It was the same in the spice market, too."

"Because of the tea tax. Tea maidens go out to collect it. You look sort of like a tea maid with that flouncy tunic you had on. Is it what they're wearing in Britannia these days? Because it looks awful. It's a shockingly bad imitation of the real thing. Matron will not be happy. Can't have counterfeits out there; she'll go daft if people are copying the temple style."

The taffeta had cost Millicent quite a penny from Swanson and George of Mayfair, and it amused her for it to be seen as inferior quality to the Roman version.

"So, the tea maidens collect taxes?" she asked, as Jana ushered her into another smaller room, this one was lit naturally through large windows that opened out into a quiet, bright courtyard. Jana pushed Millicent down on to a low wooden stool.

"And the urns sell produce in the square out front?" Millicent returned to her questioning.

"Yes," Jana answered. "You start out as an urn, and then, one day you're allowed to wear the bustle and handle money. We'll see to your hair next. You like it up, don't you?"

She sat still while Jana fussed over her locks, piling and pinning her curls into some semblance of order. "Are you an urn, too?" Millicent asked.

"No. I haven't the face or figure for it," Jana answered. "Too thin. Not like you." She gave Millicent a little pinch. "You've got the kind of curves all the tea sippers like. Bet you dance like a dream."

Millicent was mortified. Dance? "I'll be damned if I'm going to dance for tea sippers." Oh! Her hand flew to her mouth. How easy it was to slip into Sangfroid's profanity.

"You'll make a fortune and earn your bustle in no time. Then you can get out of here." There was no malice in Jana's voice, just resignation.

"How do I do that?" Millicent asked, though she had no intention of staying at all.

It was a careless question, and Jana showed considerable surprise. "Why, as a tea maid you get to keep a cut of whatever you collect. That's how you buy your way out. That's why the tea is so popular a career path with the poorer girls. You can make a fortune and start a new life, hopefully with some rich old fool in tow. Some girls have gone on to be career mistresses." She seemed impressed, while Millicent suppressed a shiver. What a horrid place this was.

The outer halls began to echo with voices and footsteps, while outside, in the leafy courtyard, girlish laughter rang out.

"Siesta is over," Jana said resignedly. "We'd better go to afternoon prayers."

"Is she here?" Millicent asked anxiously.

"Who?"

"Looselea." Sophia might actually be lodged in the same building, feted as a goddess. Wouldn't that be wonderful, in a strange way? And, if so, would Millicent be able to pry her away? Sophia must be terrified by this world; at least Millicent hoped she was. Otherwise it would be impossible to get her to leave all the adoration behind and return home.

"Britannia really is the ass-end of nowhere." Jana shook her head sadly at the question and led Millicent away. Millicent took this response to mean that the goddess was not present at her own temple. She followed Jana dejectedly. More fool her for thinking there might be an easy way out.

Young women were converging in the corridors. Together, she and Jana flowed with the throng into a massive chamber.

"Where are we now?" she asked, looking around with awe.

"The Hall of the Seven Kettles. This is where it all happens," Jana told her in hushed tones. "Kneel down here."

Around them women knelt in rows facing to the front where a pulpit, of sorts, stood to the side of a large statue. Millicent gazed dumbstruck at the icon. Not because of the exquisite workmanship or pleasing aesthetics, for there were many to appreciate in this piece of classical art, but for its countenance. Before her stood a twenty-foot marble statue of Sophia. She sat decorously on a rock, her stern features rendered smooth and creamy by the beautiful stone. Her dress was of Millicent's era, and she held a large silver teaspoon in one hand and a kettle in the other. The kettle was tipped forward and poised under the ceiling oculus, so that when filled with rainwater it poured from out of the spout into a giant marble cup and a saucer by the statue's feet. The teacup was large enough to bathe in, and Millicent suspected its purpose was that of a baptismal font. As if reading her mind Jana pointed to the cup.

"That's where the initiates are dunked once they become urns. You'll be in there soon."

Not on your nelly!

The hush was broken by rustling, as if a flock of starched birds was taking roost at the back of the room. Millicent looked over her shoulder. The last few tiers were filling up with men in snow-white, formal togas. Jana looked back too, and rolled her eyes.

"The sippers are in. Leery old goat-eyes."

"Who are they?" Millicent whispered.

"Sponsors and wannabes. Some, the richest, keep girls at the temple for their own exclusive use. They're your future clients. Do you see Cassian in the back row? He has his eye on you. The man with him will be coming here later tonight," Jana muttered disdainfully. "He's called Belarus, and he's a chronic gambler. He'd bet on how high a dog lifts it leg to piss. A couple of absolute losers. Stay away from them if you can."

Cassian caught Millicent staring and gave her a cheery finger waggle. She turned away with a shudder. She had to get away from here. Her attention was drawn to the front of the room as Cybele, the tea matron, mounted the pulpit and gazed down on the assembled. She raised her arms and began a long dirge that Millicent could only take to be a prayer.

"Oh, Looselea, look upon the dredges and despair. See the splash in the saucer. See the drips upon the tablecloth. How can we give you tea time cheer?" Cybele intoned in an annoying nasal twang. Millicent wondered if the prayer came with the franchise. It was awful.

"One lump or two." The congregation intoned back as one. Millicent was startled. She hadn't expected that.

"Lift up thy spoon and stir," Cybele droned on. "Lift up thine cup. Hear thy kettle boil. Hear thy china call, oh great Looselea."

"No more goats," the crowd answered. "No. No. Really. No more goats."

And that seemed to be that. How curious, Millicent thought. What had goats to do with anything?

"We have among us new acolytes who wish to dedicate themselves to the goddess and the indulgences of the tea. Come daughters and bathe in the waters of the perfect brew."

Several girls moved shyly to the front and queued to be immersed in the giant tea cup. Millicent saw it was filled with an ugly brown liquid. Jana nudged her.

"That means you, too," she said, unenthusiastically nodding at the queue. "You'll never get that gunk out of your clothes," she sighed. "That's why we all run around in ugly yellow tunics. The tannin ruins the linen," she complained. "Pity you couldn't have stayed white for a little longer, but I guess Cassian has already booked you anyway."

"What's in that cup?" Millicent hissed back. "And why do I have to get in it?"

"Goat urine and rainwater." Jana shoved her, more roughly this time. "Don't be a ninny. Just go do it. It's an initiation. We can wash you down again after."

Millicent rose unsteadily to her feet and shuffled after the new maidens crowding down the aisle.

"And don't swallow any." Jana whispered after her.

Cybele glowered at her. It was obvious she was dragging her feet while the other young women as good as skipped towards the teacup. Did they know they were queuing to sit in goat urine? Millicent's steps grew slower and slower.

A few feet away, to her left, a door to the courtyard lay ajar. It let the light breeze waft away the heavy odour from the teacup. Outside, she could make out the curved edge of a fountain; the shadow of palm fronds played across the stonework. Millicent fancied she could hear the splash of water and trill of birdsong. She imagined blue skies and the warmth of the sun on her shoulders. She imagined a low and easily scalable courtyard wall.

She lifted the hem of her tunic and legged it.

Chapter 20

SOPHIA DID NOT LIKE IT. She did not like it at all. The place was dusty, hot, and filthy, even for the outdoors. The lazy, persistent hum of flies merged with the equally persistent drone of old men's voices. She wasn't sure where she was. The ground under her feet was hard-packed and cracked open with drought. A crude building made from various tree parts and lumps of mud stood off to her left. Bales of straw were piled inside it, and a broody hen roosted resplendent on the topmost one. A few straggly, windblown trees grew almost horizontally along the ridge behind her. Other than that, the place was a dust bowl. That accounted for the dirt she supposed, brushing down her skirts with vigour. She had no idea how she had gotten here but assumed the machine made people travel whether they wanted to or not. It was most thoughtless.

She became aware of a tense silence fallen over her less than pastoral panorama. Bar an annoying fly droning near her ear, all was quiet; the old men's voices had dropped away. She looked up to find several dishevelled goat herders—she could think of no other occupation that required such a disarrangement of clothing—staring at her open mouthed. *How rude.* There were five rough looking fellows in all and a boy, maybe in his early teens. They gaped at her in a most alarming and unintelligent way.

"I say, where is this?" she inquired.

They started back as if she'd flung fire at their feet.

"Oh, really." She was so cross. This nonsense had gone on long enough. "Haven't you seen a lady before?" She doubted it. She would have very stern words with Hubert when she saw—and then it hit her like a pail of water, freezing her heart in a spasm of pain and erasing all sensibility. Her dearest Hubert was gone! Devoured by a monster before her eyes. And his accursed machine had catapulted her out of London to some distant goat farm. She was alone, lost, and surrounded by a total lack of hygiene.

She sank onto a boulder, her legs no longer capable of holding her. One of the men approached her cautiously in that he was shoved to the foremost by the others. He was older than the rest, more stooped and bedraggled, with mounds of dirty linen heaped around his scraggy frame. Considering the others wore strips of fabric held together by stains alone, it seemed safe to assume he was an elder, and therefore her welcome party.

He mumbled something at her from a safe distance. Sophia thought she could make out...Latin? Where in the world did they speak Latin? Had Hubert's machine sent her to Latvia! Good gracious. It also made her think of Gallo with his gentle Latin lips—words! Gentle Latin words. Her heart spasmed again. She had lost Hubert and Gallo, and all in one day. The only two people she had ever felt any genuine warmth for. And somehow she'd been careless enough to lose them both. She was an undeserving, stupid, and wretched failure of a human being. Fate had taken away all her happiness as punishment.

A tear rolled down her cheek and splashed on her dusty silk lap. She tried to shake herself out of self-pity. It was not an attractive feature, and she actively forbade it in others. Plus it was an unaffordable luxury at this moment. Perhaps later she could let the floodgates open, as a secret indulgence in her hotel room. The old man muttered again. She thought he said something about an ecstatic welcome. At least someone was happy.

She concentrated on his words, trying to decipher them.

"Welcome, lady visitor of the goatherd," he was saying. He flapped his hand at the young boy beside him, who went scurrying off towards a tiny village nestled on a distant hillside. She began to take further note of her surroundings. She was at the edge of an olive grove in a small valley. It was pretty, she supposed, in the Biblical sense, meaning there was dust and donkeys, but where was the inn? She needed to wash and indulge in a pot of much needed tea.

The valley floor was vibrant and fecund against the barren hillside where she stood. The gritty dust that seemed to get everywhere blew in hot, swirling breezes. Overhead a cloudless blue sky domed the valley with a stifling stillness broken only by the drifting of far-off honey buzzards cruising the higher air currents. The air was heavy and tranquil with the silver shiver of olive boughs and an occasional clank of a herd bell to break the peace.

The old man spoke again, "Would you like a goat, dearest magical lady?" He was clearly unsure how to address her, but she decided dearest magical lady would do for now.

"No. No goats," she said, and was pleased he seemed to understand her. Perhaps her Latin was better than she imagined. "Perhaps some tea."

By dusk the entire village had come out to welcome her and present her with their most favoured goats. In the lean-to, they had put coarse sack matting over the bales, chased out the chicken, and much to her consternation, expected her to recline. She would rather sleep tied upright to a tree than lie on that giant mouse nest.

At her feet, a filthy blanket held about a hundredweight of figs. If she saw one more fig, she'd have a fit. Olives, figs, goats, even a lopsided loom. They had brought her anything and everything they treasured, but no tea.

A fire pit had been built nearby and now its light and heat were welcoming in the early evening time. One of the goats had been dispatched, thankfully well out of sight, and it was now being roasted on a crude spit. The smell was appalling.

Sophia had been right all along to dislike travel. One did not have to experience it to know it was horrid. Stars were beginning to pulse through the twilight. Every passing second, a new cluster bloomed out of the night sky. Sophia regarded the crystalline majesty above her and sighed at its beauty. For one infinitesimal moment, she moved outside of her present woes and her soul flew towards the wondrous magnitude of the universe and was spellbound.

"My dearest magical lady, please have another fig." The elder was pressing figs upon her again. He wrung his hands in supplication. "The people wish to know which is your star? We see you look for it. Where do you live, dearest magical lady?"

How sweet. Now, if only it were Gallo asking her to count the stars and chose which one to live upon. She sighed deeply. How long must she wait before Millicent or Gallo came along and took her back home? It was awful; she had no luggage, and her silks were covered in a fine layer of valley dust. As for the stars? She waved her hand in a flamboyant gesture at the Milky Way weaving indolently overhead.

"That river of light," she said, "it's all mine." And smiled dreamily. Her audience gasped, and she was amused at their naivety. Now, if only she had a nice cup of tea, she could bear the absurdity of the moment as well as the infinite beauty of it, too.

By the next morning, the populations of several other villages had arrived with even more figs and goats. Sophia arose from her slumber to find a crowd assembled outside her holy hovel. She had eventually succumbed to the makeshift bed through a mixture of exhaustion and the simple rustic wine that washed down the spit-roasted goat…which tasted much better than she had imagined. She had quickly fallen into a deep and restorative sleep on her prickly pillow, and now awoke to find even more supplicants kneeling unnervingly close to her straw boudoir. The elder approached with some local women in tow.

"We have maidservants for you, lady of the stars. They will take you to the river and adorn you." He stood taller now and spoke with more authority. Not to her, of course, to her he was as acquiescent as ever, but he was enjoying ordering everyone else around on her behalf. Sophia had to admit, this adorning her at the river idea sounded just the ticket after a long night in a hayrick.

"What is your name?" she asked him. It would probably be a useful thing to know.

He preened with importance. "I am Volos, dearest star lady. Your servant and number one priest. And this is my wife, Despina, who will be your number one house servant and priestess. She will be matron over your handmaidens." He pointed to an eager cluster of young girls. "My daughters and nieces are at your service."

Oh, so she had a priest, a priestess, *and* servants now. Sophia warmed to the idea of worship. Foreigners were strange people; she'd have to get used to their little ways. She turned to Despina and smiled. The woman fell to the ground.

"Oh do get up and take me to the river. I need my toilette. I hope you have scented soaps." To Volos she said, "And you. Get me a cup of tea." Ignoring his nervous, crestfallen face, she allowed herself to be led away by her handmaidens.

Sophia returned unsure whether to be pleased or disgruntled, eventually deciding her handmaidens had done well by her under the circumstances. She now wore a wonderful flowing toga of the purest white. It was cool and clean and caressed her skin wonderfully after the stuffy layers of her dinner dress, which had been whisked away for laundering while she had been pumiced within an inch of her life with volcanic stone. The experience left her scuffed and bruised but undeniably glowing. Her hair had been massaged with oils until it shone and then elaborately braided and piled up on the crown of her head. She would have felt almost regal if it weren't for the growling of her empty stomach. She looked forward to her morning tea.

A concoction of lukewarm water and fresh, frothy goat milk awaited her, along with a bowl of some indescribable gruel that had figs bobbing on the surface.

"No. I need tea. Tea. Teeeea," she said, rather peevishly. But really enough was enough. "Haven't you people heard of it?" And with horror, looking out at a sea of blank faces, she realized they hadn't. She was in an Englishwoman's hell!

Luckily, Sophia had recently formed the habit of purloining a little of Hubert's fabulous Darjeeling whenever she visited Christie Mews. This was not because the Trenchant-Myres couldn't afford their own Darjeeling. *Au contraire.* They kept fine and expensive teas, but they were locked away in the tea caddy and only Mamma had the key. This left Sophia with a predicament. Whenever she visited the Misses Partridge, which was often, she had to drink the dust from the bottom of their tea caddy. They were not as domestically vigilant as Mrs. Trenchant-Myre, and as a result, the old dears' servants stole tea from them with the greatest liberty. So, when visiting, Sophia always kept a smattering of decent tea leaves in her reticule to top up her tea cup. She restocked regularly from the Aberly's equally unfettered caddy, tutting all the time at Millicent's inattention and unwarranted trust. All Sophia required was a teapot of hot water, and she could manage the rest herself. She had the tea leaves upon her person, surely these people had some sort of pot she could use?

"Have you a teapot?" she asked, loudly as this was important. Again she got the blank look she was becoming used to. She grabbed a twig and scratched the outline of a teapot in the dirt. "This is a teapot," she said.

Volos stared at her drawing. "You want this, oh lady of the dirt?"

"Yes. Yes, I do," she said, uncertain of this latest sobriquet. To fall from the stars to dirt so quickly was unsettling. Volos snapped his fingers, and a young man came forward to look enquiringly at the crude sketch.

"You do this," Volos ordered. The young man bowed, first to Volos and then to Sophia, several times, before running off towards the village.

"Hani, the potter," Volos explained. "He make this for you, goat lady."

Sophia sat back and considered a few things. Firstly, she was now the lady of the goats; was that better than dirt? Secondly, the village had a potter. What an interesting development. She lifted her twig and began another sketch. "Call him back," she said. "I want him to make me this as well."

Volos bowed deeply. "Of course, lady of pots."

The first teapot was minuscule, so she introduced scale to her sketches. The second exploded, so she explained it was to be capable of holding hot water and needed to be glazed appropriately. The third needed a tighter lid to stop the contents evaporating. The fourth moved them on to the need for a sturdier handle. Goat curds and lemon juice made a wonderful poultice for burns. The fifth needed the spout modified so as not to scald. Goat curds and lemon juice were again useful. The sixth needed the inside to be less porous as a scummy film formed on top of the water. The seventh had a pretty floral decoration and poured like a dream. Sophia filled it with water and her precious tea leaves and waited anxiously. The set of six cups and saucers she'd also had made were delightfully delicate. She was very pleased with them and favoured Hani and his family with a winsome smile. They were elated and began to manufacture her tea set for the mass market under her divine seal of approval.

The entire geographical region—all of which had come to pay goat-laden tribute—held its breath on bended knee. Sophia smiled indulgently at their childlike curiosity and pagan befuddlement. The reverence they showed her first cup of tea was almost religious.

It's funny how a nice cup of tea can put a fresh face on an old problem. For several days Sophia had been stranded in the Valley of the Goats, as it was now known due to the growing herd around her new retreat. The straw filled lean-to was a thing of the past. Instead, a rather nice, if basic, two roomed villa had been hastily erected for her in handmade mud, brick, and stone. Volos assured her marble blocks and stone masons were at this very moment trekking over the mountains to build her a spectacular temple. A temple sounded rather elaborate, but she supposed those were the sort of places people could safely stay in when travelling abroad. She took her trusty scratching stick and drew up a set of plans based on the ground floor of Farrance's of Belgrave Square to show Volos what, to her mind, best suited sensible traveller accommodation.

During one of these planning sessions, she shared some of her tea with Volos. He was impressed with the smoky flavour, and she explained to him where tea came from. In the dirt, she scratched out a rough map of China and India to the east of Europe. She looked at her little dirt map and wondered where the Urals were. She missed Captain Gallo terribly.

It was nice to have someone to talk to sensibly amid her ever shifting sea of goats. And now that the newness was off her relationship with Volos, she found she could converse easily with him and several other members of what was becoming her household. She needed this human connection. Sophia was becoming fretful that Millicent and Sangfroid, and especially dear Gallo, had not yet rescued her. She hoped everyone was safe but would have preferred for them to come searching for her quicker. She itched to be home. Being abroad was far too foreign. But wherever it was that Hubert's machine had deposited her, she knew it was best to stay close to her disembarkation point. That way, she would be easily located when the others eventually bothered to turn up. It was all very vexing.

"Please, lady of the tea, meet my grandson." Volos introduced a teenage boy. "This is Heron. He is staying here with me until he gets word to join his father in Alexandria."

"Egypt? How lovely. You will see the pyramids, Heron," she said, and indicated the boy should sit beside her. His shy gaze fixed upon the pot boiling on the fire. The steam lifted the clay lid up and down with an irregular clatter. It seemed to fascinate him.

"Ah." Sophia noticed his attention to the steaming pot. "The power of steam, Heron. See how the pressure builds up and lifts the lid? My fiancé, Hubert, did many wonderful things with steam pressure. Why, it could even be used to turn that spit." She pointed to the current goat-on-a-spit. It had become a chief staple of her new diet, along with mountain greens stewed in lemon water. There was always some poor kitchen waif turning the spit handle while their shins roasted.

The boy's eyes shimmered with intelligence. He had immediately understood her implication. Sophia concluded there was more going on in his head than most of the villagers combined.

"I like the steam, oh lady of the steam power," he said, with a reverence worthy of his grandfather. Sophia was pleased, perhaps she should teach these people some rudimentary science? After all, the youth of the valley should learn how to improve the quality of life in this barren place. And it would certainly pass the time for her. What a delicious thing to tell Millicent when next they met. That would certainly stop her crowing about free education for the wastrels and the waifs she was always fretting over. Millicent could hardly preach to the converted, now could she?

"Tea?" Sophia offered generously, despite her dwindling supply. "We really do need to source more of the stuff." She looked pointedly at Volos. Heron supped from his clay cup, savouring the unusual taste.

"We will go to China and India and get this for you, lady of the steam." Volos slapped a hand on his heart. "We will we demand it in your name," he proclaimed. "Ah. But what will we say?" he asked, a little uncertainly.

"Why, ask for tea, of course," Sophia told him. "Loose leaf tea."

"Looselea." Volos tried to wrap his tongue around the words.

"Loose leaf," Sophia corrected. "Ask for loose leaf."

"For our lady, Looselea, goddess of tea, we get more tea." He smiled in satisfaction. There was a valley full of men who would make it so. An army of acolytes.

"And steam power," Heron added. "Our goddess of steam power," he said shyly, and Sophia laughed gaily at their rustic whimsy.

Chapter 21

THE WALL PROVED LESS SCALABLE than Millicent had hoped. No matter how much she scrabbled for a foothold, she found it impossible, and she was soon dragged down into the courtyard. A furious Cybele towered over her.

"Is this how you repay my kindness?" She slapped Millicent across her unbruised cheek, though this time Millicent did not fall. Two burly slaves held her by her arms, keeping her upright despite her sagging knees. A crowd had gathered, and to the back of it, Jana stood wringing her hands with huge tears welling in her frightened eyes. Cassian and Belarus pushed to the fore, anxious to see all, eyes slick with malicious excitement.

"You are not worthy of the tea," Cybele yelled. "A little chit from the colonies, I'll have you whipped raw."

"You'll ruin her!" Cassian cried. "Let me take her off your hands. I'll give you a fair price."

"You?" Cybele turned her fury onto him, and he took a step back. "A fair price? You owe me your house, you idiot! You have nothing. Nothing." Then her eyes narrowed, as a vicious thought occurred. "Actually, she is worth more than a whipping." She gave Millicent an insolent, speculative stare. "In fact, a despoiled tea maid could be worth a lot of coin to the games master." The crowd gasped, and Millicent heard a squeak of despair from Jana.

"Despoiled!" Millicent was outraged and struggled against the hands holding her. "You, who run a house of ill repute, dare to call me desp—"

"Yes. I think I will sell you to Master Kronos," Cybele talked over her as if she hadn't uttered a word. "It's good marketing. The public needs to see a tea maid torn to shreds. They've been sullen lately. Slow to pay their taxes. This will cheer them up. I might even make it an annual thing." Her idea of marketing worked; a ripple of excitement ran through the crowd.

"I'd rather death than stay at this filthy bordello. Good riddance to you, you violent, ham-fisted lady-lout." Millicent's deprecation earned her another blow. One that left her ears ringing.

"What a delicious idea." Belarus cooed. "Two gold pieces says she's disembowelled before the quarter bell. Takers?"

"Three for a beheading." Someone in the crowd took him on.

"Shut up." Cassian hissed at Belarus. "Cybele, you know I am waiting for money from Athens. Surely we can do a deal?"

"I've been waiting on your money for over a year, Cassian," Cybele interrupted. "Is it coming from Athens by three-legged donkey?" Her joke earned Cassian the scornful laughter of her lackeys. With a satisfied smirk on her over-rouged face she signalled for Millicent to be dragged away. "Take her to the Belly, and book me a premier box for tomorrow's games. I want to see this first hand. Ten gold on a beheading," she told Belarus as she stomped back into the temple.

At least I've found the door. Millicent tried to put on a brave, if bruised, face as she was dragged away. Jana's fretful eyes told her this was trouble. If the bookmaking going on in the crowd was anything to go by, it was serious trouble.

Master Kronos smelled. His men smelled, too, but not as evilly as Kronos did. It was more than body odour and bad meat breath. It was more than the filthy stains on his uniform, or the greasy strings of hair that hung from his tonsured crown. It was as if he was decaying inwardly, and a sour and insidious stench seeped from every pore. Proximity to him was toxic. Not that Millicent had any intention of proximity. She reared backwards on introduction, swallowing down a rush of bile to her throat.

"Another prisoner for tomorrow's games. This one came in with an invoice." The soldier tossed her into a small guardroom. Kronos sat on a stool by a fire pit watching a game of dice. His men played for a prize of crusty old sandals.

"We got our lot already. Cells is crammed with felons and they're for free." He didn't look up. He slouched like a poisonous toad, oily and odious, overseeing the game. "Why'd I pay for another one, 'eh?"

"This one's a special delivery from the tea," her escort said, and gave Millicent an unnecessary dig in the ribs with his spiked truncheon, no doubt hoping for her to squeal.

She squirmed away and gave him a hard look. After a quick hike through the night streets, Cybele's slaves had carted her down to the arena. They had moved fast, as if embarrassed by their assignment, and loathed to draw attention to themselves. They delivered her to the Belly's rear entrance with the greatest deference, along with a letter from Cybele; and with obvious relief, turned for home without a backwards glance.

The night watch officer had not been impressed to have an extra administrative duty dumped on him at this late hour. He muttered as he processed Millicent in double quick time, then ordered another guard to herd her down a maze of gloomy corridors to the cells, and to Kronos.

"The tea, 'eh?" That caught Kronos's attention, and the guards at his feet stopped gambling long enough to look her over. "What have we 'ere, boys?" Kronos squinted at her. "A little urn, is it?"

Millicent did not like the sniggers that followed his remark, and she drew herself up to her full, if ineffectual, height.

"Most definitely not," she said in her primmest voice. She knew precisely what being an urn meant, and had no truck with this ribaldry.

"Where will you put her, boss?" one of his men asked.

"I've no idea." He scratched his stubbly chin and came over to inspect her. Millicent leaned as far from him as was possible, preferring to press back against the spiked truncheon. He was foul. "If the tea sent her over, you can bet she'll cost a pretty penny. She ain't any old dog meat." The guard handed over Cybele's letter, and Kronos unfolded the parchment and scanned its contents. Millicent could tell from the unfocussed flicker of his eyes that he could barely read. This was casual bravado before his men. Up close, as she unfortunately was, beads of sweat formed on his bald pate with the effort.

"Severus will be expecting something grand with an urn in the ring," another guard said. They all pondered this, then Kronos sighed heavily.

"S'pose so." He considered his options. "Put 'er with the Amazons for the meantime. That other lot will kill her if they get so much as a sniff. They'd crunch yer pelvic bones to dust, sweetheart," he told Millicent with a leer, "and spit you out. And I got other animals to do that, not a hoard of barbarians from the provinces."

"There's already a book on how she tops it." The soldier who brought her to Kronos was eager to gossip. "The big money's on beheading."

"Is it now?" Kronos looked interested at this. "What are the odds for eaten by beasts?"

The soldier shrugged. "Most reckon the barbarians will snuff her."

Kronos sucked on his yellow teeth. "Bring 'er here." He indicated they follow him down a passage that spiralled farther into the bowels of the building. He waited until they were several paces into the descent before bringing the guard up short.

"Tomorrow I want you go to the bookies and put all this," he said quietly as he handed the soldier a bag of coins, "on her being eaten alive. See if you can squeeze out extra odds on 'em starting on her headfirst."

"Wot, headfirst?" The guard repeated surprised.

"The biggest bugger will go for her first. Right for the throat, gets in the kill that way, see. Then the rest will rip out her guts."

"There's five to one odds it'll be the guts first." The young soldier smiled, fascinated at this insider information. Millicent was horrified. They were talking about her death as if she were not even there.

"Yeah. The first one pulls out her throat and chews on her face. Trust me, I see it all the time. Bet on her going headfirst." Kronos tapped his nose. "Might as well earn a few denarii if there's a book on."

The soldier looked impressed and pocketed the purse. "You gonna arrange for her to go in with the beasts then?"

"Course I am. I'll make it look legit though. You just get that whack on first thing tomorrow morning, right?"

"Right."

"How can you bargain with people's lives like that?" Millicent demanded. Kronos gripped her arm in a tight squeeze that cut short Millicent's chastisement. "Ouch!"

"You need to see this, sweetheart." He pulled her into a side passage. "The posh ones always need to see, so they understand." He smiled coldly and winked at the soldier.

The smell of faeces and rotten flesh gagged Millicent more than his rough treatment ever could. To open her mouth in this vile air was to invite disease. She pulled the neck of her tunic to cover her nose and mouth. Her eyes stung with the astringency. On either side of the corridor were cells with walls almost up to her shoulder in height. They were topped with strong iron bars. From behind the bars came the cries of wild animals. Lions, bears, wolves—any predator she could think of—roared out in desperation. The sound rose to a deafening crescendo as they moved along the stone floors strewn with filthy straw. Dung was heaped on either side of a stagnant gully that failed to flush away the dirty water, blood, and urine. The overspill filmed the floor with a layer of putrid scum.

"Hesta's tits! It stinks in here." The soldier choked out, covering his mouth and nose with his hand.

Kronos laughed, unaffected by the stench. A cart rolled past pushed by a slave, naked save for a scrap of a loincloth. Sweat traced patterns in the dirt of his body. The cart he was pushing was nothing more than a high-sided wooden box on wheels, and whatever was in it stank. Bloated blowflies hovered lazily over the contents.

"Suppertime." Kronos grinned and rubbed his hands together. "We're in for a treat." He freed a pitchfork tethered to the side of the cart and stood on the rim of a wheel to peer inside. Grunting with effort he poked about with this fork until, with a satisfied smack of his lips, he pulled out an unidentifiable hunk of rotting meat. It was thick with gristle and strings of white fat. With a practiced flick he pitched it into the nearest cage. The snarling and snapping from within rose to a crazed level. Millicent and the soldier shrank back. Kronos laughed at them, and again rummaged around in the cart for another chunk of meat.

"The trick is to keep 'em hungry but not weak. They have to perform after all," he said, and skewered another solid lump to the end of his pitchfork. Millicent recoiled into the soldier, who in turn backed off as the foul meat swept inches past their faces before being thrust into the next cell. This was a long bony hank of meat covered with grey mottled flesh. Threads of sinew dangled from one end and at the other hung a human hand. If she hadn't her back pressed against the soldier, Millicent would have slid to the floor in horror. Instead, the soldier pushed her aside, and vomited wetly into the overflowing gully at their feet. Kronos howled with laughter and climbed down off the cart.

"You are a wicked, wicked man." Millicent gasped into the fabric covering her mouth. She fought back her tears and tried to mask the terror she knew he wanted to raise in her. She would not give this evil creature the pleasure of seeing her cry.

"I am the games master," Kronos said. "I need to put on the best show possible for our divine lord on earth, Emperor Severus. Or I'll be in that bleedin' cart." He tossed the pitchfork to the slave, who fumbled his unexpected catch and dropped it. Kronos scowled, then turned his attention back to Millicent.

"It ain't easy dreaming up amusing new themes for that sadistic little godling." Kronos warmed to his rant. "He wants art, and theatrics, and splendour beyond all imagining." He flung his arms up in exasperation. "He wants an Olympics of gore and gut shredding death, with all the dramaticals of the Muses. He wants grandeur and artistry and manslaughter aplenty. And it's *me* has to deliver it." He thumbed his chest and leaned into Millicent's partly covered face. "Them that go into the arena deserve to die. They fucked up and guess what, life is hard and no one gives a shit, not even the gods. And as for this." He pointed over his shoulder to the cart. "These bastards were too lame, or stupid, or weak, to survive a bleedin' blink in that arena. They're not good enough to die in it. Therefore, they are not entertaining nor dramatical. They're only use to me is as animal fodder. So, what do you want to be, little urn, 'eh? Fodder, or fighter? You can choose here and now, 'cos either way you're gonna die." He withdrew a dagger from his belt and toyed with the point, drawing a small bead of blood from his thumb. Millicent prayed he'd contract septicaemia before the end of the week.

The slave began to push his fodder cart past them when Kronos stopped him. "And where do you think you're going?" he asked.

The slave looked down at his feet, afraid to meet Kronos's eyes. "The fodder is getting low, and Master Milo wants me to go feed the herbivores next."

"Herbivores? Herbivores!" Kronos slapped the slave around the head. "The bleedin' cattle are the fodder, you harpy's tit!"

"Not the cattle; the herb—" The slaves words stopped abruptly as he realized he had spoken out of turn and with no deference. It was too late to retract. Kronos plunged his dagger straight into the slave's heart. His whole body jerked in shock. For an instant his stunned gaze locked with Millicent's, and then he toppled towards the slurry. Kronos grabbed him before he hit the floor. With surprising strength he bundled the warm body up the high sides and into the cart.

"There's more fodder for you." He grunted with satisfaction.

"Oh, shit," the soldier muttered, shaken at the whole experience. Millicent, on the other hand, was more verbose. She opened her mouth and screamed.

Kronos raised his hand to strike her, when a bellow came from farther down the corridor. An angry, anxious shout that out-roared even the loudest beast. "Millicent! Millicent! Millicent!"

"'Ere, is that you? Are you Millicent?" Kronos hesitated, interested at this development. Millicent nodded wordlessly.

"Sounds like you got a friend?" Kronos took her arm. "Someone to show you the ropes, 'eh?" he said and dragged her towards the shouting. "Ain't that lucky."

The soft shift of the fire embers awoke Gallo. She was unsurprised such a small sound had alarmed her, even in her sleep. It was the soft, sneaky sounds that killed you.

The Belly was hardly a restful place. Beasts howled endlessly, and the animal handlers were equally as loud with their cussing and threats to their charges. But these were distant, unthreatening sounds. She considered rousing herself and saving the fire, then decided if she was going to die in a few hours she might as well get her rest. Every ounce of strength would count tomorrow. Gallo dropped her head onto her arm and curled tighter into the foetal position she preferred to sleep in; it made her a smaller target and kept her body core warm. Old battlefield habits die hard.

She tucked her chin farther into her chest, trying to get comfortable, when above the din she heard a woman scream. Not unusual, women had been screaming all night long. Toxis had delighted in telling her that local felons were sometimes butchered and fed to the animals. It kept their strength up and the taste of human blood gave an edge to their hunger. Human meat was a treat for these monsters, once tasted never forgotten. This scream was different though. It had a ring to it, a quality that triggered something in Gallo's mind. She was on her feet in a flash. Her sudden movement sent her cellmates scrambling, instantly ready for action.

"What is it?" Alkaia was at her side at once.

"I recognize that scream," Gallo said, moving to the bars and peering anxiously into the dark. "Millicent! Millicent!" She roared, so fiercely even the beasts were still for a moment. "Millicent!"

"Gallo?" The call came back, pinched and fearful. "Oh, merciful heavens. Gallo, is that you?" She could hear tearfulness of Millicent's voice, and she gripped the bars tighter. There was movement farther down the dim passage. Someone with a lantern was coming towards her cell.

"It's Kronos," Alkaia said. "Wonder what the fat slob wants?" The flicker of weak light grew steadily until the games master appeared. He dragged another person along with him. Gallo could make out the form of a woman clamped tightly by the arm, and her heart beat faster.

"Millicent?" she called again.

"It's me." The answer echoed back to her.

"Visitor for you, ladies." Kronos fumbled for his keys. "Seeing as how you all know each other, you can bunk up. I was gonna give her to the Bull men, but apparently she's worth her bustle in gold and needs to be kept in one piece for a while longer." He clanked open the door and pushed Millicent into the cell so roughly that she fell. "Here's a tea maiden all of your own, ladies." He sneered. "Mind your taxes are all paid up." Then he slammed the door and stomped away.

"Hey." Gallo helped Millicent find her feet. "Are you all right? What the hell happened? Where have you been?"

"That man is perfectly horrid." Millicent blinked back her tears and rubbed her arm where a deep bruise was already forming. "Oh, Gallo. I'm so happy to see you," she said and flung herself into Gallo's arms, much to the warrior's surprise.

"Shush," she soothed, and wrapped Millicent in a warm hug. "We've found each other, haven't we? That's got to be good. Two down and two to go. Soon we'll all be together again and can get out of here. Have you seen Sangfroid or Sophia?" she asked.

"I was hoping they were with you." Millicent snuffled into Gallo's chest.

"Is that your missus?" Hipp asked, with interest.

"No," Gallo answered. "She's my mate's missus. Well, sort of. It's complicated."

Millicent pulled away and scrubbed her eyes with the back of her hand, trying to hide her embarrassment. Gallo noted the soiled tunic; obviously a lot had happened.

"Come here and get warm." She sat Millicent down by the fire and built up the embers into a blaze. The Amazons hovered nearby, interested in this new development, but keeping a polite distance until Millicent recovered her composure.

"Where have you been?" Gallo asked gently. Whatever had happened, it had shaken this stern little woman to the core.

"I landed in a fish market, of all places. And a man called Cassian took me to the tea temple. Oh, Gallo, it's awful out there. This city is so strange and cruel, and in the centre of it sits this...this...cult that Sophia has somehow propagated. And it's terrible!"

"Have you any idea where Sophia might be?" Hope brimmed in Gallo's voice.

Millicent shook her head. "Apart from an enormous statue of her, there was no sign. I was hoping she'd be at the temple, but it's too well established. It's as if Sophia were here years and years ago when the tea religion was new. Now it's no more than a church of corruption and decadence, and the average Roman citizen hates it."

"You mean Sophia's been here before?" Gallo frowned at this. She found all this travelling through time hard to keep up with no matter how much Sangfroid explained it. And she was rubbish at explaining anything, anyway. If it wasn't a gun or a military action, Sangfroid didn't give a dung beetle's fart about it.

"I don't think Sophia is here now," Millicent said. "She was in the time machine a little bit longer than we were. It may have seemed like a fraction of a second to us, but Lord knows what it means in timeline orientation. There could be hundreds of years difference in where we landed."

"It's like me being only a few steps ahead of you on the Amoebas and ending up in the coal cellar. Look where I landed this time," Gallo said bitterly. "Will we ever find her, do you think?" She had to ask, though she knew the odds were grim.

Millicent shook her head. "I have no idea. What about Sangfroid?"

"Not a sniff." They slumped before the fire, stared dully into the flames and leaned into each other for comfort.

"Is this another messenger?" Alkaia appeared at Gallo's side, looking intently at Millicent.

"Well, she's brought no good news," Gallo said. "So I'm not sure."

"Do you worship Looselea?" Alkaia asked Millicent directly. "You said you were at the tea temple."

"I certainly do not." Millicent was adamant. "I've never seen such a crowd of ne'er-do-well reprobates in all my life. They are corrupt, and offensive, and cruel. They may as well worship rats for the way they get on."

"That's religion for you," Alkaia said.

"Well, holy rats or not, there is obviously some divine plan in place for you both to turn up here," Toxis said.

Gallo and Millicent swapped glances. If there was a divine plan in place, they were the last to know.

Chapter 22

"It's dawn." Hipp rose from her crouch by the dead fire.

"How do you know?" Millicent asked. The unrelenting gloom gave her no indication as to what time of day it was. She was exhausted; unable to sleep even a wink though those around her, including Gallo, had somehow managed to doze off. She now watched enviously as her companions stood and stretched and looked keen to face the new day.

"I can hear a different pattern to the way the guards are working," Hipp said. "Also, our firewood and food have run out. I'd say that's the end of the hospitality. Time to earn our keep."

"What do you think will happen?" Millicent asked Gallo in a low voice.

"No idea." She shrugged. "These guys are Amazons. They're here for Severus Ex's games, so I guess we go to the arena at some point and fight."

"Severus Ex?" Millicent asked.

"He's the current Emperor, and to my recollection, he's a right bastard."

"Oh." She did not know the name Severus Ex from the list of Roman Emperors she'd had to memorize as a schoolgirl.

"Sorry for cursing," Gallo said, and her sudden gallantry surprised Millicent. "I know you hate B words, but he is an

Alpha bastard. And it won't be long until you agree...even if you don't say it like I do."

"I am sure I will come up with something appropriate," she said. "Gallo, will we be out there with...with the animals?" She remembered Kronos's bet and desperately hoped Gallo would say something good, something to hold onto, that would inspire hope.

"Hell, yeah." Gallo cracked her knuckles and grinned. "But we'll have weapons, and if you stick by me, we might even stand a chance."

"We will fight with valour and die with honour." Alkaia joined them, offering a flask of water. "It's a win-win."

Millicent failed to see the first win, nevermind the second.

"If you say so, but I'm not very good at fighting," she said, though didn't add she'd been rather good at dying recently. All her attempts at rescuing Sangfroid had ended in death. How would this adventure end? Hubert had always been waiting at home for her on the other end of the time machine, reeling her in back in. He had literally been her lifeline. This time, there was no one to bring them back. They could all die here and that would be that. Hopelessness washed over her. She sank down beside the fire pit and stared at the ashes while her cellmates chatted amiably around her. A mid-morning meal of bread and water was finally delivered.

"When do we go in?" Alkaia asked one of the guards.

"You're keen." The guard sneered through his brown teeth. "You'll go in after the Bull men. They're on with the charioteers. Better be a good match. It's been a slow morning, and the crowd's bored."

"Has the Emperor arrived yet?" Toxis asked.

"Nah, probably not out of bed yet. He never arrives until after noon anyway."

"All these warriors came to fight as tribute, and he's not even here?" Alkaia was outraged.

The guard shrugged. "People tell 'im who was good and who was shit. He's only interested in the animal fights anyways. More fun."

"And we're with the animals?" Alkaia asked.

Another shrug. "Kronos decides that. But he put a bundle down on that one," he pointed at Millicent, "having her face eaten off, so I reckon you'll be with the beasts, and good luck to you." He sauntered off, whistling chirpily while they digested this news.

"Yes!" Hipp punched the air. "We got the beasts!"

"And Severus Ex will be there to see us fight." Toxis and Alkaia slapped each other on the back in congratulations.

"And why is this good?" Millicent turned to find Gallo doing a gleeful little jig behind her.

"It's what they came here for." Gallo indicated the Amazons. "I'm happy for them. But you know what would be good," she said. "What would be really good? Is if we could get a counter bet that Millicent keeps her face. We could easily swing the odds by protecting her." She slipped Millicent a sly wink.

The Amazons stilled their back slapping and listened. The smell of a wager caught their attention.

"We could come away rich." Gallo drove home her point. "Of course, it would only work if we were alive, as well as honourable."

"I like your thinking," Alkaia said. "I'd love to beat these Roman turds at their own game. Especially if Kronos lost the butt-wipe toga off his back."

"I like it, too," Millicent said. "The keeping-my-face-on part in particular, but how do we wager? I mean do we even have any money to invest?"

"Amazon's always have money," Hipp said happily. "We're great traders." She jingled a little pouch hanging discreetly from her belt. Millicent noticed that all the Amazons had them.

"Great gamblers more like." Gallo snorted. "The Amazon nation was renowned for gambling," she informed Millicent, who struggled not to look disapproving.

"It comes from living on the edge of extinction," Alkaia said. "We don't call it gambling; that sounds like we're reckless. We call it trading in odds. And this is a good trade, especially as we are in control of the odds."

"I've got no denarii," Gallo said sadly, "and neither has Millicent, or I'd be in there with you."

"We've got my face," Millicent spoke up. "Gallo and I put my face into the pot. You can't win if I run face first at a lion."

"True, but unlikely. Look, as its Gallo's idea, and your face, we'll cut you in on a share. One share split between the two of you." Alkaia cut the deal, and Gallo and Millicent agreed.

"Your face is safe with us." Hipp slapped Millicent on the shoulder and unbalanced her. "Even if you do die we guarantee you'll be a pretty corpse."

"She won't die. I won't let her. Now, how do we place the bet?" Gallo asked. "I wouldn't trust that guard as far as I could gob."

"In the Belly?" Alkaia said. "The bookie always comes to you. Guard!" she yelled, and slammed the bars until they rang.

"Yeah?" The eager, stained smile was back at the cell door. The guard was obviously fascinated by the Amazons.

"Get me a bookie. The one Kronos uses," Alkaia ordered. The guard's eyes gleamed and without hesitation he disappeared down the corridor.

"Can you hear that?" Toxis hushed them all. They stood silently and strained their ears. A rumbling permeated the depths of the dungeon. Then a soft series of crashes and a distinct roar of a thousand voices, though it was muted and sounded far off.

"Sounds like the Bull men are pleasing the crowd," Hipp said, matter of fact.

"Nobody likes the charioteers. It's like cheating having them in there." Toxis grumbled.

"Yes?" A polished voice called from the corridor. A strange man stood by the cell bars. He contrasted greatly with his surroundings in that he was clean. "You asked for me?" he said impatiently.

"We want to place a bet," Alkaia said. She went over to the bars. She towered over the man so that he nervously stepped back, though not without checking where he placed his foot first.

"I am Maximum." He cleared his throat and got down to business. "What can I do for you?"

Alkaia jingled her coin pouch, and Maximum leaned a little closer. "I hear Kronos put a big bet on with you earlier," she said.

"The tea maiden being eaten? Yes. It's an obvious hedged bet as he is the games master, but the populous have responded well. Though those not in the know favour disembowelment, so the odds are lively." He sniffed in satisfaction. "Nobody likes the tea. It's good morale for the people to see an urn savaged to death once in a while. I'm hoping it becomes a regular event."

"Oh, well, if it's good for morale..." Millicent muttered.

"Well, this purse says she won't be eaten." Alkaia jingled it again. The other Amazons jingled theirs. Maximum bristled with excitement.

"And as it's for the people...well..." Millicent continued to mutter.

"Shush." Gallo nudged her.

"Great Jupiter, is that her?" Maximum zoned in on Millicent. "Are you sure about this? She looks like fodder to me. I thought she would be bigger."

"Well, excuse me, but I happen to be the average height for an Englishwoman." Millicent prepared to launch a castigation when Gallo stilled her with a stern glance.

"Odds?" Alkaia growled, and the threat in her voice focused Maximum back on business. The odds were set and agreed, and the coin purses were handed over in exchange for a scrap of betting papyrus. Alkaia thrust the marker down her breastplate.

Maximum left quickly, weighing a lot more than when he'd arrived and looking very pleased. Another roar drifted down from the arena, louder, and more bloodthirsty.

"Sounds like the Bull men and charioteers are almost done," Toxis said. "Wonder if we're next?"

The answer came quickly. Kronos appeared and squinted through the bars.

"Ready, girls?" he asked. He lifted a heavy ring of keys from his belt and unlocked the door. His guards hovered behind him, waiting to escort the Amazons to the arena. Kronos nodded and a pile of heavy chains was thrown onto the cell floor. "Your game is dead weight," he said in a flat voice.

"Dead weight. Against beasts?" Alkaia spat on the floor. "You cheating filth."

The Amazons began to crowd Kronos forcing him out into the corridor where his guards anxiously readied their spears. He looked rattled and angry and pointed to the chains.

"You can put 'em on and fight, or you can die down here like cowards. Not much of a tribute that, 'eh? Severus won't be too pleased, now will he?"

"Dead weight is useless sport against animals. It's better to fight them freely, face to face," Toxis objected. "Every harpy's hole knows that."

"Should've thought about that before betting against me, then, 'eh?" Kronos sneered. "Think I wouldn't know what's going on in me own jail? Sort it out. I'll be back." And he slammed the door shut.

"What's dead weight?" Millicent asked Gallo.

"I have no idea." She shook her head and looked over at the irate Amazons.

"It's when two fighters are chained together by the ankle," Hipp answered. "It's called dead weight 'cos if one of you gets wounded or killed the other is stuck dragging a dead weight around the arena. Sort of shortens your life expectancy a little.

And it's crap against beasts 'cos it curtails movement. No leaps, no somersaults, no back flips, or climbing. It's crap! Just crap!" She was shaking with anger. It was a terrible insult for a warrior to die in chains.

"Kronos is a sticky bastard. He's pushing the odds in his favour." Toxis toed the chains. "What are we going to do?" she asked Alkaia.

"We work the odds, like always," she answered. "Gallo, you're with Millicent. All you need do is guard her. The rest of you, tether up and keep these two away from anything pointy, and that means weapons as well as teeth. I reckon there'll be more than beasts in with us. Kronos is a sore loser. He'll try and cheat us any way he can."

They paired up and locked the manacles around their ankles. The guards reappeared wheezing under the bundles of Amazon weapons they carried. Kronos was noticeably absent this time.

"I'd have stuck this up his arse, and he knows it," Toxis hissed, as she examined her sword blade lovingly. "I missed you, baby," she said and kissed it.

"They've had these all night. Check nothing is damaged or blunted," Alkaia ordered her warriors. The Amazon weapons were a mixture of short swords, spears, and their famous labrys axes.

"We're not allowed bows," Hipp said sadly. "They took all our weapons away when we arrived, but at least we can fight with our own gear and not their crappy junk." She ran her thumb along a blade and smiled in satisfaction at the beads of blood forming on her flesh.

Gallo snapped the cold iron manacle around Millicent's ankle. It weighed a ton, she had no idea how she could walk in it, nevermind run. And she intended to do a lot of that.

"Here." Gallo handed her a trident. "Just poke at anything you don't like the look of." She selected a sword for herself and looked at it admiringly. "Nice workmanship. I'm glad you brought extras," she told Alkaia and got an approving smile in return.

"This way." The guard swung open the door.

They clanked along the slow rise of corridors from the lower cellblocks to the arena's main passageway. Each step brought the cries of the crowd and the thumping of their feet on the stadium floor closer. The gloom began to lighten, and the smoke from the oil lanterns drifted higher on fresh currents of air.

"How did the Bull men do? Was Severus Ex impressed?" Hipp asked.

"He's still not here," the guard grumbled. They finally converged out of the gloom and into a wide, clean tunnel that had daylight pouring in from one end. The roar of the crowd was deafening. At the end of the tunnel massive wooden doors stood shut against the noise and the glare of sunlight. The arena was on the other side. Millicent's heart thumped so hard her breastbone hurt.

The doors creaked open, and blinding sunlight shot down the passageway. Dust billowed in on a hot wind, and the incessant din of the crowd rolled like thunder along the tunnel walls. Guards herded in the dregs of the previous match, while slaves hauled in several steam driven chariots. These machines were no more than huge bronze boxes with a vicious array of blades and scythes protruding from all sides. They were horseless, manoeuvred by steam, and they had been wholly battered. A few still had wheels in working order, though several had their wheels missing and had to be manhandled into the tunnel. They were weighty things and ploughed furrows in the dirt floor. Each chariot burped sad, irregular puffs of steam from small funnels. Their side panels, which once were elaborately embossed in bronze, now had great lumps of decoration torn off or bent into odd angles. Rivets had popped and seams burst open. Despite their weight they looked like toys tossed around by ill-tempered children.

Millicent was alarmed to see blood flowing freely through the open seams. She realized these were not automated chariots; men were inside to drive the machines that now served as their coffins.

Behind this limping procession came three huge men. They had the skins of black bulls draped over their shoulders like cloaks. The bull's head, horns still intact perched over their foreheads. *These are the Bull men.* Millicent had as good as expected Minotaurs, and her blood ran cold remembering Kronos's threat to throw her to them last night. They looked savage. Blood and sweat ran down their bare chests. As they drew level with the Amazons they gave each other curt nods of respect. No words were spoken. These were warrior races brought here on a madman's bidding, killing at his whim.

Bringing up the rear, and dragged through the sand by their heels, came the dead. Several of the Bull men, and two of the charioteers who had been prized out from their mechanical shells and slaughtered. These bodies were badly broken, limbs falling unnaturally, and skin split and burned by blasts of steam.

Millicent turned away. Every time she left her own timeline, she arrived in someone else's hell. On the Amoebas, she had seen such carnage that her legs became numb and heavy and her head swam nauseatingly. It was the same here. Her sweaty grasp became slick on the iron of her trident.

"You lot will go in with the felons." A guard barked out his orders.

"Why are there felons in with us?" Alkaia frowned.

"Kronos says the more the merrier. They're chained together just like you."

"They'll only get in the way." Alkaia snarled. "The whole thing is a joke. Kronos is a weak, cheating bastard. Why can't we have a good, clean fight?"

"Is it bad that there are others in with is?" Millicent asked.

"It will be chaos," Hipp said. "Kronos is piling everything in at once. It's just a gore fest."

"It's got nothing to do with us fighting honourably now." Toxis was livid. "It's all to hinder us saving you so he wins the bet. Asshole."

"It'll be okay." Gallo squeezed her shoulder. "We have a plan, and we'll stick to it."

The guards herded them through the doors and out into the heat of the arena. The crowd howled at the sight of chained Amazons. Millicent was unprepared for the actual size of the Belly, especially from her viewpoint in the naval of it. It was dizzyingly huge, capable of holding tens of thousands. And tens of thousands were there right now. Tiers upon tiers of them, rising up to dizzying heights until lost to view in the glaring sunlight. The arena floor was a rough mix of sand and grit. It slid into Millicent's delicate tea maid sandals and cut the soles of her feet like powdered glass. Blood, lumps of skin tissue, and glutinous human organs stained the centre, churning it up into a red mud field.

Half of the cavernous bowl baked in the heat, the other half sat in shadow. Millicent's eyes had barely adjusted, when a movement on the far side of the arena caught her attention. A pair of doors matching those she had just come through began to open. The crowd bayed like hounds. The noise was overwhelming as another contingent of fighters entered the arena.

"It's the felons," Toxis said.

"Keep your backs to the sun," Alkaia said. "Use your armour to blind any incoming."

On the far side, the felons were being forcibly pushed from the murk of the tunnel out into the blare and light. They were chained in pairs, just as the Amazons were. The felons looked ragged and exhausted. Weapons hung from limp hands, as if they'd already accepted their pitiful fate. They stood dazed, stunned by the vast spectacle around them. Animals poured into the arena with them, running freely. Not the fierce predators that had roared all night in the cells below, but oxen, camels, mules, and horses; all skin and bone, and staggering in shock at the noise. In their clumsy, side-stepping anxiety they barrelled into each other and knocked felons aside. It was chaotic and clownish, and the crowd laughed—a great rumbling sound that scared the poor beasts further.

"I wish Sangfroid was here," Millicent whispered. A dreadful sense of doom had descended on her. In every direction lay cruelty and bloodlust. She was surrounded by apathy and malevolence, and she could bear it no longer. She was terrified.

"Yeah, me too. She'd mind our backs all right," Gallo said, looking around her with interest.

"I don't know how you can be so casual." Millicent was amazed at Gallo's fortitude. "This has to be—"

"Oh, look. There she is!" Gallo interrupted her.

"Who?" Millicent tried to follow her gaze.

"Sangfroid."

"Sangfroid!" Millicent squealed in disbelief. Her heart hammered in her throat. "Where? Oh, where Gallo? Show me!"

"There." Gallo pointed across the arena into the far gate. "Chained to that elephant." She frowned. "Poor bastard. That's not lucky."

Chapter 23

Sangfroid felt the opposite of lucky and had done so for some time. She'd landed ass first in the middle of a guardhouse game of knucklebones. It was immediately assumed she'd jumped in to steal the winnings. At first she'd been amused they thought she'd even want to steal a ratty old cloak and some copper coins. Then they pounced. It didn't take long for her boots to be ripped off, and for her to be roughed up and dumped in a cell with the smelliest, most woebegone criminals she'd ever encountered.

"Steal yer boots, did they, son?" A grizzled old man sidled up to her as she dabbed the blood off her nose. "They oughta be locked up with us," the old boy tutted. "They think they can do whatever they want in here. It's double standards, is what it is."

"Where exactly is here?" Sangfroid asked, once again parking her disbelief that her gender had been so easily reassigned. She scanned the cell, hoping for a glimpse of untidy chestnut hair and an impossibly impractical dress, but Millicent was nowhere to be seen. She pushed down her panic and prayed that Millicent was safe wherever she was. There was no sign of Sophia or Gallo either and that worried her as well. They had all travelled here together, so why were they separated now? She wanted to regroup and get the hell out of this timeline. And she wanted her boots back.

"Got big feet, ain't ya?" The old man seemed transfixed by them. "Biggest I ever seen," he said, not without awe.

"Where are we?" Sangfroid asked again. She added a soupçon of threat to her voice. The old guy was shrunken. He looked about a hundred years old and was as skinny as a rake. He wore what looked to be a sack tied at the waist with a bit of twine. His feet were bare, filthy, and pitifully deformed. Sangfroid's darkened tone caught his attention, and he answered, "Why, we're in the Belly waiting to be fed to the lions, son." He sounded almost cheery.

"What's the Belly?" She already knew, but wanted confirmation for the leaden feeling forming in her gut.

"You're new in town." This seemed to amuse the old man for he wheezed out a laugh crossed with a death rattle. "The Belly is the biggest arena in Rome. In the whole world, in fact and we're here 'cos we've been rounded up for Severus Ex's games."

"Severus Ex?" Sangfroid frowned. This was not good. "Not Severus ex Machina?" Just her luck to materialize in the reign of one of the nastiest Emperors ever. Severus Ex was a gallstone to the gods themselves, nevermind his own people.

"That's the shit, all right," the old man confirmed. "What's yer name, son? Whatya in for? You look more like a fighter than a thief."

"I am a fighter." Sangfroid surveyed the overcrowded cell, the solid iron bars, and the hellish noises from outside. The cries of man and animal mixed into one distressed cacophony—and at top volume. "What's that racket? Sounds like a farmyard on fire."

"It's the animals they keep to feed the predators. I'm Michael, by the way. Who are you?"

"Sangfroid. What predators?"

"Sounds Gallic. Are you Gallic? That might account for the feet."

"I'm from…the Urals." Sangfroid thought it best not to mention moon base Alpha Zeta IV.

"Never heard of any Urals. Where's that? Near Gaul?"

"Yeah, near Gaul. Now, about these predators."

"They're what we fight," Michael said. "Man-eating beasts. Look around you. As if any of us could fight. We've been locked up in the city prisons for months waiting for this day. We're nothing but a sideshow to keep the crowds happy."

"So we're to fight lions and tigers and stuff?" Sangfroid felt a little excited at this.

"Severus Ex's lions and tigers, and whatever else he's had made."

"Made?"

Michael cackled. "Steam animals. You don't think Severus Ex would make it easy, do ya?"

Steam animals? The thought fascinated Sangfroid, but before she could ask more questions, the cell door slammed open. Several guards pushed into the already crowded cell and wedged a way open for a fat, greasy jailer to follow them in.

"That's Kronos, the games master," Michael murmured. "He's a right turd."

"We're low on animal fodder," Kronos said. "Need volunteers." He flicked a casual glance around the room. "Her and him and him and him." He pointed at certain people, mostly the elderly, and his guards hauled the individuals out of the cell and bundled them away.

"Oi. That's me missus!" Michael pushed forward.

"Get after her then." Kronos grabbed him by the front of his tunic and tossed him out with the others. With a hard glare he backed out of the silent room. His gaze momentarily locked with Sangfroid's and showed a glimmer of surprise.

"You're a big bugger to be in here," he said but kept backing for the door. One of his guards muttered something in his ear. His eyes immediately dropped to Sangfroid's bare feet. He nodded and was gone, the door slammed shut behind him.

"Where are they taking them?" Sangfroid asked. No one paid her any attention. People squatted in small groups on the bare dirt floor or sat alone staring sullenly into space. Others curled into tight balls to try and sleep the hours away. "Where are they taking them?" she asked again and poked the nearest person.

"You heard 'im. They're low on fodder. They'll cut 'em up and feed 'em to the beasts. Then tomorrow they'll throw the rest of us to 'em." Came the surly answer. "Now piss off and let me sleep."

So she was in a lion's den, only with steam lions that ate human flesh? Cool. But she was sorry for Michael. That wasn't right; the old coot had been harmless. And what about Millicent? Was she here? Sangfroid worried for her more than ever, which was a lot as she was never really done worrying about her. This was a vicious place, and Millicent, with all her high ideals, would be ill prepared for it. How would she survive in this timeline? Sangfroid could only hope that Gallo was close by to help her, and that they had Sophia with them as well.

The night was long and drawn out. No food or water was provided. No fire for warmth either, though the press of bodies kept the cold at bay. Sangfroid sat amid the hot fug of humanity and brooded over her missing companions.

Morning arrived and the guards were back. Sangfroid hoped they'd bring food; she was starving. Instead, they slung a selection of rusty old weapons into the middle of the cell floor and stood well back and laughed as the inmates clawed over each other to arm themselves.

At first Sangfroid was confused as to what was happening, until a body landed at her feet. The young man's neck was broken, and as she watched, the lad's fingers were peeled back and the short sword he'd been holding was ripped away. People were fighting for weapons. There weren't enough to go around. She sprang to her feet and entered the fray, using her height and strength to full advantage. She hauled out a decent looking spear. Unfortunately, an ugly bugger was hanging onto the other end. In a blink, with a quick jab and flick, Sangfroid flipped her antagonist onto his backside and claimed the prized spear as her own.

Aware Kronos was watching her from the shadows out in the corridor, she retreated to a corner to examine her booty. Her spear was not such a prize after all. The shaft was bowed, and the point was dull and chipped, but by then there was nothing else left, so it would have to do. When she looked up, Kronos had gone.

For the next few hours, her companions sat fraught and silent waiting to be called. The only sound was the constant baying from the animal pens. Some felons tinkered with their weapons, but there was little they could do to improve the rusting junk they'd been given. Sangfroid glared at her spear in growing anger. At least let a soldier die with a decent weapon in her hand. And her boots!

"Hear that?" Someone whispered. Sangfroid strained to hear and could just about make out a muted roar, like ocean thunder.

"It's begun," the man beside her said. Trepidation rippled through the cell. The games had started.

Sangfroid looked at the skinny, undernourished people huddled around her. Half of them didn't even know how to hold the weapon they'd scrabbled so fiercely for. Those who had lost out and had no means of defending themselves looked wretched and beat down already. The place stank of desperation. One man, in the far corner, lay dead. His dagger stolen from him, but not before it was used to silence him. *These games are a farce*, Sangfroid decided. There's nothing honourable about them. These people could never survive in an arena; it was nothing less than murder to throw them into one. *But then this is not battle*, Sangfroid reminded herself, *this is entertainment of the basest kind.*

The guards came for them at around midday. By now Sangfroid had become accustomed to the roar of the crowd that came and went like the tide, barely breaking the monotony in the cells far below.

"Right you lot. On yer feet." The order came. They shuffled out the cell door into the corridor. Farther on down, the animal pens were opening. Oxen and horses and even scrawny camels spilled out into the throng. They too were malnourished and nervous from being penned up too long. They skittered sideways, stomping on the hapless felons, crushing toes and knocking people to the floor or against the walls. Sangfroid side-stepped the lurching gait of an old milk cow, acutely aware of her missing boots. She hated the thought of dying without them; it was so cliché.

"You. The tall one." A shout made her look back. Kronos waved at her from the back of the crowd. "Get over 'ere."

Sangfroid pushed through the press and came to stand before Kronos and two of his guards. She towered over them; she towered over everybody. The guards shifted uneasily, and she liked that. They should feel threatened. Given the opportunity, she'd happily kill them and then go look for breakfast.

"Was yer mother an Amazon or what?" Kronos squinted up at her. His question seemed genuine enough. Sangfroid said nothing. She wasn't going to discuss her mother with this scat-heap.

"I got something special for you." Kronos continued, unconcerned at Sangfroid's silence. He turned away obviously expecting to be followed.

"I want my boots," Sangfroid said and stood her ground. Kronos hesitated.

"Yer in no position to make demands." He spat out a wad of mucus and avoided Sangfroid's gaze.

"I want my boots. They'll be no use to you when I rip your legs off."

The guards raised their swords, but it was a half-hearted gesture. Their feet scuffed the stone floor, ready to take flight. These weren't real soldiers, Sangfroid realized. These were no more that hopped up jailers and animal handlers. Their job was to bully the weak and defenceless in their last hours, to be cruel and neglectful to the animals in their care. They could no more fight than their charges could. She bared her teeth and growled. She had an impressive growl—low and dangerous—that reverberated menacingly in her chest. She could mash these snivelling little pretend men with her bare hands and best they knew it.

"Get 'im his bleedin' boots," Kronos snarled at a guard. "They're too big anyways." His face was hard set, and Sangfroid realized whatever she'd been singled out for was more important to Kronos than a pair of old army boots.

The guard returned quickly. "A name fer the boots, fair exchange." Kronos held them just out of reach. He seemed incapable of delivering cleanly on a deal.

"Sangfroid." She snatched her boots from his grasp and shoved them on. She stomped the soles on the ground with a satisfying slap and felt immediately better.

"I has a specialty for you, Sangfroid. You're a giant, see, and I has to make good use of you for Severus Ex. Can't let the Emperor get bored now, can we?" Kronos walked away, and Sangfroid fell into step beside him. "See, my predecessor bored him. Just a little, but it was enough to get his nose cut off and buried up to his neck in an anthill. Not nice. I had to watch. It was part of the promotion package." He tutted. "I was sat there for three days."

Sangfroid looked at him sourly, not interested in his sordid little shock tactics. She'd seen ants the size of houses. She'd seen ants that shat houses.

"Where you from then?" Kronos tried a new tack. "They all as big as you back home, huh?"

Sangfroid ignored the question. "What specialty?" she asked, instead.

"This way." Kronos led her farther into the area with the animal pens. He halted by a tall wooden stall. "Her." He nodded at the gates. "She's your specialty."

A serpentine tube, constructed of metal rings squirmed over the gate and tapped Sangfroid square in the chest, before worming up to her chin. It roamed over her face, only to poke her in the eye, before fumbling through her hair.

"Bloody hell," she said, ducking away. "What is it?"

"She likes you." Kronos laughed mirthlessly. The door opened a crack. Sangfroid looked aghast at the huge elephant looking down at her. Her skull was flesh but her ears and trunk were mechanical plates which slid and expanded over each other in a life-like synchronicity.

"What the hell is it?" Sangfroid asked again, swatting the trunk away. Her eyes told her it was an elephant, but logic said something else—something monstrous.

"An old toy of Severus's," Kronos answered. "But even she's boring now, so it's to the arena with her." A huge blast of steam billowed out from the elephant pen and fogged up the corridor so thickly that they couldn't see each other for a moment.

"A steam elephant?" Sangfroid was stunned. The steam began to dissipate, and she took another hard look. She had never heard of such a thing. It was amazing.

"Half and half," Kronos said. "Part real, part machine. Powered by steam and, unfortunately, hay. Except we don't have none of that, so she's in foul form."

"Yeah." The guard who looked after the animal pens spoke up. "She weren't cuddling you, she were sniffin' you out fer food. She's sneaky."

"You want me to ride her?" Sangfroid asked. She was confused. She wasn't sure if she'd be happy on the back of an elephant. She'd rather be on the ground doing what she did best—fighting for her life.

"No, no," Kronos said and nodded at his men. Before Sangfroid could register what was happening, a guard snapped a heavy manacle around her ankle.

"You're not gonna ride on her," Kronos continued. Sangfroid pulled at the iron chain attached to the manacle. It disappeared under the gate and into the pen. "You're gonna partner her," Kronos said, far too chirpily and swung the gate open wide. The chain led to a larger manacle around the elephant's leg. "She's gonna be your dead weight."

"What in Hades?" Sangfroid shouted. She couldn't be expected to fight with a damned elephant chained to her leg! But Kronos was already walking away whistling a cheery tune.

"She's a good girl." The guard told Sangfroid. "I liked her." Sangfroid noticed the past tense. "She can be a bit stubborn at times. Tends to sulk."

"What do you call her?" Sangfroid asked. The information might be useful.

"Aphrodite."

Aphrodite heard her name and trumpeted. She began to sway to and fro in her stall; the sudden movement yanked Sangfroid clear off her feet. She hit the floor with a thump that winded her completely.

"She's hungry is all." The guard helped Sangfroid back up. "Starving in fact. They stop feeding the herbivores when they come down here. It's not like they're going to fight or anything. They're just food for the predators. She's been starved for days now," he said sadly and opened the gate wider.

Aphrodite slowly lumbered out into the corridor, and Sangfroid had to dodge out of the way before she was squashed against the wall. She got a much better look at Aphrodite once she was out of the stall. She was a large, adult-sized, bush elephant, and three of her limbs were organic, the last was skeletal metal with a piston knee in polished bronze. Her concave back was wrinkled and leathery but her sides bulged with the clockwork mechanisms that seemed to push along her digestive systems and somehow power her through various steam vents. Sangfroid was unsure exactly what she was looking at in the depths of her guts, but it creeped her out. Aphrodite's metal tusks were her glory, long and curved and even in the dull light of the corridor Sangfroid could imagine how awe inspiring they would be polished to a high shine. Money had been spent on this creature's creation. She was an expensive trinket, and Sangfroid wondered at the hedonism of an Emperor who could have such a magnificent beast built, only to cast it aside like some sacrificial gambit.

"Come along now. There's a good girl." The guard began to herd Aphrodite along the corridor, encouraging her to follow the other animals. Sangfroid had no choice but to keep up. And quickly. One step for Aphrodite was three for her, despite her long legs.

They blundered up through a maze of lower corridors, following the herd of pitiful animals until they emerged into a long, wide tunnel. The gates at one end lay open and the noise from outside was terrifying. Felons were being pushed out into the arena. Sangfroid could see their stunned faces as the noise hit them almost as hard as the sunlight after days in darkness. Then the animals came bowling out after them, terrified and skittish, crushing anyone too slow to get out of their way.

Aphrodite smelled the fresh air, her trunk lifted and waved from side to side scoping out the breeze, and then she was off, moving quickly towards the gates. The noise did not unnerve her as much as it did Sangfroid, and she wondered at the clarity of the elephant's hearing. They were the last to leave the tunnel and enter the arena. Sangfroid felt physically assaulted by the electric atmosphere. Half the city had turned out for the spectacle, and the crowds rose, tier upon tier all around her. Their roaring was stupendous.

The sand bowl they were to fight in was all heat and dust, and she had to pull air hard into her lungs to breath. The light was intense after the gloom of the tunnel, and this, more than the gigantic roar that greeted her entry, spooked Aphrodite into a stampede. Sangfroid had to sprint to stay alongside her. Aphrodite barrelled through the throng, smacking into several horses and a camel. Felons were flung sideways by her, and an unfortunate ox ended up on its snout before the elephant came to an exhausted halt. The living parts of her hung slack on her frame and Sangfroid could see in the clear daylight just how famished and weak she was. In fact, all the animals looked as failed as the criminals. She was standing shoulder to shoulder with the dregs of the Empire.

On the far side of the arena, other fighters were making a grander entrance. These were true warriors, tall and fit and well equipped. Sangfroid squinted at them, her eyes aching with the glare bouncing off their armour. Amazons! The breath caught in her throat at seeing this long extinct, legendary tribe. They were giantesses, graceful and strong, and as dusky as the hills of their homeland. Sunlight spilled off their helmets and breastplates. Their weapons and teeth flashed as they paraded before their audience, and in response the crowd screamed out its appreciation. There were only a half dozen or so Amazons, but their bravado filled the arena so it felt like there were a million of them.

Sangfroid noted the Amazons were chained to each other at the ankle. What was it with Kronos and chains? Couldn't he let people just get on with it and fight? And why were the Amazons even here? Surely they were meant to fight beasts, not Amazons? She hoped so; she'd rather face a steam lion than an Amazon any day.

A third gate crashed open, dragging her attention away from the Amazons. This gate stood midway between the other two gates where Sangfroid and the Amazons had each entered. Out spilled a riot of keening, howling beasts. Lions and bears. Tigers and wolves. Hyenas, bulls—anything with sharp horns and sharper teeth. The sun blazed off their clockwork engineering and skittered across the exposed gears and cogs that churned alongside the living tissue. The hides of these fantastical creatures had been flayed away to reveal bunched muscle and sinews, and the pumping pistons that gave the animals motion. Their jaundiced eyes, maddened by pain and hunger, took in all about them with sly cunning. Oily saliva dripped from mechanical jaws that snapped in calculated time and with vicious precision. It was as if Hades had vomited up every rabid, mutant mongrel ever conceived. Sangfroid's blood ran cold. Time stood still for one chilling, hell-bent moment.

And then the crowd went wild.

Chapter 24

THE THIRD GATE CRASHED OPEN, and the bowels of hell spewed forth. The man-eaters they were to fight were automatons! Millicent felt her knees give way and began to sink to the sand, only Gallo's vice-like grip on her upper arm kept her upright, though at a severe list.

In a fast, synchronized movement, unhindered by their chains, the Amazons formed a barrier in front of them, and she lost sight of Sangfroid, though the towering elephant indicated where she was in the fray. They had been in so many scrapes together, battling alongside each other, that now it felt strange for this gory arena to separate them. Millicent felt more exposed than ever not having Sangfroid with her. It should be *her* hands holding her up, *her* strength fortifying Millicent's terror. Everything felt skewed and sinister. There was no control on this journey either in the way they had entered into it, or in how it would end. There was no Hubert on the other side to save them, and no Sangfroid beside her now. They were facing death alone, and this time there was no going back.

"Remember," Alkaia shouted over her shoulder, "your task is to keep your face attached to your skull. Anything, and by that I mean any man, beast, or automaton, comes near you, you kill it."

"You got it," Gallo shouted back. Her eagerness astounded Millicent. Together they watched as the mechanical beasts spread out and plunged into the men and women on the far side of the arena. "Hey, half those poor bastards don't even have weapons?" Gallo frowned, her rapture tainted. "That's not very fair."

"I don't think fairness is a concept of these games. I think the general idea is not so much to fight honourably as to die horribly," Millicent said. Her trident felt alien in her hand, but at least she had a weapon. She had no idea how to use it, but in the screaming chaos around her, she realized she would have to. They were close to the arena walls and Millicent gave a sharp cry as a putrid orange hit her on the shoulder. Several more landed near her feet.

"The crowd are pelting us with rotten fruit," she cried in outrage. "As if life isn't hard enough."

"They want us in the thick of it, not lurking back here," said Gallo, ignoring the missiles hurled their way. The thick of it was now a morass of screaming felons and animals that the automatons were easily carving through.

"Yooou're shit. Yooou're shit. Move your arse and take a hit." The crowd chanted behind them.

"Well, really." Millicent was flabbergasted at their rudeness. "Do they not understand tactics? We do have a plan."

The bedlam before her was terrifying. Beyond her guard of Amazons, she could make out a huge lion crunching on the head of a prone man. Its metal teeth ground his skull to pulp in seconds. According to the bookmakers that was the favoured fate for her. She felt ill.

Other felons fought to keep the beasts at bay with vain swipes of their swords and spears, their arms growing weaker and weaker and their parries less effective with each passing second. She saw several hyenas surround a man, dodging in and out, nipping and butting him as he spun with his short sword, trying to fend them off. It was an orchestrated game, and Millicent realized these creatures moved with a calculated cunning far beyond their normal nature. They were hardened to the arena and its means of providing food. They had developed new skills to bring down their quarry in this man-made feeding frenzy. And how much of that cunning had been pre-engineered through their mechanization?

Beasts of various kinds were tearing into unprotected flesh. Some fed, but most were on a killing spree. The dead and dying lay scattered about as creatures abandoned their mauled victims to go after those still trying to flee. They enjoyed the chase more than the kill, crowding in on those who chose to stand and fight. They were merciless and slow to bring about the inevitable end.

Two lions played tug of war, tearing their victim asunder. Horses and oxen, the easiest game of all, were dragged to the ground. A camel ran past with a tiger clawing at its back. The sandy arena floor became a mire with the blood and entrails poured onto it. Millicent looked for Sangfroid, but she was lost in the melee.

"Kill the urn. Kill the urn. Cut her up and watch her burn." The crowd flung out their new chant along with their pieces of rotten fruit. A tomato hit her between her shoulder blades.

"They seem to particularly dislike you." Gallo pointed out unnecessarily. "Must be a tea thing."

"More a tax thing. If they don't shut up, I'll throw this trident at them."

"That's the spirit." Gallo grinned. And again, Millicent couldn't believe Gallo's jubilation in the face of such awfulness. She was definitely a born warrior, and Millicent was glad to be chained to her.

"Millicent! Millicent!" The call finally penetrated Millicent's consciousness. "Yoo-hoo!"

She squinted up into the hostile crowd, scouring the hordes sitting in the cheap seats. Suddenly, she picked out the worried face of Jana giving her the thumbs up with a grim little smile.

In this setting, it was very heartening. She gave Jana a weak smile back and waved her trident. Jana pointed up to her left and then made a face. Millicent followed her gaze and saw Cybele sitting in a private box surrounded by her weak-chinned entourage.

"Who's that?" Gallo looked over at the box and its inhabitants.

"No one important. Just the head heifer at the tea temple," she said and turned back to the havoc at the far end of the arena. "Can you see Sangfroid?" she asked worriedly. "I can barely see the elephant in all this chaos." Gallo was taller and had a better view.

"No, but she can look after herself," Gallo answered. "Just keep an eye on the predators. They'll be turning their attention on us next." She gestured with her sword to the massacre on the other side. "I reckon that lot is the appetizer."

Across the arena, Sangfroid swung her spear into the eye socket of a huge mechanical bear. It shook its head violently breaking the shaft in half before keeling over. In a blink two hyenas tore into the living parts of the creature and saved Sangfroid the worry of dispatching it. She grabbed an abandoned sword to replace her lost spear. The hilt was greasy with blood. Looking closer she found part of a human scalp in her palm. She flicked it away and adjusted her grip. Beside her, Aphrodite trumpeted her alarm and sideswiped a lion out of her path with a whiplash crack of her trunk. She stood confused, swaying from side to side in the middle of the bloodbath. While Sangfroid was pleased she had finally stopped running, she now presented a huge blindside. She could see the elephant was not able for a fight; she had neither the strength nor sense of self-preservation to survive long out here. The sideswipe to the lion had been a lucky reflex. Already she was dead weight; if she fell over, Sangfroid was stuffed, there was no way she could move, nevermind fight with a dead elephant glued to her side.

A huge wolf rushed her, and she beheaded it with a mighty, but beautifully executed, sweep of her short sword. It lay with its mechanical legs still pumping even as its head bounced several yards away. These creatures were proving a demon to kill; it took a maximum hit to do any damage at all.

The felons were mostly done for. They lay in tattered heaps all around her. She began to worry that she and Aphrodite would soon be the only things standing. The felons hadn't managed to dispatch even one beast, she noted with exasperation, unless they'd choked one to death while it gorged on them. Sangfroid had hoped for better odds, but in reality, these hapless criminals had never stood a chance. She watched a lion drag down a horse by its throat, and another leap on a woman who didn't even try to save herself. The screaming of the animals was harder to take than the dying cries of men.

A tiger tore its way up Aphrodite's left flank—the side Sangfroid could not reach. The elephant reared in terror, nearly wrenching Sangfroid's leg clean off. She pulled a trident out from under a nearby body and hurled it with all her might at the tiger now biting down on Aphrodite's back, hoping to at least unbalance it. The tigers were big beasts and highly automated, and she doubted if a puny, blunt projectile would inflict much damage. Her luck was in. The creature lost its footing, but instead of falling off, it ripped its way down Aphrodite's side, digging its claws into her flesh to slow its descent.

Aphrodite screamed and reared even higher throwing the tiger off. The trident bounced back and landed with its prongs on either side of Sangfroid's foot. She swore at the lucky miss. The tiger followed. It crashed to the ground between Aphrodite and Sangfroid, far too close for comfort. Once it found its feet, it would be on top of her. She swung back her sword ready to make a quick and hopefully decisive strike when Aphrodite thundered back down onto all fours. Her massive metal foot landed on the tiger's chest, and with a loud pop, its metal guts sprang loose.

"Good girl." Sangfroid breathed in relief. "Now just do that twenty-seven more times."

It was all too much for Aphrodite. She continued her sag downwards and lay flat out on the ground exhausted and in shock.

"No, no, no!" Sangfroid yanked on the chain pinning her leg inches from the reclining elephant. She had barely room to move, nevermind defend herself. "Get up, you lazy cow!"

A humongous bear came lumbering up. It reared on its hind legs and Sangfroid jabbed it hard in the guts with the trident. The prongs cracked against metal plate under the belly fur and jarred her wrist painfully. She was unable to move, Aphrodite had her pinned to the spot, and her weapon was useless. This was it! Even an old soldier's luck could only last so long. The bear roared straight into her face, marinating her in halitosis and saliva, then it raised the huge claw that would finish her off. Sangfroid was aware of two things—the world around her moved into slow motion, while sound separated out and amplified until she could clearly differentiate every shrieking voice, every murmur, every creak in the entire building. And above the hullabaloo came the trill of many, many imperial trumpets.

"Severus ex Machina, your Emperor!" A voice boomed out, and the crowd bellowed approval. The central balcony filled up with slaves waving palm fronds, and soldiers ushered in a man bedecked in gold-plated armour and swathed in royal purple. Slaves wafted the greenery over his head while others threw cypress under his feet to perfume, as well as cushion each step. Severus Ex had finally deigned to arrive at his own honorary games.

Aphrodite lifted her head. Her trunk waved towards the balcony where the smell of cypress, leafy laurel, and sweet scented bowers breezed through the stench of death. She trumpeted hopefully, and lumbered to her feet following the scent of food with a shambling awkwardness. Then she took off like lightning. Sangfroid was instantly swept up with her and whisked away like linen blowing on a clothesline, leaving the bear to swipe at empty air. Aphrodite moved fast towards the scent of fresh foliage. She stomped on hyenas, crushed lions, and swept bears and wolves aside. Her concentration was on only one thing—food. She gained momentum and cannoned towards the lower terraces, focused on her goal. The spectators in the lower stalls began to panic at her relentless advance.

Aphrodite charged headfirst into the arena wall like a huge, bronze battering ram. Dust and debris flew into the air. An entire section of wall slid away. The plank seating cracked and shattered toppling screaming spectators into the arena. From the turrets on the topmost tier archers shot at Aphrodite. Their job was to shoot down anything trying to escape the arena floor. Most of their arrows bounced off her body plate or thudded into the crowd causing even more panic. The few that did pierce her living flesh made her angry but did not stop her. She ploughed on through the terraces, crushing all in her way and heading straight for the Emperor's balcony. Sangfroid clung onto her side plates as best she could. She had long ago given up on trying to keep up with Aphrodite, electing instead to jump onboard and hang on for dear life. If she lost footing, she was dead. Simple as that. She wedged her fingers between metal panels that ground against her fingertips so tightly she worried they would be cut clean off.

The avalanche of spectators that spilled into the arena were fresh meat to the predators. They renewed their attacks, some escaping up into the terraces causing uproar from the people trapped there. Arena guards began to belatedly sidle into the ring. They hugged close to the walls, timorous despite their full armour and heavy weaponry. Their fear was palpable, much to the disgust of the spectators on the other, safer side of the arena. They began to bombard the guards with anything they could lay their hands on. Stones, fruit, and seats rained down on them along with curses at their cowardice.

With an unholy roar, the Amazons charged and, despite their chains, ploughed into the morass, destroying beasts left, right, and centre, defending the hapless citizens. The crowd thundered its approval. Behind the Amazon charge, Gallo and Millicent ran to keep up. Millicent wasn't at all sure this was the wisest thing to do, but Gallo was already halfway across the arena dragging her behind, so her options were limited.

"Safety in numbers," Gallo shouted, before beheading a bear and gutting the hugest wolf Millicent had ever seen. She looked at the cogs and gears spilling out of the wolf. It was more hellhound that lupine, and she had no doubt an evil mind had created it.

"Hey," Gallo told her. "Watch this." She picked up a putrid pomegranate that had rolled near her feet, and with a strong right arm flung it straight at Cybele's box. It landed in the matron's lap, much to her alarm. Immediately, she leaped to her feet and exited her box with a flurry of her followers. Gallo crowed with delight then turned back to business. "Keep up with the Amazons, they're your protection," Gallo ordered, and charged on.

"I thought you were my protection?" Millicent puffed along beside her.

"I have your left flank, but believe me, they," Gallo nodded at Alkaia and her warriors, "have everything else."

"Where is the elephant?"

"What?"

"I've lost sight of the elephant," Millicent said, craning her neck to see. The arena was filling with smoke. Kronos's men had wheeled in tar barrels and set them alight. Millicent was unsure how this was meant to ease the confusion. It had no effect on the animals whatsoever and managed only to blind the warriors fighting them. A hail of arrows whistled overhead.

"What on earth are they shooting at?" Millicent asked.

"The predators. Citizens have fallen into the arena; they can't have the great and the good of Rome guzzled by mechanical beasts." She swiped at a second wolf and cursed as it leaped out of reach.

"They'd destroy their own mechanical beasts?"

"They can always rebuild them with the salvaged parts." Gallo swung the broad of her sword flat across the back of a hyena. It yelped and turned on her and she sank the blade hilt-deep into the exposed gears of its muzzle and prized its jaw off.

"There's your elephant." She swung her sword point towards the stalls on the far side of the arena. Millicent's gaze followed the dripping blade, and there was the elephant, bristling with arrows like a mammoth hedgehog but still lumbering steadily through the tiers of seats. It was heading directly for a brightly bedecked balcony where all was in chaos.

"Where's Sangfroid? Wasn't she was chained to it?" She squinted through the oily smoke, and then saw her, clinging to the side of the animal trying to keep away from the stomping feet, and ducking any incoming arrows. "Oh Lord, she still is!"

Gallo roared with laughter. "She's making a run for it right through the Emperor's balcony. Told you she'd be all right. I wonder if we should follow her?"

Millicent considered this. Piles of bodies lay between them and the breach the elephant had made in the wall. All around them guards ran hither and thither while Kronos, resplendent in his games master finery, screamed out orders, then counter orders, then countered the counter orders, his face a contortion of fear and fury. Under his direction, nothing but confusion and clownishness unfolded. The Amazons swept all before them. Everything fell to their blades. Beasts and guards alike were enemy in the smoke-filled morass. Only the thankful citizens felt their mercy and were allowed to escape unscathed.

A guard's head rolled up to Millicent's feet like some macabre rugger ball. Repulsed, she kicked it back into the smoky abyss. Out of the fug another guard came charging in, sword raised and a demented war cry howling from his throat. To her fevered mind, it was as if the head had somehow re-animated to a full-sized man and came at her hell-bent on revenge. Millicent blindly levelled her trident, and he ran into it at full tilt. There was a snap as his armour buckled and gave way. A popping sound reverberated along the shaft and into her arm as his flesh sank into the prongs. He staggered, grunted in shock, and fell to his knees, wrenching the weapon from her numbed grasp. She gawped at his lifeless form. Horror rose within her, enveloping her senses in a sickly dreamlike haze. Reality became a tunnel of distant noise and narrowing light.

"Well done you." Gallo walloped her on the back and sent her staggering. The thump pulled her back to the here and now, to the arena in all its destruction. It stung like cold water.

"I knew it. You're a friggin' natural." Gallo yanked the trident out of the guard's chest and thrust it back into Millicent's unwilling hands. It was the last thing she wanted, but already Gallo was loping away, dragging them deeper into the smoke smeared battlefield. Millicent hopped along after her, pushing through the clash of steel and the harrowing cries of animal and human, her fingers glued to the trident with the blood of her kill.

When Aphrodite finally reached the palm fronds, peace prevailed. Satisfied, she stood and munched on all the garlands and foliage she could find. The Emperor's balcony had long been evacuated of his honourable personage, and the remaining Imperial guards had a commander wise enough to let the elephant graze quietly. Sangfroid took the opportunity to slink away. In the ruckus of Aphrodite's ascent, the chain had wrenched loose. Now she hunkered under a wooden terrace, hacking at the manacle pin with an arrowhead. Around her spectators were being hastily ushered out, the games had come to an impromptu close.

"You. Out now!" A spear tip dug into her back, placed perfectly to puncture a lung with the slightest pressure. This was an Imperial guard, not the riff-raff who worked for the arena. Sangfroid stood slowly, appreciative of a well-handled weapon, and let herself be escorted back to the arena. The guard marched briskly past the mountain of bodies being unceremoniously slung onto open wagons. The predator carcasses—and there were far more than Sangfroid expected—were cleaved apart, the mechanical joints and innards dug out for salvage. She was prodded across the arena towards the group of Amazons. The high death toll of the steam beasts suddenly made sense. The Amazons had annihilated them. Amazons despised the unnatural.

"Is that all's left?" Kronos stomped up and down looking more smelly and bedraggled than ever in his outlandish costume. He tried to swagger before an Imperial commander, though his fear and uncertainty showed in every step. Kronos was in trouble, and Sangfroid wasn't at all surprised. The games had been a debacle. If it hadn't been for the Amazons, these automated predators would be prowling the streets of Rome by now, gorging on anything they could find. There was an anthill somewhere with Kronos's name on it.

Sangfroid turned her attention to the Amazons. Close up they looked to be a strong, close knit crew. She'd be more than happy to have warriors like this in her unit. *They'd show a squid a thing or two, I'll bet.* To the rear of the Amazons, she thought she saw...*did she?* She blinked the smoke out of her eyes and looked harder. Was that Gallo lurking at the back like a big weed, laughing at her? And beside Gallo stood a dwarf woman. No. Not a dwarf...a normal sized woman. A normal woman among a stack of big Amazonian weeds! Gallo and the Amazons towered over her, but there was no doubt that it was Millicent! Her Millicent! She began to run towards her, but after two strides it became a hobble, and then a serious limp. Aphrodite had nearly torn her leg from its socket.

Millicent hobbled forward to meet her. Gallo followed, still chained to her by the ankle. Sangfroid swooped on Millicent and lifted her into the air in a huge swirling hug of joy. Round and round she spun, holding her tightly, until Gallo squawked for her to stop as she had to skip around and around with them.

"Oh, Millicent," she said, and immediately ran out of eloquence, so she kissed her. She kissed her as though their lives depended on it. She melted into the softness of Millicent's mouth, aware of the scrape of her own chapped lips. The sweet, sweaty scent of Millicent filled her senses despite the acrid smell of smoke and gore clinging to her own body. She rejoiced in the kiss, the closeness, the momentary nirvana it provided.

"Oh, look. Romance." The Amazons began to catcall and make kissy-kissy noises that broke through her stupor. Sangfroid pulled back and found herself face-to-face with a very startled and flushed Millicent. Sangfroid had kissed her, and she was livid. Her throat went dry. Squarely, she met Millicent's sparking gaze and scoured it for clues. There were hundreds, but she couldn't read any of them.

"I can't believe you're here," she managed to say. Her arms refused to let go. "You smell of oranges?"

"Rotten oranges." Millicent did not step immediately out of her arms. Sangfroid could feel exhaustion in the slackness of her body. She had found a comfort in their embrace, too. Even if it was not openly acknowledged. "The crowd pelted me. They thought I was a tea maiden."

"A what?"

"It's a long and tedious story. The main thing is we are all together at last, except for Sophia, and I have a theory about that."

Always with the theories. "Does this mean we can get the hell out of here?" she asked.

Now Millicent did step back, her face a flurry of thought. "I'm not sure how we can. There's no one back home to work the time machine."

"How in Tartarus did you end up in the arena?" Gallo slapped her on the shoulder. "Isn't it fantastic?"

A lowly trumpeting interrupted their debriefing. Aphrodite lumbered slowly towards them prodded on by guards with long spears. She was limping and her skinny flanks ran red with blood.

"Hey girl." Sangfroid reached up to rub the fleshy knoll above her metal trunk. "Did you enjoy your grub?" Her heart felt heavy for the animal so abused, yet so gentle in spirit. Millicent joined her and gingerly patted a shoulder before gaining courage to stroke a wizened, whiskery cheek.

"She's very sweet, Sangfroid," she said, as if reading her mind. "But a Colossal squid has already nearly destroyed the house. What would a mechanical elephant do? We can't take her back. We can't even get ourselves home."

"I know, but I hate this world and the way it treats animals. And felons," she added as an afterthought remembering Michael.

"It treats the poor and needy just as badly. It's a hateful place," Millicent agreed.

"Line up, you shower of scum," Kronos yelled, unwittingly reinforcing their words. They shuffled together in a sort of row as Aphrodite was led away to the animal pens.

"Commander Pullo of the Imperial Guard believes the Emperor's would-be assassin is hiding among you lot," Kronos said. He was obviously cranky at having to spew out this balderdash, but was under orders to comply. The Imperial command could squash him flatter than a turd fly if they chose to.

The commander stepped forward and brushed Kronos aside. He was a tall, impressive man bedecked in the regalia of the Emperor's finest. His lorica held a swirl of sigils and emblems across his chest relaying the might and majesty of Rome under

Severus Ex. "We know the elephant was a decoy, a means to get an assassin close to the Emperor." His tone was clipped, cold, and impatient. "And we know one of you is behind this attempt on the Emperor's life. So, these are the options. Continue to harbour the assassin, and you will all be killed here and now. Or, the assassin surrenders, and the rest of you are spared." His eyes flitted from one to another, gauging the reaction of his words. They were met with a stony Amazonian silence. He puffed through his nose. "What's it to be?"

Millicent grabbed Sangfroid's hand and held on tight. The Amazons bristled at the ridiculous accusation. Commander Pullo took another step forward to make his formal charge. "I want the one called Sangfroid for attempted assassination of the Emperor by means of a mechanical elephant." More silence. The commander waited a heartbeat then barked out, "Who is Sangfroid?"

Another heartbeat, and Sangfroid slipped free of Millicent's grasp and stepped forward. "I'm Sangfroid."

The commander nodded with satisfaction and went to turn away.

Millicent stepped forward. "I am Sangfroid!" Her voice rang out loud and clear. Her chin defiantly tilted. Sangfroid frowned. The commander halted.

Millicent glared at Gallo, who, after a confused blink, realized what she had to do and also stepped forward. "I am Sangfroid," she bellowed at the Imperial commander.

The Amazons exchanged swift, furtive glances. Then, they too, stepped forward as one, and all called out in unison, "I am Sangfroid."

Commander Pullo's lips thinned to bloodless slits. He glared at Kronos. With a grumpy sigh Kronos came forward.

"You are a dozy lot," he said, moodily. Nothing was going well today. "Sangfroid, get over here." He looked directly at Sangfroid and pointed at a spot before him. "I know who you are. You're the only bleedin' man in the whole bunch, fer Jove's sake."

Chapter 25

Gallo moved protectively towards Sangfroid, and Millicent stayed glued to her side. "We can't be separated," she hissed.

"You and me, babe." Sangfroid took her hand and squeezed it. "All the way."

"Not that." Exasperated, Millicent tugged her hand free. "I meant the three of us can't be separated. We might never meet up again and be stuck here forever."

All three stood proudly defiant waiting for Commander Pullo's next move. The Imperial soldiers shifted uneasily. The arena guards looked twitchy, and the Amazons simply glowered. Hands drifted to sword hilts or curled tighter around spear shafts and ax-handles. The air was sharp as pinpricks. Static energy roiled around them, as if an electrical storm was brewing. It prickled the skin and dried the mouth and made muscles and tempers twitch. Millicent suddenly realized this was much more than just a drama-laden, atmospheric standoff. There actually *was* an energy field gathering around them.

Her scalp tightened and the ground under her feet felt loose and insubstantial. A sickly feeling of foreboding grew in her stomach. She toppled. The sandy floor of the arena tilted up to meet her as she fell headlong towards it. *I know what this is. But how on earth can it be happening? How could—*

She never finished her thought; the world around her went black. It spun wildly out of control and swirled away from her. The heat and dust, along with the horrid coppery smell of blood dissipated. Another warmer smell came rushing in, a comforting one. It held oil and leather, the spicy tang of sweat...Millicent slowly opened her eyes and found herself nose deep in Sangfroid. She was clutching her tightly, arms wrapped around her waist. "I'll never get used to this," she muttered against Sangfroid's breast.

"Oh? I kinda like it." The smile in Sangfroid's words made Millicent pull away. It did not do to bury one's nose in a soldier's chest. Stepping away, the surroundings immediately came into sharp focus. They were in Hubert's laboratory, standing next to the time machine. The drapes were closed and a fire crackled in the hearth. Gallo had landed flat on her back on the chaise and was struggling out of its feathery depths into a sitting position.

"I'm getting good at this." She patted the soft fabric looking rather pleased. "Better than the coal hole."

"How did we get back here?" Sangfroid asked, looking around the room. "Not that I'm complaining."

"I'm not at all sure." Millicent was troubled. "Unless Hubert has somehow set his machine to automatically recall time travellers. Though I'm sure he would have mentioned it if he had done. It would be a marvellous advancement, and he was never slow to brag."

The door opened, and Edna entered carrying a silver tray of drinks. She moved as slowly and as carefully as ever, head bowed in total concentration on her feet. The crystal decanter and glasses tinkled tremulously with each step.

"Thank you, Edna," Millicent said and tried to pat her hair into some semblance of respectability before the hired help. She noted Sangfroid and Gallo's eyes light up as the decanter of whiskey was deposited on an occasional table. Their love affair with her timeline's alcoholic beverages had not diminished.

"Were you expecting us?" She found it strange for Edna to be so circumspect. Usually the girl was a ditherer. And it was very peculiar for her to be in the laboratory at all. The room spooked her, and Hubert had always been adamant that she should never enter as she was a notoriously clumsy girl.

"Yes, ma'am. The master said he'll be along directly and to bring out the best malt," Edna said.

"The master? Professor Aberly is here?" Millicent's heart pounded. Could Hubert still be alive? Had they arrived back before his untimely death and, better yet, could they avert it altogether? She took an eager step towards Edna, anxious for more information.

"Why yes, ma'am," Edna said and turned to fully face her. "The master's upstairs in his rooms."

Millicent took a step back in alarm. Though Edna spoke, Millicent was unsure where the words were emerging from. Edna had no mouth. In fact, Edna's entire visage was missing. Her face was no more than a bronze clockwork mask. She had no human features—no nose, mouth, or eyes...yet her face seethed with tiny mechanical movements as if the metal itself were alive.

"Skatos!" Gallo gawped.

"I don't think we're home yet." Sangfroid gently inserted herself between Millicent and the Edna machine, though it gave no indication of being dangerous. With a soft whir, Edna turned and left the room, slipping past the man who now stood in the doorway.

"She is quite harmless," he said. "A mere service device; nothing more."

"Hubert!" Millicent made to run to him, then hesitated, for although it looked like her dear brother, there were subtle changes that disconcerted her. He looked leaner, and his hair was very awry; no longer oiled down and respectable, it shot violently into the air as if voltage ran through it. His gilt eyeglasses were of smoked glass and strangely styled, and his clothes had a severe, dapper cut that was totally unlike his usual wardrobe. Gone were the bulky tweeds with overstuffed pockets and saggy elbows, these were now replaced with well-tailored worsted wool.

"Hubert?" she repeated, uncertainly.

"Oh Millicent, dearest, you look as if you've been through the wars." He reached out for her with brotherly affection, and she accepted his embrace, conscious of her filthy Roman tunic pressed against his new, unsettling elegance.

"It's true; I do feel as if I've met my Waterloo and barely scraped through." She sniffed away her tears. This was not the time for self-pity, no matter how inviting the concept. There were too many questions rampaging through her mind, and she began with the foremost.

"What have you done with Edna?" It opened a floodgate. "I thought you were dead. I thought Weena had eaten you. Did she not eat you? And where is Weena? And why do you look so different? Did you bring us back here in the time machine? Where is Sophia? Is she here? Please let her be here. And why did you order the good whiskey for these two?" She indicated Sangfroid and Gallo. "You know they will only guzzle it."

Hubert laughed. His easy confidence a new thing, too.

"All is well, Millicent. Let us sit by the fire, and I will tell you everything. Here, let me pour you all a…" His words trailed off as it became evident at least two of his guests had already helped themselves to the whiskey and were now sitting by the fire in comfort with their glasses brimful. "Um, let us join Sangfroid and Gallo." He guided Millicent to the chaise and presented her with a glass holding a thimbleful of spirits. "Purely medicinal," he murmured.

"Yeah, medicinal." Gallo raised her glass in salute.

"Feeling better already." Sangfroid raised her glass, too.

"What happened, Hubert?" Millicent persisted. "The last time we saw you, Weena had devoured you. And then Sophia inadvertently started the time machine and took us all off to a dreadful alternative Rome. Though Lord knows where she is now. She was not with us. She was slightly ahead of us, which I assume means she arrived even farther back in history." She spluttered over her first sip of whiskey, then found its harsh warmth secure and soothing.

"Firstly, we need to locate Sophia and very soon. Secondly, Weena did not devour me. As a young female, she has a soft pouch in her mouth where she can keep her young. Not unlike a pelican," Hubert explained.

"Pelicans keep food in their pouches." Millicent pointed out, unwilling to be so easily placated. She had seen her brother swallowed by a huge space squid, something one did not shrug off lightly.

"Um. Yes. Perhaps that was the wrong analogy," Hubert conceded. "Anyway, Weena has this pouch thingy to hold her young when she travels. Remember, she's from the Cat's Paw nebula in Scorpius Major, an enormous gaseous galaxy where space squid swim about in shoals and keep their infants close until they can cope on their own."

"Like whales in a pod." Millicent was intrigued. She imagined the Cat's Paw nebula as a huge space ocean marbled with lazy curls of current. A wonderland where magnificent space beasts ploughed the deeps; much as she dreamed of cryptids navigating the inky fathoms of her own planet.

"Yes, except whales don't keep their young in their mouths," Hubert said.

"Neither do pelicans," Millicent countered.

"Forget all that. If she didn't eat you, where did she take you?" Sangfroid interrupted. "You said they put their young in their mouths to go travelling. So, where did you go?"

"Ah. Yes." Hubert shifted uncomfortably. Now that she was used to this fine-feathered version of her brother, Millicent could relax, for she sensed the older version, with all his awkward mannerisms and wonderful kindness, was not far beneath this new, shiny surface. His travels had not changed him that much. "Well, um…" he stuttered to a halt, unsure of himself and what to say next.

"That bad, 'eh?" Gallo said, gently. Millicent was impressed with this uncharacteristic sensitivity. Gallo's rough edges had certainly begun to soften. "We had it rough, too," Gallo continued with her newfound empathy. "We were thrown into the gladiator arena. With Amazons! And steam-powered lions. And tigers and bears, too. They had steam powered everything!" Her excitement grew. "And Millicent had to work in a brothel."

"What?" Hubert jerked in his seat. Millicent closed her eyes.

"And I was chained to an elephant," Sangfroid butted in.

"A brothel?" Hubert said.

"And accused of trying to assassinate the Emperor." Sangfroid warmed to her theme. "Like I'd come at him with a steam elephant." She snorted with disgust into her glass.

"A brothel?" Hubert blinked hard for several seconds, focusing on Millicent who sat slumped in her chair.

"A spear and a good view is all I'd need if I wanted to stiff an Emperor," Sangfroid said.

"I fought alongside the Amazons." Gallo began to compete with Sangfroid. "I took down three steam wolves single-handed. And two lions."

"A brothel?" Hubert stared harder.

"Believe me, it was a flying and very unwelcome visit," she assured him. "The place was called the High Tea Temple of Rome. It is a cross between a tax office and a bordello, and we owe it all to Sophia. I have no idea how she instigated such a twisted, self-serving religion, but she somehow managed it."

"She's a gem," Gallo murmured into her glass.

"Can we be sure it was Sophia and not some far-flung look alike?" Hubert asked.

"There were several crossovers with our own culture that could not be explained in any other way." Millicent listed on her fingers, scones, teacup statues, bustles, and the unmistakable similarity of the Goddess Looselea to Hubert's fiancée. "Though I found the prayer to her unfathomable. It was very goat centric."

"Sophia does not like goats. She detests animals of any kind," Hubert said. "She can barely cope with humans."

Millicent suppressed a snort. "I am certain she had a hand in the advancement of the Roman Empire's technology in that other timeline. I'm sure of it. She has done something. It's too coincidental to be otherwise."

"Your evidence is circumstantial, but I can't ignore it. Weena and the squid have their own suspicions, too."

"Suspicions?" Millicent asked, very alert.

"The space squid feel there is something fundamentally wrong with the Roman Empire."

"Only because we're winning the war," Sangfroid said.

Hubert ignored her. "They suspect a time continuum has been breached," he said. "They can feel a temporal ripple spreading across the universe, but it seems to travel only as far as the Roman frontline. There it stops."

"More evidence of chronological mischief making." Millicent frowned. "The anomaly is somehow attached to the Roman Empire." She blinked rapidly as if to clear her mind. There were other issues at stake, and so much to talk about. "But you must tell us more about your adventures with Weena. And what on earth has happened to Edna?" she asked. "Is she steam-powered too?" The thought was unsettling.

"It is not Edna as you know her, but an automaton made more or less in her likeness."

"How on earth did you find the time for that?"

"First, let me explain what this place is, for it is not what you think," Hubert said and sat back in his seat nursing his glass.

Dark thoughts flitted across his face. "You remember I left the dinner table and went upstairs." He began his story. "Once I understood Weena's intentions were to take me travelling, there was little time to warn you. We had to be opportune. She had sensed a small fracture in time that would release her from here and was intent on taking me with her. I tried to let you know I was safe, but I see now I failed to convey my acquiescence, leaving you to fear the worst."

"Your shoes on the landing did indicate a premeditated act, and after the shock subsided, I suppose it did prompt me to go over your notes," Millicent said. "Unfortunately, before I could properly peruse them, Sophia started up the time machine. The very thing we didn't want to happen had occurred. She was whisked away to Lord knows where; certainly farther back in time than where we ended up. Presumably she started her cult in some primordial soup kitchen, and we inherited the whole dreadful mess."

"Millicent, have you ever thought that if we were to fix Sophia's *mess*, this world might no longer exist?" Hubert said. "In fact, might *never* have existed."

Millicent was surprised. "Of course it would exist. Why would we not exist?"

Hubert stared at her intently for a moment. "You're assuming this is *your* world," he said. He stood, went over to the window, and set his hand upon the drape cord.

"Whatever do you mean?" Millicent stood, all alarm. She did not like the ominous tone in Hubert's voice.

He pulled the cord and the drapes swung open on the most garish sunset Millicent had ever seen. The sky glowed a vulgar, haemoglobin red.

"Good gracious, what a jarring sunset." Millicent went over to the window to take a better look. "Oh, it's not a sunset. What on earth has happened to the London skyline?" As far as the eye could see, chimneystack upon chimneystack crowded in, all rising to hundreds of feet. Some billowed thick black smoke, while others blazed, spitting out spikes of fire so hot the flames burned white in the centre.

"Industry. Fierce and uncontrollable industry," Hubert answered. "This is the new beast. Factories instead of arenas, production engines instead of steam lions, and as always, the poor and the unfortunate are fodder for the machines."

"What is this place?" Horror coloured her words. "It can't be home."

"This is the London I returned to after my travels with Weena," Hubert said. "I have been here for several months trying to locate you using your temporal footprint. The time machine thankfully held a horological residue. I finally succeeded in pinpointing you and hauling you all back. I have managed to find Sophia, too. And as you suspected, she is more pre-historic than yourselves. Considerably so."

"London? But it's horrid." Millicent was too astounded at the sight before her to grasp all that Hubert implied. "This has to contravene every by-law of the Public Health act. I shall write to the Board of Health immediately."

"There is no Public Health act, Millicent. In this London, there are no philanthropists to push for sanitation or the provision of clean water," Hubert said. "All of that occurred in another London, our London. A place that no longer exists."

"This looks more like something from a period in my world's history." Sangfroid peered over their shoulders with little enthusiasm. "Massilia, Palma, Antioch. Boring old ancient cities poisoned into extinction by industry." She looked out at the mess. "And now here's Londinium, another cesspit." She squinted at the hunched figures out on the pavement. The once refined, beech-lined Christie Mews was now a shuffling crush of pedestrian traffic. Everyday workfolk trudged along the smog-filled streets in head hanging misery. Their feet swilling through a mire of mud and refuse that clogged the gutters and flooded out over the pavements. Steam trams rumbled past, loaded with crates of raw materials heading for the maze of mills and factories. The air was rank, claustrophobic, and thick with despair.

"Look at the smog. It's green! How the hell do folk walk around in that," Sangfroid said. "My lungs would fall out my backside."

"Life expectancy is not an issue here. Those are not folk," Hubert said. "At least not as we know them." Sure enough, a dull gleam from under a headscarf or cap gave away the true nature of the workers.

"They're all automatons." Millicent gasped. "Like Edna."

"Not quite," Hubert said. "These are steam people. Part flesh, part machinery. The poor, the criminal, the dispossessed, all crudely engineered into mechanical slavery. An entire populous of them. Ground down through ill repair and overwork."

"Surely this can't be London's future?" Millicent said in horror.

"This isn't the future. This is 1862," Hubert answered quietly. "This is the same year that Weena swallowed me, and you followed Sophia to an ancient alternative Rome, and this is what we have returned to. Something has gone disastrously wrong."

"Are you sure this is your own timeline?" Sangfroid asked. "It looks more like the industrial cities from *my* past. Brutal places. Technological expansion was at its peak then, and the automatons bore the brunt of it."

"Yes. I suspect this is another element of your timeline's history, a London, or Londinium if you like, with an equivalent date to that of our own and obviously with its own set of social issues." He looked at Millicent for confirmation, as if the habits of the other Hubert were ingrained in this version of him, too.

"Yeah, but these are hybrids." Gallo pointed to the rag-tags trudging along outside. "Where we come from, they are banned."

"Why is that?" Hubert asked.

"Steamheads were outlawed eons ago. Bio-engineering humans is essentially unethical," Gallo said. "Plus they tend to kill you." This was added with a shrug. "There was a great steam slave uprising once, led by a semi-automate called Sparkitous. Lesson learned, don't build a super race, then try to enslave it."

"Bio-engineering?" Hubert sounded intrigued. "How would one go about that?"

"Please focus, Hubert," Millicent scolded. "This is no time for tangential thinking."

"Looks like history is repeating itself here," Sangfroid said. "In Londinium 1862."

"Yeah," Gallo agreed. "If this city depends on steamheads, then it's written its own death sentence. Steam slaves always end up venting, and, boom!" She threw her arms in the air with great gusto. "The mother of Vesuvius!"

"So you agree, this is a part of your timeline's past?" Hubert asked.

"Not this technology." Sangfroid glared moodily out the window. "I agree with Hubert, something's gone wrong, and I think I know why we've landed here."

"And why would that be?" A familiar voice asked from the doorway. They turned in unison as Millicent entered the room. At least it looked like Millicent, except that, like her brother, this was a coolly confident, better dressed, and much more sophisticated version.

"Ah, there you are." Hubert moved towards the newcomer. "Millicent, please meet Millicent. This is you," he told his sister, "only a little sideways."

Chapter 26

"This is impossible. You are counterfeit. You cannot be me," Millicent blustered. Her cheeks blazed at the stupidity of her statement. This woman was the spitting image of her. Of course it could be her. Had she not witnessed her own duplication in time during their escape from the Amoebas? Then, there had been two of her racing through the same timeline. She had accepted that possibility, but standing face-to-face with another version of herself was something else altogether. Nevermind it was a swished up, highly polished version of herself.

She was at once acutely aware of her grubby face and blood-speckled tunic compared to this other, pristine, and annoyingly self-satisfied Millicent. The warm smile that greeted her was as cloyingly superior as it was infuriating. The newcomer had a relaxed, almost feline charm that Millicent could not in any way equate with herself. It was beyond all imagination and so had to be false.

"Now that's just creepy," Gallo muttered. "Two frocks. Soon we'll be a friggin' boutique."

"Granted, it must be difficult for you to contemplate," the new Millicent said and waved a languid hand at her elegant ensemble. "But please rest assured that, as doubtful as it may seem, I actually *am* you. Imagine me as an advanced version."

She sauntered over to join her brother. Millicent frowned at the sway of her hips. It seemed not only uncalled for, but totally unnecessary for ladylike propulsion. Her frown deepened as she noticed Sangfroid's gaze fixed upon it, too.

"Hubert, I demand an explanation." Millicent had to stop herself from stamping her foot. First, he dismantled her favourite parasol, then he tinkered with the servants, and now this. It was too much. The cynical, cool assurance of this new Millicent utterly dismayed her. She was like the new Hubert; the same, yet different, and somehow...better?

"Have you been making automatons of me?" she demanded.

"No, dearest. This really is you, only from a different time dimension." Hubert tried to soothe her. "I can see where the confusion lies."

"It's weird." Sangfroid was squinting back and forth between the two. "But I can sort of tell the difference."

Millicent's face flamed. The difference was obvious. This new Millicent was a trollop. Over curved and over confident, and dressed in a sophisticated way that somehow displayed it all to full advantage. Her hair was gloriously styled and shone like spun copper. Millicent self-consciously patted her own bedraggled locks and dislodged a smattering of sand onto the carpet. She was acutely aware of the grimy Roman tunic that barely covered her scraped knees. She was as tattered as one of Mr. Dickens's urchins and not nearly as effervescent.

"What do you think?" Sangfroid asked Gallo, who took a huge gulp of whiskey and glared from one Millicent to the other.

"I can tell you this ain't medicinal anymore." She indicated her glass. "Seeing two of them makes me queasy. Prof, does this mean there'll be other versions of us popping up all over the place? Because that would be as much fun as an asteroid up the Vestals."

"It shouldn't happen, but obviously does, and usually with careful planning," Hubert said. "On this occasion, Millicent," he indicated the newcomer, "has made a concerted effort to meet you. She has been so kind as to help me out with my algorithms. It is because of her intervention I eventually found you."

"Must you call her Millicent? I mean it's all so confusing," Millicent said, aware of the whine in her voice but unable to stop it. "I cannot believe she is not some sort of enhanced automaton." She shot the new Millicent a sharp look that easily slid off the over-curved surfaces.

"I assure you I *am* you," the other Millicent answered, a little too smoothly. "But should you wish to test me, I can reveal some of our darkest secrets as proof, like the time you unpicked the seams in your underdraw—"

"I do not need to test you!" Millicent interrupted hurriedly. "I accept you are nothing more than a timeline anomaly." This was offered rather grumpily. "Furthermore, I suggest you be referred to as Millicent number two until all this is over. It will make life, if not easier, at least a little more accountable."

"I think you'll find, in this timeline, I am nearer to the original." The other Millicent looked equally mulish. The Millicents squared up to each other, and the temperature in the laboratory seemed to rise by a few degrees.

"Hubert," they said simultaneously and turned on him with alarming synchronicity. He stepped back, startled.

"Um…Um," he said, stuttering into his diplomacy mode. "Er. I…I think the earlier Millicent may have a harder time adjusting. Would it really hurt to differentiate in such a way?" He pleaded with his swishier sister.

"Very well," the new Millicent said graciously after a short contemplation. "I concede to being Millicent the second for as long as this visit lasts." She gave an ingratiating smile at her counterpart that somehow managed to remove any sense of victory the other may have assumed.

"You were about to share your adventures with Weena, Hubert." Millicent2 seamlessly moved on to other business. "I'm sure our guests will be very interested in your findings."

Hubert's face grew grim, and he moved back to the hearth and took a seat. The others followed likewise.

"Millicent." He took care to look directly at the original, grubby version of his sister. "Have you ever thought that if we were to fix Sophia's *mess*, Sangfroid and Gallo may no longer exist?" he said. "In fact, might never have existed."

Millicent was surprised. "Of course they would exist. They would exist in their own timeline. Granted, it may not be as technologically sophisticated as before. If Sophia had not interfered, then surely that other timeline would have more or less evolved at the same rate as our own, wouldn't it?"

"You're assuming these timelines run parallel," Hubert said.

"Yes, I suppose I am. But why do you say Sangfroid and Gallo might not exist?" The thought was disconcerting.

"Yeah, why?" Sangfroid asked. Neither she nor Gallo looked happy at the idea. "Constantly killing me is one thing, but not ever existing is a whole new dice game."

"We're assuming that Sophia somehow projected the ancient Romans onto an advanced technological path that made them capable of deep space exploration by, in our calendar, as early as 1957. Far sooner than we could reasonably expect mankind to travel into space."

"Just because *you* can't do it doesn't mean the rest of us can't," Sangfroid said.

"Please, let me explain," Hubert said. "This is not a competition between our cultures. The problem is this, if Sophia went back to a predetermined point in time, and if she then accidentally introduced a new technology to your ancestors, there is a probability that she split off from one timeline and took you all off in an unnatural direction. Like grafting a new branch onto another plant." He looked to see that they all understood.

"Okay," Sangfroid conceded. "So maybe we're from the same plant, and maybe we grew off in different directions, but our branch is nearer the top, so we should take it as the norm."

"Why do you say that?" Millicent demanded.

"Because we're the more advanced civilization."

"You are not. We barely survived your bloodthirsty world. Anything capable of killing, they put a steam engine in it and let it loose," she told Hubert.

"Please listen." Hubert ignored their bickering. "If Sophia *did* interfere, we cannot deny that the changes she wrought produced an even more powerful and successful Roman Empire. If we change anything, we cannot ensure how the future would unfold for that other timeline, and whether the conditions that brought Gallo and Sangfroid into existence would prevail. Why, their timeline might never have come into being at all."

Millicent sat very still. She did not like Hubert's prognosis. Her mind immediately flew to Sangfroid. She did not like the idea that this woman she had gone through so much to save might eventually not exist anywhere in the universe at all. How fruitless the struggle would have been. How empty she would feel. Her thoughts drifted of their own accord to the kiss they'd shared in the arena. The dry tang of Sangfroid's mouth on her own and the divinely inappropriate flutterings and murmurings of her body in response—She broke away from the thought, fighting against the blush she knew flooded her face, and corralled her mind back into order.

"Then why can't we let that timeline be? Let it stand as Sophia left it and simply return Sangfroid and Gallo to where they belong?" Any world where Sangfroid was safe was a welcome compromise, despite the madness outside the window. Let that cruelty remain a part of Sangfroid's history, as long as she was *in* its future. That was all that mattered to Millicent. "Can we leave them back far enough so they'd be safe? Back on their troop ship, before the Amoebas was attacked, and the whole rigmarole with our timeline began?"

"Ah, the Quintus Prime." Gallo sighed, dreamy-eyed at the mention of the troop ship. "She may be a rusty old turd tub, but she's home. To the Quintus!"

"The Quintus!" Sangfroid joined her in a toast.

"I knew you'd come to that conclusion," Hubert said, continuing his conversation with Millicent as if the other two hadn't spoken. "Previously, I would have agreed. Until Weena took me back to the Amoebas, and I saw the outcome of the battle for myself."

"Did we win?" Sangfroid asked eagerly.

"'Course we did." Gallo gave a confident smile. "We always win. It's getting boring."

"As we now know, two organisms can exist simultaneously in the same timeline as long as they constitute separate entities coming from separate temporal states," Hubert continued.

"Huh?" Sangfroid said.

"He means an entity can exist in duplication within a singular modal of existence," Millicent explained.

"Huh?"

"You can be two people in one place at the same time." Millicent2 put it more succinctly.

"Ah." Sangfroid went back to her whiskey.

"This meant that Weena and I could hide in the nearby gas fields and wait until the battle for the Amoebas reached its conclusion. Despite the fact that Weena, in infant form, was already onboard and trapped in the Beta labs."

"Just as I saw myself in duplicate in the same laboratory," Millicent said. "We already know this can happen."

"That is not my point," Hubert said, quietly. "It's not a nice thing to return to a place where you know something awful happened."

They sat silently as the embers settled in the hearth and waited for Hubert to begin his story—

He was with Weena, and she was sliding gracefully through space. Her body rippled softly. Her long, tendrilous arms delicately wove the interstellar propulsion that drew them steadily closer to a distant metallic dot. The dull, pewter sheen only caught his eye after they had travelled towards it for some time. He knew it had to be the Amoebas.

To their right, a huge shoal of space squid undulated away from the ship towards a vaporous mass on the southern edges of the nebula. Weena adjusted her route to outflank them, then homed in by a circuitous path on the abandoned ship. Through the thin skin membrane of her pouch, Hubert could now clearly see the research ship. It spun listlessly in space like a broken Christmas ornament, dangling at an obscene angle, all sense of convention and order stripped away. As they approached, the magnitude of the destruction became apparent. The hull was blackened and scorched. Large sections of metal casing had melted or were completely blasted away. From out of these gaping holes, the ship's contents haemorrhaged into the vacuum around it. Fragments of everyday life hung around the breach, spinning aimlessly within the stir of escaping oxygen. A micro-turbine, a chair, a bottle, and unsettlingly, a shoe, drifted past them before disappearing into the void.

The ship was a wreck. There could be no survivors left onboard. He could only hope the majority of the crew had managed to evacuate safely. Weena manoeuvred carefully through a jagged tear on the port side, slithering past the debris cluttering the opening. She was not fully adult yet and could still fold herself into the smaller fissures. The ship was slung sideways making navigating the corridors disorientating for Hubert, but Weena flowed through them easily, bringing them directly to Beta hangar where the main battle had taken place.

Hundreds of bodies floated freely in the cathedral heights, angelic in their loose, splay-limbed flight. Below, others lay glued to the floor, hunched and twisted like melted gargoyles. Hubert was desolated by the many souls so casually surrendered to this echoing, airless chamber. He hated the futility of this kind of bloodshed and could not understand why Weena wished him to see this horrifying aftermath. Mankind had always waged wars, and the outcome was always monstrous and wasteful. And then a particular body caught his eye. It was a woman, large formed with corn-coloured hair. The emergency lights played across the brass of her uniform. She drifted quietly past on her back, a huge gash across her chest exposing the snapped ribs and a tatter of lungs. Sangfroid's lifeless eyes stared blankly up at the hangar ceiling. Hubert's throat tightened with a strangled sob as Sangfroid's body grazed against another poor soul, and slowly spun away.

"Why are we here?" He gasped. "What is all this for?" His eyes were wet, and he was not ashamed. In answer, Weena rippled against him in empathetic gentleness and softly swam away to the far side of the hanger. There, in the farthest corner and far from any exit, he saw Gallo. She was unmistakable to him. Tightly hunkered against the wall, her head turned aside and eyes closed as if sleeping. From the chest down she was covered with a thick black liquid. Squid ink. It had glued her into the corner, and he could only imagine the fumes had asphyxiated her. His heart weighed heavy. Neither of his friends had escaped the carnage. The futility of it cast him further into despair.

Weena took him away from the hangar and down a darkened corridor to the Beta labs. She went directly to the small lab annex where they had first met and showed him, stretched out and seared to the table, the charred skeletal remains of her infant self. She had not survived either—

Millicent's stifled sob brought Hubert out of his dark tale.

"Are you saying we all died?" Sangfroid said, flatly. "No one got out? Not even Weena?"

"No one." Hubert shook his head. "It was a terrible thing to see."

"I'll bet." Sangfroid was not amused.

"So basically, left to their own devices, Gallo and Sangfroid die, and the squid don't manage to save Weena." Millicent scrabbled about her person for a handkerchief. A rose scented hankie was thrust into her hand. She dabbed at her eyes and blew her nose fiercely, then stiffened on realizing Millicent2 had provided the exquisitely tatted square of lace. She composed herself quickly, and with a murmur that was almost a thank you but not quite, she tucked the stained scrap into her rope belt to launder later.

"Are you suggesting they only survive if we intervene?" She turned to Hubert.

"I'm suggesting they may only exist because Sophia intervened," he said.

"Note how it's always about them and what they do," Sangfroid told Gallo. "They have to be at the centre of everything."

"I remember drawing fire into the far corner to let Travis get the techies out." Gallo offered. "It was stupid thing to do. Makes sense I didn't make it." She shrugged. "What were you doing before Millicent arrived?"

"I was gonna make a run for the Kappa exit," Sangfroid said.

"And as I pointed out at the time, a huge squid was guarding it. I made her climb around it using the bulwarks," Millicent said. "I told her she wouldn't stand a chance running for the exit. And obviously you didn't." Millicent addressed this final part to Sangfroid, satisfied with this proof that her logic had been flawless. "Once I arrived, you both survived long past the point where you got yourselves killed through ridiculous decision making."

"When she came," Sangfroid nodded towards Millicent, "we got out of the hanger and found you in the corridor checking out weapons."

"Yeah. I ran too, after my gun jammed," she said. "There was a helluva commotion on the far side of the hanger. It took the squid's attention was off me, and I got the hell out."

"How serendipitous. I wonder what caused that diversion." Millicent2's dulcet tones glued Sangfroid's attention to her.

Millicent seethed.

"I suspect there are optimum time points for interacting with another timeline," Millicent2 continued. "And, as you found out in Rome, others when it's downright dangerous."

"Precisely," said Hubert. He seemed pleased with this conclusion. "Optimum time points where we can skew probable outcomes into a more favourable direction." Anticipating the question already forming on Sangfroid's lips, he added, "In other words, places where we can fix the odds." His face darkened in warning. "Extremely dangerous places. And that's where I'm sending you."

Chapter 27

The door opened, and Edna entered. The lamplight bounced off the high curve of her bronzed forehead.

"Supper is served." She creaked into an ungraceful curtsey.

"I was unsure if you'd have an appetite after your adventures, but I had Cook coddle some eggs and set out a selection of cold cuts just in case," Hubert explained.

Sangfroid and Gallo were out the door in an instant, almost knocking the Edna machine sideways in their haste.

"Are you sure you aren't in some way responsible for these household automatons, Hubert?" Millicent asked as she and her brother followed more sedately. "It would be so like you."

"No. Not at all," he answered. "It is a normal convention for this era. I find it fascinating, though. Granted, I did take Edna apart for a good look. Cook, too. It was most interesting."

"Hubert. I forbid you to dissemble the servants," Millicent scolded. "It's unsavoury."

"But the research has to be done," Millicent2 said in Hubert's defence. "We need to ascertain what has happened here and how these creatures operate."

They followed Sangfroid and Gallo into the dining room where the sideboard was laid out with a light buffet.

"Our servants are safe. They are fully automated." Hubert warmed to his theme. "In that they are all machine with no living parts. But the cities working populous," he indicated the nightmarish world beyond the house, "are part human, part mechanical. I suspect the fully automated servant is a luxury and the steam powered worker, or hybrid as Gallo puts it, are the common-place industrial models."

"You should be safe enough." Gallo bit into a chicken thigh, then continued with a full mouth. "But I can't speak for the rest of the city. There's a possible meltdown situation here."

Millicent2 moved to where Millicent stood by the buffet and murmured, "I need to talk to you. Perhaps later, in private." She helped herself to several cold cuts, a slice of quiche, and a hefty spoonful of piccalilli.

Millicent studied the generous helping on her companion's plate. "My, what a robust appetite you have." She picked out a few morsels for her own plate. "Are there food shortages in your time?" she asked with fabricated concern.

"No. I just enjoy my food," Millicent2 answered with a smile. "It must be reassuring for you to realize you finally fill out." She spread Ardennes pâté on a finger of bread and butter and paused to say, "Oh, and don't worry, you get hips, too," before popping the lot into her mouth. She picked up her plate and glided away like a well-oiled serpent. Millicent's hard stare bore holes in her counterpart's back, but to no discernible effect.

"Hey." Sangfroid ambled over, a cheery smile on her face and an over-filled plate in her hand. "Glad to see you two getting along." She glanced down at Millicent's modest supper plate. "You'll need more than that to keep your strength up."

"Oh, shut up." Millicent stomped off to eat alone.

"So, Prof, what's the plan to get Sophia back?" Gallo asked anxiously. "We'll need to get going soon. She's been on her own too long. It could be dangerous, even if she is a goddess." She was filling her pockets with bread rolls and drumsticks. A bottle of wine disappeared into the copious inner pocket of her uniform jacket.

"Hey, it's not a picnic." Sangfroid frowned at Gallo's squirreling of food.

"You saw the muck we had to eat last time." Gallo's brow darkened.

Sangfroid hesitated, then began to fill her own pockets. "At least you got muck. I was as starved as that elephant."

"Poor Aphrodite." Millicent re-joined them, scowling at their bulging pockets.

"Yeah. I wonder what happened to her," Sangfroid said.

"Chow for the big cats," Gallo said bluntly. "Not that she had much on her in the first case. More like a bag o' bones, poor old cow."

"I can reset the time machine to let you travel to Sophia's expected co-ordinates." Hubert brought the conversation back on track. "And recalibrate to within a few days either side."

"A few days," Sangfroid exclaimed.

"It's the best I can do given I wasn't there at the outset to take accurate notes," Hubert replied. "And I have a suspicion that time has a different acceleration rate in other timelines than it does here. You said you spent a full night in the arena cells but in reality you were gone for several weeks."

"You said you had her co-ordinates?" Millicent was anxious. "How far into the past did she go to build a religious cult?"

"Very far. Hers was the original destination in the machine. You all piled in afterwards and missed her drop off point by a several hundred years," Hubert explained.

"How careless of us." Millicent knew she was being snide, but really, Sophia was more than a nuisance. A sudden thought occurred. "Where is Weena? The house seems empty without a gargantuan tentacle coiled around it."

"Weena is safe. This is not a good timeline for her to be in. What if someone were to find her and tinker with her biology? I have no wish to see a semi-automated Colossal space squid," Hubert answered.

"A semi-automated Colossal space squid as opposed to a wholly organic one," Millicent said dryly. "It bears no thinking about. But where is she now?"

"She's in our original timeline of 1862. In Loch Ness, no less," Hubert said, smugly.

"Oh Hubert, what a brilliant place to hide her." Millicent's congratulations made him smile broadly. "She shall become a cryptid! It is all too clever."

"Yeah. Great fun. Can we rescue Sophia now?" Gallo's impatience was growing.

"I was never happy leaving her behind," Sangfroid said, morosely.

"We never leave a soldier down," Gallo confirmed their space marine creed. "Unless she's dead, then nobody wants her anyway. And we don't know she's dead yet," she added a little anxiously.

"No, we damned well don't!" Sangfroid sounded determined.

"I hope she's not dead." Millicent felt guilty. She had not been as worried for her soon to be sister-in-law as she should have. She had assumed godhood would provide Sophia with protection, but that assumption could be wrong. After all, many ancient peoples sacrificed their gods, and who was to say Sophia hadn't manifested herself to one of those tribes? She could even now be neck deep in some huge cannibal cooking pot. Millicent's guilt bubbled to the surface along with the imagined stew.

"I hope she's still out there trumpeting away angrily." Sangfroid had a distant look in her eyes.

"I'd like to think she is," Millicent reassured her, then after the faintest hesitation said crossly. "You're talking about that elephant, aren't you."

Sangfroid looked at her in surprise as if she would be talking about anything other than Aphrodite.

Gallo glared. "Hey!" she said. "I was manacled to your frock, and I looked out for her, even when an entire automated zoo was trying to eat her face off. The least you can do is help me find Sophia."

"I am *not* a frock." Millicent ground her teeth. "I am more than a frock."

"I should hope so." Millicent2 regarded the grimy tunic Millicent was wearing. "More than *that* frock at least, but I suppose this rag is fitting for the destination."

"So, let us begin our rescue." Again Hubert tried to herd everybody back onto the topic. "Follow me, please." He took command and made his way back to the laboratory. "No time like the present," he joked over his shoulder. "Depending, of course, on where the present happens to be." And his smile dropped away.

Chapter 28

Millicent2 turned towards her study rather than Hubert's laboratory. Sangfroid hung back, then followed her.

"You're not going with us?" She hesitated at the study doorway.

"No. It's not my place to go. I belong elsewhere and need to get back," Millicent2 answered.

"Exactly how far into the future do you belong?"

She smiled. "What a curious question. What thought is behind it?"

Sangfroid came farther into the room, and trying to look casual, picked up a geological knick-knack from a side table. "Just interested." She shrugged, and idly tossed the weighty rock from hand to hand. "What's this?" she asked pausing to examine the odd shaped stone.

"Fossilized mammoth dung." Millicent2 gently removed the rare specimen. "A Christmas gift from Hubert." She set it safely on the mantelpiece. "Tell me, what are you worried about?"

"It's just that…it's just…" She composed her thoughts. "Am I dead or alive where you come from?" she demanded. "I'm getting bored with this being killed then not killed then killed again thing. It sort of…well, sort of…"

"Kills the romance?" she proffered.

"I'm not sure if the romance is alive and kicking in the first place." Sangfroid grew sullen. "I'm not sure of anything anymore."

"Do you want to go home?"

Sangfroid's broodiness intensified. "What's home?" She snorted. "If it's the Quintus Prime and the Space Corps, then it looks like I'm toast anyway." She rounded on Millicent2. "Look, it's hard to be romantic when you've been told you're dead. It's not much of a future to offer a girl."

"Oh, Sangfroid." She reached to cup her flushed cheek in her cool palm. "There will always be a small corner of time for us."

"For us?" Sangfroid echoed. "There's an us?" They stood looking at each other for a moment. "I knew you were going to say that. Everything about you is so déjà vu," Sangfroid murmured. "All this time-jumping has pulverized my head. It's hard to know what's real anymore, so I try to follow my gut, but that only confuses things more."

"If you feel it, then it is probably real. Trust your gut."

"Am I going to lose you?" she asked bluntly. "That's what scares me most. And I'm a frontline marine, so not many things do."

"I can't tell you that. Time is fluid, things change, and there's much I don't understand either," she said. "I can only suggest you do what I do, and go with your feelings. Like this." And she stood on tiptoe and kissed Sangfroid full on the mouth.

Sangfroid started as if lazered, then sank into the kiss as if it was the most natural thing in the world to taste the plump softness of Millicent's lips and to feel the delicious yield of her body against her own. Sangfroid tightened her arms around her, drowning in the intoxication, and would have inadvertently squeezed the last ounce of breath out of her but for Millicent2 gently pushing her away. Reluctantly, she broke the kiss but kept her hands clamped on Millicent2's waist. She couldn't let her go, sure the loss of connection would break her into little pieces.

"I shouldn't have done that," she said, "but I've missed you so much."

"Missed me? So I'm with you in your own timeline?" Sangfroid was delighted. She lowered her head and breathed in the scent of Millicent2's hair.

"Until I get back there, I really have no idea." Millicent2's answer was cryptic, and before Sangfroid could question her further, Gallo's bellow came rolling down the hall.

"Sangfroid! Move it! We're all ready to go here."

"You'd better go before Gallo explodes like the mother of Vesuvius all over Hubert's laboratory." She stepped out of Sangfroid's clasp. "Everything is so fragile at the moment." She pressed her fingers to Sangfroid's lips, staunching the flood of questions. "Time has run out for me here. You'll have to trust me; we are meant to be together. I can tell you no more than that."

"But we're together now, right?" she asked again. "Somewhere, somehow?"

Millicent2 tapped the breastbone over Sangfroid's heart, and smiled. "Always. Time is merely an inconvenient circumstance."

"Where the hell has Millicent gone now?" Gallo's voice thundered. "Anyone would think this was a spa day and not a bleedin' rescue mission."

"Go. If you don't, then there will be no future to squabble over." Millicent2 shooed her away.

"On my way," Sangfroid called to Gallo, and with a lingering look, allowed herself to be ushered out of the room. The door swung shut behind her, only to swing slowly back open a moment later. Millicent stood in the doorway quivering with indignation.

"I saw your embrace," she said coldly to Millicent2.

"Delectable wasn't it."

Millicent coloured brightly. "You knew very well I could see you, yet you deliberately continued your vile seduction. You are a brazen, heartless, hussy."

"*That* is going in the book." Millicent2 promptly pulled a small, well-used notebook from her reticule and proceeded to scribble in it while Millicent looked on in outrage.

"But I jest." Millicent2 stopped scribbling and riffled the pages of the notebook. "I keep calibrations in mine, not other people's profanities. This book holds the three-dimensional waypoints of every place I have ever visited. Latitude, longitude, and time-span disparity."

Millicent looked blankly at the book, then said, "You kissed her."

"Of course I did." Millicent2 gave a well-worn sigh. "She's a big, kissable brute."

Millicent glowered. "You had no right. You can't go leaping about in time kissing…people."

"Kissing *your* people, I think you mean?" Millicent2 raised an eyebrow. "Isn't that better than leaping about in time and killing them?" Then she added, "It's just so hard to resist, especially when she's all brand new and squeaky clean." A dreamy look came to her eye that Millicent didn't like at all. She gathered herself into a ball of seething hauteur and scrabbled for the moral high ground.

"You better not have filled her head with romantic twaddle and…and all that kissing nonsense. She's hard enough to handle."

"Surely you can't blame me for making the most of it," Millicent2 drawled. "Soon she may not even exist."

"What do you mean?"

"Sangfroid and Gallo are destined to die in their own timeline, no matter what you do, no matter how hard you try, you know you can't stop it. And neither do they belong here. They exist because of an anomaly that you created when you first started Hubert's machine. You, my dear, are like the chicken and the egg." Millicent2 stared intently at her. "So now they are going back to rescue Sophia and, in doing so, ultimately seal their fate and the fate of their great race. No deity, no steam power, no future." She let Millicent absorb this for a moment, before continuing, "If Sophia's influence on the ancient world succeeds, then they die in battle on the Amoebas. You cannot change that. And if there is no Goddess Looselea, then they may not even exist at all. Did you not think of that? How damned brave they are?"

"Yes. Of course I have considered it," Millicent said quietly. She was at a loss as to what to do. "What I am also considering is your place in all of this. What have you to offer asides from excessive confusion and loose lips?"

"Why, have you not realised? I am here to help you. You have to find out how all this started. How did you end up in the time machine in the first place?"

"I was trying to dis-embroil my parasol from the mechanism. Hubert was very free with my summer accessories."

"No. Think back. The machine was in gear, the great disc was spinning and steam filled the air, what happen next?"

"I was pushed!" Millicent said, with equal measures of anger and puzzlement.

"Exactly. And you need to find out who and why. You are approaching a pivotal point in time, my dear. A dangerous waypoint. A crossroads where entire destinies can fly off into multiple directions. One false step and you can create conditions where you yourself could fail to exist. Someone forced you into that first false step. I came here to direct you, you must trust me. I am you, I am your future, your destination."

"I'd as soon crawl through the sewers of London in a perpetual loop if you are my destination." Millicent was affronted. "You are loose and abandoned and far too flirtatious for your own good. I mean, kissing at a time like this. I could never be you. I have no idea what bizarre future you hail from, but looking out these windows, I can believe a suitable aberration exists somewhere for a woman like you."

Millicent2 looked her squarely in the eye. "You can stop this self-deprecation right now," she said. "You are going on a very dangerous journey, so I advise you to listen to me, *carefully*, as I've not much time left."

Millicent gawped. Before her stood a cold, iron-willed woman, with determination wrapped around her like steel bands. The light dimmed in the little study room until there was nothing but gloom, and they were haloed in the centre of it.

"When you find Sophia, an event will happen that will fundamentally change everyone's lives," Millicent2 said. "You will have to make a decision then and there, and you will have to be brave." The room sparked with energy. It fizzed along Millicent's skin, raising the fine hair on her forearms. She knew what this was. A time portal opening up around them.

"Millicent." Sangfroid was calling. Her voice rang up the hallway.

"If Sophia starts her religion there is no turning back." Millicent2 was speaking rapidly, but her voice sounded faint and percussive, as if she spoke from far away. "When you see the tea, you'll know." The air began to stir, brushing across their faces, ruffling tendrils of hair. Sangfroid's footsteps drew closer.

"What tea? What are you talking about?" Millicent said. Her throat felt tight. She had to force the words out. Millicent2 oscillated before her eyes, weaving in and out of focus.

"The decision is yours," Millicent2 said. "Only yours."

"Millicent." Sangfroid stepped into the study. "What the Hades are you doing? We have to go."

"I was just…" Her words trailed away. She was alone. Millicent2 had gone.

Wordlessly, she followed Sangfroid out into the hallway, churning over Millicent2's last words before any could be forgotten. *A pivotal time point. A dangerous crossroads. Only your decision.* Anxiety clawed at her. She had no idea what Millicent2 had meant. She was obviously referring to Sophia and the tea religion. That was the anomaly they were heading straight for.

The churning drone of the time machine came down the hall towards her. The gas wall-lights spluttered in the draught stirred up by the whir of the huge disc. Light shone from Hubert's open laboratory door and laid an oblong of yellow across the parquet flooring. She followed Sangfroid towards it as if in a dream. None of it felt welcoming.

Chapter 29

Loose shale shifted under Millicent's sandals. She lurched forward and would have fallen if not for Sangfroid who grabbed her elbow to keep her upright. They were standing on an incline high above a wide valley floor. The hillside was windswept and barren and dry, crumbling earth eddied around their feet like tidal water. This high up the valley, the landscape as strewn with boulders and drought-hardened, scrubby plants. It was hot and desolate, but below them the valley looked as lush and green as any Eden.

Olive groves shimmered a soft silver in the afternoon light. Dirt tracks criss-crossed the fields and followed riverbanks, knitting together the clusters of farm buildings and vineyards that dotted the valley. Wisps of blue smoke spiralled upwards from thatched roofs, and across the tops of the trees came the distant clang of herd bells. Towards the top end of the valley a group of sprawling buildings sat centred around a larger structure. The smoke over these buildings was dense and rose high before drifting away. All the meandering valley tracks eventually converged and headed towards this focal point.

"Let's head for that village," Sangfroid said. She pointed to the olive terraces, fifty feet or so below them. "There's a track down there. We'll follow it." She offered her hand to Millicent as they began the slippery descent.

They reached the lower slopes quickly. The terrain was now less hazardous, and they could move faster. The greenery grew thicker, and insects droned contently in the clumps of wild lavender. The occasional bleat of livestock drifted up from the fields below.

"We're not alone," Gallo said quietly, staring straight ahead.

"Where?" Sangfroid kept walking, her gaze fixed ahead of her.

"Half a klick west."

"What?" Millicent swept the hair from her damp brow and looked all around her. "What is clicking?"

"It's a measure of distance. Be discreet." Gallo nodded towards the rim of the valley. Millicent squinted into the late afternoon sun, seeing nothing but sunspots and dust motes. Then she saw him—a scruffy old man leaning on a shepherd's crook. A few goats milled around him, and he had a look of abject horror on his face. He stared at them open mouthed.

"Hey. You," Sangfroid called out. The old man turned heel and shot off down the hill.

"Hey," Sangfroid yelled again, but the old boy was not for stopping. Goats scattered before him as he disappeared into the groves below.

"He looked very alarmed," Millicent said.

"Yeah. Guess we look weird." Gallo looked down at her clothes. She and Sangfroid were in the tattered uniforms they refused to set aside. Millicent still wore her tunic and sandals.

"I'm not so sure," she said. "That old man had a tunic not unlike like mine. He was clearly not happy with us. I wonder what worried him so much."

"We shouldn't be here, and he knows it. I wonder who he's run off to inform," Sangfroid said. "We might have a meet and greet up ahead." She shared a knowing look with Gallo. Millicent sighed. They had come to find a friend. Couldn't it be nice, just this once?

They pressed on down the hill, following the track the old man had taken and keeping an eye open for any other valley inhabitants. The olive terraces flattened out quickly and soon they were walking through olive groves on the valley floor. What had looked like dirt tracks from above turned out to be irrigation ditches dusty with drought and choked up with straggly undergrowth. Cicadas filled the air with cheerful chirrups as Sangfroid led her party deeper into the groves in search of tree shade.

The first stone hit Gallo on the shoulder. With a grunt, she turned and immediately crashed off in the direction it had come from. More stones thudded on the ground around them. One struck Millicent on the thigh and the sting of it stopped her in her tracks. Sangfroid pushed her behind a tree for shelter.

"Are you okay?" she asked.

"Yes. It just stung a little," she said, looking anxiously after Gallo. She had disappeared towards the nearest irrigation ditch.

"Stay there," Sangfroid ordered and bounded off after Gallo. She had taken barely five paces away when the bushes rattled madly, and Gallo surged forward holding a small boy by the scruff of his neck.

"His friends scattered like rats in a barn blaze," she said and gave the boy a shake. The youngster looked about the size of a barn rat in her grip. A miserable barn rat. He was sheet white, and his legs trembled so hard Gallo's grip seemed to be the only thing holding him up.

"Never go into battle with a pack of weasels for back up." She shook him again. "You're only as good as the soldier standing next to you." She shook him some more to emphasis his stupidity. "Remember that."

"Where do you live, boy?" Sangfroid used her growly voice. The boy grew paler, and Millicent felt sorry for him despite the bruise rising on her thigh. He had to crane his head right back to look wide-eyed between Gallo and Sangfroid on either side of him.

"A...Are you giants?" he asked.

"Yes. And we eat our enemies." Sangfroid scowled. Gallo picked up the cue.

"So what are you?" she demanded. "Friend, foe, or dinner?"

"Friend!" The boy responded quickly. "I didn't mean it. Honest."

"What do you think," Sangfroid asked Gallo, still playing the game.

"I don't need a friend." She shrugged. "I am hungry though." She rubbed her stomach. "Seriously, I am. It's like I haven't eaten in ages," she told Sangfroid, who nodded in agreement. The boy trembled.

"What I do need is a scout," Gallo added, as if in afterthought. "Someone who can navigate this valley from one end to the other. Someone smart who knows his way around."

"I can do that." The boy squeaked, but was ignored.

"Nice idea." Sangfroid scratched her cheek. "But I'm feeling peckish, too. I could do with a small boy for lunch. Maybe even two! Where did your weasel friends go?"

Millicent suppressed a smile at the tactics.

"I live over there." The boy pointed through the grove to where a puff of smoke spiralled idly on the breeze. "My mum will give you food."

"Over there?" Sangfroid looked in the direction the grubby finger pointed. A dog barked, and the olive trees rustled expectantly. "Show me," she said.

Gallo let the captive go, and he ran for his life. After several yards, he stopped and looked back to make sure they were following.

"It looks like we have a scout after all," Millicent said. "Let's hope the adults around here are more welcoming than their children."

"If they're not, then Gallo will shake 'em into surrender." Sangfroid offered Millicent her arm while she worked the stiffness out of her thigh.

"Aye, Decanus," Gallo answered happily. "Shake, rattle, and roar."

"Mom!" The boy led them into the enclosed yard of a small holding. A couple of scrawny dogs barked but hadn't the energy or interest to leave their shady spot to go snap at the strangers. Instead, their tails lazily thumped up clouds of dust and their tongues lolled. "Mom, I brought giants home for dinner."

A tired looking woman came to the door. She didn't look much older than her son.

"What is it now, Magnus? You know…" Her words trailed away when she saw his companions. She paled.

"Come here," she said quietly and held out her hand for him to go to her side. He did so grudgingly, reluctant to move away from his trophies.

"I found them near the ditch," he said, refusing to hold her hand. "They're giants and they're hungry. Can I be their scout? Can I?"

"Jana?" Millicent blurted in surprise. The woman was the spitting image of the girl from the tea temple. The woman stared back at her with no recognition.

"I am Jana, but I don't know you," she said. She was very respectful, even as she slowly edged herself between her child and her visitors. Her speech, looks, mannerisms, everything reminded Millicent of the Jana she had met at the temple baths.

"How strange," she murmured. "It's like people get recycled throughout these timelines."

"She could be a direct ancestor of your friend," Sangfroid pointed out. "We mean no harm, ma'am." She stepped forward. "We just need some directions. We're heading for the village to the north of here. Are we on the right track?"

"We've got to feed them, Mom, or else they'll eat me." Magnus refused to lurk behind his mother and came out from behind her to place himself firmly on the menu. Mother and child were both very thin. Jana being the gaunter of the two. To Millicent it was obvious just by looking around the yard that food and supplies—in fact, *everything*—was in short supply. These people were not well off. The farm buildings had a make-do-and-mend feel. The repairs she could see were shoddy and amateurish. A donkey standing in the shade of a lemon tree was so thin its ribs stuck out. Even the guard dogs were spent, panting among the bedraggled chickens whose grubbing in the dirt seemed the only industry about the place.

"Where is your husband," Millicent asked, a germ of concern growing in her. The place was in too much disrepair. It was practically falling down.

Jana's eyes hardened. "My husband has gone to fetch tea for She Who Must Be Brewed For," she said with a bitter undertone that was hushed if not repentant.

"She who must be what?" Millicent asked.

"Brewed For," Jana repeated. "She is our deity, and one year out of five, the men of the valley must go and serve her. They travel east to bring back her tea. It is a hazardous journey but each family must send an able bodied man."

"She Who Must Be Brewed For?" Sangfroid said frowning.

"That's Looselea, that is," Gallo said cheerfully. "It's the old name for her. Hey, we've found Sophia. That was easy."

"I'm confused," Millicent spoke quietly to Sangfroid. "This place is the tap root of the cult I saw in Rome. Now we're hearing she is demanding servitude from the people who live in this valley. We need to find out exactly what Sophia is up to."

"Can they stay to dinner, Mom?" Magnus whined, tugging on his mother's arm.

Millicent noticed the dull colour on Jana's cheeks as she awkwardly tried to hush the child. *There is no food to spare.*

The thought both angered and humbled her. She felt a flash of anger at Sophia, dragging a working man away from his farm and leaving his family to struggle.

"Give them your food." She pulled a linen napkin wadded around a hunk of roast beef from Gallo's pocket. "They have nothing."

Sangfroid began emptying her pockets, prodding Gallo to do the same.

"Where we come from," she said, "giants bring dinner with them, and it's not always small boys." She winked at Magnus and got a big, gap-toothed grin in return. Jana's face grew redder, but her eyes flashed at the abundance springing from her visitors' pockets.

"You…you must sit and eat with us. Even if it is mostly your own food." She sounded flustered and apologetic and directed them to a bench under the rickety veranda. She ducked inside her doorway and returned a moment later with a jug of wine, a rough homemade loaf, and a plate of olives.

Gallo and Sangfroid fit their long legs under the bench with difficulty. Millicent supposed they truly were giants to the small, undernourished woman and boy who regarded them warily from the other side of the table. Together they broke bread, and the tension eased as they shared their impromptu meal.

"Why don't you eat the chickens?" Gallo asked bluntly, watching the old boilers pecking around the yard.

"We will. As soon as we get some chicks to replace them, but the cockerel has disappeared. I think a fox got him." A thin thread of anxiety laced Jana's words.

Sangfroid watched the expression on Magnus's face as he bit into the beef. "Where are your nearest neighbours?" she asked Jana.

Millicent was reading Sangfroid's mind; where was the community here? If the menfolk were routinely peeled away from their farms, surely friends and neighbours should rally round?

Jana gave a dry laugh. "My neighbours are in the same position as we are. Wives, widows, all trying to hold their rundown homes together until their sons and fathers and husbands return. But it's been years now and still no word."

"Years?" Millicent caught Sangfroid's eye. How long had Sophia been here? There was obviously an anomaly in the time flow just as Hubert has predicted. Sophia had only been gone from her own time for several hours, yet here it was years. They had been in Rome for two days, but to Hubert it had been months. What would the impact of the years spent here be on Sophia? Millicent wished Hubert had travelled with them; he might have some ideas how to proceed.

"Can you tell us a little about She Who Whatsit?" Sangfroid asked.

"She came from the stars," Jana began. Millicent snorted and quickly turned it into a cough. Jana looked at her speculatively before continuing. "And she chose this valley above all others because of the beauty of our goats—" Sangfroid's snorting interrupted her this time, along with Gallo giggling quite openly into her mug of wine. Magnus giggled too, though he had no notion of the joke. "What?" Jana asked. "What's so funny?"

"We know She Who Must Be blah blah," Millicent said.

"And she's not very fond of goats." Gallo grinned widely.

"Well, she's made a fine fortune out of them." Jana snapped and immediately regretted her words. She looked furtively around, as if the olive groves were full of eavesdroppers.

"I take it you cannot speak openly," Millicent said quietly. "Tell us what has been happening in the valley, Jana. Truly what has happened? Your words are safe with us."

"Why are you here? People like you—"

"Giants, mom. They're giants," Magnus interrupted. "Not that one." He pointed at Millicent who was the same height as his mother.

"They are not giants," Millicent informed him primly. "They are very greedy soldiers who are too big for their boots."

He immediately dropped his interested gaze to Sangfroid and Gallo's boots.

As an afterthought, Millicent added. "And ignore their language. It's unwholesome for young ears."

"Why are you here?" Jana asked again, impatiently. "You say you know her. Does that mean you are gods, too?"

"See," Millicent turned to Sangfroid and Gallo. "I told you so. She's set herself up as this Looselea person and caused all this commotion, nevermind what her cult gets up to millennium down the line."

"We always believed you," Sangfroid said. "It was Hubert who was sceptical."

"Unbeliever," Gallo muttered.

"No, we're not gods." Millicent turned back to Jana. "Nor giants, or anything mythological. We simply want to meet with...with this lady you're talking about and bring her back home where she belongs." Millicent watched Jana's face carefully. Some people didn't like it when you tried to topple their belief system. Jana's face lit up. Then again, some people were natural insurgents. If you were lucky, they were on your side.

"She sends the men away to fetch her infernal tea all the way from Chin," Jana said, and as if a floodgate opened, all Jana's worries and resentment poured out. "All our animals are leased." She cast a hand around the farmyard. "That's why we can't just eat them. They have been given to her by people outside of this valley, and now she has so many she leases them to the farmers so we can sell the milk and cheese. But there are so many goats in this valley the dairy market is saturated and therefore worthless."

"That's not very sensible," Millicent agreed. It sounded just like Sophia and her impractical mind-set. The woman could well be heaven sent, for her feet were seldom on the ground.

"Some have made a fortune off her temple," Jana said. "But the poorer people see nothing of it. If anything, her worship leaves us worse off. There are many in this valley who would like to see her return to wherever she came from."

"She Who Must Be Returned," Millicent murmured. But how? Sophia sounded very ingrained.

"Is the temple that tall building you can see from the hillside?" Sangfroid asked.

Jana nodded. "Is that where you are going. You'll find her there, but her followers will be with her."

Sangfroid shrugged. "We're old friends. She'll be glad to see us." She stood indicating the end of their meal. "Can you show us the right track to get there?"

"Can I be your scout?" Magnus leaped to his feet "Please," he whined.

"You can take them to the temple track but no farther," Jana said sternly. "They can find the way easily from there."

"You'll set us safely on our way." Gallo mollified him. "Like a good guide."

"Thank you for the food," Jana said shyly, and clasped Millicent's shoulders in a farewell gesture. "I wish you well."

"Thank you, Jana," Millicent answered, and again inwardly marvelled that this woman, or the essence of her, had passed through the ages of this strange timeline. Time travel was such a curious thing. On an emotional level she felt she was travelling in ever decreasing circles rather than stretching out across the universe. It saddened her that this Jana's progeny would become enslaved to the tea temple religion she abhorred so much. At least this Jana was a freewoman, poor as she was.

With Magnus as their guide, they quickly found the main valley road. It was wide and heavily rutted. A lot of traffic obviously moved along it though it was quiet at this time of day.

"You have to leave us here," Sangfroid told Magnus. "But we might come back this way later. If we do, maybe we'll see you then."

"Here, boy." Gallo dug in her pocket and pulled out a small jackknife. At least it was small in her hand. In Magnus's hands it looked weighty and jokily over-sized. The boy's eyes shone. "And remember, a good soldier is always shrewd when it comes to picking his companions, as well as his fights." Gallo tapped him on the forehead. "It's big brains that wins battles, not big balls."

Never lifting his gaze from his prize, Magnus traced the pattern on the hilt with a grubby finger.

Millicent watched as he traced the Þ symbol. She frowned, she had seen this before somewhere.

"T…thank you, sir," Magnus mumbled in awe.

"Away with you, whelp." Gallo gently pushed him in a homeward direction.

"Where did you get that knife, Gallo? What does the engraving mean?" she asked.

Galo shrugged. "It's from the Parabellum. You get 'em free, like a drinks promotion thingy."

Millicent had no idea what a drinks promotion thingy was, but she was certain she had come across that symbol before on their travels.

"Was that wise?" Millicent asked, as they watched Magnus disappear among the olive trees. "A knife like that is hardly common place in this age."

Gallo shrugged. "Once we get Sophia out of here, this world soon won't exist, so why not cheer the little beggar up. Everything here will collapse without its godhead and take the future with it." She turned and trudged onward, shoulder to shoulder with Sangfroid, unflinchingly towards their own extinction.

Millicent followed, biting her lip at the cruel inevitability of it all. Every step they took doomed this timeline's future and condemned Sangfroid and Gallo along with it. How would it end? Would they simply disappear, blown away like smoke while she was whisked back to Hubert's laboratory? She fretted these past few days would be wiped from her memory, or survive dreamlike and unformed on the edge of her consciousness. She could imagine the void all too readily. Her life spread out before her, empty and sterile, and inconsolably dull. The thought was unsettling. She did not want to lose any of this. She watched Sangfroid's strong back—the stretch of her uniform across her shoulders, her dark-blonde hair curling at her collar—and finally admitted she did not want to lose her.

Ahead, she could make out the straw thatch of houses. Many houses. Up close, what had seemed like a small, rustic village, turned out to be a larger municipality. Hopefully, Sophia would be in residence, and they could find her quickly and take her home...and it would all be over.

How could it end like this? Millicent's mind was buzzing. Millicent2 had warned her that her actions could change everything for good or bad, and here she was, approaching the crossroads, the optimal point in time, and she was still clueless as to what to do. Gallo and Sangfroid accepted that returning Sophia to her own time would destroy her religion and with it their culture and probable existence. What alternative had Millicent? Allow Sophia to remain here? Let this timeline unfold as it may? Hubert and Weena had both warned against it. This timeline was the anomaly, and she was standing at the root of it. But if she could redirect all their future lives, how could she do it? And would it be for the better?

Chapter 30

The geese greeted them first. Guard geese. Loud, raucous, and flocking towards them at great speed.

"Hold up," Sangfroid ordered.

Gallo stiffened. "I don't like geese," she said. "Sneaky fuckers. They dodge when you kick 'em."

Behind the geese came the old shepherd they had seen on the slopes.

"Told ya I wasn't drunk. See." He pointed them out to several other old men who followed him as far as the town gates. These men were marginally better dressed and Sangfroid hoped they were the town dignitaries. They could grab Sophia quicker if the town nobs took them straight to her. She smiled and tipped them a friendly nod. They responded by shuffling into an uneasy huddle and gawping even harder at the monstrosities that had popped up on their doorstep.

"Real live giants," the shepherd continued proudly, as if he were presenting a freak show. "And a littl'un." He squinted at Millicent. "Probably their body slave."

The town guard arrived carrying spears and cudgels and hovered in the background looking very unhappy at seeing real live giants with their body slave on the doorstep. The two groups stood facing each other outside the rickety town gates.

"We come in peace." Sangfroid opened with the greatest lie in the universe. She checked out the guards' weaponry with a casual, practiced eye and wasn't worried. There was nothing there she and Gallo couldn't snap with their bare hands, including the guards' necks.

"Welcome," an elder called back from a safe distance. "I am Volos, magistrate elect of the great city of Sophopolis. Tell me, where are you from?"

"They're from the next valley," the old shepherd butted in, excitedly. "I saw them come over the mountain. They've come to steal our goddess!"

"Quiet, you old fool," Volos scolded. "How can they be after our goddess? Where are their goats, 'eh? They can't lure her away without offerings."

"Maybe they don't need goats," one of the elders spoke up. "They have a slave girl. Maybe a serving wench is their offering." As one, the old men settled their cataract-clouded gazes on Millicent and examined her like a fatted calf.

"So what? Slave girls have been offered before." Volos shook off the comment. "She Who Is Never Impressed wasn't that bothered."

"She's very scruffy for an offering." Another elder pointed out. "Very substandard."

The debate continued. "But she's not a local girl. This one has been chosen especially to please. Look at her colouring." Yet another pointed out. "It's the same as Looselea's. Pasty Celt complexion with squirrel red hair."

"Excuse me, but I happen to be auburn," Millicent said. "And my skin tone has been remarked upon as pale but interesting."

The old men glared, and Sangfroid placed herself deliberately in between Millicent and them. "This is *my* slave girl," she said in a severe tone. "She is not a gift."

"Are you selling her then?" Volos asked. "Looselea might like her."

Behind her she could make out Millicent's snort of exasperation.

"Maybe." Sangfroid scowled menacingly to show it was unlikely this lot could afford her prized possession.

"Must I be socially embarrassed every time I visit your accursed timeline?" Millicent muttered.

"We have come to pay tribute to Looselea," Gallo said.

"Where are your goats then?" The old shepherd asked, not as easily cowed as his municipal representatives.

"I don't need goats. Tell her the giants of the Urals have come to see her," Gallo boomed in her best angry giant voice. "And be quick about it."

Volos looked uncertain but nodded for one of the guards to deliver the message.

"You know of our goddess?" he asked uncertainly.

"We are great friends, and she will be glad to see us," Sangfroid confirmed.

This threw the elders into an even tighter huddle. Intrigued as they were, they also seemed very nervous. Where there many attempts to steal their goddess? Why would anyone want to make off with Sophia? The notion amused Sangfroid, she'd have just as happily left her here, but Gallo seemed smitten, and Hubert was adamant she be returned to her rightful place before the universe disappeared up its own black hole.

"So…" Volos struggled to fill the silence. "You're from the Urals? Where's that then?"

"Land of giants and mighty amphitheatres." Sangfroid was dismissive. "Miles from here. Looselea knows of it."

The guard reappeared and murmured in Volos's ear. Volos stood aside and with a low bow and sweep of his arm showed them the open gateway. "Please, mighty giants of the Urals, and attendant, welcome to Sophopolis. The goddess awaits."

"Have you brought my luggage?" Sophia greeted them. Then she saw Gallo and blushed. She patted at the folds of her toga with nervous hands.

"No dear. We've come to collect you, not deliver luggage," Millicent said, looking around her with interest. Sophia's villa was the largest building in the town and centrally located at the head of the one and only plaza. The sunlight diffused through latticed window shutters, and in the late afternoon, the walls were bathed with a pearly incandescence. The effect was cool and welcoming after the dust and heat outside. There were a few reclining benches scattered across the expanse of stone floor, and a small fountain tinkled tranquilly in the corner. The room was minimal, quiet, and stylishly eloquent. Millicent could not equate it with Sophia in any way. Had her ordeal changed her for the better?

"This is a very lovely place, Sophia. Are you staying here?" she asked.

"The locals built it for me. They are very darling, but I miss my knick-knacks," Sophia said. "The place needs a bit of clutter. I don't suppose you brought any Wedgewood with you? They try so hard, but the tea sets they turn out are just not up to specification, no matter how much I explain, and the Chin imports never arrive in one piece." A familiar whine entered her voice, which Millicent found most comforting. This was indeed the Sophia she knew.

"We have come to take you home, Sophia, to your own Wedgewood and knick-knacks," Millicent said as her trepidation grew. Sophia was not focusing her thoughts and sensibilities as expected. She had supposed Sophia would be eager to return home. This was becoming more of a home visit than a rescue.

"Oh, I can't leave now," Sophia exclaimed, confirming Millicent's growing doubts. "It is the eve of my festival. My inaugural. I'm a goddess you know. These people love me. Your timing is very auspicious. In fact, I may have a role in it for some of you." She laid her hand on Gallo's arm and bestowed an awkwardly flirtatious smile on her hero. "But first let me offer you some goat canapés. It's the region's specialty."

"Thanks, but we've already eaten. Look, we need to go, Sophia." Sangfroid was her usual blunt, bossy self. "There's a time-flux window thingy opening up and we need to be ready for it."

"You want me to go through a window? Whatever for?" Sophia was not impressed. "I refuse to leave just yet. The festival will run for the next three days, and I must be here. I am, after all, the guest of honour."

Millicent could see exactly what was going on. Sophia had finally found a situation that matched her ambition. Here, she was the brightest and the best, because she could declare it so. At last she'd found a place she could rule with her iron will, her beady eye, and her own brand of peculiar logic. It would be like winkling a crab from under a rock to get her away from here.

"We haven't got three days." Sangfroid was getting tetchy, and Millicent knew this could only end in stalemate…or dungeons. If Sophia had any. Sophia would be obstinate just to prove her authority, and Sangfroid had the ambassadorial finesse of a caribou. Between the two of them, nobody would be going anywhere.

The guards stationed outside the villa door peeped in, made nervous by the raised voices. Millicent now realised that Sophia meant something to these people. She was a godhead, and they may not want to let her go. It was a delicate situation. Too delicate for Sangfroid to stomp all over with her muddy old military boots.

"You simply have to give us a tour, Sophia," she said, ignoring Sangfroid's stupefied look. "The town looks intriguing. And I must hear all about this festival. It's in your honour, you say?"

Sophia immediately took her arm and spun them both around to face another door on the far side of the room.

"Yes. I am to be officially deified, though I have been as good as a saint to these people already. The preparations are all through here," she said, her voice full of excitement at the possibility of showing off. "But first you must come and see my factory."

"Factory?" Millicent was incredulous. "You have a factory?" What had Sophia been up to?

"Yes. I've always wanted one. They're all the thing."

"Whatever do you need a factory for?" Millicent asked. Behind her Sangfroid seethed. She could feel her itching to grab Sophia and stomp back to the mountains with her over her shoulder like some Neanderthal. They had only a few hours before Hubert began to call them back, and judging by the amount of guards dotted around the place, it would be a hard task to simply whisk the local deity away. This mission needed a high level of skill and subterfuge. She slid a sideways glance at Gallo and Sangfroid and realized she was on her own.

"Why, I need a factory to make tea," Sophia said. "You have no idea how hard it was to get a decent cup of tea here when I first arrived. It was almost impossible."

"Tea? You make tea?" Sangfroid asked.

"Yes. We refine it. We import the raw leaves from China. I pointed my men in the general direction, and they eventually found it. I have successfully opened a trade route, though it is a tediously long one." She led them outside towards another building. It was square and squat, built in rough stone and much more rustic than the villa. Millicent would have assumed it was an olive press except that Sophia had already pre-warned her of its use.

Another guard—they really were everywhere—flung open the doors for them to enter. They were immediately assaulted by a tsunami of steam and noise.

"Open the vents!" Sophia waved her hand before her face to dispel the fug. "Good gracious, must I tell you everything.

The Tea Machine

Where's Heron?" she demanded from a worker who appeared out of the swirling miasma.

"He's with Volos, tending to the ceremonial fountain, my divineness."

"Volos is my festival coordinator," Sophia explained. There was a lot of yelling and loud banging, but eventually the overhead brass vents opened, allowing sunlight to blaze through the board slats and the steam to dispel. The factory floor was revealed as a long, low room lined with huge iron drums which rotated and roared like masticating brontosauri.

"These are the rollers." Sophia gestured to them with pride. "Luckily the leaves are withered enough by the time they arrive. We spread them out on special mats on the ship decks and let the sun and wind dry them out en route."

"You're making tea? Actual loose leaf tea?" Millicent was surprised. "I thought you imported it as a consumable?"

"We do, but in its raw state. Here we roll it, and oxidize it. Let me show you the macerator machines." She led them deeper into the building. "I am very lucky in that Volos's grandson, Heron, is a very capable boy and can follow my instructions to the letter. He's so intelligent."

"Sophia," Millicent mulled over her next question carefully, "when you say you are treated like a goddess here, do they call you by another name? Perhaps Looselea?"

"Why yes. After the loose leaf tea I have created a market for."

"You actually prepare the tea here?" Gallo asked. "It must be a massive operation."

"So far we have produced nearly ten tons. We distribute sacks of it to the various temples that seem to be popping up all over the region. Volos sees to that." Sophia whisked them along on her tour. "It's a very profitable export industry. We sell the teapots as well as the tea."

I'll bet it is. Millicent remembered the bitterness in Jana's words back at the impoverished farm. Sophia and her sidekicks were commercially exploiting the people under the context of worship.

"And here is the venue for my first ever festival. Though I hope there will be many more. It would be wonderful if this could become an annual event." Sophia brought them out into the main plaza again. "I have instructed the local women how to makes scones, and of course, there will be tea enough for everyone."

Several men were working around the central fountain. Millicent noticed Volos, and when he spied them, he approached with a young man at this side.

"Ah, I believe you have met Volos already," Sophia said. "But let me introduce Heron, one of my most favourite of the young Latvians." Millicent caught the word and realised Sophia, for all her meddling, had no real clue as to where she was geographically, much less time wise.

Both men bowed low as they approached. "Oh wonderful lady of the tea leaf, we have completed the fountain for tonight's opening ceremony," Volos said.

"Oh how clever. I knew you would." Sophia clapped her hands in delight. "You have arrived just in time," she told Millicent. "In a few hours, we begin my festival when the waters of the town will run with tea, and this fountain will be at the heart of it. Heron is such a clever young man." Heron glowed at her praise and bowed again, even lower. "He has a bright, bright future," Sophia added.

The waters of the town will run with tea? Millicent considered this. She had been warned by Millicent2 to look out for the tea, was this what she meant? And now that she had located it, what on earth was she supposed to do?

Evening fell quickly in Sophia's corner of the world. It was as if the sun suddenly collapsed behind the mountains, exhausted after another day of shining down on everyone.

Sophia had arranged bathing water and clean togas for her guests, so that they might look decent for her grand event. It was not as sumptuous as the bathing spa Millicent had experienced before, but the cool, clear water was a godsend in such a parched, dusty place.

"We have to get her out of here," Sangfroid spat out in frustration. "Time is running out."

"Everywhere she goes, she's surrounded by guards," Millicent pointed out. "You can't just grab her."

"Oh, can't I?"

"They're guarding her for a reason," Gallo said, her face dark and brooding. "Sophia's the major commodity in this neck of the woods. She's their golden goose, and they're not going to let her just up and walk away with her friends, no matter how much they blag on about her being a goddess."

"Gallo is right. Sophia's a captive here whether she knows it or not," Millicent agreed. "I wouldn't trust that Volos as far as I could toss him. He is behind all this deification nonsense, and probably behind all the scams going on, too. I'd wager anything on it."

"So what's the plan?" Gallo asked. "Given that the prof could call us back at any minute."

"Grab her and run," Sangfroid answered. Millicent sighed but knew better than to argue this particular point when she hadn't a counter suggestion. She could only hope inspiration would come to her at the appropriate moment.

They were collected by another contingent of armed guards and herded into the plaza where they took up places of honour beside the fountain. The sky above was a bejewelled canvas of stars, and the plaza reflected this back with hundreds of burning torches. It looked very festive. Drummers kept up a steady, ominous beat on animal hide drums, and a local chorus hummed along with them in something akin to a droning lament, at least to Millicent's ears.

Sophia appeared on the steps leading down from her private villa, resplendent in a snow-white gown and bare feet. The drum beat increased to hysterical levels, with the chorus launching into a high-pitched wail. Volos mounted the steps and, with a low bow, greeted his goddess partway to escort her to the fountain. Above the calamity of the music, Millicent was aware that the melodious tinkle of the nearby fountain. Suddenly the fountainhead changed from musical babbling to an ugly gurgle as the crystal clear waters began to spew darkly. At first Millicent was unsure what she was seeing. The rush of the fountain tore her attention away from the arrival of Sophia, now promenading under a canopy of palm fronds towards the centre of the plaza.

The waters were staining the colour of tea! This was exactly what Sophia said would happen, and now Millicent2's words rang in Millicent's head. *When you see the tea you will know what to do.*

On the ledge by the fountain lay a rough cloth for towelling, and Sophia's sandals sat beside it. Millicent remembered the ceremony for the new urns at the tea temple in Rome. They were more or less baptised in the tea water. This was it! This was where that ritual had originated; she was here at the founding moment. It had to be at this very point in time that Sophia became ritually deified, and her religion took over the ancient world, not so much for its divine truths as its pragmatic capitalism.

Volos brought Sophia to the edge of the fountain. The dreadful music had reached a crescendo, the elders of Sophopolis were gathered around their goddess chanting their supplications, and the air began to crackle with energy. Hubert was beginning to reel them back through time! Still unsure what the correct action should be, but completely out of time for enlightenment, Millicent yelled a warning to Sangfroid and ran full pelt at Sophia, catching everyone off guard. She hurtled against Sophia plunging both of them into the tea fountain where they flailed about entirely inappropriately in the brown stained water.

Millicent was immediately aware of the clamour. Sophia screamed, the guards yelled, Volos roared, and the singers finally shut up. She heard the slap and crunch as Sangfroid and Gallo grappled with the guards, tossing them aside as they fought to protect her and Sophia. The tea water smelled brassy and above that came the coppery tang and mechanical hum, and the skittering electrical current that hailed the incoming storm.

"You've ruined everything." Sophia's wail overrode the queasy sensation, and Millicent made a lunge to grab hold of her. "It was going to be beautiful and you ruined it for me."

From behind she heard the splash of Sangfroid and Gallo leaping in to join them. They had to cling together; they had to leave this place together.

"You have always resented my natural ability to make friends…" Sophia continued, heedless of the change in the air around them.

Millicent had to call on her better nature not to let Sophia go again. The yelling and screaming around them began to fade away as Millicent's vision darkened and swirled, and the world collapsed about her.

Chapter 31

Hubert gawped open mouthed. "Where did you come from?"

Millicent regarded him with shrewd eyes. His hair was oiled into a sharp central parting. His tweed jacket sagged around his paunch, the pockets misshapen with pencils, handkerchiefs, and interesting shaped stones, and of course, string bulged out of every pocket.

"We're home," Millicent declared as she flopped onto the nearest seat. "Really home." This was *her* Hubert, not some slicked up, slimmed down, futuristic phantom. They had landed in *her* timeline, in *her* 1862.

Gallo carefully placed Sophia on the couch. The events at the fountain combined with the return journey had been too much and threw her into a fainting fit.

"My head hurts." Sophia burst into consciousness with a complaint and sat bolt upright, gazing around stupefied. "We're home already? Did I sleep the entire journey? Was I ill?"

"Yes," Millicent answered distractedly. "You fainted with heat exhaustion. Best not to speak for the next hour or so."

"You're all soaking wet." Hubert was astounded. "And what's that smell?"

"Tea. Putrid tea water." Sangfroid scowled and shook her squelching boots. Gallo handed her a tumbler of whiskey that calmed her somewhat. They squelched over to the straight backed seats by the drinks table, and sat there sulking, dripping all over the carpet.

"Hubert! You're alive!" Sophia realized he was among them and flung herself in his general direction. He fumbled the catch, steadying her by the elbows. His face a mask of confusion. "I've had the most awful time in Latvia," she bawled.

"Latvia?" He pulled a clean handkerchief from one of his copious pockets and handed it to her, guiding her skilfully towards Millicent.

"Yes. I was just becoming accustomed to the peasants and their rustic ways when Millicent arrived a ruined my holiday. *And* just as I finally had things running properly. Latvians are a terribly disorganized people with an uncommon fondness for goats."

"But…" Hubert was lost for words. "But…"

"For a leading figure of the European scientific community, you seem very incurious." Millicent knew she sounded tart, but really, they had just reanimated in his laboratory in complete dishabille and all he could say was *but*?

"But," he began again, then added, "what on earth?"

Millicent sighed and accepted the small glass of malt Gallo presented her. Another was pressed on Sophia.

"Purely medicinal," Gallo murmured and winked.

"Why aren't you dead?" Sophia homed in on Hubert now that her fiancé was standing before her in the rudest of health. "Last time I saw you, that awful mollusc creature had swallowed you. It was most upsetting. I was quite overcome."

"Ah, but you see Weena didn't devour me." Hubert became animated now the conversation had drifted into known waters. "In fact, I—"

"Weena has a pouch in her mouth like a pelican," Sangfroid interrupted. "He sat in there and she took him to the Amo—"

"She spat him out." Millicent gave Sangfroid and Gallo a stern look. Sophia was still oblivious to the true nature of their travelling. If her intellectual lassitude and cerebral conceit allowed her to steadfastly believe she had visited Latvia, then so be it. If she were ever to be informed as to the fantastical nature of her journey, then Hubert could be the one to explain it to her, preferably in private, and in a room far away. Millicent was in no mood to rehash their adventures for Sophia's benefit.

"I hope you washed thoroughly." Sophia looked at Hubert with distaste. "When we are married, I shall forbid any experimentation where you are eaten. It's too embarrassing. How will I explain it to my society ladies?" She arose with the greatest dignity available to a woman in a tattered, tea-stained toga. "I need to bathe, have Edna prepare a guestroom and send home for more clothes. Discreetly of course." And with that she marched out into the hallway to the splintered staircase.

"I was right, of course. The stair carpet is ruined." Her words drifted back to them. "And this balustrade is dreadfully bent." This was followed by a furious tutting that dissipated as Sophia's tired footsteps moved farther up the stairwell.

"Latvia?" Hubert turned to Millicent for explanation.

"Pre-history to you and I," she answered wearily. "I can only assume her mind has blocked out anything she cannot understand, or that did not make sense. Which will be about just everything that happened."

"Pre-history? Good grief." Hubert was dumbfounded.

"The grief was indeed good and liberal. But we managed to nip her deification in the bud, and hopefully put paid to her meddling with historical timelines once and for all. The fact that we are here and not in alternative London more or less proves it."

"What alternative London?" Hubert asked.

"That is a story that will have to wait until I, too, have had a bath." She was too exhausted to go into it in any depth right now, especially as she had already done so with an alternate Hubert in an alternate London. All seemed to be well with this more humdrum version of her brother, and she would report all to him after she'd had a good rest. She was bruised to the bone and needed a few hours recuperation.

Unfortunately, Hubert was full of news and determined to share at once. "Weena didn't eat me, you know. After she gathered me in her pouch, a curiously gentle experience I might add, she took me—"

"To the Amoebas," Millicent said, her voice thin with weariness.

"And we were all floating about dead," Sangfroid said and flapped her hands like a bird.

"Fallen in brave battle," Gallo added happily.

Hubert looked lost. He gazed from one to the other. "How did you know that?"

"You told us before." Sangfroid sounded bored and poured another snifter for herself and Gallo.

"I did?" Hubert instinctively turned to Millicent for context.

"There was an alternative London," she said. "Another 1862. A horrid place. Hopefully it only existed for a short while. We met with an alternative version of you while we were there."

"An alternative London. Like this one, only not?" Hubert looked dumbfounded.

"Yeah," Gallo said, "like this one, only different. It had automatons instead of people. And huge factories all over the place and skat like that."

"Automatons?" Hubert looked like he might cry at missing such an opportunity.

"Legions of them," Millicent said. "An entire workforce."

"Waiting to rise up and rip their human masters' hearts out." Gallo warmed to her theme. "They always do that."

"A London full of automatons. I would have loved to have seen that." Hubert was very put out.

"You were there as a future version of yourself," Millicent told him.

"It hardly compensates." He paused, lost in thought. "You mean there's a new world order still to come?" he suddenly asked.

"I certainly hope not," Millicent said. "It felt more like a concurrent effort. One running in parallel. Hopefully, by removing Sophia at the opportune moment, it no longer exists."

"But Gallo and Sangfroid are still here, so things can't have changed." Hubert pointed out.

"Maybe we've nowhere else to go," Sangfroid said. "Maybe this is it for us."

"What about Weena?" Millicent asked. "Have you hidden her in Loch Ness yet?"

Hubert looked at her blankly, then said, "What a wonderful idea. Sheer genius. How clever of you, Millicent."

"If she isn't there already, then where is she?" Millicent asked.

There came a screech from upstairs, and she sighed. "She's still in the guestroom, isn't she? The one Sophia is using."

"I'm afraid so." Hubert moved towards his machine, his hands already working out a calculation on his brass slide rule. "Loch Ness," he muttered to himself. "Brilliant. Now, if I could only get there yesterday…"

Millicent remedied Sophia's ablution and apparel problems before turning her attention to her own. She had bathed and rested for a few hours, awaking to a household quiet in the dawning of the day. She quickly dressed and made her way downstairs.

The house had a tranquil, melancholy air, and she was surprised to hear the murmur of voices in the front parlour. Passing by, she could make out the timbre of Sophia and

Hubert in hushed conversation. Quietly, she carried on to her study at the rear of the house, wanting to prolong this time alone to reassemble not only her thoughts, but her entire being. She allowed herself to sink into the familiarity and security of her surroundings before turning to her small bureau and the bundle of neglected correspondence that had gathered over the last few days.

Only three days yet it feels like a lifetime. She paused. In her heart she knew it was a lifetime. At least the parts that counted. The parts that constituted the whole, the parts that forged and formed her into who she was today, in this precise second. And she had come through it toughened and restructured at a cellular level. A lifetime of lessons in three days.

Her notebook lay on the bureau. Usually she kept it in her reticule, but she did not carry that around with her anymore for fear of losing it in some foreign timeline. It fell open, and she prepared to scoff at her naive efforts to repair Sangfroid and Gallo's bad language. But on flicking through the pages she found lists of figures and personal notes rather than alphabetized expletives. She frowned. This was Millicent2's notebook. How had she managed to plant it in her bureau and in this timeline? Has she been sashaying all over my house? Millicent was outraged.

Then she remembered Sophia's sighting of her on the stairs when she had actually been in the study. Had Millicent2 been travelling back and forth managing the whole sorry adventure from the get go? She was so engrossed with the cramped lines full of spidery handwriting and co-ordinates, she barely heard the light tap on the door. Here, in her hands, she literally held a time map to multiple pasts and futures all running on parallel lines. What did it mean? Why had this been left for her to find?

The door swung gently open, and Sangfroid stepped in to the study.

"The house is busy this morning, despite the early hour," Millicent murmured distractedly.

"Cook's up. The smell of bacon is coming from the kitchens," Sangfroid said. She sounded upbeat but forced.

Millicent checked the mantelpiece clock. "Is it me or does time seem to move faster now we're back."

"I've noticed it before," Sangfroid said. "It's like a kind of overspill. It gets back to normal soon enough." She came farther into the room and began to roam awkwardly, picking up this and examining that and putting Millicent entirely on edge. Millicent wanted to sit quietly and think, and she couldn't do that with Sangfroid loitering behind her, fumbling with every movable object in the room.

"What is it you want, Sangfroid?" she asked with a thin veneer of patience.

She set down the whatnot she was toying with. "This is fossilized mammoth dung," she said, clearly grasping at conversational straws.

"Are you referring to the geological specimen or the situation in general? Please, get to the point and stop all this rattling about. What do you want?"

Sangfroid took a deep breath and came towards her. Then she did the most peculiar thing. She sort of lurched, as if her leg had given way under her. She regained her balance looking annoyed.

"There's too much furniture in this room," she announced and began to rearrange Millicent's mother's furniture to clear a space on the floor before Millicent's desk.

"What on earth? Stop abusing the furniture."

In answer Sangfroid lumbered down onto one knee. "Millicent," she began.

"What on earth are you doing?" Millicent sat bolt upright.

Sangfroid blinked a little stupidly at the interruption then barrelled on, sticking to some predetermined schedule.

"Millicent, I don't know why it is, probably some timeline freakishness, but it's like I've known you forever, and I feel deeply for you." She took a breath and as an afterthought grabbed for Millicent's hand. "Millicent, I know I maybe should have asked your brother for your hand first, but he's busy in the front parlour with Sophia, and once, not so long ago, he said he wouldn't allow it, but anyway, Millicent, I love you. I think I always have and I know the other you, that is… we have a future together. You told me so yourself. Will you marry me? We can do that where I come from even if it's not the norm here," she added.

The mantelpiece clock ticked, stretching out the silence in the room. A bird started its morning chorus in an overhang of wisteria outside the window.

"I'll be really good to you," Sangfroid said uncertainly. "Really good."

"But, Sangfroid." Millicent flicked through Millicent2's notebook, to a particular page and holding it up for Sangfroid to see. "We are already married."

Excerpt from

Parabellum

by Gill Mc Knight

(Book two of The Teatime Chronicles; Coming 2017)

The soft folds of material moved freely against her flesh. It was not an unpleasant feeling, and the narcotic fibres of the cloth relaxed her as she pushed tentatively through the crowd. She felt light-headed with a strange kind of euphoria, and now she understood why the robes were called Naili, after the tribe famed for its belly-dancing. Her skin felt alive, it pulsed and crawled deliciously with every movement. It made her want to move more to enhance the pleasure further.

The room was noisy, and a haze of cooling vapour hung high over the heads of the crowd, its purpose to keep the temperature at an ambient degree. It was necessary; heat pulsed off the bodies she tried to slither past with minimum contact, except she found herself attracted to the body heat. She forced herself to keep pushing onwards; she had to find a way through, a way out. Somewhere under the layers of sensation, a small, sober, inner voice, inhibited to the point of muteness, was warning that this could not, would not end well.

Strangers smiled leerily at her. Several raised their glasses in friendly salute, others reached out to gently pat her arms and shoulders in a mild greeting. She was confused. Who were these people?

The haze above her head cleared for a moment, like cloud breaking under thermal winds, and the purple blaze of a bright and brazen neon sign, several feet high, flashed down on her like an omen of ill-boding. Millicent's small, sober, inner voice broke loose and howled in dismay. Parabellum. She was on the troop ship, Quintus Prime, in the Parabellum bar.

"Hey." Gallo barrelled out of the crowd and grabbed her by the forearm. "There you are. Come on." And pulled her back into the thick of it, cleaving a path towards the far corner. "Found her," she called to a group of soldiers. They were all lean and lithe and louche, sitting around a drink-laden table in the relaxed manner of cheerful ne'er-do-wells.

"Sangfroid," Gallo cried and drew Millicent forward amid catcalls and laughter. "Here's your birthday present. We all chipped in, but she has to be back at the brothel before midnight or it's extra."

Before she could draw a breath to protest Millicent was flung onto the lap of a blonde woman soldier. She looked up into Sangfroid's amused grey eyes and failed to see the person she knew so well. This Sangfroid laughed even as her lips found the pulse point of Millicent's throat and sucked on it lasciviously. "You," she murmured against Millicent's hammering pulse, "are better than cake."

About Gill McKnight

Gill McKnight is Irish but spends as much time as possible in Lesbos, Greece, which she considers home. She can often be found traveling back and forth between Greece and Ireland in a rusty old camper van with her rusty wee dog. Gill enjoys writing, roses, and by necessity DIY.

CONNECT WITH THIS AUTHOR:
Website: www.gillmcknight.com

Other Books from Ylva Publishing

www.ylva-publishing.com

Banshee's Honor
(revised edition)

Shaylynn Rose

ISBN: 978-3-95533-103-0
Length: 379 pages (153,000 words)

Warleader—in Y'Dan, this is a title of pride, of honor, and of joy. Oathbreaker—a word branded only on those whose crimes are so heinous, all must know of their crime. Both of these names have been given to Azhani Rhu'len. Only one of them is right.

The Secret of Sleepy Hollow

Andi Marquette

ISBN: 978-3-95533-515-1
Length: 166 pages (45,000 words)

Graduate student Abby Crane schedules a research trip over Halloween weekend for Sleepy Hollow, in search of material for her doctoral thesis and answers about her long-lost ancestor, Ichabod Crane. Local folklore says he disappeared at the hands of the ghostly headless horseman—or did he? With the help of the attractive Katie McClaren, Abby finds much more than she ever thought possible.

SECOND NATURE
(2nd revised edition)

Jae

ISBN: 978-3-95533-030-9
Length: 496 pages (146,000 words)

Novelist Jorie Price doesn't believe in the existence of shape-shifting creatures or true love. She leads a solitary life, and the paranormal romances she writes are pure fiction for her. Griffin Westmore knows better—at least about one of these two things. She doesn't believe in love either, but she's one of the not-so-fictional shape-shifters.

THE CAPHENON

Fletcher DeLancey

ISBN: 978-3-95533-253-2
Length: 374 pages (165,000 words)

An emergency call to Lancer Andira Tal has shocking news: there is other intelligent life in the universe, and it's landing on the planet right now. The aliens sacrificed their ship to save Alsea—temporarily.

Alsea is now a prize to be bought and sold in galactic politics. But Lancer Tal is not one to accept a fate imposed by aliens, and she'll do whatever it takes to save her world.

Coming from Ylva Publishing

www.ylva-publishing.com

The Wallops
Gill McKnight

The villages of High Wallop and Lesser Wallop have graced either end of the Wallop valley since medieval times. And competition between the two has never ceased since, especially over the famous Cheese and Beer festival.

As head Judge of Show, Jane Swallow has always struggled to keep peace, friendship, and equanimity within the community she loves, but this year everything is wrong. Her father has just been released from prison and is on his way to Lesser Wallop with the rest of her travelling family and their caravans.

Her job is on the line, and her ex-girlfriend from a million years ago has just moved in next door.

Her life is going down the drain unless she can pull off some sort of miracle.

Parabellum
(Book two in The Teatime Chronicles)
Coming 2017
Gill McKnight

Married life is hard; especially on a troop ship thundering through Scorpius Major on the hunt for a squid hive. But it's not as if Millicent Sangfroid, nee Aberly can return home. Number five Christie Mews in under attack, as is the whole of London, from the steamslave riots. Sophia has gone to join the Amazons, and Severus ex Machina knows who Millicent is and has set his Imperial guard to find her—if only she knew who *he* was. Then maybe she could stop this whole frightful mess.

The Tea Machine
© 2015 by Gill McKnight

ISBN: 978-3-95533-432-1

Also available as e-book.

Published by Ylva Publishing, legal entity of Ylva Verlag, e.Kfr.

Ylva Verlag, e.Kfr.
Owner: Astrid Ohletz
Am Kirschgarten 2
65830 Kriftel
Germany

www.ylva-publishing.com

First edition: November 2015

No part of this book may be reproduced, scanned, or distributed in any printed or electronic form without permission. Please do not participate in or encourage piracy of copyrighted materials in violation of the author's rights. Thank you for respecting the hard work of this author.

This is a work of fiction. Names, characters, places, and incidents either are a product of the author's imagination or are used fictitiously, and any resemblance to locales, events, business establishments, or actual persons—living or dead—is entirely coincidental.

Credits
Edited by Jove Belle
Cover Design & Printlayout by Streetlight Graphics

CPSIA information can be obtained
at www.ICGtesting.com
Printed in the USA
BVHW030228120221
599990BV00009B/48